STREET BROTHERHOOD

CALUMET EDITIONS

Minneapolis

First Edition July 2025
Street Brotherhood: Rise of the Underground.
Copyright © 2025 by A.D. Metcalfe
All rights reserved

This is a work of fiction. All of the characters, names, incidents, organizations, and dialogue are either the products of the author's imagination or are used fictitiously.

10 9 8 7 6 5 4 3 2 1
ISBN: 978-1-962834-48-3

Cover and book design by Gary Lindberg
Cover art by Nathalie Erika Langner

Praise for *Street Brotherhood*

"A. D. Metcalfe has done it again! Her quick-witted, page-turning writing style makes *Street Brotherhood* a must read. Metcalfe's characters jump off the pages, pulling you into their vivid world. Do not miss the ride!"'

–Steven Manchester, #1 bestselling author, *The Menu & Ashes* .

"The characters are fierce, the dialogue is sharp, and Metcalfe's storytelling will have you glued to your subway seat."

–Darina Sikmashvili, author, screenwriter and director

"Youth culture has always shaped New York. For over two centuries, the city has been the pre-eminent field of dreams for young Americans of all cultures. Street Brotherhood brings to life this sense of possibility, of yearning, of dreaming beyond what exists today. And Metcalfe's hero, Johnny Alvarez, joins a pantheon of seekers—real and fictional—who we will forever associate with the Big Apple. Caught up in the moral complexity of underground life, Johnny pursues his dreams in a way that is both timeless and universal. The terrain for the impassioned storytelling may be the city's gritty streets, but this is a story that can be found up and down the boroughs. Metcalfe's gift is to let us time travel. I urge you to take the trip."'

–Sudhir Venkatesh, Columbia University Professor, sociologist, ethnographer, and author of, *Gang Leader for a Day*

"A. D. Metcalfe's *Street Brotherhood* is a page turner, gritty, fun, funny, badass. Rarely do you get empowerment and tragedy in the same breath. This book rips."'

– Josh Boardman, author and Founder of Hewes House

"A real New York story as told by a real New Yorker."

– Al Diaz, author, artist

STREET BROTHERHOOD

Rise of the Underground

A.D. Metcalfe

**CALUMET
EDITIONS**

Minneapolis

For Leslie

Also by A.D. Metcalfe

Street

CHAPTER ONE

Johnny Álvarez sat on the trunk of a parked car, his weathered high-tops propped on the bumper. He dragged on a Marlboro as students poured from the doors of Roosevelt High, a boxy five-story composition of brick, concrete and security grates. The institution, which consumed most of a block on West Nineteenth Street, had recently been referred to as one of New York City's most troubled schools. Truancy was rampant. There were drugs, assault and batteries, reports of rape. To the Board of Education's disappointment, no one had yet considered arson.

Johnny was starting tenth grade relatively unscathed. He had a measured demeanor, but if fucked with, his dark, steely eyes would lock onto a would-be aggressor, revealing a simmering rage that made even the densest of goons retreat. Additionally, his reputation from junior high had accompanied him here, where rumor had it, he beat a kid damn near into a coma just for messing with him.

But Johnny didn't flaunt it. Unwanted attention could lead to someone wanting to speak to his parents or digging into his records. From there, they might discover that his application papers were forged, that John Avalon, the name he was using, was fake, and that his address was a vacant apartment in a tenement on 180th Street.

Johnny flicked his butt into the gutter as Jarrod King and Clyde Demarco, his second and third in command, broke from the stream. Both were white, brown-haired, and sinewy, but where Clyde still clung to a shred of innocence, Jarrod had given up long ago.

"How'd you get out so early?" Jarrod extended a hand for the gang shake.

Johnny shook back, then did the same for Clyde. "My English teacher lets us out early on Fridays."

"Shit, we had an algebra quiz, but couldn't leave till everyone was finished."

"You got a test the second week of school?"

"Such bullshit," said Clyde. "But we were both done in like twenty minutes, so we did a bunch of homework."

Johnny clucked his tongue. "Some scholarly motherfuckers over here."

Chico Velasquez appeared next, Puerto Rican, stocky, olive complexion. They slapped skin all around. "Yo, hermanos, we still gonna look for that tunnel up in Riverside?"

"Why not." Johnny finger-combed his black curls. "Nothing else to do."

"Is it part of the subway?" asked Clyde.

"Nah," said Jarrod. "Supposed to be some kind of train tracks buried under the park. I heard there's a lot of cool graffiti in there."

"Sounds mysterious," said Chico. "We need to throw up some of our own shit."

"Yeah." Johnny slid off the trunk. "Start putting our name out there. Soon as everyone gets sprung, we're meeting the rest of the crew uptown."

As the four teens leaned against the car, Mario Washington burst through the door. He was a wiry, dark-skinned fifteen-year-old with a big loose afro. His arms flailed in frustration. "Ain't that always the way? Soon as you got some shit you wanna do, these teachers hold your ass up." Nearby students scowled but moved aside. "And why are we talking about the 1500s in 1975 anyway? Maybe I give a shit about the Renaissance on a Monday, but not on a fucking Friday!" He gave the gang handshake all around. "I mean, we got someplace to *be*, right?"

"We do." Johnny pushed away from the car to head for the door. "Let's hurry-up the others."

◇◇◇

The seventeen members of the Dogs of War came from their respective schools and jobs to meet at Seventy-Second Street and Riverside Drive.

Pedestrians veered aside as the gang entered the park, following the gentle curves of tree-lined footpaths that paralleled the Hudson River.

Jarrod broke off. He stopped in front of a steel door cut into the swell of a small hill. It was bound by a thick chain and padlock, but the lock was broken. He unfastened the door and tried to pry it open, but it was wedged in the dirt. "Someone gimme a hand. This might be it."

Johnny and Clyde went to help. With their combined strength they managed to open it partway. Clyde stuck his head inside. "This looks promising."

"Cool," said Johnny. "Let's go."

They took turns squeezing through the opening. Inside, a lopsided section of diamond-plated stairs led to a wide tunnel with two sets of tracks. Were it not for the patches of light bursting through the occasional street grates above, it would have been pitch-black. Rats scurried into the shadows as the gang fanned out, heading north to explore the tunnel's depths. There was a lot of litter, mostly booze bottles, beer cans, and undergarments. Some crew members pulled out jumbo markers to tag *Dogs of War* amid the existing graffiti before jogging to catch up with the others.

"Man, it's creepy in here," said Mario.

"Creepy to you," said Jarrod. "Five-star digs for the homeless."

"Then where the hell are they?"

"The rats ate them," said Clyde.

"Don't even play like that." Mario scooted toward the center of the group. "You know I hate rats."

"If they ate everybody, they're probably full," said Johnny.

"I don't give a shit. They'd chew my face off for the fun of it."

"If they ate your face, it'd be an improvement," said Chico.

Mario hissed. "Yo' mama didn't mind my face when she was sitting on it."

"My mother wouldn't touch your raggedy ass, but those rats will." Chico grabbed Mario's sleeve and whipped him toward an unlit section by the wall. Mario let out a girly shriek and sprinted back.

As the group got deeper into the tunnel, they slowed to admire the more brightly colored murals of graffiti. Some had exquisite details with 3D lettering. Others were accompanied by expertly drawn cartoon characters.

"We should come here with better supplies, throw up a big piece of our own," said JJ, a small-framed, towheaded eighth grader.

"Definitely." Johnny tapped Mario. "You finish the template for our gang tattoo yet?"

"Close," said Mario. "I finally perfected the German shepherd. He's snarling, wearing an army cap, with *Dogs of War* written below."

"Nice. Let's make appointments to get inked." Johnny turned to Clyde. "How much we got saved?"

In addition to being third in command, Clyde was also the gang's treasurer. Being the only male in an apartment with three sisters and a single mother who worked multiple jobs, he was granted the luxury of his own room, one his siblings were loath to enter, so privacy was guaranteed. It was the safest place for Johnny to stash the money he had been earning, running drugs for a dealer called the Brick.

"Between what's hidden in the Twister box in my closet," said Clyde, "and what I've been sneaking into my savings account, somewhere around fifty grand?"

Jarrod grunted. "That ought to cover it. If not, I'll chip in my allowance."

"Your drunk-ass parents don't give you no allowance," said Chico. "Their government checks barely make it from the mailbox to the liquor store."

"I can't argue." Jarrod hawked a loogie onto the ground. "The stench of cheap gin and Pall Malls makes me gag whenever I walk through that door. I can't wait to get the fuck outta there."

"Hang tough," said Johnny. "Shit's gonna change. I'm tired of crashing on all you guys' couches and holing up in that vacant apartment. Getting our own place is a priority. Something big enough for everyone and not just some rental." Johnny punted an empty bottle of Wild Irish Rose and it clanged down the tracks. "The Brick's gig is good, and it's regular money, but he's not interested in expanding his clientele. Banking more dough is gonna require branching out."

"We could get jobs after school and on weekends," said Clyde.

"Fuck that. Three-fifty an hour washing dishes? We'll be thirty before we save enough." Johnny's feet shuffled in the dirt. It was easier to put aside his circumstances when he was with his crew. But his homelessness, the risk of getting busted and sent to foster care—or worse, back to his family—those things were never far from his mind. He spun around. "We're losing daylight. Let's get outta here."

Halfway to the exit, the crew heard voices reverberating through the tunnel. As they got closer, they saw a large group lingering near the door. Johnny signaled to duck into the shadows.

"You think they're trouble?" Jarrod whispered.

"Not sure." Johnny fingered the folding knife in his pocket. "Is anyone packing, just in case?"

"I got my blade."

"Me, too," said Mario.

As the boys skulked closer, they counted twelve men. They were boisterous, drinking from brown paper bags and passing a joint.

"They seem kinda drunk," said Leon Waits, a Black tenth-grader with short dreads and thick glasses.

"Good," said Clyde. "That means they'll be easier to take down."

"And they're loud and rowdy," said Johnny. "Those kinds of people tend to be weak on the inside."

Mario wagged a thumb at Johnny. "The Colombian Confucius, over here."

"Go ahead, make fun, but you gotta gauge your opponents. I've always found it's the quiet ones who are most dangerous."

"Should we wait until they go?" asked Leon.

"They don't look like they're leaving any time soon." The idea of being trapped in a dark, damp place was too familiar for Johnny. He did not want to put his crew at risk, but if they were stuck here much longer, it might trigger some claustrophobia. When a loud belch echoed from the group, followed by a round of laughter, he waved an arm. "C'mon. Just stay cool, follow my lead."

When they emerged from the darkness, Johnny saw that the men ranged in age from late teens to early thirties. Many wore layers of street clothes, but some had jackets with matching logos: two crucifixes side by side, so one looked like a shadow of the other, the letters DC printed below.

"Lookie here," said one of the men. "The rats in this tunnel sure got big." The others turned.

"Oh, shit," called another. "Musta been a breakout at reform school."

Johnny ignored the comments and led his boys toward the exit, but a few men blocked the path. Others ambled closer. One stepped in front of Teddy Edwards, a white sixteen-year-old with a chunky build. "What you got there, gringo?" He pointed to the jumbo marker sticking out of Teddy's back pocket. "Lemme hold that shit." He grabbed for it. Teddy turned, but the guy was able to snatch it anyway.

"This kid got one, too," said another man with Chico. "What the fuck are *you* tagging, your ABCs?" He spat out a laugh and others joined in.

"You kids didn't think you could pass for free, did you?" a guy slurred, sidling up to JJ. He wrestled him into a headlock for a few moments before releasing him, but it looked more playful than threatening, so Johnny let it slide.

"They should give us their milk money," someone shouted.

"No one carries milk money no more, you dumb fuck," said the man with Teddy.

"Maybe if he finished past sixth grade, he'd know that," hollered another.

As the older crew shit-talked each other, Johnny sized them up. His eyes landed on a light-skinned Latino, standing by the tracks. He was mid-twenties, with wavy short-cropped hair, and a medium build. His air was calm but authoritative. That was their leader right there. Johnny stepped toward him. "You gonna let your men jack up a bunch of kids for some cheap markers?"

"Hey César, this one over here ain't no kid." One man held Tito Juarez by his jacket. At nineteen, Tito was the oldest and tallest member of Johnny's gang. "Where you from, hermano?"

Tito's green eyes remained emotionless. "El Salvador."

"Damn, I didn't know the tunnel went *that* far." He smirked, then poked Tito's chest. "You the one running this class trip?"

Johnny spoke up. "Look, man, we're not out for trouble."

César's face pinched, giving Johnny the once-over. "This is *your* crew?"

"Yeah."

"You ain't got no colors, no patches. What are you, like, a *starter gang*?" He sneered, then closed the gap to emphasize the modest height differential. "You at least got a name?"

Johnny stood firm. "The Dogs of War."

"Dogs of War, huh?" César snorted. "Ain't that some Shakespeare shit?"

Johnny shrugged.

"And who the fuck are you?"

"Johnny."

César's eyes swept over the boys. "You got yourself an interesting group here, Johnny. *Negros*, *blancos*, *Latinos*, a couple of thugs, some geeks... You trying to be a gang or the United Nations?"

Johnny didn't answer.

César's eyes narrowed. "How'd you know it was me?"

"Huh?"

"You said these were my men. How'd you know that?"

"Good instincts, I guess."

A smile began to form on César's face but he wiped it away, turning to his crew. "All right, let 'em pass. Like the kid said, they ain't here for no trouble."

The men grumbled, but moved aside. Johnny tipped his head to César, then followed his brothers through the door. Once outside, they cut through the park to the street.

"What the fuck was that about?" asked Jarrod.

"I don't know, but I think we came close to getting our asses kicked," said Clyde.

"Not with my man here." Chico slapped Johnny's back. "He knows how to defuse a situation."

"It's not that hard," said Johnny. "Just don't be a dick."

"There's our recruiting slogan right there," said Mario.

"We better recruit more people if we keep getting into shit like that," said Clyde.

"There's a line of guys waiting to join," said Jarrod. "As soon as we know they're cool, they're in."

"Did anyone see the lettering on those jackets?" asked Teddy. "DC, with the crosses. That's tagged around the city a lot."

"Straight up," said Mario. "I see it all over the subways and shit."

"What's it stand for, the Double Crossers?" asked JJ.

"I doubt a gang would call themselves that," said Johnny. "It's probably Spanish for Dos Cruces."

"Well, excuse me." JJ clutched his chest. "*Our* families didn't teach us to speak fifty fucking languages."

"Only five. Three fluently," Johnny said, then expelled a disgusted laugh. "But that's all they taught me. That, and how to take a punch."

CHAPTER TWO

When Johnny arrived at Washington Square Park, it was busy. People had come out in droves to enjoy the warm fall weekend. One of the Brick's teenage joint-slingers was patrolling the fountain and Johnny gave him a nod before cutting over to a tree-lined finger path.

In the southwest corner, the dealer was at his usual spot at one of the granite chess tables, mid-game with Russ, a guy Johnny had met before. The Brick—or B, as most people called him—was a Black man in his fifties with a short salt and pepper afro, and a goatee. He was tall, thin, and always dressed sharp. His real name was Rick, but only his closest friends called him that.

Russ was a little older, darker-skinned and heavyset. He wore sweats and a Yankee cap. The Brick had captured most of Russ's pieces, but that was standard regardless of the opponent.

Johnny walked over. "Hey Russ, 'bout time you gave this guy some pointers on his weak-ass game."

"I know you ain't talkin' about me, motherfucker," the Brick said, not looking up from the board. "Why don't you and that smart mouth of yours lay down some cash, if you're so damn confident?"

Johnny stifled a laugh. "I would, but it goes against my code to take money from senior citizens."

The Brick raised an eyebrow at Russ, who grinned into his shirt. "This kid's about to find out that I ain't got no code when it comes to smackin' a minor upside his head." He turned to Johnny and smiled. "What's up,

Colombiano?" He held out his palm and Johnny slapped him five. Russ did the same. "Are you and that band gonna play today? I'll bet you'd make some good scratch on a day like this."

"We should, but since school started, it's hard to get motivated."

"You oughta hit the clubs, do some open mic nights. Your group got a name?"

"Temper."

The Brick pursed his bottom lip. "Temper. I like it. Lemme know when you get that first recording contract." He snickered. "So, Colombiano, to what do I owe this pleasure?" He slid his bishop across the board to take Russ's knight.

"I was wondering if we could talk a little business." Johnny bobbed his head toward Russ, to see if it was okay to speak in front of him.

The Brick clicked his tongue. "Sit your ass down, boy. You know he's cool."

Johnny sat. "I like to check, in case things change."

The Brick looked across the table. "That's what I like about this kid, Russ. He's polite, professional, and always looking out." He faced Johnny. "So, what is it? Are you ready to take over my empire?"

"Not *this* year."

"You sure got some big *cojones* for a young pup." The two men grinned.

Johnny's eyes swept the area to make sure no one was within earshot. "I was just wondering if maybe you had a way to earn some extra money."

The Brick's smile faded. "What the fuck are you into?"

"Huh? Nothing."

"I know what I pay you, and it's more than most adults make." The Brick shook a Newport into his mouth. "What are you, fifteen?"

"Yeah."

The Brick's head wagged so hard it was difficult to light the cigarette. "Why's a kid like you need so much money? You into something I gotta worry about?"

"No."

"Because if you are, that shit could bite me in the ass. You know that, right?"

"Yeah, but—"

"I finally find someone reliable," the Brick said to Russ. "Someone who'll pick up my inventory without skimming off the top, not like these other motherfuckers who're only out for themselves."

"I'm not—"

"And you should see this kid shoot. Whenever I take him to the range, the boy don't miss a target. Says he's been shooting since he was a baby or some shit."

"Eight," Johnny muttered. "I started shooting pellet guns at eight."

"And now he comes here with some harebrained idea that he needs to compete with the Rockefellers?" The Brick took a deep drag of his cigarette to calm down, then threw an arm over the backrest to face Johnny. "So? Why you need so much damn money?"

"For a place. For me and the gang."

"Hmm." The Brick stroked his goatee. "That's a *great* idea. I think it's high time you and that gang of yours settled down, maybe got yourselves a nice split-level Colonial in the suburbs. Big lawn, pool, maybe a detached carriage house..." He turned back to Johnny. "So, what are you thinking, the Hamptons, or further north, like Pine Hills?"

Johnny didn't need to understand the specifics to get the sarcasm. "That's not what I meant. Right now, we're all spread out. Some are in bad family situations. It'd be cool to have our own place."

The Brick regained seriousness. "I hear you, but what exactly do you think you're gonna afford in this city?"

"I've saved a lot. We don't blow money on stupid shit. And I see a lot of run-down buildings, ones we could probably fix up ourselves."

"Oh, you want a whole building, do you?" He pointed his cigarette across the table. "Russel, do *you* own a building?"

Russ spit out a laugh. "Nope."

"Huh. Me neither. We're grown-ass men and we don't own a building."

"I'm not talking about a skyscraper." Johnny sighed. "More like one of those abandoned-looking warehouses. How much could something like that cost?"

"A hell of a lot more than you got."

"That's the point. If I could just get a few more regular runs, it'd help."

The Brick stomped out his cigarette and squeezed Johnny's shoulder. "Look son, you see what I'm dealing with here because you're making my pickups. It ain't a huge operation, but I'm good with that. Greed is how you end up in jail."

Johnny knew asking was a longshot. In the year he had been doing this, nothing ever changed. Once a month, Tito, the only legal driver in the gang, would take Johnny to a house in Harrisburg, Pennsylvania, where he would pick up ten to fifteen pounds of weed. Every other month, it was an address in Hamden, Connecticut for a kilo of cocaine. Each run paid $500. "Maybe you know someone?"

"My competitors ain't gonna want some referral from me."

Johnny's shoulders slumped. "I get it."

"Look, kid, you're hard-working, resourceful, and you got your crew. I'm sure you'll figure something out." The Brick turned back to the chess game, but it had been so long, he forgot whose turn it was. None of them had the game on their mind, so all three just stared at the board.

"This has got to be the most boring match I've ever seen," a female voice said, snapping them out of it.

"Margaret." The Brick stood. "What a pleasant surprise." He kissed her cheek. "Mm-hmm, you are looking fine, as usual."

"Thank you." She brushed the floral-patterned dress hugging her hourglass figure, then put a manicured hand on Russ's back. "Hello Russell, how are you today?"

"A lot better now," he said, scooting over. "Care to sit?"

"I'd love to, thanks." She smiled at Johnny. "And how is *this* handsome young man?"

He grinned. "I'm good, Margaret."

She swept a long black curl behind her milky white shoulder, then removed a silver cigarette case from her purse. When she plucked out a Virginia Slim, all three dug through their pockets for a light, but Johnny was fastest. He struck a match, cupping it with both hands. She dragged in and blew a dainty stream of smoke to the sky. "So, what's the problem here, a stalemate?"

"Nah," said the Brick. "We were just talking about other things."

"Am I interrupting?"

"Not at all. Your boy was just asking how to make a few extra bucks." He stuck out his bottom lip. "Maybe next time he sleeps over, you could throw him a stipend for tidying up. You know, clean the oven, vacuum, or some shit."

Russ's face dropped. "Say what?"

Johnny smirked into a shoulder.

"I didn't tell you?" The Brick said to Russ. "She gave motherfucking Little Ricky here a key to her penthouse." He wagged a thumb toward the brownstones overlooking the park on Waverly Place. "Said she feels sorry for the kid, thinks he's got trouble at home, needs a couch to crash on from time to time." He tipped his head back and laughed. "Man, has he got her snowed."

Margaret winked at Johnny before turning to the Brick. "Maybe if you weren't so jealous all the time, things would've worked out differently for us."

"*I'm* not jealous," Russ cut in. "For the record."

"And besides," Margaret continued, "I'm barely ever there. He works hard and tries to do well in school. Sometimes he needs a quiet place to do homework."

Johnny bowed his head. "Thank you, Margaret."

The Brick waved them off. "I don't know what you two got going on, but it ain't right."

"If you want to start a rumor that I'm having an affair with Margaret, I'm totally down with that."

"And who knows," said Margaret. "He's handsome, rugged, and he's got the whole macho street thing going on. How long can a girl resist that?"

The Brick hissed. "This motherfucker's gonna be mayor before he's eighteen."

Margaret looked at Johnny. "So, Mr. Mayor, where's your entourage today?"

"We're meeting up later to check out some party in Brooklyn." Johnny flashed a grin. "Would you care to be my date?"

"Russell, you witnessing this line of bullshit?" The Brick coughed. "The *balls* on this kid."

Margaret feigned consideration. "I'll bet going to a party with you and your gang would be a blast, but I'm seeing a client tonight, and unless you're able to cover the two grand I'll lose by canceling..."

Johnny glared at the Brick. "Another reason I need more money."

It was the Brick's turn to look smug. "And she's worth every penny."

Margaret smiled. "Oh, B, you're so sweet." She stood and put a hand on Johnny's shoulder. "And you're welcome to crash whenever. You won't disturb me. I never bring clients home."

"Thanks, Margaret." Johnny also stood. "I better get going, too."

"All right, Colombiano," said the Brick, holding out his palm, "I'll catch you on the flipside."

Johnny gave him some skin, nodded to Russ, and headed out of the park.

CHAPTER THREE

The Dogs of War met outside Brooklyn's Nostrand Avenue subway station and looked for Pacific Street. "Whose party is this again?" asked Johnny.

"Betsy Tanner," said Rafael Barrientos, a brawny Dominican eleventh grader. "She goes to Roosevelt. I've seen her checking me out, but she ain't my type."

"She's not gonna mind the whole crew showing up?"

"Tough shit if she does, right?" Rafael stopped in front of a three-story Victorian row house. "I think this is it."

When the gang entered, they doubled the number of people already there, teenagers mostly, drinks in hand, talking and laughing. Some of the crew wandered off into subgroups, but Johnny stood by the foyer. While the house was spacious, the décor was utilitarian and understated. By the door was a sunroom overlooking the street. In the living room, furniture had been rearranged to create extra space, with folding chairs set out for additional seating. A middle-aged man in a tie-dye shirt stood by the stereo thumbing through albums, his hips rocking contrarily to a Steely Dan song. The adjacent dining room had assorted chips, dips, and other snacks set on the table.

"Damn, my family could use a place this big," said Clyde. "Then I wouldn't be bumping up against my sisters all the time, or having to pee in the kitchen sink because they're hogging the bathroom."

"No shit," said Rafael. "But at least your grandparents don't live with you."

"True, but grandparents don't menstruate at the same time."

Johnny sighed. "Maybe this is what crossing the bridge gets you."

The three of them set off toward the kitchen. Wine and liquor bottles filled the counter. More food had been placed on a round table in the corner, a vegetable platter, and what looked like spinach pie cut into triangles. Two kids leaned into the open refrigerator which was stocked with beer and sodas. Some students Johnny recognized from Roosevelt were in the garden patio out back. A woman, presumably Mrs. Tanner, was passing a tray of finger sandwiches.

A tawny-haired white girl in frayed bellbottoms and a Rolling Stones T-shirt latched onto Rafael's muscular arm. "Rafi, you came." She swigged from a plastic cup.

"Hey Betsy." He smiled. "Hope you don't mind; I brought a few friends."

"Cool." She looked over the group. "I've seen you guys around school, mostly out on the block, acting rowdy, heckling kids."

"Guilty," said Clyde.

"That's fine, as long as you don't target *me*."

Johnny nodded. "I'll cross you off the list."

"Great." Betsy took another gulp from her drink. "Help yourself to anything. My mom's trying to make sure everyone eats, so they don't get too drunk, and my dad's pretending to be hip by playing DJ."

"What's up with that?" said Clyde. "Don't most kids have parties when their parents are away?"

Betsy waved the air. "Not my folks. They're total hippies. Their philosophy is that it's better for teenagers to drink and smoke pot at home, supervised, instead of out on the street."

"So, it's safe to spark up?" said Johnny.

"Hell yeah, as long as you share."

After Betsy flitted off, Johnny and the others grabbed drinks. More people continued to arrive, raising the energy and volume in the house. In the hallway was a door leading to a basement that had been converted into a game room. There was a pool table, ping pong, and a dart board. A handful of gang brothers were playing rounds against some other kids. More guests pulled beer from a second fridge or lounged on beanbag chairs.

Johnny watched the shenanigans until hunger pangs lured him back up. He grabbed some sandwiches and sat with Tito and Leon in the garden to eat. After, he lit a joint and the three passed it around. Betsy stumbled outside, fresh cocktail in one hand, pulling a girlfriend with the other. The friend was tall, with platinum blonde hair, and skin as smooth as alabaster. Her makeup accented her steel-blue eyes and full lips. She wore a low-cut top with a tight mini skirt, and appeared to be just as drunk as Betsy.

Betsy stopped in front of Johnny. "Hey, how about a toke?"

He forced his gaze from the blonde. "Sure." He passed her the joint.

Betsy puffed, handed it to her friend, then batted her lashes. "Don't suppose you got anything stronger."

Johnny did have cocaine on him, perks from his work. Though he only smoked weed, the blow was handy to have because you never knew when you might need some leverage. Johnny eyed the blonde's long legs, and the thin material of her shirt clinging to her breasts. *Or an icebreaker.* "Yeah. I got something stronger."

The two girls pawed each other, giggling.

"But not here."

"My room," said Betsy.

He grabbed his beer and stood, grinning at his brothers. "I'll be back."

Betsy led them up the stairs. "It's Johnny, right?" she said, half turning around. "This is my best friend, Sherry. At least she used to be."

Sherry clicked her tongue. "Stop it."

"What? You never hang out anymore."

"Because I'm trying to go to school *and* work."

"Your glamourous work. You're too good for the rest of us now."

Johnny stayed out of it, enjoying the view from behind.

When they got to Betsy's room, she brushed the decorative pillows from her queen-size bed. She and Sherry sat against the headboard, Johnny on the edge, facing them. He pulled a small packet from his pocket. "Have you guys done this before?"

"A few times," said Betsy.

Sherry's proficiency answered his question. She already had a matchbook from her purse and was rolling a dollar bill. "Pass me an album," she said to Betsy, who complied. Johnny poured out a small pile. Sherry chopped it into lines and snorted one. Betsy did the same, then passed it to Johnny, but he waved a hand.

"You're not gonna join us?" she asked.

"Nah, that's all right. You guys go ahead."

It didn't take much convincing. They took turns doing the rest.

Sherry patted her nostrils. "Damn, this shit is so much smoother than what I'm used to."

Johnny nodded. "It's pretty pure."

"Where'd you get it?"

"Around."

"What are you, like, a dealer?"

"No. I just have access to good shit."

"Access?" Sherry turned to Betsy and they both sneered. "What the fuck does that mean?"

Johnny sipped his beer. "Look, I don't mind sharing, as long as you don't advertise it. Especially around school, okay?"

"Sure, whatever." Betsy flicked a wrist.

Sherry made like zipping her mouth closed, and the two burst out laughing.

Don't make me regret this. "So, how long have you known each other?"

"Since grade school," said Betsy. "We both lived on the Upper West Side. But a few years ago, my family moved downtown and I changed schools."

"We still hung out a lot," said Sherry. "Until they moved to Brooklyn last summer. Now it's harder."

"But her parents also hate my artsy-fartsy parents because they're too permissive." Betsy rolled her eyes. "They think I'm the bad influence. If they only knew."

Sherry grimaced. "My folks are sort of religious."

"Why'd you stay at Roosevelt?" Johnny asked Betsy. "Aren't there better schools around here?"

Betsy shrugged. "I made friends there, and I didn't want to transfer again. I'm gonna graduate soon anyway."

Sherry giggled into her hand. "Sometimes I play hooky from my lame all-girls Catholic school to spend the day with her at Roosevelt."

"The teachers are so braindead they never notice," said Betsy.

"And there are hot boys."

Betsy backhanded Sherry's arm. "She says she's there to hang with me, but I know it's just to cruise."

Sherry looked at Johnny. "Last time I was there I blew a guy in the janitor's closet."

Johnny choked on a mouthful of beer.

"What, you've never heard of the janitor's closet on the third floor?" said Betsy. "It's legendary. Kids go in there all the time for a quickie."

"Wow." Johnny swiped his forehead. "How've I missed that?"

Betsy turned up her palms. "It's unlocked all morning because the guy is in and out of there, filling mop buckets and shit. At fourth period, he goes on break and locks the door, but you've seen the guy, right? He's seconds older than dirt and looks like he's inhaled way too much cleaning fluid."

Johnny laughed. It was the truth.

"So, if you want to use the closet, you stick a wad of gum or a folded piece of paper in the latch to hold it open before he locks it. He never checks, just hits the button on the knob and leaves, but the door can still be pushed open. Then, you can flip the deadbolt from the inside so nobody walks in on you."

"And you did that?" Johnny asked Sherry. "Who was the guy?"

Sherry pointed a thumb at Betsy. "Some kid in her biology class. I don't remember his name."

"What about you?" Johnny asked Betsy.

"I've had sex, just not in that closet."

Johnny wagged his head. "I'll never think of the third floor the same way."

"Zach Reed from my math class claims he had a three-way in there, but nobody believes him."

"It *is* pretty dark," said Sherry. "Maybe he thought it was a three way, but it was just the feather duster tickling his balls."

Johnny cracked up. "You girls are nuts. But next time Sherry plays hooky in our school I want to know about it."

"Don't hold your breath. She's too busy modeling to hang out anymore."

"Ugh." Sherry tipped her head back. "Stop being such a drag."

"That's the work you're doing?" Johnny asked.

"Yeah."

"And she just got a spread in Seventeen Magazine." Betsy squeezed Sherry's cheeks between her fingers, making fish lips. "I mean, look at her. Isn't she beautiful?" They both laughed.

"Yeah. She's beautiful," Johnny said, but they didn't hear him over their giggles.

"Who wants more drinks?" Betsy jumped up. "I'll make a run. I gotta pee anyway."

Johnny drained his beer can. "I'll take another."

"Me, too," said Sherry.

Once they were alone, Johnny searched for something suave to say, but found himself dumbstruck.

"You've got a cool vibe," Sherry said, examining him. "Your eyes, they're so dark and intense. Like sexy, but scary at the same time."

"Really?"

"Yeah. I can't tell if you want to fuck me or kill me."

"What's that supp—"

Sherry leaned forward and kissed his mouth. Her lips tasted like beer and strawberry lip gloss. When she offered her tongue, he did likewise, caressing the nape of her neck. After a long moment, she pulled away and stood up. "I gotta pee."

When she left, Johnny clutched the swelling in his pants. *Definitely fuck.*

When Sherry returned, Betsy was behind her. "We gotta go downstairs, shit's getting wild. C'mon!"

The girls disappeared into the crowd, but Johnny saw Jarrod and Chico flagging him over. Jarrod's eyes narrowed. "Did I just see you come down from the bedrooms with two chicks—one being, like, six feet tall?"

Johnny stroked his chin. "Hmm, did I?"

"Shut up. Who the fuck is that?"

"Betsy's best friend."

"She's hot as hell."

"Did you bang them?" asked Chico.

"Jesus. No." Johnny laughed. "Not yet, anyway."

The three weaved through the house taking inventory. Mario, JJ and Leon were in the sunroom, sharing a joint with Mr. Tanner, who looked hammered. The Martinez brothers, Alex and Andre, were on the front steps, making out with some girls. In the back garden, Tito and Betsy's mother gazed at each other, deep in conversation. He cradled one of her hands, petting it tenderly.

"Fucking Tito." Johnny wagged his head. "Mr. Mumbles hardly says a word till he gets with an older woman. Then he really lays on the charm."

"Good thing the dad is in the other room," said Jarrod.

"Who knows," said Chico. "Those parents are pretty loose. Maybe they're swingers."

Jarrod nodded toward the stairs. "I heard someone say there's partying on the roof. Wanna go look?"

Johnny shrugged. "Sure."

On the second-floor landing, he cocked an ear toward Betsy's room. It sounded like several girls were in there, laughing and talking. He kept hiking upward. At the other end of the hall, the bathroom door opened and Sherry came out.

"Hey, where are you going?" she asked. "Can you help me with something?" She tipped her head toward the bathroom.

Johnny turned to Jarrod and Chico. "Meet you up there?"

Chico winked. "Not if you're lucky."

Johnny doubled back and Sherry closed the door behind him. The bathroom was narrow. A lime green tub with a peace sign shower curtain stood opposite the sink. The toilet was under a window with frilly curtains. Sherry put a hand on the counter to keep from swaying. "How much to buy the rest of that bag?"

Johnny looked her over, biting his bottom lip. "I'm not a dealer."

She flashed a smile. "Then just give it to me."

"I'm not doing that either."

"Why?" She put both hands on her hips, teetered, then regained balance by half sitting on the counter.

"Because you're already fucked up."

"So what?"

"So, if you pass out, people might start asking questions. I don't need that shit coming back on me."

"Oh, right. Mr. Paranoia over here." She rolled her eyes. "Everything's a big secret. What are you, a fucking fugitive or something?"

Sort of. "Look, I just don't need the hassle, okay?"

"I'll blow you for it."

Despite the matter-of-fact way she said it, the words still made his groin tingle. But it wasn't worth it. "I gotta go."

As Johnny turned for the door, Sherry lunged at him, groping his pockets in search of the packet. The unexpected ambush triggered Johnny's reflexes. He spun around, grasped her wrists, and shoved her against the sink.

"Asshole. I was just playing around." She tried to pull free but he was too strong, so she relaxed in his grip and smiled. "Mmm, you like it rough, huh?"

"No. Just don't fucking grab me."

She licked her lips, blue eyes glimmering. "I think you do."

"I really don't."

Sherry leaned in. He let her kiss him, but kept hold of her hands in case it was a ploy. She had to crouch to accommodate the four-inch height disparity as their mouths sucked and nibbled. When Johnny released her,

Sherry's fingers dug through his mop of curls to claw at his scalp. It was forceful, but felt better than he would have guessed. She pulled his head back by his hair, running her lips and tongue up and down his throat. Johnny's hands found her breasts and buttocks and she arched into his touch. But when she sank her teeth into the thin skin of his neck, he shoved her away. "Jesus! What the fuck is wrong with you?"

She gave him a lopsided smirk. "What's the matter? Can't handle a little pain?"

More than you fucking know, bitch. He touched the spot where a welt was already forming. Her bite was trivial compared to the violence he had escaped at home. But it still pissed him off. Almost as much as it turned him on.

Johnny took hold of Sherry's head and kissed her. She slid down her panties and lifted her skirt. Sitting on the counter, she pulled him between her legs, then raked her fingers down his back. Johnny winced as her nails clawed the old scars. He ignored the discomfort by pushing up her shirt to gnaw on her breasts as they pounded into each other. The act was forceful, violent almost.

As they caught their breath, Johnny felt he should offer some tenderness, but she pulled away to fix her clothes. "Wow, you're fun. Most guys won't play that rough. It's like they're afraid they'll break me or something."

"You're nuts." Johnny closed his pants. "In a good way. But I'm still not giving you any drugs."

She waved a hand. "Fine. I can get it other places. Your shit is just way better." When she opened the door, it sounded like someone had commandeered the stereo from Mr. Tanner. Disco was thumping, punctuated by whoops and cheers. "Sounds like shit's getting crazy down there." Sherry flashed a smile. "See ya, Jason."

"Johnny."

"Whatever."

CHAPTER FOUR

"Please, Tito," said Jarrod, hanging on his arm. "Please tell me you fucked Mrs. Tanner last night."

Tito grunted as they hiked with the rest of the gang across Central Park's Sheep Meadow. "This motherfucker's like the El Salvadorian Lurch." Jarrod shook his head. "How do you say, '*You rang,*' in Spanish?"

"Forget about him." Chico sidled up to Johnny. "I need to hear about this guy. There's no way that tall, waspy, white-bread bitch screwed your drug-running, gangbanging, orphaned ass is there?"

Johnny grinned. "*Si, señor.*"

"How much chloroform did it take?" asked Mario.

"You don't need chloroform when you got blow," said Clyde.

"True." Johnny stopped at a section of grass away from other people. "But I think she's crazy enough to fuck me without it."

The crew members sat cross-legged in a circle. Eric Hanson, a white sixteen-year-old with mousy hair, massaged his temples. "I can't believe you're making us spar with hangovers."

"Speak for yourself," said Maurice Steinberg. He was a year younger, with kinky reddish hair and glasses. "I feel great." He flexed his biceps, then puffed out his cheeks like he was about to puke. Some others in the circle gagged at the sight.

Johnny looked at his brothers. "Trouble doesn't give a shit if you're hung over. It finds your ass whenever, so you need to be prepared. Besides, soon it'll be too cold to have these sessions. We gotta practice while we can." He pointed to Mikey Mahoney and Patrick Ryan, two members with a significant size difference. They stood to face off in the circle. "Clyde, set your watch for three minutes."

On "*go*," the two began. The goal was to be prepared for anything, so all styles and combinations were fair game. When the round was over, opponents would stay in the center to receive feedback from the group before the next pair was picked.

They had been there a while when Johnny noticed a man watching from the tree line. He was mixed race, weathered and unshaven. He wore a long-sleeved T-shirt with camouflage cargo pants, both of which looked like they hadn't been changed in days. Johnny tried to focus on the match in progress, but the guy kept shuffling closer, scratching his beard and talking to himself.

Clyde leaned into Johnny. "Homeless?"

Johnny shrugged. "Might want some change."

After the guy made a few passes outside the circle, Johnny put up a hand to stop the round. He turned to the man. "Can we help you?"

"That little white kid, there," the guy pointed to JJ, who had been fighting Oscar DeJesus. "He's got a good right, and ducks quick, but he's disorganized and can't take a punch. The Mexican boy's kicks are weak because he isn't centered." His voice was gravelly, his gestures exaggerated. He went around the circle, identifying and critiquing the previous fighters. His comments were lucid and accurate.

"What's your name, man?" Johnny asked.

"Horatio, but people call me Tio."

"You know a lot about fighting, huh?"

"Hand to hand combat was my specialty in 'Nam."

Johnny looked over his crew. Their expressions mirrored what he was thinking. He smiled at Horatio. "You want to coach us? We'll pay you."

Horatio clicked his tongue. "You think I'm a charity case?" He wagged both hands. "You're the ones who need charity fighting like that."

Johnny stood. "I didn't mean to insult you. But you seem to know your shit, and we wanna learn to fight better."

Horatio shifted his weight from side to side, his face contorting like it was short circuiting.

"If you want to hang out and watch, that's cool, too. No pressure." Johnny returned to his spot on the grass, shooing a few of his brothers over to make an extra space. "Where were we? Oscar, JJ, continue."

As the round restarted, Horatio inched over and sat down. Up close, the musculature beneath his baggy clothes became apparent. He twitched and winced at some of the blows, releasing an occasional sound, but with each fight, his comments grew more detailed and commanding. Soon, he was in the circle, laying hands on the boys to fix their positions, and demonstrating hardcore tactics to immobilize their opponents. Horatio occasionally launched into an off-the-wall rant, but the crew indulged him because the instruction was worth it.

At one point he pitted Johnny against Rafael. Johnny was fit and agile, and had been taking karate classes sporadically for years, but Rafael was larger, and lifted weights as a hobby. When they squared off, Johnny took the offensive, lunging at Rafael with punches, then throwing a roundhouse kick, all of which were deflected.

"Hold up," Horatio said to Johnny. "You're pretty good with your feet, and that's your best defense against a bigger guy like this, but you gotta get in there." He looked at Rafael. "And you, you're gonna have to do more than block." He stood between them, acting out maneuvers, then let them practice a moment before resuming.

When Horatio called to start, both of them applied the suggestions without holding back. Blows were landing hard. The brothers in the circle winced and gasped. Just before the round ended, Johnny threw a jab, catching Rafael on the side of his head. Rafael shook it off, and stepped into a punch that connected with Johnny's cheek. Johnny spun at the waist from the impact, but managed to keep his feet planted.

"Oh shit," Rafael put a hand on Johnny's shoulder. "I'm sorry, man."

Johnny waved him off. "I'm fine. We're good."

"Damn right, you're good," said Horatio. "If you boys *really* wanna fight better, you're gonna have to take punches, you hear?"

As Johnny sat to watch the new combatants, he found it hard to concentrate. The fatigue from fighting combined with the pain radiating throughout the side of his face made memories hard to suppress.

◇◇◇

Johnny's pace decelerated as soon as he turned onto the dead end. Delaying the walk would not change the inevitable, but at this point the reflex was involuntary. He stole glances at the modest Miami houses, their clotheslines and chipped bird baths. The scorched grass was trimmed, borders lined with flowers and bushes. The neighbors, some of whom Johnny had known all of his eleven years, were proud of their tiny plots. Nice folks, living normal lives.

They used to try to be friendly with his parents, but that had become futile long ago, so Johnny had taken it upon himself to overcompensate, being extra nice and cheerful to reduce suspicion. And when they asked why they had not seen his brother, Johnny peddled the same story his parents told the school: Orlando was staying with relatives in Tampa.

Johnny fished the keys from his pocket as he approached the last house on the street. Unlike the others, this one hadn't seen a paintbrush or a lawnmower in as long as he could remember. Inside, however, it was compulsively tidy.

When Johnny entered, he was surprised to see his father on the sofa. Usually, it was his mother who was home in the afternoon. On weekends Miguel and Aylin barely crossed paths as they came and went to their second jobs. What was even more peculiar was that there were three beer cans on the coffee table. The Álvarezes almost never drank. Money was too tight. But even if it wasn't, they were generally averse to doing anything amusing.

Johnny tried to slip into his room, invisibility always being the safest strategy, until he heard Miguel's voice.

"*Javier, ven aca.*"

Nowadays, Miguel only ever addressed Johnny to punish him, so his voice had the power to make the boy's innards liquify. He crept across the living room and stood, keeping the coffee table between them.

Miguel scooted to the edge of the couch, pointing at the floor in front of him. "I said, come *here*."

Johnny shuffled closer to stand at his father's knees. Miguel was handsome, tall, with dark brown eyes and black slicked-back hair. Johnny had inherited his best features.

"What's the matter, son? Are you afraid?"

"N—no."

"Have you done something wrong?"

"I don't believe so, Papá." Johnny dipped his eyes and saw that Miguel's knuckles were marred.

"What time are you supposed to be home?"

"Five o'clock."

"What time is it now?"

Johnny glanced at the clock on the wall. "Five minutes to five."

Miguel patted the coffee table. "Sit down."

There were strict rules about putting one's feet or ass on the table, so Johnny hesitated.

"Sit down. I won't hit you."

Johnny did as told.

"Are you a good boy?"

"I try to be"

"Not like Orlando."

"No."

"He made me miss work again. I was supposed to be at the gas station by four o'clock." Miguel drained what was left of his beer.

"Where's Mamá?"

"She got stuck at work because someone called in sick." His eyes narrowed. "Your brother was yelling so much that I couldn't leave. The neighbors would hear."

Only then did Johnny notice blood on his father's dark-colored shirt. "What did you do?"

Miguel leaned into his face. "I shut him up."

Johnny swallowed. "How?"

Miguel barked out a laugh. "I didn't kill him, if that's what you're asking. But somebody should. That boy is the devil."

Johnny could not argue.

"We'd all be better off without him. Isn't that right?"

The Álvarezes had always been somewhat reclusive, regimented and aloof, but Orlando's condition had been making things worse. Johnny wondered why they didn't commit him to some loony hospital instead of locking him in the cellar. He suspected it had something to do with money, or perhaps their vehement animosity toward institutional authorities.

"Your brother hurts you, doesn't he?"

The comment halted Johnny's breath. All the times he had been released from the cellar, sometimes bleeding and bruised, his parents had never said a word. Having the abuse acknowledged now offered Johnny a flicker of solace, which quickly turned to anger. It was, after all, his father who always ordered him down there in the first place.

A glimmer appeared in Miguel's eyes. "Don't you want to get even with him?"

Johnny peeled his tongue from the roof of his mouth. "What do you mean, Papá?"

"What if I got a gun? You could shoot him."

Was his father serious or drunk? "Where would you get a gun?"

"I'll find one."

"What if I miss?"

Miguel shrugged. "Don't miss."

"But Papá—"

Miguel swiped a hand over his head. "You're always shooting those damn pellet guns. It'll be just like that."

If Johnny could have willed himself dead, he would have.

"Javier, be a man. You'd be doing it for your family."

There was only so much posturing Johnny could manage before yielding to the psyche of an eleven-year-old. "Papá, I—I can't." His shoulders convulsed as he choked back tears.

Miguel watched in disgust as Johnny struggled to pull himself together. He sighed, leaning back. "Fine. Go to your room."

Johnny got up to walk away.

"Javier. One more thing."

As Johnny turned to face his father, Miguel's swooping arm backhanded him across his cheek. Johnny spun at the waist from the impact, but kept his feet grounded. The physical pain was always more bearable than the emotional.

"From now on, you'll come home at three o'clock. Then, if Orlando is acting up, you will entertain him so I can go to work."

CHAPTER FIVE

Johnny and Jarrod walked up the stairs to Tito's apartment on Nagle Avenue. Since graduating high school, Tito had been working full time at his cousins' garage. Jorge and Julio had a repair and body shop in the Bronx, and paid Tito enough to afford a cheap place. It was a small roach-infested one-bedroom that overlooked the IRT elevated subway line. It was luxurious compared to the vacant apartment on 180th Street, where Johnny had been squatting the last three years, with no electricity and scant heat. He still slept at Clyde's or Jarrod's occasionally, since they both lived in Chelsea, closer to school and the gang's hang outs. Margaret's penthouse apartment was always a delightful retreat, but he was cautious about wearing out his welcome there.

Johnny stuck his key in the lock. "Your parents won't miss you if you stay over on a school night?"

"Those drunks?" Jarrod sucked his teeth. "Doubtful. But if they do, fuck 'em. It's even more depressing there than here. At least the company's better."

In the narrow kitchen, Tito stood at the stove, cooking curried chicken with rice. He caught Johnny's eye. "That thing's been making noise since I got home from work."

"What thing?" Johnny asked.

"That thing in your bureau."

"Shit. The pager." Johnny went to a dresser beside one of the foldout sofas. He opened the top drawer to dig around some socks. "In six months, this thing hasn't buzzed. Why is Marco calling me now?"

"I don't know," said Jarrod. "Because even coked-out lunatic drug lords get lonely from time to time?"

"Shut up, I'm being serious." Johnny looked at the screen. "Eight calls from the same number."

"You're calling him back?"

"Why wouldn't I?"

Jarrod swiped a hand over his face. "Um, I don't know. Maybe because the one time you met him he almost killed you?"

"That's because he had some bad history with the Brick, but I smoothed shit out."

"The fifteen-year-old diplomat," Jarrod muttered.

Johnny dialed the number.

"Háblame."

Marco's voice jolted Johnny. He had forgotten how similar it was to his father's. Both from Colombia, their Spanish had a similar cadence and melodic tone. "It's Johnny, I just saw your page."

"Are you on a pay phone?"

"No."

"Always call from a pay phone. Where are you?"

"Manhattan."

"Where?"

He didn't want to say the address. "Uptown."

"Meet me in two hours. Port Authority."

"What are you doing in town?"

"Never mind. Just meet me."

"I'll be there."

"Of course, you will. Come alone."

The phone clicked and Johnny stared at the receiver.

"Well?" said Jarrod. "Was it him?"

"Yeah."

"What's he want?"

Johnny cradled the phone. "He didn't say. Just said to meet him at Port Authority in two hours."

"You're gonna meet a guy like that, and not even know why?"

"He probably wants me to run some product or something." Johnny found a small path amid the clutter to pace. "Look, we've been talking about this. Trying to find new opportunities, banking more money to get a decent place to live."

"Johnny, he's a fucking supplier. Not some mid-level dealer like the Brick."

"Exactly. Instead of humping small amounts to a guy hawking loose joints in the park, why not go straight to the source?"

Tito stood in the kitchen's doorway. "New opportunities are good, but getting involved with that guy could be dangerous."

Jarrod flopped on a couch. "Yeah, why take a risk like that?"

"It could be riskier if I don't go."

"Really?" said Jarrod. "How's he gonna find you? Even *you* don't know where you fucking live."

"You just made my point." A train passed outside, rattling the windows enough to halt the conversation. When the steel wheels screeched toward the station, Johnny winced. "I can't do this anymore. I need something to change."

"Okay, but do you know how fucked up things will be for us if you die or go to jail?"

"I know you'll be in charge."

Jarrod's eyes narrowed. "That's not funny."

Johnny sat next to him. "I just feel like this guy could be our ticket to move up. Is he high and paranoid? Sure, but for some reason he likes me, wants to take me under his wing or some shit."

Jarrod huffed. "Or peck your fucking eyes out."

"Dinner is ready," said Tito. "You can eat before you go."

"Great," said Jarrod. "I'd feel much better if you got slaughtered on a full stomach."

◇◇◇

Tito drove the three of them to Port Authority in the used Dodge van the gang had bought from Jorge and Julio's shop the previous year. It still had EZ Exterminating printed on the sides, with pictures of belly-up rats and roaches. As they pulled to the curb, Johnny double-checked the pockets of his hoodie for the pager and a pack of Marlboros. No weapons, because Marco forbid them.

Tito and Jarrod offered to wait, but Johnny said that might trigger Marco's paranoia. "And don't drive around the block a hundred times either," he said. "Just go home and I'll call as soon as I'm clear."

"You got it, man," said Jarrod. "But you know I gotta tell Clyde what's what."

"I know." He gave his brothers the gang handshake, then exited the van.

Johnny lit a cigarette and stood by the Port Authority's main entrance. It was impossible not to recall the first time he had walked through those doors. Twelve years old, alone, scared. But free. It had taken courage to flee that Miami house. Also, luck, because strength and opportunity would never have been enough to immobilize his eighteen-year-old brother. And if the first bus had been going to Nashville instead of New York City, his life would be very different.

Three cigarettes later, a black 1962 Lincoln Continental pulled up. It had tinted windows and New Jersey plates. Marco was behind the wheel, waving him in. "Come. Lock the door."

Johnny obeyed. The car's interior was plush, with white leather seats, spotless maroon carpeting and faux wood panels. "Wow, nice ride." He swiveled like he was admiring it, instead of checking the surroundings. The back was empty. Only a trench coat lay over the seat, but beneath it was the outline of a rifle. Johnny stiffened and faced forward. "Maroon and white, huh? Classy choice."

Marco shrugged. His thin, twitchy frame looked uncomfortable driving, and he was overdressed for mid-October, wearing a gray sweater-jacket and scarf. A thermal cap with earflaps framed his pale, pock-marked face. "Show me." He wagged a finger at Johnny while merging into a lane of slow-moving traffic.

"I know the drill." Johnny pulled up his pant legs. "I'm not packing." He unzipped his hoodie and lifted his shirt to reveal his empty waistband. Marco, however, had a .38 tucked into the front of his trousers.

When Marco nodded, Johnny leaned back, stealing glances of the man as he navigated Midtown. He was leaning over the wheel, head toggling between rearview mirrors, hands locked at ten and two. This big drug kingpin, driving like a little old lady. "If you need directions, I can help. I know the city pretty good."

"I've been thinking about you a lot." Marco's focus remained on the road. "Ever since we met last April."

Johnny cocked a knee to face him. "If you missed me, you could've called sooner."

Marco slammed the brakes to avoid some jaywalkers. "*Ay, cabrón. Fucking city.*"

"The horn is more common here than the turn signal."

"I hate this place. I should be home in Santa Marta."

"You came from Colombia just to hang out with me?" The comment came out more flippant than Johnny had intended, but Marco didn't seem to be listening.

"The pollution. All this noise and potholes." He cringed. "You should visit. I have a beautiful home. It's on the beach, secluded, peaceful."

Johnny brushed the bench seat. "Lemme guess, the interior is maroon and white?"

Marco zigzagged on side streets until the less-congested Twelfth Avenue, then sat back. "You think you're a fucking smartass, don't you?" He pulled the .38 from his pants and pointed it at Johnny's head, eyes flitting between road and gun. "Maybe the Brick puts up with that shit, but I would advise you to stop mocking me."

Johnny choked on a breath. "I—sorry. I get sarcastic when I'm nervous. And you haven't told me why I'm here."

"I have a personal matter." He returned the gun to his lap. "I need your help."

Johnny exhaled. "How?"

"I need you to shoot a guy."

"Me?" Johnny shrunk back. "Why don't you do it?"

"I'm no good with distance. My hands shake."

"Don't you have people for that?"

"They aren't too sharp. And besides, I want to see what you're made of."

Right now, Johnny thought, the answer was Jell-O.

Marco turned onto Riverside Drive. At 116th Street, he pulled to the curb and idled. "Check out the gear in back. Make sure you're good with it." His edgy gaze left no room for debate.

Johnny crawled over the backrest to examine the weapon. It was an M40 sniper rifle with a silencer. The Brick had taken Johnny to firing ranges a handful of times. He was a good coach, and Johnny's natural talent made him a quick study. The man had quite a collection of pistols and rifles. Some similar to this one, so the feel of it was not completely alien.

"You gonna be okay with that?" Marco pulled a vial of white powder from his pocket and took a snort.

"I don't know. I guess, but—"

Marco lowered the tiny spoon to glare at Johnny through the rearview mirror. "You bragged to me about your aim, said you killed a guy with one shot."

"I shot a guy who was gonna shoot *me*. Not some random stranger." Johnny lay the rifle on his lap. "And I only ever handled something like this at a range."

Marco yanked the cap from his head. "Well, you better fucking figure it out." He loosened his scarf. "I didn't come this far to have you back out."

"Who am I shooting?"

"A guy who owes me money. The bigger kick in the balls is that he just bought a place in that building. It's setting a bad precedent." Marco pointed to a brownstone down the block, then checked his watch. "After work, he has drinks at this bar on Broadway. He should be coming home soon. I thought it'd be fun to blow his head off in front of his brand-new apartment." Marco launched into a cackling fit, punctuated by snorts.

Under other circumstances, Johnny would have found the laugh comical, infectious even.

Marco hooked an arm over the backrest, grinning. "What's the matter, smartass, you didn't think that was funny?"

Johnny's brain was spinning. His eyes fixated on the floor, searching for a way out of this.

Marco's voice softened. "Listen to me, *muchacho*. I like you. Too many people are phony, one dimensional. Not you. You've been through some bad shit, but from those experiences you took away strength, not self-pity. I respect that." Marco lifted Johnny's forehead with the barrel of the .38, forcing their eyes to meet. "But I will still take you the fuck out. Understand?"

As Johnny watched Marco's dilated pupils quiver, and beads of sweat form on his pasty skin, he got it. It wasn't just about being able to afford a place. Marco had never even mentioned money. Johnny wanted to come here. He was drawn here, despite being fully aware of this man's temperament. But why?

Then it hit him. It was familiar. The unpredictability, the terror, never knowing if you'll get out alive, all such poignant reminders of home sweet home. It was pretty twisted, really, this delusional notion that if Johnny could just ingratiate himself to this man—this lunatic who spoke like his father and acted like his brother—that maybe it would reconcile all the shit from his past.

Johnny blinked. "Yes, sir. I understand."

Marco withdrew the gun to look out the windshield. "He usually comes down 116th. When he turns the corner, I'll drive by and you'll get him."

"You're gonna be moving?"

"Listen, I'll do what I have to, and you'll just fucking kill him, okay? I told you; I shoot just fine close up."

"Whatever," Johnny mumbled. *Not like the added pressure will affect my aim or nothing.*

They sat in silence, Marco staring at the street while Johnny prepared. He readjusted to a kneeling position, then lined up objects in his sights through the tinted window.

"He's coming."

A man in his late fifties, dressed in a navy-blue tweed coat, was sauntering toward Riverside Drive. On his arm was a woman. The two huddled together against the chilly night air.

"He's fucking *with* someone," said Johnny.

"If you have to, take her out, too." Marco shifted into drive. Johnny flipped up his hood and lowered the window several inches.

The couple turned onto Riverside, and the Lincoln rolled forward. Johnny struggled to center the man's head in the telescope, but it was bouncing too much. He tried the chest instead. As the pair approached the building, the guy let go of the woman's arm to fish in his pockets. They paused at the bottom of the building's steps, laughing, but the woman was blocking Johnny's shot.

Marco stopped the car. "Shoot him."

"She's in the way."

"So?" Marco's hands clawed the backrest like an anxious puppy. "What are you waiting for?"

Johnny peeled his eye from the scope. "Shush!"

Marco sat back.

Johnny resumed his focus. The guy had found his keys and was proceeding up the stairs, his date close behind. Opportunities were running out. "Beep the horn."

"Huh?"

"Honk the fucking horn."

Marco pumped his palm into the steering wheel. The couple stopped at the door and turned toward the street. Johnny fired. The man clutched his chest. His date reached out as he began to sway. Johnny was going to shoot again when the man collapsed. The woman had to jump aside to avoid being knocked over as his body rolled down the steps.

Marco sped away from the curb, laughing and slapping the dashboard. Johnny melted into the back seat, the gun heavy in his limp hands. Cold air blew through the cracked window, cutting the numbness.

"You did it!" Marco bounced like a giddy child. "Get up here." He patted the seat beside him.

Johnny folded forward, stifling the urge to vomit, but the gun was in his lap. He began to slide the rifle back under the coat, then had the impulse to wipe it with the jacket's flannel lining. He crawled up front.

"You didn't lie about your ability, that's for sure." Marco pulled off near 179th and Broadway. "A headshot would've been better, but you still got him." He reached over Johnny's knees to pull a paper bag from the glovebox. "There's ten grand, but with skills like that you should be charging more."

Something about the comment's presumptuousness annoyed Johnny. Especially after having been threatened with death to perform the task. Not puking had seemed easier than keeping quiet. "Charge?" He turned to Marco. "You never even told me why the fuck I was meeting you. Just took me hostage, forced me to kill a guy, and now you're tossing me ten grand?"

"You're not a hostage."

Johnny cradled his head. "It kind of feels that way."

"I don't want you to think of me like that." His finger traced the steering wheel. "I believe we have a connection, a universal bond, like kindred spirits."

This guy was even loonier than he thought.

Marco looked at Johnny. "I don't like many people. They don't get me. But there's something different about you, something intense, some plane of understanding. I want you to trust me."

"Then don't be sticking a gun in my face all the time."

Marco fanned the air. "I'm sorry for being so strict, it was just a really important job, and I needed it done right."

"I would've done it right without all the threatening." Johnny opened the bag to peek at the cash. Drained and confused over what had just happened, he felt there was nothing to lose. "And for future reference, I charge twenty."

"You're worth all of that." Marco looked up and down the street. "Where can I drop you? I gotta get to Jersey and ditch this car."

"I'm good here."

"You sure?"

"Yeah."

Marco extended his hand. "Thanks, and sorry if I scared you. You're a good kid, Johnny."

Johnny returned the handshake. "Don't worry about it." He stuffed the paper bag in his undershirt, zipped up his hoodie, and stepped out of the car.

"By the way," Marco said before Johnny closed the door. "Seafoam and ecru."

Johnny ducked to look at him. "Excuse me?"

"The interior of my home," Marco winked. "The colors are seafoam and ecru."

CHAPTER SIX

Streets were empty, the storefronts dark behind steel grates. Even car traffic was light. The sick feeling in Johnny's stomach remained, and this was not a safe place to be carrying so much cash. He needed to put his head down and get to a phone booth. The first one he found had the receiver ripped from its box. The next one was intact, so he called Tito's.

Jarrod answered on the first ring. "Where the fuck are you?"

"181st and Broadway."

"We're on our way."

"I'll be walking uptown."

The EZ Exterminating van was hard to miss barreling down Broadway, and Johnny flapped his arms. It screeched to a halt and he jumped inside. Jarrod and Tito were full of questions, but Johnny couldn't answer yet. Once in the apartment, he grabbed a beer, lit a cigarette, and sunk into the couch. Tito sat across from him.

"Clyde's waiting for an update," said Jarrod, dialing the phone.

Johnny guzzled from the can. "Tell him I won't be at school tomorrow."

"You're never absent."

"He's cutting school?" Clyde could be heard through the receiver.

"You guys go," said Johnny. "Tomorrow I gotta lay low. We'll hook up after."

"Fuck that," said Jarrod. "I'm not going either. It's already late and we haven't heard the story."

Johnny pulled the paper bag from his shirt and shook it out on the coffee table. Loose fifties and hundred-dollar-bills poured into a pile.

"I gotta go, Clyde," said Jarrod. "Cash is falling out of his clothes." He rounded the sofa to perch beside Tito. "What the fuck?"

Johnny drained the beer, stubbed out his Marlboro and ran down the basics.

"He had you kill a guy?" Jarrod swiped his face. "You think you'll get made?"

"I doubt it."

"What if they find Marco, would he give you up?"

"They won't find him. But all he knows me by is Johnny, and that's not my birth name."

"It won't hurt to have the crew on high alert just in case. That lady might've seen something."

Johnny tipped his head back, allowing the beer buzz to merge with all the other feelings.

"You going to be all right?" Tito asked.

"It's pretty fucked up, shooting someone for no reason."

"But that guy wasn't innocent," Jarrod said, sorting the bills. "He ripped off Marco, right? You gotta be pretty stupid to cheat a guy like that. If you ask me, he should've been expecting it."

Johnny shrugged.

"He was gonna die one way or another. At least you got paid."

Everything being said was true, and Johnny appreciated Jarrod's attempt to rationalize it. But he hadn't pulled the trigger.

After Tito retired to his room, Johnny and Jarrod made up the foldout couches. They stared at the shadows bouncing off the ceiling as street sounds seeped into the room.

"You sure you're okay?" said Jarrod.

Johnny readjusted his pillow. "You're afraid I'm gonna have one of those episodes, aren't you."

Jarrod propped on an elbow. "Well, that little joyride *did* contain all the ingredients for some Álvarez family flashbacks."

"I thought I might slip a little, but then I realized something." He rolled over to look at Jarrod. "Maybe all that shit I went through in Miami made me more comfortable in whacked out situations."

"The way I'm comfortable around drunks?"

"Yeah." Johnny expelled a disgruntled laugh. "Back then, I learned to stuff shit down. Maybe I need to do that here, pack what happened away with all the other crap."

◇◇◇

When Johnny and Jarrod woke, Tito had already left for work, but there was a note saying they should come by if they were bored. The auto body shop was on 233rd Street in the Bronx, so they took the 1 train, grabbing a *New York Post* on the way. They thumbed through it twice, but didn't see anything about the shooting.

When they got to the garage, Tito was wrenching under a Buick. Julio and Jorge examined the engine of an older model Chevy. Both men were late twenties, rough-looking and streetwise, but their quality work was well-respected in the community.

Jorge clasped hands with Johnny. "How's it going, man?" He gave Jarrod a nod. "Cousin Tito showed me his tattoo. Your crew's got a bad-ass design."

"Thanks." Johnny brushed below the shoulder of his left arm, where he had recently been inked. "We're happy with it."

Julio walked around the front of the car wiping grease from his hands. "When you get sick of riding around with pictures of dead vermin all over that van, let us know. We'll paint it for you."

Jarrod laughed. "We kinda like it."

Johnny kicked Tito's foot and he rolled out on the creeper, jutting his head toward the back room. Johnny and Jarrod followed him to a basin where he lathered his hands. "I've been keeping an eye on the TV back here," he muttered over the running water. "There was one report, but it didn't say much, only that the victim was a forty-five-year-old bank manager, single, no suspects or motives."

"Nothing about witnesses?" Johnny asked. "Or the car?"

"No."

"The cops might know more than they're saying."

"Don't worry," said Jarrod. "The gang will protect you."

When the three returned to the bay, Jorge and Julio were consulting with a man who kept glancing at them. Finally, he broke from his conversation to wag a finger. "It's driving me crazy, but where do I know you kids from?"

Johnny noted the double cross patch on the sleeve of his jacket. He met his eyes. "The tunnel."

"Riverside Park." He snapped his fingers. "Now I remember. The *Dogs of War*." He howled at the ceiling. When he realized no one was sharing his mirth, he inflated his chest and stepped closer to Johnny. "And you are *El Presidente*, right?"

Johnny remained neutral.

"I see your tags all over town now. You must be trying to make a name for yourself." César outstretched his arms. "You think you can hang in the big leagues?"

Johnny thought about how he had just impressed a murderous drug lord. He visualized the guy he had shot tumbling down the steps, for the first time without guilt. Johnny raised an eyebrow and shrugged.

César turned to Jorge and Julio. "You know these pups?"

Julio jutted his chin at Tito. "That one's our cousin."

"Hmm." César folded his arms at Johnny. "You stakin' a claim anywhere in particular, young gangster?"

Johnny stuffed his hands in his pockets. "Not really. I just float around."

"So, you ain't got no family, no roots?"

"Nope."

César stroked his chin a few times. "No shit. You're true street." He pursed his lip. "How old are you?"

"Fifteen."

César spat out a laugh. "You're carrying a lot of weight for fifteen. You sure you can handle it?"

"I can handle it." The words came out snippier than Johnny had intended. He didn't need to be rankling any gang leaders after what had just gone down, so he recalibrated his tone. "We just do our own thing, man. We're not trying to tread on anyone."

César cast a glance over the three of them. "When you amateurs get tired of playing in the sandbox," he slapped the emblem on his sleeve, "come join a real gang." He zeroed in on Johnny. "What's your name again, little brother?"

"Johnny."

César put out a hand and Johnny shook it, then nodded at the others before leaving the garage.

Jorge gave Johnny the once-over. "Damn, brother, you just got props from César Aguilar."

"He seems like a decent guy," said Johnny. "But his crew was bent on hassling us when we bumped into them before."

"We hear a lot of that," said Julio. "But we've been working on César's cars a while, and he's always been straight up."

"Truth," said Jorge. "But I don't recommend joining that gang. The Crosses got quite a rep."

Johnny sucked his teeth. "There won't be any joining."

Tito and Jarrod agreed.

Johnny felt the pager buzz in his pocket. He looked at the screen.

"You need the phone?" asked Tito.

"Nah, I'll go outside." Johnny tapped Jarrod. "C'mon."

They jogged to a pay phone across the street. Johnny dialed and Marco answered. "Can you meet me?

"I guess. When?"

"Soon. Twenty minutes."

"Yeah."

"The place I dropped you last night."

"Okay."

"Why aren't you in school?"

"Seriously?" Johnny made a what-the-fuck face at the receiver. "You're gonna lecture me about attendance?"

"You're right. Be there."

The phone clicked and Johnny hung up.

Jarrod turned up his palms. "So?"

"He wants to meet."

"Are you fucking kidding?" Jarrod rolled his eyes so hard his head and neck followed. "You're gonna be murdering for this guy every goddamn day now?"

"It didn't sound like that."

"It didn't sound like that last night either." Jarrod stormed a tight circle. "Jesus, fuck, Johnny. How do you know he's not gonna shoot you for being a witness?"

"He wouldn't do that." Johnny sighed. "Look, I don't know how to explain it, but we made a connection. Like, he thinks we come from the same cosmic stardust or some shit." He started back toward the garage. "I'm trusting my instincts on this one."

Jarrod followed. "All right, but I'm coming with you."

Inside, Johnny told Tito he needed to use the van, but Tito looked concerned. "Can you wait for me to get done here?"

"Not really."

Julio gestured from across the bay. "Hey Cuz, if you need to leave early, you can finish that Buick up tomorrow."

◇◇◇

Tito crept the van toward the intersection on Broadway where Marco had dropped Johnny. There was more traffic now. Stores were open, delivery trucks double-parked, people bustled. As they neared 179th Street, a police car idled by the curb.

"You never see cops in this city," Jarrod said, wedged between Johnny and Tito. "What the fuck are they doing here now?"

"I don't know." Johnny's leg bounced against the door as he looked for the Lincoln.

"Has it been twenty minutes yet?"

"It doesn't matter, he's always late. Go around the block."

"You think they're onto something?"

46

"Jesus, Jarrod, I don't know, but if Marco sees them there, he's gonna freak. He's super paranoid."

"He might think you called them."

Johnny glared at him. "Yes. And then he *will* kill me. But what exactly am I supposed to do?"

"We will stand with you," said Tito.

"Whatever." Johnny bit his thumbnail. "I'm not even sure how he's coming. Knowing that lunatic, he might just parachute onto the sidewalk."

When Tito circled back, the cop car was gone, so he pulled to the curb. All three got out and lit cigarettes. After ten minutes, a yellow taxi flanked the van and tooted the horn. Johnny waved at it to go around. The rear window rolled down and he saw Marco was in the back. "Shit, that's him."

Jarrod and Tito positioned themselves between the cab and Johnny.

Marco dipped his head to look over his sunglasses, then motioned for Johnny to come closer. When Johnny tried to squeeze by his brothers, they moved with him toward the gutter. Marco held up his hands to show that he was only holding a paper bag.

"I'm good, guys, really," Johnny said, then walked alone to the taxi.

"You've got some fiercely loyal friends there," said Marco.

"I know."

"Must be nice."

"Having people? Knowing you got each other's backs? Yeah, it is." Johnny locked eyes with Marco. "You can trust me."

"You proved that last night." Marco smiled and handed Johnny the bag. "And now you can trust me because I'm making good on my debts." He looked up and down the street. "I gotta go, but I want to work with you again."

"You know how to reach me." Johnny put his hand through the window and Marco shook it before the taxi pulled away.

"I didn't expect him to look so frail," Jarrod said, returning to the van.

Johnny groaned. "He doesn't look frail whacked out on blow with a gun in your face."

Jarrod held the door for Johnny, but he waved him off and hopped in back. He sprawled out to finger through the money. It looked like an additional fifteen grand. Johnny set the bag aside, then folded forward to ease the enormity of his feelings. There was remorse over having killed a man, but also pride for having done it so adeptly. Marco's instability was terrifying, but that made pleasing him even more rewarding. And then there were Tito and Jarrod, who had stepped between him and Marco, neither of them knowing what might go down. Though all of the Dogs of War pledged to protect each other, their loyalty had never been tested like that. Even Marco had commented on their valiance.

CHAPTER SEVEN

The mid-January sun was already low in the sky by the time Roosevelt let out. Any passing clouds lowered the temperature. Crew members gathered at their usual spot to wait for the others. Some bobbed to keep warm while more draped over parked cars. They smoked cigarettes and passed a bag of sunflower seeds, alternately puffing and spitting shells.

Mario stepped in front of Johnny. "Fuck. Not this kid again."

Johnny peeked around him to see Hector Sarno, a dark-haired tenth grader with a toothy smile.

"You gotta set him straight, man. Otherwise, he's gonna keep nagging us."

Johnny exhaled through taut lips. "I know."

"How's it going," Hector said to the pair before exchanging nods with the others. His eyes settled on Johnny. "Hey, you mind if I get a word?"

"Of course." Johnny extended an arm toward the gutter. He followed Hector across the street, where they leaned against the doorway of an apartment building. "What's up?"

Hector stuffed his hands into the pockets of his pressed jeans. "So, I was just wondering," his weight shifted between his clean white Adidas, "is anything going on with my status?"

Johnny raked fingers through his hair. "I've been meaning to talk to you about that." He looked at Hector. "It's not gonna happen."

Hector's face flushed. "How come? We've gone to the same schools since junior high."

"That's right."

"And this year, I've hung out with you guys, we shot hoops, played baseball—"

"It's nothing against you personally, Hector. I like you. *We* like you." Johnny eased his discomfort by glancing across the street. Some of his brothers were play fighting, more were egging them on.

"You just recruited a bunch of new guys. Why not me?"

Johnny took a deep breath and faced him. "We were asking around, and heard your dad's a cop."

"Huh?" Hector took a step back. "Yeah. In Queens, but so what?"

"How come you never mentioned it?"

"Because I don't get along with the guy, I hardly ever see him."

"I would've preferred hearing it from you." Johnny bit his lip. "But still, it's too big a risk."

Hector tapped the brick wall with his toe. "Please. Let me prove myself. You want me to fight someone, steal something?"

"That's not what the Dogs of War are about."

"Then what? Just gimme a chance."

"I'm sorry Hector. The vote was no." Johnny watched him deflate, on the verge of tears. Johnny offered his palm. "Look, man, we're still friends, okay?"

Hector took a moment to regain his composure, but then latched onto Johnny's hand. He flashed a hint of white teeth. "If my dad dies in the line of duty, will you reconsider?"

Johnny laughed. "Yeah, man. Definitely."

Hector smiled with him before disappearing down the block.

When Johnny returned, Clyde approached. "How'd he take it?"

"He seemed upset, but I think he gets it." Johnny shook his head. "But even if his pops weren't NYPD, there's something off about that kid."

As the school block thinned out, Johnny saw that Jarrod had stepped away from the group to put moves on a dark-haired tenth grader who lived in his building. Since Christmas break, they had been getting chummier. Her name was Michelle. She was bold and brash, and her shit-talking rivaled the gang's. Two of her girlfriends waited nearby. A few crew members began trading dance moves in front of them, to see who could get the best reaction. Only one girl appeared amused. She had a chunky build, a round face accented with pastel makeup, and spiky blonde hair. The other's hair was auburn, layered and loose below her shoulders. She was taller and slim, her clothes plain by comparison, and she wore no makeup. An obligatory smile was pasted on her lips, but her eyes kept drifting elsewhere.

When a couple of the boys tried to get the girls to participate by grinding closer, Johnny curled his tongue and whistled. The whole crew looked up. With one nod, he indicated it was time to go. Everyone ambled down the block, Jarrod arm in arm with Michelle, her two friends following behind the group.

"That's a powerful whistle."

Johnny turned to see the taller girl behind him. He decelerated to walk beside her.

"The school should hire you and ditch that bell. It'd probably be more effective."

Johnny grinned into his chest. "I'd have to charge extra for fire drills."

She laughed. "Hi. I'm Jessica." She looked around for her friend and saw she was chatting with Leon and Teddy. "And that's Danni."

"Johnny."

"Yeah. We're in the same science class this term."

"I didn't notice." Closer now, he could see that her eyes were hazel with dark lashes, her complexion smooth and glowing. Makeup would have been a waste.

"You guys got a pretty big clique."

"Yeah. We're all from the same orphanage."

Jessica's brows furrowed a moment. "Shut up."

It required effort for Johnny not to stare at her. "So, besides being a connoisseur of whistles, what do you like to do?"

She laughed. "I sketch and paint. Sometimes I take an art workshop after school."

"That's cool. How'd you get into that?"

"I loved drawing as a kid, and my parents always encouraged it, so I just kept at it." She pulled her coat tighter. "It probably sounds boring."

"No. Some of us are into that, too." He grinned. "Except we put *our* shit on the subway."

Jessica faced him. "You joke, but graffiti *is* art. I love the different styles. A lot of it's very creative." She touched his arm. "It requires real talent."

Johnny looked at her hand and she pulled it away. They both realized they were on the avenue, and that the group was starting to split off toward various modes of public transport.

"I guess I'll see you in class." Jessica smiled. "But maybe you won't see *me*."

Johnny shook his head. "I won't make that mistake again."

CHAPTER EIGHT

After a Saturday night of loafing around and smoking weed, the Dogs of War sauntered out of Washington Square Park. It was late, and some brothers could not break curfew, but the rest headed down West Broadway, past avant-garde clothing stores and cavernous galleries, all of which had already closed.

Rafael stopped in front of one gallery's display window. Track lighting illuminated its showcase piece: a glossy white box the size of an end table, with a red ball of equal proportions perched on top. "Who *buys* this crap?"

"Opulent motherfuckers," said Mario.

"I should spray-paint a basketball, glue it to a milk crate, and sell that."

Mario sucked his teeth. "Nobody'd buy art from a graffiti-writing scofflaw."

A smattering of people spilled from a bar on Broome Street, laughing, some poshly dressed, others more Bohemian. Once they tottered off in different directions, Jarrod tagged the Dogs of War insignia on a phone booth with a marker. "What should we do?"

"I got something to show you guys," said Johnny.

The bourgeoisie abruptly ended at Canal Street, a loud, grimy thoroughfare with kiosks full of second-rate knockoffs and kitschy crap. Johnny hooked a right. After a few blocks, he cut away from the clamor of Holland Tunnel traffic to Desbrosses Street, which was deserted and cobblestoned. On Washington, he turned south and stopped mid-block.

"What are you doing?" asked Clyde.

"Sometimes, when I'm alone, I like wandering around down here."

"Why?" asked Patrick.

"Listen." Johnny tipped his head toward the sky. The winter chill was refreshing on his cheeks, warmed from walking. "It's so quiet. No people, no traffic, and you can smell the river a block away." He paused from his meditative state to see confused faces staring at him. "Really? You don't get it?" He turned a full circle with arms open. "Look around. It's mostly warehouses and loading docks. Monday through Friday, anonymous truck drivers coming and going. Dead as a motherfucker nights and weekends. No shops, no supermarkets, no one even parks their cars around here."

"And we care why?" said Rafael.

"Because there's nobody to give a shit if we commandeer a place." Johnny turned to a derelict five-story building. It had a wide stoop with three granite steps leading to a steel door. The ground floor windows were blacked out and barred. The ones higher up were industrial-sized and caked with soot. "I first noticed this building two years ago, and *that's* been there the whole time." He pointed to a faded FOR SALE sign inside a second-floor window. The company name, RealCorp, was legible, but some digits of the phone number were obscured by dirt.

"Do you know how much they're asking?" said Patrick.

"I tried calling, but I'm not getting the numbers right. I want to break in and get a closer look."

"We got enough money?" said Mario.

Johnny shrugged. "It's exactly what we've been saving for."

Jarrod jiggled the front door. "We're not getting in this way."

"Did you look around back?" asked Rafael.

"Yeah." Johnny went to a void between an adjacent building. It was blocked by a seven-foot-tall wrought iron gate secured by a giant padlock. "There's a fire escape back there, but I couldn't reach it. With some help, I could probably climb up, pry open a window."

Mario walked toward the gate and looked down the alley. It was narrow and barely illuminated by the dim streetlights. Two rats darted from the gutter, and he shrieked. "Fuck that!" He bolted behind Chico.

"It's just a few," said Rafael.

"That's what they *want* you to think, but there's probably a whole army in there, waiting. Haven't you seen that movie, Willard?"

"Some of us should stay out here anyway, keep watch," said Johnny. "Once I'm in, I'll open the front door."

"I'll go with you," said Jarrod. Patrick, Clyde and Leon also volunteered.

Johnny grabbed the iron bars and hoisted himself over the gate. When he dropped to the other side, squeaks echoed in the darkness. He stomped around to chase off any lingering rodents. When the others were clear, they rushed single file through the narrow alley until they came to a wider gap behind the building, which dead-ended. The backdoor was also bolted.

The crew stood, assessing the fire escape. The drop-down ladder was pulled up to the first platform, more than fifteen feet high. Leon shook his head. "What now?"

Johnny stroked his chin. "Didn't we pass a construction dumpster a few blocks back?" He called to the boys out front, telling them to go find something they could prop against the wall. Several minutes later, Rafael, Chico and Mario were passing a dented metal garbage can and a long two-by-six over the gate. Johnny angled the board against the building on the upside-down can.

"Who the fuck's climbing that," said Jarrod.

"I used to climb palm trees in Miami," said Johnny, spotting a piece of pipe in a corner. He stuck it in his waistband before giving his brothers a nod. They circled around to steady the apparatus before helping him on. Johnny began to shimmy up the board. It kept shaking, but the brothers held tight. The end of the plank was a few feet shy of the steel grating, but Johnny used a downspout to hoist himself onto the fire escape's landing.

The windows were five feet wide and ten high, with panels of wire mesh glass. Johnny tried to push one open, but could see it was latched. He smacked the pane above the lock with the pipe. Some glass chunks rained into the alley, and the boys below ducked. The second blow made a hole big enough to unlock the window. After some jiggling, it opened a few feet and Johnny crawled inside.

The moon provided just enough light to find the staircase, which dumped him at the front door. Johnny flipped the two deadbolts and let his brothers in, then walked down the hall to open the back. When everyone was inside, they began exploring what they could see.

The ground floor might have served an executive function once, but all that remained were battered shelves, file cabinets and desks. Under the staircase was a musty boiler room that housed an archaic furnace, electrical panels, and assorted maintenance gear. Jarrod spotted a flashlight on a utility table. It still gave off a dim glow, so he led the pack to the upper levels. Each had two separate lofts, with very few divider walls, and random pieces of furniture. It was hard to see much else, so they reconvened on the second floor, where Johnny had broken in.

An overhead light flickered on.

"What the fuck was that?" said Rafael.

Clyde stood by the door, his hand on a switch. "Didn't anybody *try* the lights?"

Mario laughed. "Bunch of idiots."

"Wow," said Chico. "They're still on the grid."

Johnny wandered the length of the two-bedroom unit, his jaw agape at the high ceilings, water-stained with blistering paint, and spider webs spanning every corner. The hardwood floors were scuffed and gouged. At the far end, a peeling Formica counter corralled some filthy kitchen appliances. But all Johnny saw was potential. He inspected the bathrooms. Each had yellowed tile, calcified claw-footed tubs and rusted fixtures. The stuff uptown in Tito's apartment wasn't much better.

Obliquely, in the center of the main space, was a single oversized black leather sofa, sunken from the weight of countless asses. Leon plucked a small tuft of stuffing from a torn seam. Using his palm as a launching pad, he blew it into the air. It spiraled a few times before landing near a dead water bug. "It's a bit of a fixer-upper."

"Who better to fix it?" said Johnny. "We're at seventeen members and growing. A good cleaning, some paint...this place can fit all of us." He searched his brothers' faces. "Aren't you guys itching to get out of your homes?"

"I'd love to." Leon ran a hand over his short dreads. "I never know when the TV's gonna be gone because my thieving drug-addict brother sold it for a fix." He picked at a small hole in his houndstooth sweater vest. "But realistically, if I move out now? My mother could have a problem with it, and I don't want to bring heat on the rest of you."

"He makes a good point," said Johnny. "Some members might have families that care enough to cause problems. But that doesn't mean they can't be involved and stay over as much as possible."

"My parents are too drunk to notice if I'm gone," said Jarrod.

"Mine, too," said Patrick.

"We've got three generations crammed into one apartment," said Rafael. "Me moving out would be a blessing. Besides, I'll be seventeen in a few weeks, so what can they do?"

Clyde half raised a hand. "I hate to be a killjoy, especially while you guys are already picking out drapes, but what if we can't afford this place?"

"I still make runs for the Brick every month. So, with the twenty-five grand I just got from Marco, that should put us up near eighty," said Johnny. "And he said he wanted to work with me again, so there could be more."

"Sure, go kill some other people. Then you won't have to worry about a place to live because you'll be in prison."

Johnny closed his eyes to avoid rolling them. "Marco just wanted to see what I was made of. He's got other work." He turned to Chico. "Your dad's the super in your building. Think he'd help us get shit up and running?"

"Hell yeah. And we can trust him."

Johnny smiled. "Your parents have always been cool with me. The gang, too. Ask if he'll come by to look at shit."

Chico nodded.

Johnny tore a strip from a crumpled paper bag, then went to where the sign was hanging. He copied the correct phone number with his graffiti marker and tossed the sign on the floor. After letting everyone out the front door, he locked it, and exited from the window, lowering the fire escape's retractable ladder so getting in again wouldn't require the same acrobatics.

CHAPTER NINE

Tito and Johnny stepped out of the van on Washington Street. Other than an increase in traffic on the West Side Highway, the neighborhood was as desolate as it had been the night before. Now, in the light of day, Johnny could look for evidence of residential tenancy. Between the loading docks, he checked doors for names and apartment buzzers, then stood in the middle of the street to see if there were curtains or plants in the windows above.

After a few blocks, he met Tito back at the van. "Anything?"

Tito shook his head.

"Me neither. I'll go let you in."

Johnny climbed around back, then up the fire escape. As he opened the front door, Chico's parents were pulling to the curb in a rusty Pontiac Tempest, with Chico in the back. The car was packed with tools from the building on East Fifth Street, where the Velasquez family lived.

Luis's large frame unfolded from behind the wheel. He produced a woolen cap from his stained canvas jacket to cover his balding head. "Can't you just play in traffic, like other kids your age?"

Johnny laughed, walking over to shake his hand. "Thanks for taking the time to come."

"Your crew is always helping me paint apartments and move furniture in my building. It's the least I can do."

"If you could just tell us what we're dealing with, that'd be great."

"Pops is the master," said Chico, rummaging in the back of the car. "He can fix anything."

58

"In Puerto Rico, replacing wasn't an option for us." Luis readjusted his bold framed glasses, one of the plastic ear pieces held together with electrical tape. "I learned how to repair out of necessity."

Lucinda had climbed from the car, tightening the wool coat around her short, stout figure. She ambled in front of the building, her dark eyes evaluating every corner. Johnny hung back as Tito and Chico led Luis to the boiler room with some tools. He switched to Spanish. "I didn't realize you were so interested in property maintenance."

Lucinda's gaze never left the bricks. "I'm interested in whatever you do because it involves my son."

"You know that a lot of my boys are in precarious living situations. I just want to make a stable home for us."

She faced Johnny. "Chico *has* a stable home."

"I know. I'm not taking him from you."

"But he will choose to be with you. That is why I need to know what is going on with this place." She patted the dark bun atop her head. "Chico didn't give much information when he asked Luis to come here. So, I'm asking you. Will you be staying here legally or illegally?"

Johnny had always known Lucinda to be staunchly anti-establishment and distrustful of most, hence her alliance with outliers. Her refusal to speak English was a small act of rebellion, though Johnny suspected she understood more than she let on. They had a strong connection from the first time they met. She was the only person outside his gang who knew the truth about his birth family, and was one of few adult confidantes. "I'm hoping legally. It's for sale."

"For sale, is it?" She stroked her chin. "How many pockets does a person have to pick to make that kind of money?"

"Lucinda, I'm not—"

Her hand went up. "I know you boys get money. More than tips from those little shows your band puts on in the park. And I don't want to know the details, but if you have enough for this?" She eyed the sky and crossed herself.

"We don't have that kind of money, but I still want to contact the owner, see what a downpayment would be. Or maybe we could rent it cheap, in exchange for fixing it up, keep working to buy it one day. But only if Luis thinks it's worth it."

"You have big dreams, *muchacho*. And I believe you are capable of attaining them. But you must be smart, not impulsive. Patience served you well when you needed to escape your Miami home. Use it now while building a new one."

When Lucinda's hand reached up to cup Johnny's cheek, he braced. It always freaked him out a bit, like she could read his thoughts through her fingers. He tried to remain neutral while stuffing down the memory of how much he had been paid to kill a guy.

"Your ambition could entangle you with someone dangerous. Someone you believe cares about you and roots for your success." Her eyes pierced his. "But ultimately you may become just as trapped as you were with your family."

Marco?

"If you do not reconcile your traumatic relationships, you will be destined to seek the same patterns." She took a step back. "I know you avoid what happened to you in that house, but you must face it, or it will destroy you."

Tito and Chico emerged, followed by Luis, who was covered in soot and wiping his face with a handkerchief. "So, it's not *too* terrible. I turned the water on, and can probably get the furnace running, but you're gonna need a new one at some point. The pipes are old and a lot of them should be replaced, but I can order that stuff from the warehouse to save you money."

"Me and the crew will help you," said Johnny. "We'll work around your schedule."

"It might take a while." Luis scratched his head. "And you know, if you start using utilities, those bills are gonna show up somewhere. People will investigate." His eyes landed on Chico. "You could be charged with trespassing."

"I'm making some calls. We're gonna be legit." Johnny stepped closer to hand Luis a pair of hundred-dollar bills.

"What's this?" he asked.

"Take it, please, for your time."

Luis pocketed the cash and shook Johnny's hand. "Thank you. We'll always look out for you boys. You know that."

Johnny caught Lucinda's eye. "I do."

CHAPTER TEN

Johnny and the crew were camped out in front of Roosevelt waiting for the bell. They were already discussing how great their jam sessions could be in the warehouse, planning crazy parties and picking roommates when Johnny saw Sherry. It was hard to miss her platinum blonde hair and fire engine lipstick in the sea of students. She and Betsy were joking with some other kids. When she spotted Johnny, she halted mid-laugh, grabbed Betsy's coat sleeve and snaked through the crowd.

"Hey..." Sherry trailed off.

"It's Johnny."

"I knew that."

Betsy clicked her tongue. "She totally didn't."

"I figured," he said. "To what do we owe this pleasure? Is Catholic school not taking attendance today?"

Sherry flicked a wrist. "They've been up my goddam ass lately. But I managed to sneak out. So," she fingered the lapels of Johnny's coat, "you got anything?"

"It's not even first period."

"Right?" said Betsy. "She's incorrigible."

"I've only got six hours of freedom before I have to return to the convent." Sherry batted her eyes. "Please help me make the best of it, like one line, just to get till lunch."

Johnny looked around, lowering his voice. "Calm down."

"How 'bout your friends?" She threw a hand toward the crew. "Surely one of these hoodlums is carrying something."

Mario peeked over Johnny's shoulder. "Who you stereotyping? We be some *erudite* gangsters over here, you dig?"

"I'm sure." Sherry rolled her eyes. "Ruffian rocket scientists."

"Bitch, I'm American." They all laughed.

As Mario and Sherry bantered, Johnny saw Jessica walking down the block. Her cheeks were flushed from the cold and her long auburn hair bounced with every stride. He tried to catch her eye, but she looked at the ground, filing through the entrance with a hundred other kids.

Johnny refocused. "Look, if a joint will do, I got one of those."

Sherry bit her lip. "Only if you smoke it with us."

"I have a test first period," said Betsy. "But you guys go ahead."

Some of the brothers were peeling away as Johnny contemplated.

"Come on," Sherry said melodiously, fingering Johnny's curly hair.

"Fuck it." He spun to cross the street. She followed.

On the next block, they ducked under the steps of a brownstone, stood in the basement's doorway and lit up. Sherry took a deep puff, savoring the taste before exhaling. Johnny's drag was more conservative, and when she passed it to him again, he only pretended to inhale.

"Do you always hang out with so many guys?" Sherry tapped the ash off the joint.

Johnny shrugged. "I guess I'm just popular."

"Some of them are cute."

"Oh yeah?"

"I like that rugged street boy look." She pressed up against him. "It's hot." Her hand cupped his crotch.

"Jesus." Johnny flinched. "Don't they teach foreplay in Catholic sex-ed?"

Sherry laughed. "Who's got that kind of patience?" She unfastened Johnny's pants to slip her hand inside. She stroked his penis, gentler this time, and he let her. Their mouths connected and he massaged her breasts under her shirt. It did not take long to ejaculate, and once he did, Sherry wiped her hand on the front of his jeans. "You got another joint you could give me for later?"

Johnny repackaged himself in his sticky briefs and zipped up. "Uh, yeah, I guess." He rifled through some pockets and handed one over.

"Thanks." Sherry trotted up to the street. "See ya. I'm off to find Betsy."

◇◇◇

In the cafeteria, Johnny saw Jarrod sitting with Michelle as she finished her lunch. Danni and Jessica were eating across from them. He ducked behind Jessica to whisper into her ear. "You couldn't say hello? That's so cold."

She cringed at his closeness. "You looked busy. I didn't want to interrupt."

He caught a whiff of her fruit-scented shampoo, and straddled the chair beside her. "I'll always make time for you."

"The competition looked pretty steep."

He raised an eyebrow. "Not from where I'm sitting."

She bit her cheek to keep from smiling. "Is that your girlfriend?"

"Nuh-uh, nope. No."

She cocked her head. "So, that's a no?"

Johnny laughed. "I met her at a party a while back. We're just friends."

"I see." Jessica's face flushed as she balled up her lunch bag. "Would you and Jarrod maybe want to hang out with us this weekend? Like, see a movie or something?"

"Fuck, yeah," blurted Michelle. "Let's do it."

Jarrod's eyes mirrored what Johnny was thinking. Despite the precarious status of the downtown building, the crew still planned to go there to clean and start listing necessary repairs. "We can't."

Michelle's face sank. "Why not?"

"Sometimes we work weekends for my uncle," said Johnny, dusting off his go-to lie. "He's got a moving company, and he throws us a few bucks for helping him out. But otherwise, I'd love to."

Jessica twitched a shoulder. "No problem. Whatever."

Alone in the hallway, Jarrod leaned into Johnny. "You like that girl?"

"Why?"

"She doesn't seem your type."

He thought a moment. "Maybe that's why I like her."

Jarrod stopped in front of his classroom, smirking. "So, what's your uncle's name again?"

Johnny laughed. "Did we ever give him one?"

"If we're gonna keep using him as an alibi, we ought to make something up."

"What do I call my phantom uncle?"

"How about Casper," Jarrod suggested.

"I like it," said Johnny. "And his last name could be *Amistoso*. That means friendly in Spanish.

"Casper the friendly ghost. We should be able to remember that."

CHAPTER ELEVEN

At the end of the week, Johnny approached the lunchroom with a few brothers. Jessica was standing alone by the door. "You want to eat with us?" he asked.

She looked at her shoes. "Actually, I was hoping we could do something else."

Her voice was hard to hear over the cavalcade of kids, so Johnny waved the others ahead. "Is everything okay?"

"Yeah." She smiled. "Come with me."

Jessica led Johnny against the flow of students to the stairwell. He sensed her nervousness as they got off on the third floor and walked down the hall. She stopped by the janitor's closet, waited for a pair of teachers to pass, then pulled him inside.

"What the fuck are you doing?" Johnny's foot got hung up on a squeegee and he kicked it away.

She flipped on the light. "Haven't you heard of this place?"

"Yeah." Bleach and pine assaulted Johnny's nostrils, forcing him to breathe through his mouth. "But how have *you*?"

"I just thought, you know..." She bit her lip, fiddling with the front of his shirt.

Johnny looked at this pretty girl trying hard to appear plain. Did she even know what type of guy he was? Did she care? His hormones fought to override his queries. And the conditions. His hands found her waist. Their mouths connected. She caressed the back of his neck. As enticing as it was, her kiss felt forced, amateurish. Her tongue stiffly swirling his, like a brush cleans a toilet.

Johnny's hand migrated up her shirt, exploring the satin of her bra before cupping the firmness of her breast. Her hips pressed into the swelling in his pants. Johnny's body was rife with desire, but his brain kept arguing how wrong it felt. In this shitty closet cluttered with mops and buckets, separated from hordes of students by a single gum-covered door. An acceptable location for Sherry, but this girl was different.

Voices swelled in the hallway. Johnny and Jessica froze until they realized it was just an argument between a few girls over a borrowed sweater. They grinned and resumed fondling each other. Jessica opened Johnny's pants and dropped to her knees. She wrested his erection from his briefs and guided it to her mouth. Watching her made him weak, but her inexperience and discomfort with the task were difficult to ignore. He pulled away and guided her back up.

"What's the matter, was I doing it wrong?"

"No, sweetheart, you're not doing anything wrong. I just can't do this here."

"Why not?"

"Who told you about this place?"

Jessica's eyes dipped. "Michelle. She said she comes here with Jarrod sometimes."

He sighed. "Why did Michelle mention it?"

"She said it would make you more interested in me."

Johnny pressed down the swelling in his pants. "Michelle doesn't know me. And besides, she's a party girl, which is fine for Jarrod, but maybe I'm not into that."

"I'm sorry. I just thought—"

"Look, I do like you. You're smart and creative, and you have opinions about things." Johnny cast a glance around the closet. "You're better than this."

She laughed. "Yeah, but my allowance won't cover a room at The Plaza."

He kissed her. "Maybe I can figure something out." Jessica fixed her shirt while Johnny fastened his pants. "Come on, let's get out of here. We still have time to eat lunch before the next period."

Johnny tried to pay attention in class, but his mind kept drifting to the strawberry scent of Jessica's hair and how her lips felt on his skin. Was he crazy? Who refuses a blowjob? And from a girl he even liked. His boys would have given him so much shit. As torturous as it was for him, he thought Jessica must be feeling worse. It couldn't have been easy for her to make a move on him, only to be rejected.

At the end of last period, he sprinted to a classroom on the fourth floor. He spotted Jessica through the window, listlessly stuffing her notebooks into her bag. She waited for the majority of students to leave before slogging out the door.

"Hey."

Jessica looked up.

"That must be one sad fucking class."

She half-smiled. "I gotta go."

He reached for her arm but she pulled it away. "Jessica, what's the matter?"

"I just, I gotta go." She disappeared into the stairwell.

Outside, Johnny sidled up to Clyde. "Hey, what time does your sister Tiffany leave for work?"

"It depends what day it is. Why?"

"And when do Cecily and Claire get home from school?"

Jarrod overheard them and laughed. "Johnny wants to use your place as a fuck den."

Clyde recoiled. "Say what?"

Johnny grinned. "Sort of."

Jarrod hung an arm over Clyde's shoulder. "Don't worry, he'll screw in your *mom's* bed. She works so much, that mattress ain't even broke in yet."

Johnny shook his head at the sky. "See? *This* is why we need our own place."

"Why don't you use Tito's apartment?" asked Clyde.

"The junkies nodding in the hallway, the crazy couple next door threatening to kill each other, the giant cockroaches..." He rolled his eyes. "The janitor's closet would be more romantic."

"What's the deal?" asked Clyde. "You wanna cut out early one day and use my room?"

"Yeah."

"Just be out by two-forty-five. Claire and Cecily are hardly ever home before three. I'll check with Tiff to see what her work schedule is."

"Thanks."

"You've still got the keys, right?"

"Yeah."

Clyde grinned. "I'll bet if you gave Tiffany a bag of coke, she'd leave the house at 6 a.m."

"For coke?" said Jarrod. "That girl would tickle your balls with a feather *while* you fucked Jessica, then make you both lunch. And change the sheets."

Johnny laughed. "I'll keep it in mind."

CHAPTER TWELVE

Tito turned the van onto West Thirtieth Street, which bisected a rail yard and a vacant lot. A blue Oldsmobile Ninety-Eight was pulled over and Tito parked behind it. Johnny got out of the passenger seat to see the Brick doing the same. Joe Jackson, the dealer's nephew and driver, popped the trunk before joining them. He was tall and muscular, with a short-cropped afro. Johnny had met him three years earlier, when he first started running errands for the Brick.

The three gathered on the sidewalk and shook hands.

The Brick turned to Joe. "I could've sworn I hooked this motherfucker up with a counterfeit driver's license, but he still likes his ass to be driven around." He glowered at Johnny. "You trying to emulate me, boy?"

Johnny shrugged. "I drive, but I don't risk it when I have your cargo."

"That's why I like you, kid. Always thinking." The Brick looked up and down the block, then nodded to Tito, who set a large duffle bag in the Oldsmobile's trunk. He shut it and returned to the van. The Brick shook his head. "A man of few words, that one."

"Don't I know it," said Johnny. "But when he does talk, it's worth listening."

The Brick leaned against the car. "So, how's the real estate business treating you? Do I need to start shopping for a housewarming gift?"

"It's bullshit." Johnny swiped his face. "I found this old warehouse for sale downtown. It'd be perfect, but I keep calling to ask what the deal is, and all they say is someone will get back to me. I'm still waiting."

"You witnessing this shit?" The Brick slapped Joe's chest. "Fucking kid thinks he's the Harry Helmsley of high school."

Joe grinned. "If anyone could pull it off, it'd be him."

"Damn straight." The Brick jutted his chin at Johnny. "I suppose I'll be working for *you* before long."

Johnny folded his arms. "Have Joey bring me your résumé and I'll take it under consideration."

"Right." The Brick's eyes narrowed. "I hear you two have been hanging out lately. That's a dangerous combination."

"If Joe joins the gang, he'll be the only one working on a business degree."

The Brick smiled, then cast his eyes downward. "Look, I got a bit of bad news."

Johnny's brows furrowed. "You don't want me and Joe hanging out?"

"No, nothing like that." The Brick flashed a palm. "In fact, he might have more time opening up here shortly."

Johnny's eyes toggled between Joe and the Brick. "What's going on? You're not retiring, are you?"

"Let's just say I need to take a medical leave of absence."

Johnny's stomach dropped. "How come?"

The man shared a tight-lipped smile with his nephew. "They found a spot on my lung."

Johnny blew out a breath. "But they can treat it, right?" Whoever *they* were.

The Brick rocked his head. "Only time will tell."

Was it that serious? Johnny tried to get a read on Joe, but years with his uncle had taught him to be stoic. As concerned as Johnny was for the man's health, it was the worst possible time to lose his only steady source of income.

The Brick put a hand on Johnny's shoulder. "I know you got big dreams, son, but you're young. You got time." He pushed off the Olds. Slipping into the seat, he handed Johnny a paper bag from the glove box. "I put a little something extra in there for you, due to the short notice and all."

"Thanks." Johnny stuffed the money in a coat pocket, trying to think of something to say. "I hope it goes well."

"Me, too, Colombiano." He picked a newspaper off the floor. It was folded open to a page. "You hear about this?"

Johnny looked. "What?"

"Four months ago, some guy was shot on the Upper West Side." The Brick flicked the paper with the back of his hand. "New details were just released."

Johnny's insides ignited.

"The guy was a bank manager, and, as it turns out, corrupt as a motherfucker. Used his branch to launder money. And sell cocaine." The Brick wagged his head. "Back in the day I used to know this creep." His eyes locked onto Johnny's. "And so did Marco."

Johnny labored to keep his expression neutral. "Yeah, so?"

"I sent you to that crazy cokehead for a one-time transaction, but I hope that was it. You do *not* want to get involved with him. Because this?" He flapped the paper. "This has Marco's name written all over it."

CHAPTER THIRTEEN

At the end of February, the Dogs of War took advantage of the warm Sunday to play basketball with some recent recruits. They met at the court on Sixth Avenue, above the West Fourth Street subway station. The games started out competitive and physical, with shoulders being thrown and a few "unintentional" trips, but as the afternoon rolled on, the crew was trading more insults than moves. A timeout was called for a few volunteers to make a run for cigarettes and drinks.

As Johnny stood on the sidelines, watching the remaining members take practice shots, a dozen men jogged up from the subway station. They spread out around the court, fingers hooked in the chain-link fence. The double cross emblem was evident, stitched on clothing and tattooed on exposed skin.

These fucking guys again? Johnny blew a warning whistle to his brothers, and they stopped to look. The men filed around the corner entrance and fanned out. A husky guy ripped the ball from Maurice's hands. "You don't have a problem if we play, do you?" He tossed it to a comrade, then shoved Maurice to the ground. Jeff Tate, a burly redhead, lurched to his defense and got clocked in the face by another man. Mario tried to retaliate, but two Crosses grabbed him by the arms.

Johnny's brothers looked to him for a cue. He could see guns in a few waistbands, so he shook his head.

"What's the matter," said the one holding the ball. "You pussies don't want to play us?" He dribbled a small circle before dunking it through the hoop. Another Cross grabbed it, bounced it a few times, then winged it hard at Clyde, who ducked before it hit his head. Other Dog brothers endured a shove here and a smack there, but they heeded the warning not to retaliate.

Johnny stood motionless. There had to be a way to keep this from escalating. He forced himself to remain calm while hunting for any opportunity.

When Eric, Chico and JJ returned from the store, a beefy man with a shaved head and thick gold chains perked up. "Check this shit out. It's our delivery." His cohorts zeroed in on the new targets as he swiped the three boys inside the court. He grabbed the paper bags and dumped them out. Cans of soda and cigarette packs rained onto the ground. Crosses grabbed what they wanted.

Johnny was approached by a guy with a slight build and curly dark hair. He had a large mole beneath one nostril. An attempt to camouflage it with a wispy mustache only made it more intriguing as the mole hairs fought to desegregate by vining around the others. "I recognize these fucking kids." He clamped a hand onto the nape of Johnny's neck. "They're those wannabes from the tunnel." He laughed, shaking Johnny hard enough to make his head wag. "And *this* fucker is their king."

Johnny continued to evaluate the situation. The closest gun was in the belt of a guy several yards away. If he sprinted, he might be able to grab it, but that could incite chaos. Allowing a beating might be the only way out of this. It wouldn't be the worst thing he had experienced. But it might be for his boys.

Some Crosses began to drift closer to Johnny, their expressions belligerent. The Mole Man shoved Johnny toward them. Hands reached out to grab him when someone whistled. Everyone turned. César Aguilar was entering the court flanked by more Crosses, a basketball tucked under his arm.

His men parted as he walked up to Johnny. "What's up, little brother? You giving my boys a hard time?" César put an arm around Johnny and ruffled his hair. "How 'bout it, young gangster, you been considering my offer?" He assessed his men as they loomed over the younger kids. "From where I'm standing it's looking pretty good." He grabbed Johnny's wrist and pushed up his sleeve. "And you know what else would look good?" Using his index finger, he drew two crosses on the inside of Johnny's forearm.

"No disrespect," said Johnny, "but like I told you, we're just doing our own thing."

"And how do I know your thing ain't gonna bleed into my thing?"

César's hold on Johnny's arm was getting tighter. It shortened his breath. Made the court seem smaller. "I guess you'll have to take my word."

"Your word, huh?" César noticed the thick scarring around Johnny's wrist. He ran a thumb over the disfiguration, and Johnny winced. He grabbed the other hand to see more of the same. César's face softened, and his lips quivered like he was going to say something. Instead, he released his grip, then weaved amid his gang. "From now on, hands off *Los Perritos*, you hear?"

Some Crosses scowled, but César shot them a look.

"I'm telling all of you. Dos Cruces will not fuck with the Dogs of War. Anyone with a problem can answer to me!" He circled back to Johnny. "Now take your crew the fuck outta here so we can play."

The younger gang filed toward the gate when the bald-headed man with the chains spoke out. "Hey kid, don't you want your ball?" He stood in the center of the court eyeing Johnny, the basketball balanced in his meaty mitt, a .45 tucked in front of his pants.

Clyde leaned toward Johnny. "Just leave it. Let's go."

But Johnny couldn't. Not after César's declaration. He needed to demonstrate that he trusted the man's word. And if he was full of shit, and they dropped him right there, at least his brothers would be safely out of the gate.

Johnny straightened. He walked past the piercing stares and posturing bodies, César's included. He stopped in front of the bald man, holding his gaze a moment before taking the ball, then turned to retreat through the crowd.

Once the crew was a few blocks away, Mario took the basketball from Johnny. "You couldn't get our butts and soda back, too?" He dribbled a few paces. "Weak."

Johnny laughed. "At least I didn't get us shot."

Chico matched Johnny's stride. "What's that César guy's deal with you anyway?"

"I don't know." Johnny rubbed his wrists. "Maybe he was tied up in a cellar, too."

"You think César's word is gonna hold?" asked Clyde.

Johnny shrugged.

"I know we're trying to save up for that loft," said Jarrod, "but we might want to consider buying more protection."

"If shit had *really* gone down," said Mario, "we wouldn't have stood a chance."

Chico tapped Johnny's arm. "You shoot good enough to pick those fuckers off one by one if you wanted to. Just saying."

"We could also mow them down with machine guns." Johnny waved him off. "But that's not how to play it. I've got respect for César. He's just surrounded by too many bullies. In time they'll probably forget about us and move on."

CHAPTER FOURTEEN

Johnny was standing outside Roosevelt bantering with his brothers when he saw Jessica coming down the block. He flicked his cigarette butt into the gutter and jumped up to intercept her. "Just checking to see if you're still brushing me off."

Her face puckered.

"I'm serious." He twitched a shoulder. "Because then I could move on. You know, maybe rescue other girls from trying to suck dicks in a broom closet."

Jessica rolled her eyes. "Stop it."

"Stop what?"

"It was embarrassing for me, that's all."

"For *you*?" He scrunched his face. "Imagine how embarrassed I was when my boys found out I refused a blowjob?"

She cracked a smile and Johnny pulled her in for a hug. His mouth found her ear. "If you want to be together, like *really* together, I have a key to Clyde's apartment. It's not far, and no one will be there this afternoon."

"Seriously?"

"If we duck out at lunch, we'd have a few hours at least."

"I've never cut school before." She chewed a thumbnail.

"Think about it." Johnny pulled her hand away and kissed it. "We'll meet by the cafeteria. If you wanna go, we'll go. If not, we'll just eat together." He smiled, then spun toward the school's entrance.

◇◇◇

Jessica leaned against the wall outside the lunchroom, head hung. Auburn tresses obscured her face, but as Johnny neared, he could see that her cheeks were flushed. He swiped a lock behind her ear. "What's the verdict?"

"Let's go." She turned toward the exits.

"Oh, shit. Really?"

"Yeah."

Johnny made small talk as he led Jessica to Eleventh Avenue and Twenty-Eighth Street, but his body was humming with desire. He let them into the lobby of the six-story walk-up. On the fourth floor, he put an ear to Clyde's apartment door before unlocking it.

Jesica dropped her bookbag and coat by the dining table and looked around. The apartment was cluttered but clean. Johnny peeled off his coat and opened the refrigerator. "You want something to drink?"

"Sure."

"Apple juice or Coke?"

"Juice, but I'll share it with you." She leaned on the counter, watching Johnny pour a glass and take a gulp before handing it to her. "You really know your way around this place."

"There was a time when I practically lived here. Jarrod, too."

"How come?"

"We'd be hanging out together, it'd get late, so we'd just crash here. His mom has always been cool about it."

"It's a pretty small apartment. How big is his family?"

"A mom and three sisters."

"That's some tight quarters." Jessica turned the glass in her hands. "Didn't you want to go home?"

"It's too long a story." Johnny took the juice from her and set it on the counter, then leaned in for a kiss. Unlike in the janitor's closet, her touch seemed less scripted. He guided her down the hall toward Clyde's room. Inside, they kicked off their shoes. Johnny pulled up Jessica's sweater while she unbuttoned the flannel top over his long-sleeved tee. They both wrestled to shimmy off their jeans as they groped and tongued each other. Johnny ripped back Clyde's quilt and laid Jessica down. She looked so beautiful against the sheets, her hair fanned out around her head, hazel eyes looking up at him. "Are you sure you want to do this?"

She nodded. "I'm sure."

Johnny crawled beside her. They continued to disrobe, taking time to explore each other with hands and mouths. Once their bodies united, they rocked in unison until Johnny felt Jessica's breath catch, and he allowed himself to release. Breathless, he rolled onto his back. Jessica draped over him, her head on his chest.

"No one's ever done that to me before," she said.

"Wait." Johnny kinked his neck to look at her. "That was your first time?"

"No, I mean, people have done that—just one person. Actually, twice. But he never made me feel like that." She nuzzled deeper into him. "He didn't make me cum."

"Maybe you weren't ready."

"I thought I was. I mean, I wanted to. It just didn't turn out like I expected."

Johnny smiled. "Maybe the guy was an asshole."

Jessica laughed. "He wasn't as nice as you."

His smile faded. "I'm not nice."

"Sure, you are." Jessica rolled onto an elbow to look at him. "Do you know the first time I saw you?"

Johnny shook his head.

"Well, I had *seen* you before, but this was the first time I really noticed you. It was last year, the middle of ninth grade. I was new and freaked out because I wasn't prepared for how rough Roosevelt was." She caressed Johnny's chest. "Anyway, I was in the staircase between classes and it was mobbed, like always, when I got shoved hard from behind. I was about to fall flat on my face, but someone caught me. It was you. At first, I got scared because I knew you were one of the tough kids." Jessica bit her lip. "I thought you'd get mad at me for banging into you, but you didn't. You seemed concerned and asked if I was okay. That's when I realized you weren't just some thug." Jessica smiled. "I've been noticing you ever since, but you probably don't even remember that."

"Sorry." He touched her cheek. "A lot of shit goes on in those staircases, and I've shoved people, too. But they deserved it."

"I'm not surprised you don't remember. Back then I had frizzy hair and braces. You noticed me eventually."

"Yeah." Johnny rolled on top of her. "I noticed you eventually."

When they were too weak and woozy to have any more sex, they got up to dress, but neither was ready to separate. They wandered the streets together, arms looped to fend off the early March chill.

"What sign are you?" Jessica asked.

"Huh?"

She laughed. "When's your birthday?"

Lying about it had become so routine Johnny's heart rate didn't even waver anymore. "April first."

"Really?" Jessica hopped in excitement. "Mine's on the ninth. We're both Aries."

"Oh yeah?" He forced a grin. "Great."

Jessica rattled on about rams and fire signs, what their personality traits were, then touted her opinions about which newspaper had the best horoscopes. Johnny tried to keep up with it all, but couldn't get past the theory that one twelfth of the global population was having the same exact day.

On East Thirty-Eighth, Jessica stopped walking. "This is me. Do you want to come up, meet my parents?"

Johnny browsed the fifteen-story Italianate style building. *No fucking way*.

"You could stay for dinner." She tugged his arm. "Aren't you hungry? We never ate lunch."

He was hungry, and decent home-cooked meals were hard to come by. He decided it might also be fun to see Jessica's world, observe the dynamics of a normal family. He'd just have to keep the lies straight. "Do I look okay to meet them?"

"They're not royalty. You don't have to dress."

"That's not what I meant." Johnny cocked his head. "I don't want to look like I just fucked their daughter."

Jessica pulled him into the lobby. She waved at the blue-suited man behind a semi-circular desk. "Hey, Freddy."

"Good afternoon, Miss Jessica." Freddy bowed his head, but gave Johnny a quick once-over before they stepped into an elevator.

Jessica pressed the button for the eighth floor. "He's the nicest doorman we have," she said as they ascended. "They're all decent, but he's been here the longest and knows everybody."

"How long have you lived here?"

"All my life."

Johnny could not imagine such stability.

Inside the apartment, hardwood floors led down a hallway lined with closets. They tossed their bags on a chair in the corner, and Jessica hung their coats.

"Honey, is that you?" a voice called from within.

"Yeah, Mom, and I brought a friend from school. Is that okay?"

"Of course."

Jessica's home looked lived-in and comfortable, the layout functional, with furniture that was well-worn but good quality. She ushered Johnny to the galley kitchen, where her mother stood at the counter chopping vegetables. She was thin and pallid, with layered red hair. Her casual business attire consisted of a white shirt under a pink sweater vest, with beige, polyester bell bottoms.

"Mom, this is Johnny."

Her face opened. "Oh, I thought you meant Danni."

Johnny folded his hands in front of him. "Hello, Mrs. um—" He shot Jessica a wide-eyed look. She mouthed *Baxter* while pretending to scratch her face. "Mrs. Baxter. Nice to meet you."

She fanned the air. "Please, call me Carol."

Jessica walked behind the counter to nose around. "What're you cooking?"

"Just boring old meatloaf with mashed potatoes." Carol over-dramatized abashment.

"Is it all right if Johnny stays?"

"Sure, um, of course."

"Great." Jessica kissed her cheek. "I'm gonna show him my room, okay?"

Jessica spun to leave, and Johnny fell in line behind her. Down another hall she pointed out the bathroom and her brother's room before opening her door. The walls were light pink. A flowery lavender quilt covered her brass frame bed, which was cluttered with stuffed animals. Posters of pop singers were taped above it.

Johnny drifted inside, mouth agape.

"What? You don't like it?"

"No, it's...great." He plucked an elephant from the bed. The stuffing was so deteriorated the head and trunk flopped to the side. "I've been thinking of redoing my room like this."

Jessica laughed and fell into his arms. Their hug became a kiss, which evolved to groping, until they heard Carol announcing that she had made hot chocolate. "It might be safer to do homework." Jessica pulled away. "You could help me with my Spanish."

Johnny smiled. *"Sí, no problema."*

They brought their books to the dinner table. Carol set two steaming mugs in front of them, then turned toward the living room. "Chad, have you met your sister's friend?"

A younger fair-haired kid sat on the floor watching TV. He offered a wave and Johnny nodded back. "He's still in junior high," Jessica muttered. "Next year he'll be joining us." Her eye-roll summarized their relationship.

The pair had finished Jessica's Spanish assignment and were onto their science homework when Mr. Baxter walked in. He had a Clark Kent vibe, but it was all nerd. No super powers. Nor was he hiding any muscle under that pastel blue leisure suit. He set down his briefcase, eyed Johnny and gave Carol a peck on the cheek.

"Walter, this is Johnny, Jessica's friend from school." When Carol said his name, there was a hamster-like inflection.

Johnny stood and outstretched his arm. "Hello, Mr. Baxter."

Walter forced a smile and stepped closer to shake hands. "From Roosevelt, huh?"

"Yes." Johnny sat back down.

Walter kissed the top of Jessica's head and she beamed at him. "What's your last name?"

"Avalon."

"You don't live around here, do you?"

Here it comes. "No, I'm up in Washington Heights."

"That's a long commute. Aren't there schools in your neighborhood?"

"Yes, but most of my friends live downtown and go to that school."

Walter glimpsed at the books and squeezed Jessica's shoulder. "Are you helping him with his homework, sweetheart?" He snickered. "She's such a brainiac, you know."

What a dick.

"Actually, Dad, he's helping me."

Before Walter could object, Carol ordered the table be cleared and set because dinner was ready. Johnny and Jessica jumped up to comply. Chad also shuffled in. When everyone was seated, she brought out the food. Johnny's mouth watered at the pile of meatloaf slices, the steaming mashed potatoes and buttered carrots. Johnny was so hungry he could have shoveled in half of it. Instead, he labored to keep pace with the others. "Thank you for inviting me."

"You're very welcome." She dabbed her mouth with a napkin. "Is your mother a good cook?"

"Sort of, but she works late a lot."

"What do your parents do?" asked Walter.

"My mother's a receptionist at Columbia Presbyterian, and my dad's a security guard at a building in midtown."

"Cool," said Chad. "Does he carry a gun?"

Walter scowled at Chad, but Johnny laughed. "No, just a walkie-talkie."

"Which building is it?" Walter pressed.

Think fast. "He just got that job, and I haven't seen him to ask because it's a night shift."

"I see." Walter poked his carrots with a fork. "And where are you from?"

Johnny understood the question. Walter didn't care if he had lived in, say, Bensonhurst or Weehawken before moving to Manhattan. He wanted to know which third world country his people were from. It was so predictable that Johnny had to sip some water to stop smirking. If Walter wanted to know his ethnicity so badly, he'd have to work for it. Maybe with the added bonus of looking like an ass in front of his daughter. "I'm from New York."

Walter's brows furrowed. "No, I mean, are your parents Hispanic?"

"They're originally from Colombia, but my mother is half Turkish."

"Is English your second language?"

Have I not been speaking clearly, motherfucker? "I was born here. It's my first language." He held Walter's gaze. "But I'm also fluent in Spanish and Turkish, and pretty good at French, German, and Portuguese, too." Johnny popped his last piece of meatloaf in his mouth. "Carol, this is *so* delicious."

"Have more." She piled slices on his plate.

"I'll have more, too," Chad said, grinning.

After dinner, Johnny thanked Jessica's family before she walked him to the elevator. "That wasn't so bad, was it?"

"Your mom's nice."

"Stop." Jessica swatted him. "My dad's not that bad. He's a little..."

"Tight-assed?"

Jessica laughed. "Yeah. But he'll loosen up. He's just overprotective."

Not the word Johnny would have chosen, but if Jessica wasn't ready to see her father's shortcomings, who was he to point them out? He wrapped his arms around her. "This day was amazing." They hugged until the elevator came, and he peeled away.

In the lobby, Freddy put up a hand. *"Mira, un memento."*

Johnny went over. *¿Qué quieres?"*

"Don't you live uptown, near Dyckman?"

Johnny nodded.

"I thought so, because I'm on Vermilyea, by 204." He wagged a finger. "I've seen you in that funky-looking van. The one with dead bugs and rats on it."

Johnny laughed. "It's pretty conspicuous. Might be time to paint it."

Freddy clutched his chest. "You'll break my heart. That thing always cracks me up."

An elderly woman came into the lobby with a full shopping cart, and Freddy stepped from the desk to help her into the elevator. He had a slight build, late twenties, probably Dominican by his accent.

"Jessica says you've been here a long time," Johnny said when he returned.

"Six years." He nodded. "She's a nice girl. I've always looked out for her. Her brother, too."

"Cool." Johnny brushed the desk. "So, what's with the parents?"

A dimple appeared in Freddy's cheek. "Let me guess, the father wasn't so happy to meet you."

"You got that right." They shared a grin.

"Basically, he has that thing where when you ain't got a lot, you shit on people with less to make yourself feel better."

"That's a thorough diagnosis." Johnny pursed his bottom lip. "You into psychology or something?"

"Sociology. But it's just a hobby for now." Freddy twitched a shoulder. "One day I'd like to pursue it, maybe go to college. But that shit takes time and money, neither of which I possess at the moment." He opened his arms to his station. "I'm too busy being New York's greatest doorman."

"It's important work. Someone has to protect these families from what lurks in those streets." They laughed and Johnny offered a hand. "Hey, man, it was really nice meeting you."

Freddy shook back. "Same."

CHAPTER FIFTEEN

By the end of March, Chico's father had been to the warehouse several times, repairing and replacing parts. With the help of gang members, the loft now had heat and hot water piping to all the units.

Johnny was still getting the runaround whenever he called RealCorp: they were a global company, the agent representing that listing was based abroad, the time differential, blah, blah, blah. But at least he wasn't hearing *no*.

The precarious building status didn't hinder the crew's enthusiasm for fixing it up. They scrubbed a bathroom here and a kitchen there while waiting for Luis to do his thing, but once they got going, it was hard to stop. Soon they were replacing lightbulbs and washing windows. The mere prospect of having their own apartments prompted somewhat of a scavenger hunt. If a mattress or dresser were spotted on a curb, they would swing by with the van to grab it. Before long, it became a full-on competition, with each Dog brother hunting for more and bigger stuff. Some even combed the Village Voice classifieds: *If you can haul it, you can have it.*

When grabbing a slice of pizza, salt and pepper shakers might disappear from the counter. If the place was crowded enough, maybe even a napkin dispenser. At diners, silverware found its way into pockets. Ditto ashtrays and water glasses. "I thought the busboy was out sick today," one waiter said to Jarrod, Clyde and Mario as they paid their check. They just shrugged, hoping the motion didn't cause their coats to clink. Meanwhile, the booty accumulated in piles around the loft, even though everyone knew it might be for naught.

Ever since having sex, Johnny and Jessica couldn't keep their hands off each other. Johnny kept checking with Clyde to see if his apartment was safe to use, but Jessica was afraid of getting busted for missing too many classes. On April first, she arrived on the school block beaming.

"Hey Birthday Boy." She gave Johnny a hug.

He hesitated a moment before hugging back. "Shit, I almost forgot." He did forget.

She handed him a colorfully wrapped package.

Leon edged over. "It's your birthday?"

"Yes," Clyde said through gritted teeth, dragging him away.

Johnny moved from his crew to open the gift. It was a black Aerosmith T-shirt. "How did you—"

"I asked Michelle to ask Jarrod." She held it against him for sizing. "She said you guys have a rock band. Don't you like that group?"

"Yeah, sure. Thanks."

"So," Jessica picked a fingernail, "can we duck out at lunch?"

"I thought you didn't want to get in trouble."

"It's a special occasion. I'll take the risk."

"Fuck that." He pulled her close. "I'll tell you it's my birthday every day."

In Clyde's bedroom, they explored new ways to experience each other. Between the sex, they lay entwined, caressing and talking, but Jessica was starting to inquire about his tattoo, what it represented and why he got it. The questions about his home life were also becoming more pointed. His deflections were successful, only because she was too polite to press, but he knew if they got closer that would change. He could already feel her fingers lingering over the scars on his body, but he wasn't ready to worry about it yet. Unpleasantness was too easy to avoid in her arms.

In the lobby of Jessica's building, she tried to get him to come up again, but he said he had to help his uncle with the moving company. Good old Uncle Casper.

"Fine, but next weekend you're coming to dinner."

"Huh?"

"Every birthday my parents take me to my favorite restaurant. It's a few blocks from here. We're going next Friday." She folded her arms. "You have to come."

"With your parents?"

"The food's really good."

Johnny searched the ceiling for an excuse.

"It's my birthday." She kissed him and backed into the elevator. "I should get what I want."

When the door slid closed, Freddy had his arms folded. "What's the matter, one dinner with the Baxters was enough?"

"You heard that shit?" Johnny swung by the desk to slap him five. "There might be a fistfight at the next one."

"Aw, c'mon." Freddy laughed. "The old man ain't so bad. And besides, his girl is worth it."

"That she is," Johnny said before heading out the door.

It was still early, so he took the train to Washington Square Park. He did a lap to see if any brothers were hanging out. He also checked the chess tables, but the Brick was absent, too. Maybe he had started cancer treatments. Johnny pondered the deficit that would put in the park's availability of loose joints.

He lit a cigarette and flopped down on a bench near the arch. His muscles were still lethargic and spasming from the sex. The feeling was intoxicating, different from anything he had felt before. That made him nervous.

"You got an extra cigarette?" Margaret sat beside him. Even dressed down she looked stunning in blue jeans, a cashmere sweater and peacoat.

"For you? Anything." Johnny pulled a pack of Marlboros from his pocket and shook one out, then lit it for her.

Margaret drew in some smoke and crossed her legs. "I haven't seen you on my couch lately. I'm starting to take it personally."

Johnny cocked a knee to face her. "It's a fine couch, really. And the view from there is spectacular."

Margaret frowned. "Are you seeing other couches?"

He laughed. "Yes, now that you mention it. Tito got his own place a while back. I've been crashing there."

"You're really moving up in the world."

"If that's what you call it."

"I haven't seen your boys around much either."

"We've had some other projects going on."

"Sounds mysterious."

"Not really. Just working on fixing up a place."

"Yours or someone else's?"

"I'd like it to be mine, but no one returns my calls."

Margaret tapped the ash from her cigarette. "If you need help, one of my clients is a real estate lawyer."

"Are you shitting me?"

"Nope."

"He'd help a bunch of kids buy a run-down warehouse without asking where the money came from?"

Margaret shrugged. "He's married with three young children, yet he screws me once a week, so his morals can't be that strong. He'd probably do it if the price was right." She winked. "And if I asked him nicely."

"Wow." Johnny squashed out his butt with his sneaker. "I might take you up on that."

"One problem solved." She patted his knee. "What else is on your mind, girl trouble?"

Johnny shrunk back. "How the fuck—"

She laughed. "It's my business, sweetheart. I can smell it on you." Margaret brushed a black tress behind her shoulder. "Have you found yourself a girlfriend?"

"Sort of."

"Sort of?"

"She's in my school. We just started seeing each other."

"And?"

"I don't think I'm good for her."

"Why not? You're good-looking, smart, hardworking..."

"But she's a nice girl, and I'm a street boy."

"Lots of nice girls have bad boy fantasies."

"But is it okay to be with someone if they think you're something you're not?"

Margaret hung an arm over the backrest. "In my line of work, I see a lot of liars and cheaters. Some of them are nice guys, at least in certain ways. But most women understand that men are basically dogs." She flicked her butt into the grass. "And you have a dog permanently tattooed on your arm, so what does that say?"

Johnny smiled. "You make a point."

"If you're worried about it, she must mean a lot."

"I think she does."

"Well then, give her what you can without giving up who you are. If it's enough she'll stay. If not, you move on."

"You make it sound so simple." He exhaled a long breath. "It's her birthday next week and I don't even know what to get her."

Margaret perked up. "She's an Aries?"

"Jesus. You too with that shit?"

"Listen, women like astrology." Margaret tapped her chin. "That means her birthstone is a diamond. You could get her some jewelry, unless you think it's too soon."

"Me? I don't know jack shit about jewelry. And what the fuck's a birthstone?"

"Don't worry about it. I could help you pick something out. It'll be fun. How much money you got?"

"A couple hundred."

Margaret wagged her head. "Of course, you do. I know who you work for." She stood. "Come on. I know a place near here."

CHAPTER SIXTEEN

"What's that?"

Clyde's face appeared over Johnny's shoulder and he snapped closed the black velvet box.

"Oh shit. Is that for Jessica?"

Jarrod squeezed in beside Clyde. "What's going on?"

Johnny turned to face them. "It's nothing."

"C'mon, lemme see." Clyde grabbed the case and Johnny let him, knowing it was futile. Cracking it open, he revealed a petit cable link gold chain. "Oh snap. Where'd you find this?"

Jarrod fingered the heart pendant dusted with diamond fragments. "Damn. That's a serious gift for a chick you just started banging."

"I know," said Johnny. "Margaret helped me pick it out. She was so excited it was hard not to get caught up in the moment." He took back the box and stuffed it in his coat pocket. "It's stupid. I shouldn't even give it to her."

Clyde's chin pointed down the school block. "You better figure it out because here she comes."

From a distance Jessica looked more radiant than usual. She had accented her eyes with some liner and shadow. Her cheeks and lips were rosier, too, but that could have been attributed to the hike from the bus stop. Johnny was about to catch her attention when something else distracted her and she halted. Johnny craned his neck to see her talking to Hector. He must have said something funny because they were laughing. Then they began exchanging materials from their bookbags.

Jarrod backhanded Johnny's arm. "What the fuck's she doing with that weasel?"

"I don't know."

"You think he's moving in on purpose, to get even for denying him membership?"

Clyde sucked his cheek. "He doesn't have those kinda balls."

"No, he doesn't." Johnny's fingers curled into fists. "And he's not that stupid. But he might blab about our gang status."

"Does Jessica *not know*?" Jarrod's arms flung out like wet spaghetti. "How is that even possible? It's not like we're hiding it."

"But we don't flaunt it, either. Not around school, anyway." Johnny's weight shifted. "Does Michelle know?"

Jarrod twitched a shoulder. "She's never flat-out said anything to me, but I think it's pretty obvious."

Johnny checked the block. Jessica and Hector had resumed walking. When she saw Johnny, she redirected toward him.

Hector gave them a nod. "Hey, guys. How's it going."

"Good." Johnny smiled through a clenched jaw.

"I'll see you in class?" Jessica said to Hector. He took the hint and bowed out.

"You know him?"

"Just from Social Studies. Why?"

"No reason."

Jessica bit her lip. "Are you jealous?"

"No." Johnny's eyes held hers. "I'm not jealous. But you do look exceptionally beautiful today." He cocked his head. "Is it a special occasion?"

"Fuck you." Jessica fell into him and they hugged.

"Happy Birthday, baby."

"You're still meeting us for dinner tonight, right?"

"Yeah."

Her weight pressed the gift box into Johnny's hip. Was he really going to do this? The necklace would only lead her on, complicate things. He could just give her the card. Even without Margaret's help, he had combed through a stationary store, bypassing the corny Hallmark crap for something more elegant. He found one with a serene watercolor depicting a pond full of flowers. It was blank inside, but he had put a lot of thought into his handwritten message: *Your beauty, your touch, and your kind heart make me aspire to be the person you think I am.* That ought to be enough to impress any girl.

As Johnny's brain toiled to convince him otherwise, his hand reached into his pocket. "I got you something, but you can't open it here."

Jessica stepped back at the sight of the velvet case.

Johnny slipped it into her bookbag. "I mean it. And definitely don't let your parents see it."

She cocked her hip. "You don't really expect me not to look, do you?"

"Yeah, I actually do." Johnny remained stone-faced. "Unless you want some dipshit to steal it." He retrieved the card from an inside pocket. "But you can open this whenever." He kissed her. "C'mon. We gotta get to class."

◇◇◇

Johnny slowed to look in the picture window of Jake's Tavern on East Thirty-Ninth. Pendant lights rappelled from the ceiling toward cloth-covered tables. Amber diamond-point candle holders, flanked by salt and pepper shakers, held court for the place settings, each adorned with a starchy napkin folded into a pop tent. A bar, still bustling with remnants of the happy hour crowd, was off to one side. Despite the restaurant's casual vibe, it was nicer than any place Johnny had ever eaten.

He spotted the Baxters at a round table in the center of the dining room, where a waiter was passing out menus. Jessica was donned in a pink cowl neck sweater and slacks. Thankfully, not too fancy to upstage his black button-down shirt and jeans: the nicest thing he owned. On closer inspection, he saw the gold chain around her neck. *Motherfucker.*

Johnny leaned on the brick wall by the entrance. He could still bail. It wasn't like her parents were expecting much from him. But then he flashed on his deranged family—his former family, as he liked to call them—and everything they'd put him through. His alliances with killers and drug dealers popped into his head, and how he had handled himself when faced with Dos Cruces. For what? To be intimidated by the parents of some run-of-the-mill, middle-class nuclear family?

Johnny pulled open the door, nodded to the hostess at the booth, and beelined to the Baxter's table. Jessica smiled, pulling out the chair between her and Carol.

"You made it," said Carol.

"I did." Johnny patted her back, then extended a hand to Walter. "Thanks for including me."

"It's our pleasure." Walter almost sounded convincing.

Chad half-stood to stick his doughy mitt into the mix. Johnny shook it too, then sat. He wasn't sure if it was appropriate to kiss Jessica, but since she had betrayed him, it was easier not to. "Hi," he said flatly, his eyes toggling between hers and the heart pendant.

She returned a sheepish smile.

Walter took command of the table. "So, Johnny, this place has great steaks. Or, if you like Italian, the best chicken parm. But Carol swears by the veal Marsala, don't you dear?" He gave her a plastered-on grin, as if saying, "How am I doing?"

Carol rolled her eyes and opened a menu.

While they perused the selections, the waiter brought a basket of bread and filled the water glasses. When he took everyone's order, Johnny went with a steak and French fries, and Jessica ordered the same.

Carol took a slice of bread and passed Johnny the basket. "We couldn't help but notice your birthday gift."

"I love it." Jessica's hand brushed her neck. "And it's my birthstone. How did you know?"

Johnny stabbed at the butter dish with his knife. If he could cram a slab of bread into his mouth, that might delay the ambush a few moments.

"Real gold, huh?" Walter stroked his jowls. "And are those diamond flakes?"

"Dust," Johnny mumbled through masticated bread.

"Must've been pretty expensive."

Chad coughed out a laugh. "He said you probably stole it."

94

Carol and Walter's heads snapped toward Chad, and Johnny almost spit out a few crumbs.

Chad shrugged. "What?" He slurped some Coke through a straw.

Walter put up a hand. "All I meant was—"

"As I *explained* to my father, you work." Jessica directed a measured tone toward Johnny. "I told them about your uncle with the moving company, and how you're always helping him after school and weekends. That's how you could afford the necklace." Her face softened. "Which, by the way, is the loveliest thing I've ever received." She raised her eyebrows at her father, then planted a kiss on Johnny's cheek.

It was difficult to hear Jessica regurgitate the lies Johnny had fed her, but worth it to make Walter look like a dick.

The tension was interrupted when the waiter brought out the food. "So, Johnny," Chad said between bites of his fish and chips. "I hear Roosevelt can be kinda rough, like, fights breaking out sometimes." His tongue swiped a blob of tartar sauce from his lip. "Have you ever had to kick anyone's ass?"

Carol lay a hand on Johnny's arm. "Forgive him, please. We suspect the hospital may have switched some babies at birth."

Johnny laughed, then looked at Chad. "Nobody ever messes with *me*." He forked a French fry into his mouth.

"For the record, Johnny is a straight A student." Jessica hacked at her steak.

"Really?" Walter's head cocked at Johnny. "Do you plan to go to college when you graduate?"

At least he said *when* instead of *if.* "I doubt it."

"But he could if he wanted to," Jessica added.

Walter wouldn't let it go. "Your parents must be very proud of you. Don't they want to see you get a good education?"

Johnny shrugged.

"Maybe they could help you apply for scholarships, have some of your teachers write letters of commendation..."

Listening to Walter rattle on about the resources available to help the underprivileged, Johnny's jaw got so tense he couldn't chew. He had never said word one about his family's financial status. Not even to Jessica, who went to the same shitty-ass public school. Furthermore, Johnny was probably sitting on more money right now than Walter had ever saved in his whole life.

Johnny watched Walter pontificate, so smug and patronizing. Who the fuck was this asshole to assume he was that bad off. He visualized pulling a 9mm from under the table. He could feel the weight of the gun in his hand, the power of it. He centered the barrel on Walter's forehead. *I got your letters of commendation right here.* Locking his elbows, he squeezed the trigger. The bullet propelled above the table in slow motion, connecting just above the bridge of Walter's stupid fucking glasses. The impact sent him and his chair crashing backward. Blood, brain and skull fragments sprayed everywhere, including all over Chad and Carol. Surrounding diners pointed and laughed. As the bartender came around to pop a bottle of champagne, Johnny realized Walter had stopped talking. He also noticed the tension in his jaw was gone. "Thanks for those excellent suggestions." He carved off a hunk of steak and forked it in his mouth. "I'll look into it."

After dinner, Jessica lingered with Johnny to put some distance between her and her family. Carol turned before crossing the street. "Johnny, are you sure you don't want to come up for a piece of birthday cake?"

Johnny waved. "Thanks, but I better get home." He lowered his voice and looked at Jessica. "You know, so me and my parents can get busy on those fucking college applications."

Jessica thumped him in the chest. "Stop. It wasn't that bad."

"It was pretty bad."

"If only Chad had kept his mouth shut."

"Chad?" Johnny's face scrunched. "Your brother was my biggest ally tonight."

Jessica's head dipped toward her feet. "Look, I didn't think showing them the necklace would be that big a deal. Was I supposed to hide it forever?" She faced Johnny. "But it also never occurred to me that it cost so much. My dad guessed over a hundred bucks. Maybe one-fifty."

"And I have the receipt, okay? In case that asshole needs to see it."

Jessica checked her family's distance before laying her palms on Johnny's coat. "I'm sorry I put you in that position. It was selfish and insensitive."

Johnny didn't know what to say. People didn't often apologize for hurting him. And he'd been hurt a lot. It generated a strange combination of feelings. But when Jessica parted her lips to kiss him, they all flowed to his groin. His hands slid inside her coat and pulled her closer. They continued to make out as pedestrians sidestepped them.

"I better go," Jessica said, stepping back.

"Yeah, okay." Johnny closed his coat.

CHAPTER SEVENTEEN

Johnny headed down Park Avenue. The idea of taking the train all the way to Tito's was unappealing. It was still early enough to show up at Clyde's, but it was so chaotic there with all his sisters and their friends. Maybe Margaret's was the best bet. She was hardly ever home and he had a key. It was a hike to the Village, but the walk might help him figure shit out.

Why did Walter bother him so much? Johnny didn't need his approval. And as adversaries went, he was pretty benign. He was just looking out for his daughter. Who could fault a guy for that? He increased his clip, stomping out his frustration on the pavement. Maybe what really pissed him off was that Walter was right. Even if it was for the wrong reasons. Fact was, the man should be suspicious. Jessica, too.

Was it worth the risk? There were plenty of girls he could hit up to get laid. Sure, Jessica was intelligent, fun, and interested in what he had to say, but so were his Dog brothers. And he didn't have to pretend for them. Maybe it boiled down to what he had written on her card. *I aspire to be the person you think I am.* But did he? Really?

Johnny cut through Union Square Park and waited at Fourteenth Street as cars whizzed by in both directions. It was mostly taxis in the evening, but a black Ford Galaxy with its base thumping gunned it to make the yellow light. As Johnny started to cross behind it, the car skidded to a stop, then reversed. The driver was hanging out the window looking at him. It was the big bald guy from César's gang. A quick inventory counted one man riding shotgun and another in the back.

98

Johnny sprinted across the street to University Place as tires peeled out. The car had made a U-turn to follow him against one way traffic. *Hands off the Dogs, my ass!* At the next two intersections, Johnny turned right, then left, hoping the car would be blocked by other traffic. Or, if he was lucky, smash into some garbage truck.

Johnny stole a quick peek. The Galaxy had slowed enough to let out its passengers. On Twelfth Street, he turned again, struggling to find another gear as the footfalls closed in. The block was residential, tree-lined with brownstones, and no pedestrians to be seen. Headlights were approaching, but no one in this city would stop for someone being chased. At least the car would block Big Baldy in the Galaxy, and give Johnny a minute to deal with these two fuckers.

Running past some trash cans, Johnny yanked over a barrel, but it wasn't enough to slow his pursuers. He felt hands grab the back of his coat. Before he could spin to defend himself, an arm wrapped around Johnny's neck. He clawed and pulled, but his head was locked in the crook of this asshole's elbow. The other guy caught up. It was the slight-framed Cross with the mole under his nostril. He tried to take hold of Johnny's legs, but Johnny squirmed and pedaled. The captor leaned back enough to lift Johnny's feet off the ground, further restricting his breath. Johnny kicked out with as much force as he could muster. His sneaker connected with the Mole Man's face, and he doubled over, clutching his nose.

"Fucking grab him already," ordered the one holding Johnny.

"He busted my nose!" Blood dripped between the guy's fingers.

The two yelled at each other as Johnny tried to wriggle free, but he was growing lightheaded. It was no use. He let himself go limp. Honking and hollering could be heard down the block. Big Baldy and the other driver were having a standoff, but all of the sounds began to muffle into one. Buildings and parked cars closed in, making Johnny feel even more trapped. His vision narrowed and blurred. Then everything faded to black.

◇◇◇

Flickering images stampeded through Johnny's mind like some psychedelic slideshow. The stairs: rough-cut planks and 2x4s. Furniture from Orlando's bedroom, still out of place in the cellar after so long. The crudely constructed bathroom beside the workbench, the only remnant from before Miguel had constructed this subterranean jail.

Johnny can feel the air, smell it. Damp and stagnant. The nauseating scent of his brother's musky pheromones hovering with the lamb chop his mother had fed him for dinner. And then there's Orlando, always a little paler and doughier whenever Johnny has the misfortune of being locked up with him. This time, he has a nylon belt. Who the fuck knows why. He doesn't have to worry about his pants getting loose. He doesn't exercise. Why their parents haven't taken it away is the bigger question. Maybe they're hoping he'll hang himself. *Depressed teen commits suicide in cellar. Such a tragedy. An epidemic, really.* Then they would be free of him and his psychosis, without the culpability.

Orlando is grabbing at Johnny, who bobs and ducks in the small space to get away. Orlando is six years older, bigger, unfit. Johnny is spry. Where the advantage lies is that Orlando has nothing but time. He can just wait this shit out. And if by some miracle of God, Aylin or Miguel release his captor before he gets a chance to carry out his sadistic bullshit? Oh well. There'll always be a next time.

Johnny knows this by now, and weighs how much to resist, because sometimes it only makes things worse. Sometimes, resigning reduces Orlando's hostility. But this time, instead of flogging Johnny with the belt, Orlando puts it around his neck, gets behind him and pulls tight. Johnny gags, chokes, claws at the belt. Orlando doesn't have the ends wrapped in his hands, so they slip through his fingers. He won't make that mistake again. Now Johnny really can't breathe. His eyes won't blink. His ears are muffled. He is pulled backward into Orlando's chest. Johnny can feel his brother's hot breath, and shudders at his closeness.

◇◇◇

A car door shut. Then another. There was talking and some laughter, dragging Johnny into consciousness. *Those aren't cellar sounds.* His eyes were too heavy to open, and his head was throbbing, but there was something soft under him. Leather? He cracked a lid and bright sunlight pierced his pupil. Blinking a few times revealed a high ceiling, water-stained with peeling paint. He rolled his head to the side, seeing a big, empty room, vaguely familiar, but the perspective was odd.

The voices grew louder, more distinguishable. Those were his Dog brothers. This was an apartment in the loft. Johnny clung to the black leather sofa cushions and pulled himself to sitting. Rubbing the pang in his temples, he looked at the window by the fire escape, the one he had climbed into that first night. It was locked, the broken glass pane covered with cardboard and duct tape. How did he get in? He then remembered they had started leaving the back-alley door unlocked to make coming and going easier.

Johnny stood, taking a moment for the wave of dizziness to pass. Everything ached, and his neck was stiff. How could a flashback make you hurt so much in real life? He shuffled to the stairwell and looked down. Some brothers were filing in with cleaning supplies and any goods that had been pilfered during the week. Johnny tried to call out, but only emitted a croak. He whistled instead.

Mario looked up from the foyer. "What're you doing here already?"

He forced out the words. "I don't know."

Clyde appeared beside Mario. "Why don't you know. Where'd you stay last night?"

"Not sure."

Clyde bounded up the stairs. "Did you have one of those episodes?"

Johnny backed into the apartment, still dazed and disoriented. Gang members followed.

Clyde's eyes widened. "Holy shit, what the fuck happened?"

"I blacked out. Had another flashback." Johnny massaged his neck. "This time I remembered Orlando choking me with a belt. I just woke up now, when I heard you guys."

"No." Clyde pointed into the room. "I meant what the fuck happened *there*."

Johnny turned to see his blue nylon flight jacket on the floor. It was covered in what looked like blood spots. His four-inch folding Buck knife lay beside it, also soaked.

Jarrod inspected Johnny's black shirt. "Did you get stabbed?"

"I don't know." Johnny unbuttoned his shirt and pulled it open. There was some dried blood smudged on his lower back and side, but no one could find any wounds.

"If you didn't get stabbed," said Clyde, "who the fuck did?"

Chico lifted the coat by its collar. "Weren't you out to dinner with your girl?"

The reminder felt like a gut-punch. Johnny sunk into the sofa, replaying what he could remember. "The dinner went okay. I wanted to kill Jessica's father, but I didn't." He squinted at the ceiling. "No. I'm sure I didn't."

Johnny's brothers gathered around.

"After Jessica left with her family, I walked downtown, trying to decide where to crash..." Johnny's head fell between his knees. "Fuck."

Clyde sat beside him. "What?"

"Dos Cruces." Johnny clawed his scalp. "That big bald prick with the chains. The one that was taunting me with the basketball. He was driving a car. Two others were with him, the one with the mole and some other guy. They came after me." Johnny leaned back, rubbing his throat. "Somebody got me in a chokehold. Another tried to grab my feet. Like, maybe they wanted to throw me in the trunk?"

"Jesus, fuck," said Jarrod. "What happened then?"

"That's the last thing I remember."

"Because they knocked you out?"

"I don't think so. I think it's because I flipped."

"Oh Christ." It was Clyde's turn to fold forward.

"Um, what are you talking about?" said recent recruit, Ramón "Ray-Ray" Reyes.

Clyde raised an eyebrow at Johnny, who gave him a nod. "For those who don't know, you're gonna need to, because it's on us to protect him." Clyde looked at the newer members. "Everyone's already hip to Johnny's situation, just maybe not his condition."

Johnny circled his wrist, motioning to get on with it.

"A lot of the shit that happened in Miami was so bad Johnny blocked it out. I've read up on this stuff at the library, and it's a common way people cope with trauma. Especially young kids." Clyde picked at his fingernails. "But sometimes, things trigger flashbacks, and that can send him into a fugue state—"

"A what?" said Dwayne Reynolds, a chunky mixed race fourteen-year-old.

Jarrod rolled his eyes. "Clyde read a few textbooks and now he thinks he's a connoisseur of mental health."

Chico's face contorted. "A corner sewer?"

"A connoisseur. Someone who knows a lot of shit about shit." Jarrod scanned the crew. "What he's trying to say is, if you mess with Johnny—and *especially* if you try to restrain him—he might go batshit crazy and fuck your ass up."

Johnny laughed. "I like that definition better." He stood. "Now, did any of you thieving bastards shoplift a bar of soap and a towel? Because I need a fucking shower."

"Probably." JJ trotted downstairs to look. The others also dispersed.

Clyde hung back. "You can't remember anything?"

"Maybe after a shower and a coffee run, but right now? No."

"Because it looks pretty serious."

"Yeah, I fucking know, all right?" Johnny's eyes narrowed at Clyde. "But what's lodged in the forefront of my mind is Orlando, and having to remember the sick shit he did to me."

"I get it." Clyde put up his hands. "It's where these episodes started. So, if you confront that, maybe they'll stop."

Johnny swiped his face. "It's a nice theory."

◇◇◇

Johnny stood under the hot water. Blood slid off his skin, discoloring the puddle at his feet before swirling down the calcified drain. He turned his face toward the nozzle and closed his eyes. What the fuck happened? He tried to place himself on that street, conjure up some details of the car and those men, anything to jumpstart his memory. But his brain kept bouncing to Miami instead.

Johnny usually remembered the parts leading up to the cellar. It was afterwards that was fuzzy. But like Clyde said, his mind had been shielding itself from the abuse. Now, with time and distance, those previously purged details were emerging. Sometimes, apparently, in the most inopportune moments.

On that day, Johnny recalled, he hadn't wiped his feet properly, and a few bits of dirt got tracked into the house. How old would he have been? Eleven, maybe, meaning Orlando had been locked up about a year. It was hardly a punishable offense for most kids. And the crumbs were barely visible to the average person. Not his father. That prick had an eagle eye when it came to dirt. Or maybe he was looking for excuses to dispose of Johnny too. From Miguel's point of view, it must have been a win-win. The little kid's out of your hair, and the older one has a distraction to shut him up.

In the beginning, Johnny had to piss his father off pretty bad to get tossed in the cellar. But it started happening with greater frequency. Also, for the dumbest shit, which was allowing Orlando to hone his tormenting skills. Or so it seemed from the timeline Johnny was sewing together with each new revelation. His body was a good resource for mapping out this demented chronology. The disfiguration around his wrists and ankles from the short strands of rope. His parents must have deemed those too benign when readying Orlando's new chambers. The lash marks across his back from an extension cord. And the numerous scars from the box cutter his brother kept hidden. Some earlier revelations had uncovered Orlando's fascination with hanging Johnny to a rafter by his hands or feet, and slicing his skin just to watch the blood drip.

This flashback exposed something even more disturbing, if that were possible. Orlando choking Johnny with a belt suggested he had shifted from physical abuse to attempted murder. The thought made Johnny shudder and he pushed it away. Fuck all this reconciliation shit. If his brain knew enough to block it out back then, why the hell did he need to examine it now? Whatever horrors remained uncovered should stay that way.

Shutting off the water, Johnny reached for the fresh towel on the toilet tank. His Dog brothers had also produced a shower curtain, along with toothbrushes and paste from the pile of supplies. He pulled on his jeans and shoes, but left the bloodied shirt balled up on the floor. The bathroom was looking pretty decent after having been scrubbed, and Luis's plumbing survived its first test run. He stepped into what had the potential to be a bedroom. It was bigger than Tito's whole living room. He pictured a bed, some dressers, maybe even a table and chair. Closets filled with all of his stuff, instead of being stored at various places throughout the city. Stability. *That's what'll stop these batshit episodes.* Maybe, for once in his life, if he had a safe, steady home, it would fix everything. He felt connected to this second-floor apartment in particular, since it was the first one his feet had touched when breaking in.

It was going to happen. He could feel it.

CHAPTER EIGHTEEN

"Have you remembered anything yet?" Clyde asked Johnny, as crew members assembled on the block outside of Roosevelt.

"Nah. I've been racking my brain all weekend." He lit a Marlboro. "Did those textbooks say something about losing one memory to get another?"

"Not that I saw, but I could—"

"Don't waste your time." Johnny blew a stream of smoke to the sky. It was so frustrating to have blocks of time just vaporize in an instant. It made him feel angry and reckless.

When he saw Jessica peeling away from Michelle and Danni it eased the tension in his gut. "How's your dad?" Johnny asked, flicking his butt into the gutter. "Has he recovered from his charity dinner with the underprivileged immigrant kid?"

"Are you still on about that?" Jessica rolled her eyes. "And my mom really likes you."

Johnny fingered the necklace's pendant before tucking it under the collar of her sweater. "It's safer there. Also closer to your heart."

She smiled and kissed him. "When can we be together again?"

"Aren't your parents at work? We could go fuck in their bed."

Jessica laughed. "I'm not that ballsy."

"I'm working on something," Johnny caressed her cheek, "so we won't have to keep cutting school and sneaking around."

"Like what?"

To avoid answering, he put his mouth on hers. While they kissed, Johnny heard a thumping bass. But there were thousands of cars in the city

106

with souped-up sound systems. It would likely fade off down some distant avenue. When it grew louder, his head jerked up. Some brothers sensed his tension and followed his gaze.

Johnny pushed Jessica away. "Grab your friends and go."

"What? Why?"

"Please, baby, just go inside. I'll meet you later."

Jarrod must have said something similar to Michelle, because she and Danni were heading for the entrance already.

A black Ford Galaxy turned onto Nineteenth Street, and the Dogs of War huddled together. "Should we scram?" asked Chico.

"No," said Johnny. "I need to know what the fuck happened, but everyone be ready to scatter if they start shooting."

As the car neared, he could see the big bald guy's hands on the wheel. The one with the mole was hanging out the passenger window, stalking the block.

"I don't see guns, or anyone in back," said Johnny. "But someone could be hiding."

Mole Man spotted the Dog brothers, but they held their ground, watching from behind parked cars. The driver leaned across his gang mate to glare out the passenger window. When he zeroed in on Johnny, he idled, revving the motor. Johnny locked onto his eyes. Other kids stopped to look at the loud annoying car. Big Baldy made a gun with his thumb and forefinger, stretched it out the window, and aimed it at Johnny's head. Johnny stood unflinching, even as fragmented images of the lost night began to flicker in his brain.

The big Cross pulled the mock trigger in slow-motion, overdramatizing the recoil, but Johnny only smiled. Once the intended message had been delivered, the Galaxy's tires burned rubber before it disappeared down the street.

Mario put a hand on Johnny's shoulder. "You all right, man?"

Johnny collapsed into a squat, face in hands. "I think I know," he mumbled through his fingers.

Jarrod crouched beside him. "Know what?"

Mario's head swiveled. "What *I* know is those motherfuckers might circle back with a machine gun."

It was a possibility, but right now Johnny was more interested in his memory returning. He pressed his eyes closed. "Someone put me in a chokehold."

Clyde bent a knee. "One of those guys?"

"No. Someone I've never seen before." Johnny squinted toward the school building. "I could barely breathe, so when Mole Man came close, I kicked him in the face. Hard enough to take him down for a minute. I got a hand in my pocket, flipped open my knife and just started stabbing behind me, wherever I could reach. When that man let go, I spun around and jabbed him a few more times in the stomach." Johnny scanned the faces of his brothers. "The car was boxed in by another driver, but I knew that big bastard would be coming. So, when the other guy tried to grab me, I sliced him, maybe in the arm. Then I ran." He pinched his temples. "I had this feeling like I needed to keep running. Like nowhere would be far enough away. Next thing I knew, I was by the loft."

"Did you say anything to them?" Clyde asked.

Johnny stood up with the others. "I don't think so. Why?"

"How did they know where to look for you?"

It was an important question, and not having an answer made Johnny feel like he was being strangled all over again. He pushed off toward the doors. "We better get to class."

At lunch, the gang decided that Johnny should lay low, and that all of them would stop meeting on the block before and after school. Instead, they would spread out, blend in with the other students to see if Dos Cruces planned to make these drive-bys a daily event. Jessica, Danni and Michelle were told to be wary, but were given scant details. Only that a random bunch of thugs appeared to be looking for trouble in the neighborhood.

◇◇◇

Through the remainder of April, there were no signs of Dos Cruces. The weather was getting nice, and Johnny could not bear being cooped up any longer. Since the gang had not had a fight circle all winter, they picked a Saturday to meet in Sheep Meadow. Johnny called Horatio to join them.

The Dogs of War gathered early and spread out on the grass to discuss business. Johnny stretched his hamstrings. "Tito's gonna be late. He had to help his cousins finish a car. But we can begin."

Joe Jackson was there, and provided an update on the Brick. "He had surgery and it went well. They're gonna do some chemo and radiation as a precaution." He pursed his lip. "It'll be a long recovery, but everyone is optimistic."

"Give him our best," said Johnny. "And let me know if there is anything I can do." He looked around. "Who's next?"

Jarrod put up a hand. "Our band needs to start rehearsing again. I'm sick of serenading the walls of my bedroom." He circled his shoulders. "One late welfare check, and my drunk-ass parents might start piecing off my drum kit for booze money."

"He's right," said Patrick. "We could at least hit Washington Square on weekends. Make a little scratch and get some practice."

"The loft will be an amazing studio," said Clyde. "I can't wait to move my guitars and amps in there."

Teddy reached for his toes. "I've seen ads for open mics. If you want, I'll be the band manager and sign Temper up."

"You're on," said Johnny. "Being holed up the last few weeks, I've been writing some shit. Dumped all that anger over what I could and couldn't remember into five songs' worth of lyrics."

Jarrod laughed. "About time your batshit craziness worked for good."

"I can't wait to see them," said Clyde. "Temper ought to be more than a cover band. We need original material."

JJ pointed across the field. "Hey, is that Tito? Does he have an actual smile on his face?"

"I didn't know he had an expression other than deadpan," said Mario.

Johnny felt a combination of nerves and excitement welling inside him. "Sit the fuck down and spill it," he said as Tito neared.

Tito plopped down. "You gave RealCorp the garage number."

"Yeah, because someone is there all day to answer the phone."

"They called this morning."

"And?"

"I spoke to the agent. It is still for sale."

Johnny gritted his teeth. "Tito, do not make me hurt you. Are you gonna tell us or what?"

His lips curled in the corners. "They want ninety thousand. As is."

The gang cheered, slapping each other five.

"Holy shit," said Johnny. "I gotta call Margaret, get with that lawyer." He looked at Tito. "Did you get a number?"

"Mm-hmm."

"We'll need to pull the money together, see if we got enough."

"Wait." Joe put up a hand. "How are you even *close* to that?"

"You see how I live." Johnny plucked his long-sleeved polo, *Ace Hardware* embroidered above the breast pocket. "I shop at the Salvation Army. I load up on food from the school cafeteria. I saved a lot of what your uncle paid me. Plus, there were a few side jobs for big money." He poked at the grass. "This is what I've been working for."

"Where are you keeping it?"

"Some in Clyde's savings account. More hidden in his closet. Tito's stashing some at his place."

Joe swiped a hand over his brush cut. "You do know I'm a business major, right?"

"Tested out of high school to start college early." Johnny cocked his head to the sky. "Let's see, if you're eighteen now, should be halfway through your master's already."

"Shut up." Joe tsked tongue. "I was on-call for my uncle too much, and classes aren't cheap. I take a few night courses."

"What are you saying, you want to be our financial manager?"

Joe raised an eyebrow. "I'd probably have to be a member to do that."

"Are you shitting me?" Johnny slapped both knees. "We've hit it off since the day we met. I've always wanted you in." He held out his hand and Joe clasped it tight.

"Meeting adjourned," said Jarrod. "The master has arrived."

Horatio was walking toward them in full conversation with himself, gesturing for both sides. His gait was choppy and his complexion seemed ashier than usual. When the crew stood to greet him, he returned to lucidity. "You multiplied."

"We did." Johnny stepped up to shake his hand. "It's been too long."

"It wouldn't be if you pussies trained in the winter. What's a little cold weather to a bunch of punks like you?"

"It wasn't the weather," said Clyde. "We've been working."

"A little renovation project," said Chico.

Jarrod patted Horatio on the back. "I don't suppose you know anything about framing, in addition to hand-to-hand combat?"

Horatio cocked his head. "What, like carpentry?"

"Yeah."

"I've swung my share of hammers."

Johnny stifled a smile, afraid getting too excited would jinx their luck. If the loft deal went through, they would need more walls in those bare units to make rooms for everyone. The loner seemed a low risk for ratting them out to any authorities. Still, Johnny kept the details vague. "We've been cleaning up this old warehouse, but the landlord wants some extra work done. We'd cut you in if you could help us."

"Where is it?"

"Downtown, in the middle of nowhere."

"Whatever." Horatio flapped his hands. "I'll think about it, but first we do this." He looked around at the gang. "Is there anything in particular you want to address?"

"Yeah," said Johnny. "I want to learn to get out of a chokehold."

CHAPTER NINETEEN

Jessica folded her arms. "I'm starting to think you're blowing me off." She gazed at the school building.

"Really? You're gonna be like that?" Johnny sighed. "I told you. Clyde's sister took a later shift, so we can't use his apartment."

"Don't *your* parents work?"

"Yeah, but my dad works nights, so he's sleeping right now." Even the thought of a fabricated dad gave him chills.

She cocked her head. "How come I've never met your parents?"

"Jesus Christ." Johnny stormed a small circle and stood in front of her. "Because they're fucking assholes, okay? And I hate them." His emotion required no dramatization.

"I just think it's odd that you've never brought me to your neighborhood, shown me where you live."

Johnny draped himself over the hood of a parked car. "Why are you doing this?"

"Doing what?"

He took a long breath before facing her again. "Look, I'm as frustrated as you are, but I told you, I'm working on something."

She rolled her eyes. "Right, another big secret you won't share with me."

Johnny took hold of her shoulders. "Can you please stop it." He waited for her tension to release. "This weekend is supposed to be beautiful. Me and the boys will be in Washington Square throwing down dance moves to

112

make a few bucks. You should come. It'll be fun." He pressed his hips into hers. "Between sets I'll take you behind a tree and fuck that grumpy mood right out of you."

Jessica laughed, then put her mouth on his and they kissed.

"Shield your eyes, Betsy. We got some X-rated shit going on here."

The familiar voice caused Johnny stomach to flip, but he wasn't immediately sure it was bad. He looked up to see Sherry grinning, elbow cocked on Betsy's shoulder. She wore tight jeans, a low-cut top and a cropped jacket. Her blonde hair and makeup were better suited for clubbing than school. Betsy was understated, in a tie-dye T-shirt and cargo pants.

"Haven't seen you in a while." Johnny kept an arm locked around Jessica's waist.

"And it doesn't look like you've missed me, either." Sherry raised an eyebrow at Jessica.

Johnny gestured with his free hand. "Um, Sherry, Betsy, this is Jessica."

"Hi." Jessica articulated every element of the monosyllabic word.

"How's it going?" Betsy waved and smiled.

Sherry looked Jessica up and down. "She's pretty. I'm glad you found someone so nice."

Johnny could feel Jessica pulling against his grip. "So, what're you guys up to?"

"You know, same old shit." Sherry fanned the air. "But you look busy. Maybe I'll catch you later, like if you're out smoking a joint at lunchtime." She looped her arm in Betsy's. "Nice to meet you, Jessica," she said over her shoulder.

Johnny loosened his hold and Jessica pulled away. "I thought you said you barely knew her."

"I do."

"Seems like something more to me."

"I can't help that."

"And what did she mean about meeting you at lunch?"

Johnny wagged his head. "Baby, I'm not doing this. I'll see you later."

When Johnny, Mario and Ramón walked out of their last period class, Sherry was in the hall. She poked a finger in Johnny's chest. "You doing anything after school?"

"I don't know, why?"

"My parents won't be home until nine." She pouted. "And I'll be all alone."

Johnny clicked his tongue. "You poor thing."

"Why don't you ditch little goody-two-shoes so we can hang out."

"Damn, brother," Mario said, looking Sherry over. "If you don't go, I will."

"Me, too," said Ramón.

She crossed her arms, which accentuated the swell of her breasts. Johnny bit his lower lip. "If I go, will you keep your mouth shut?"

"Absolutely not." She pressed her tongue in her cheek to simulate a blowjob.

Mario slapped Johnny's back. "I think your afternoon plans just changed."

Johnny checked down the halls and Sherry rolled her eyes. "If you don't want to be seen with me, I'll be waiting on Tenth Avenue." She fluttered her fingers at the boys. "Toodeloo."

Johnny leaned against the wall. It had been weeks since he and Jessica last had sex, and it was making him crazy. He put a hand on his crotch. And why did Sherry always have to make it so easy?

"Why are you still standing here?" asked Ramón.

"Yeah, man," said Mario. "If Jessica asks, we'll pull out the Uncle Casper story."

Now, his brothers were making it even easier. "All right." Johnny put his hand out for the gang shake. "I'll catch you later."

As he rounded the corner, Sherry stepped off the curb to wave an arm. A taxi veered over. They slipped in and she told the driver to go to Eighty-Fifth and West End.

"You were able to sneak away from Miss Sour Puss?"

"Don't do that."

Sherry slid towards the door and cocked a knee. "We're pretty sensitive, aren't we?"

Johnny faced her. "You know, you *could* get what you want without being such a cunt about it."

"Where would the fun be in that?" She looked in his eyes, as a hand drifted to the crotch of her jeans.

As Johnny watched her caress the denim, the tingling in his groin eclipsed his guilt. When he caught the driver watching her in the rearview mirror, he sat up to focus out the window.

Sherry stuffed bills through the Plexiglass partition before Johnny could pay. He followed her under a long green awning stretching from the curb to a building. The main doors were thick glass behind ornamental wrought iron. Inside, a spotless red carpet stretched the length of the lobby. An elderly man in a maroon uniform stood at the counter. Sherry took Johnny's arm and breezed past him. "Hey Albert, this is the messenger from my dad's office. He's picking up some papers." The man nodded, waving them through.

"Isn't he going to notice when I don't leave in five minutes?" Johnny asked once they were in the elevator.

"That senile old fuck?" She pressed the button for the eighth floor. "Doubtful."

When Sherry opened the apartment, Johnny's mouth dropped. A spacious living room was brightened by a line of windows, each one dressed with lacy beige curtains and thick braided gold rope. The overstuffed sofa and chairs were a matching mocha suede, positioned around a black marble coffee table the size of a daybed. In its center, a triangular marble ashtray looked like it weighed thirty pounds. White shag carpeting covered the entire room. Opposite the sitting area was a mahogany liquor cabinet with fancy stemware tucked behind double glass doors.

Johnny stepped away to give himself a quick tour. There were pictures of Jesus everywhere—addressing his disciples in the hallway, holding a lamb in the dining room, meditating by the bathroom. Each one matted in an oversized gold-leaf frame. Above every door was a cross, on every end table a bible.

Johnny wandered back to the main room shaking his head.

"What's your problem?" Sherry tossed her coat and purse on the arm of the couch. "Afraid of a little religion?"

"A *little?*" Johnny hung his jacket on a dining chair.

"Don't blame me. I didn't decorate this shithole." She walked into the kitchen. "You want something to drink?"

"Sure. Whatcha got?"

Sherry grabbed a steak knife to unlock the liquor cabinet. "How about some Vodka?" She yanked out a bottle and brought it to the kitchen, then poured generous portions into two water glasses. She topped them off with ice and a splash of orange juice and handed one to Johnny. She drank hers in a few chugs and refilled it. "You got any blow?"

Johnny took a pull off his drink, then fished in his coat pockets. A paper packet was tucked in the cellophane of his Marlboros. "You're in luck." He tossed it on the counter. "Is it okay to smoke?"

"I don't give a shit." Sherry tapped some powder onto the counter and carved four lines. She snorted two of them with a rolled dollar bill, then offered it to Johnny. When he declined, she inhaled one more.

Johnny lit a cigarette, watching her absorb the wave of euphoria. As she leaned against the refrigerator with eyes closed, he thought he was understanding her better. The drugs, the booze, the promiscuity. All rebellion for her strict upbringing. She probably grew up feeling trapped and repressed, suffocated by her family's principles. He sure could relate to that. She was also harboring a good deal of rage. "How come your parents let you model?"

Sherry pushed off the refrigerator to light one of Johnny's cigarettes. "The only thing they love more than Jesus is money. Once they realized what a cash cow I could be, they relaxed their morals." She sucked in a deep drag. "They want me to be this virginal, God-fearing person, but it's okay to pose in provocative clothes if it brings them the dough."

"You don't get that money?"

"Nope. My father appointed himself manager, so he controls the finances."

"Wow." Johnny tapped some ash into the sink. "How did you get into all of that?"

"When I was little, I started doing kids' clothing catalogs. That led to offers from fashion magazines. Now that I'm older, they want me to look sexier. My father decided to allow it because it pays so much more, even though it rattles that giant stick up his ass." She gave a disgruntled cough. "Most of the money goes into a trust, which I can't touch till I'm twenty-one. But he pays himself a huge salary out of *my* earnings and throws me a paltry allowance."

"That's fucked up." Johnny shook his head. "You do all the work, and he takes the money."

"Right? Just like a pimp and a prostitute." She laughed. "I point that out every chance I get." Sherry crunched on an ice cube. "But I know enough people in the business now, so I've been making cash deals on the side, and he doesn't know a fucking thing about it."

"You really hate him, don't you?"

"I hate them both. It's a miracle they left me alone tonight, but there was some important dinner they *had* to attend. And I've been pretty obedient lately so they let it slide." She extinguished her butt with tap water and topped off both drinks. "I'll be eighteen in a few months and they can go fuck themselves because I'll finally be free. Keep the money for all I care, but I'm so outta here."

As Sherry catalogued more grievances, Johnny envied the volatility of her emotions and how unrepentant she seemed about it. Maybe if he screamed out every injustice he had ever faced, bore his trauma to the world, it would stop those episodes. And when he turned eighteen, would his chains be off, too? He wouldn't have to hide anymore, use an alias, or worry about social services. Johnny had a lot in common with Sherry. But was that a good thing? What he liked most about Jessica was that she was nothing like him.

Johnny was so deep in thought that he didn't notice Sherry had stopped talking. She leaned over and slapped his face.

"What the fuck?" He grabbed her wrist.

She grinned, batting her eyes. Johnny backed her against the counter, and they began pawing each other. Their mouths and tongues pressed together as they ripped off articles of clothing. She wrestled him toward the dining room, pushing a placemat aside to sit at the head of the big oak table. It was probably her father's spot, but the inappropriateness of it only titillated Johnny more. He pulled off her panties and stood between her legs. As he thrust into her, the salt and pepper shakers, brass candle holders and a floral centerpiece all rolled to the floor.

The act was rough and frenetic, but when it was over, Johnny felt a small chunk had been carved from his simmering rage. After a short rest and another drink, she lay him on the shag carpet in the living room and straddled him until they were both shaky and breathless. When she went to the kitchen to light a cigarette, Johnny followed. He pulled a dishrag from the oven handle to wipe his dick. "Do you even care about me, or are you just getting even with your parents?"

Sherry shrugged. "What's it matter?"

Johnny smiled. "I guess it doesn't."

"Good." She went to use the bathroom. When she came back, she chopped out another line. "You know what's confusing about you?" She snorted it. "I can't tell if you're a nice guy pretending to be bad, or a bad guy pretending to be nice."

Johnny grinned. "What's it matter?"

"I guess it doesn't." Sherry laughed. "So, why don't you get high? Don't you ever want to make all the bullshit disappear?"

"I get high, just not on that. I smoke a little weed, drink a bit."

"You won't do the hard stuff because you're afraid of losing control."

"Maybe." He scratched his chin. "When I was a kid, I felt like I didn't have any control. I like it better this way."

"I get it. So, when are we gonna fuck all over *your* parent's stuff?"

Johnny didn't answer.

"Can you go one more time?"

He twitched a shoulder.

She took his hand and walked him down a hall, into her parents' bedroom. The décor was in line with the rest of the house—dark wood, black marble, and gold leaf. The king-sized bed had a red velvet cover with pillows accenting the brass headboard beneath the obligatory Jesus paintings.

Johnny released her hand. "You expect me to get it up in this ugly-ass room?"

"It's hideous, right?" She cracked up. "Come on, let's show this fucking mattress something it's never seen before." She hopped on the bed and posed on all fours, wiggling her ass like a porn star. The profaneness of it was an extra turn-on, and Johnny rallied for a final round. After, they dressed and returned to the kitchen to finish their drinks.

"You should probably go," Sherry said, rinsing the glasses.

"Okay." Johnny grabbed his coat and stuffed the Marlboros in his pocket. "You want the rest of that?" He nodded toward the almost empty packet of cocaine.

"Yeah, thanks. I'll see you around."

Johnny wanted to kiss her goodbye, offer some ritualistic display of affection, but she seemed suddenly cold and detached. So, he left.

CHAPTER TWENTY

Washington Square was bustling. Benches were full of folks enjoying the sunny May weekend. Musicians had set up throughout the park, their different styles blending at the whim of a breeze, occasionally interrupted by the screeches of children zooming around the fountain. The dealers were making their rounds too, laundry-listing all the ways people could get their heads straight.

The Dogs of War gathered under the arch. After a brief rehearsal, Teddy set up a boombox and cued a mixtape made from his extensive record collection. Mario stepped up first. His convulsive moves, which resembled a seizure, immediately drew a crowd. When he dropped to the ground and flapped like a fish, the audience cheered. He hopped up and threw it to Oscar, who could spin and twist like a top. Chico could pop and lock, but it was more his comical expressions that got people going. Johnny and Jarrod incorporated gymnastic style tumbling into their moves, and Leon had a knack for the liquid robot. The energy was infectious and people were eager to toss cash into the buckets passed around by other members.

During a break, the brothers fanned out. Some went to get drinks. Johnny was sitting on a bollard smoking a cigarette when he saw Margaret. She was trying to look casual in beige capris and a black sweater, but with her face and figure, it was hard not to stand out. She flipped a black corkscrew curl behind her shoulder. "No rock and roll today?"

"We didn't feel like schlepping our instruments around," said Johnny. "Besides, we need more practice, but we don't have a place to rehearse."

She smiled. "I have news about that."

"Really?" Johnny flicked his butt away. "You talked to that client guy?"

"Yes, Thomas. He thinks it'd be a hoot to help you out."

"What does he want in return?"

"There's not much he won't do for me." She batted her eyes. "But if you could hook him up with some blow, I'm sure he'd appreciate it."

"Hell yeah, I can do that." Johnny stood to contain his excitement. "The Brick sometimes gave me coke as a bonus. I've still got a stash because we don't use it." He paced a few steps. "What else does he need?"

She fished in her purse for a pen and a grocery receipt. "The property's address, the name of your contact and a phone number."

"It's 430 Washington." Johnny's eyes swept the park and he pointed at Tito. "Tito took the call from the RealCorp agent. He's got that info."

"Okay, I'll get with him." She jotted down the address. "Thomas will also want to know who he's representing."

"What do you mean?"

"You probably don't want *your* name on the deed, for obvious reasons. But you could create some sort of business title." She grinned. "Something that doesn't scream, 'Here's a bunch of minor's living in a gang den paid for with drug money.'"

Johnny laughed. He thought for a moment, then snapped his fingers. "How about PDG Enterprise?"

Margaret shrugged. "Sounds innocuous enough. What's it stand for?"

"*Perros de Guerra*. It's Spanish for Dogs of War, but no one will know that."

She wrote it on the receipt. "I'll let you know when we get to the hard part, where you need to cough up the cash."

Johnny grew serious. "Thank you, Margaret. You have no idea how much this means. If you ever need anything, like if one of your clients starts hassling you or something, me and my boys are on it."

"That's comforting."

Johnny spotted Jessica walking across the park with Danni and Michelle. She had on makeup, a prettier top than usual, and her auburn hair shimmered in the sun. He had not expected her to show up after their little tiff, and seeing her felt uncomfortable. Especially since his muscles were still achy from his escapade with Sherry.

The girls stopped where Jarrod was standing with a few Dog brothers. Michelle passed him an open quart of Ballantine in a rolled down paper bag. He took a big swig, then open mouth burped before kissing her. Michelle punched him in the chest. Danni cracked up, but Jessica appeared indifferent. When she saw Johnny, she broke away.

"Am I interrupting?"

"No." Johnny shook his head. "Jessica, this is Margaret, a very good friend of mine."

Margaret bowed her head. "It's a pleasure to finally meet you. Johnny talks about you *all* the time."

Jessica shrunk back. "Really?"

"And you are even more beautiful than he described." She leaned closer to examine Jessica's heart pendant. "What a *gorgeous* necklace. Where ever did you get it?"

Johnny rolled his eyes.

"He got it for my birthday. Isn't it lovely?"

"It's as lovely as you are, my dear. He sure does have good taste." She brushed a hand over her sweater. "But I'll leave you two lovebirds alone. I need to speak with that gentleman."

As Johnny and Jessica watched Margaret head toward Tito, a wave of awkwardness settled over them.

"She seems nice," said Jessica.

"Mmm." Johnny swiped the ground with his sneaker.

"At first I thought that might be your mom."

"I wish," he muttered into his chest.

"Look," Jessica's weight shifted between legs. "I'm sorry."

Johnny lifted his head.

"I know you haven't been deliberately blowing me off. I was just feeling sorry for myself." She stared off. "And then that gorgeous blonde showed up. I guess I didn't have to be such a bitch about it."

He fucked Sherry all afternoon but she was apologizing. How the hell did that happen? Either way, it wouldn't hurt to ride the wave. "Now that you mention it, you might have been the bitchiest of all the bitches that ever bitched."

She put a hand on her hip. "Surely not *all* of them."

He pinched the air. "It's pretty close."

Jessica laughed and fell into his arms. He buried his face in her sweet-smelling hair.

"I would've apologized yesterday, but heard you had to work," Jessica said as they pulled apart. "Your uncle must be busy lately."

"Yeah." Johnny swiped the corners of his mouth. "He is. And having me and the boys at his disposal has really been a godsend." Johnny cringed at *godsend*, a word nonexistent in his daily lexicon, but she didn't seem to notice.

"I would have called, but I don't have your phone number."

"It gets shut off a lot because my parents don't pay—"

She put up a hand. "You don't owe me an explanation." She stuffed a piece of paper in his pocket. "I just wanted you to have mine, in case you ever felt like calling. For any reason."

"Yeah, because old Walter would probably love to hear from me."

"You never know. Maybe if you had called him, he would've met you down here, done some fancy footwork and a couple of head spins."

"I'm sure." They both laughed.

When Johnny saw his crew warming up for another set, he brushed some hair from Jessica's face and kissed her. "I better go. You sticking around?"

"Of course."

As the music started, Mario nudged Johnny. "That can't be good." Margaret had returned and was chatting with Jessica on the sidelines. "What could they possibly be talking about?"

Chico leaned over. "My guess is that your girl's getting some career counseling." He grinned. "To swallow or not to swallow, that is the question."

"Daddy, guess what," said Mario, mimicking Jessica. "Johnny introduced me to a real live prostitute today."

Chico did likewise. "Hey Margaret, what's the going rate for an Around the World?"

Johnny rolled his eyes. "Fuck you both." He stepped away to perform, putting extra energy into his moves and tumbles, wowing the crowd.

CHAPTER TWENTY-ONE

Tito turned the van onto Washington. It was slow going navigating the box trucks backed up to loading docks, their noses blocking the narrow street. A tractor trailer had to park diagonally, forcing cars to drive on the sidewalk. Workers shouted to each other over gurgling diesel engines as dollies and handcarts clanged across diamond-plated steel.

"It's a lot different on the weekdays," said Clyde from the back seat.

"No shit." Johnny turned to face him. "But we couldn't ask for less nosey neighbors."

"And by five o'clock it'll be deserted again," Jarrod added.

Tito found an empty spot and pulled over. The four climbed out after Johnny grabbed the backpack with the cash. He had collected all of the savings, his money, gang money, everything accumulated since landing in New York almost four years earlier. It was going to wipe them out financially, but everyone would just have to step up and stay alert for earning opportunities.

Margaret and the lawyer were waiting on the block. "Been here long?" Johnny asked over the din.

"Not at all," said Margaret. "Johnny, meet Thomas Dickerson."

Thomas stepped forward to shake hands. He was fair and slight, a bit on the short side, wearing a tailored suit and tie. His face, however, was so plain Johnny thought if he blinked, he might forget what it looked like. In high heels, Margaret towered over him, stunning in a pinstriped jacket and knee-length skirt, both of which hugged her curvaceous figure. Her white blouse was unbuttoned to highlight her ample cleavage. Completing the lawyer look, she had chosen some bold-framed cat-eye glasses. It was an effort not to gawk.

Johnny introduced the others, then thanked Thomas for coming.

"Are you kidding?" he said. "I'm dying to see what's up with this place. But which one is it? Nothing's numbered around here."

Johnny smiled. "That's a good thing." He led them to the correct door. "Let's go inside. It'll be quieter."

"How'd you get keys already?"

Jarrod sucked his teeth. "We don't need no stinkin' keys." He made sure none of the truck drivers were looking, then vaulted over the gate into the alley. Within a minute, he was opening the front door.

"You kids are resourceful," said Thomas. He put a hand on the small of Margaret's back and ushered her into the foyer. Jarrod's eyes landed on her ass as she passed and he emitted a grunt. Johnny glowered at him, then opened the apartment to the right. "So, basically two units per floor. A lot of open space."

Margaret ran her fingers along an industrial steel desk and some dented file cabinets. Thomas peeked out the barred windows, then walked to the kitchenette at the far end. He bounced on the balls of his Italian loafers. "Floor might need replacing."

"That stuff's not important," said Clyde. "We've got an army of laborers."

"And we had someone check the furnace and plumbing," said Johnny. "It's all functional."

Thomas looked at Margaret. "Where'd you find these kids? I wish mine had half the chutzpah."

"What can I say?" She shrugged. "I know some interesting people."

Whenever Margaret spoke to Thomas, it was with a loving tone, fawning even. Johnny was impressed with her ability to make this little guy, a nobody, feel like such a hero. How much must he be paying her?

They walked across the hall, around the piles of stolen goods and things found on the street: mattresses, end tables, chairs, and anything else deemed usable. Thomas chuckled. "Moving in already?"

"Would that be a problem?" asked Tito.

"I doubt it. After talking to the seller's lawyer, my take is that he can't wait to dump this place." He picked up a tarnished candelabra. One of its five cups was missing. "Where do you find this stuff?"

"That was on the Lower East Side," said Jarrod.

He set it down, shaking his head. "The guy wants out of New York, and this place is his last tie. Once those papers are signed, there'll be no looking back."

"How long will that take?" asked Johnny.

Thomas pursed his bottom lip. "His lawyer suggested they could make it work within the next few days. Maybe a week?" He wandered back into the hall and looked up the wooden stairs, not a single step level with another.

Johnny held Margaret back. "Can I trust him with all this cash?"

She adjusted her glasses. "I believe all people have the potential to be dishonest."

"That's not what I was hoping to hear."

"That's why I always peek in their wallets." She smiled. "Then I know where they live, or if they're lying about who they are." She put a hand on Johnny's arm. "I also warned him that you weren't somebody to fuck with."

"He's not getting any blow until I have papers in hand."

Johnny locked up after everyone had moved onto the sidewalk. "You guys need a ride somewhere?"

Margaret glanced at the belly-up rat on the side of the exterminator van, its eyes x-ed out. "Thanks, but we'll get a cab."

"Okey-dokey," said Thomas. "I'll just need the money, and then we'll be in touch after the closing." He extended a hand.

Johnny searched the lawyer's eyes for a sign. Could he really be trusted? It wasn't like there was an abundance of options. Johnny supposed if he did get screwed, he could always adopt Marco's strategy: wait outside this fucker's house and assassinate him. But that didn't guarantee he would get the money back. Johnny shrugged off the backpack and handed it to Margaret.

◇◇◇

For the next week, the gang spent every free hour at the loft. They decided who would room together, and claimed apartments. Through Luis's connections with other building supers, he caught wind of apartments that were being vacated, and the crew was able to pick through what remained before it hit the curb. He even found two pairs of used industrial-sized coin-operated washers and dryers, all of which he hooked up in the loft's boiler room.

Johnny confiscated a queen-size mattress for his bedroom, a wobbly end table, and made some shelves with boards and bricks. Tito volunteered to be his roommate, and once the paperwork was finalized, they could add the contents of his uptown apartment to the mix.

Joe and Rafael took a ground floor unit, saving the desk and file cabinets since Joe would be handling the finances. They were both avid body-builders and had enough barbells and weight benches to make their place look more like a gym. Johnny thought it didn't hurt to have the gang's biggest muscle living by the front door.

Clyde and Jarrod picked a third-floor apartment. One night while they were scoping out the neighborhood with a bunch of brothers, they saw a ten-foot-long bar outside a shuttered tavern near Chambers Street. Together, they managed to haul the thing to the loft and up the stairs to their unit, figuring a bar would go best where most of the jamming was taking place.

Chico, Mario and Ramón moved next door to them, in the apartment with the least outdated kitchen. The appliances all worked, and it had a large, tiled island with a basin sink. They made tables from old doors, big enough for communal meals.

Horatio was paid to consult with the gang about renovations. Despite his gruffness and occasional rants, he had a good eye for space, and offered practical, affordable solutions for the boys' domiciliary visions. He also mapped out where they could construct hidden storage areas in the walls and closets, as soon as there was money in the till for building supplies. While he was there, Horatio had the crew continue their fighting practice. He raised the level of intensity and provided strategies for lethal maneuvers.

CHAPTER TWENTY-TWO

Johnny waited in the hall for Jessica's last class to let out. "You got a few hours? I want to show you something."

Her face scrunched. "What is it?"

"It's a surprise." He took her hand, then led her to the 1 Train.

"Where are you taking me?" she asked when they got off at Canal Street, but Johnny would not answer.

On Washington, he produced a set of keys and unlocked the steel door.

"Johnny, what the fuck?"

"C'mon." He walked Jessica to his second-floor apartment, tempering his excitement. "We found this guy, a friend of my uncle. He's letting us hang out here in exchange for doing some work. Cleaning, painting, whatever. Basically, keeping an eye on the place till he can get back to the city."

"And how long's that?"

Johnny only shrugged.

She wandered around, looking at the high ceilings, giant windows and mismatched bits of furniture. "Wait. This apartment or the whole building?"

"All of it."

"And who's *us*?"

"You know, my boys, the crew."

She folded her arms. "And what happens when it's fixed up? Do you get the boot?"

"I don't know." He laid hands on her shoulders. "Look, you know shit's not good with my parents, and it's not just me. Jarrod's folks start drinking the minute they get out of bed. Mikey's stepdad is a perv. Clyde's mother works three jobs, and Mario lives in a tiny apartment with his mother, sister, and her screaming infant. His bedroom is the couch." He ran fingers through his hair. "Do I need to keep going?"

"No. I get it."

"The arrangement is kinda sketchy, but right now it's all we got."

Jessica sat on the leather sofa. "About that."

"About what?" Johnny sat beside her.

"The 'we.'" She picked at a fingernail. "When you guys were doing your dance thing in the park, I noticed some of you have the same tattoo. What's up with that?"

Johnny leaned back and sighed. "I guess you want to lay it all out today, don't you?"

Jessica cocked a knee. "I guess."

Hadn't Margaret said something about giving people what you can without giving up who you are? This was everything he had ever wanted. His own place, with a family he built. People who shared his vision and had his back. As much as he liked Jessica, the Dogs of War would always come first. Maybe it was time to find out if that was enough for her.

"I thought you knew the deal."

"Well, I'm not an idiot." Her eyes swept the walls. "But there's 'let's call ourselves a gang for fun,' and then there's an organized group of criminals with a defined hierarchy." She looked at Johnny. "Which one are you?"

He held her gaze. "The second one."

"What criminal shit are you into?"

"You see us. We work for our money." Johnny pinched the corners of his mouth. "And nobody's looking for trouble."

"Who's in charge then? Because around school, some people think it's Jarrod."

Johnny smiled into his chest. "I'm actually okay with that. I don't mind being in the shadows." He stood and went to the kitchen. Jessica followed. He opened the fridge and pulled out two Budweisers. "You want one?"

"Sure." She popped the top and took a swig, looking at the appliances. "That is the oldest stove I've ever seen. Does it even work?"

"I don't dare try it. The best kitchen is upstairs, so we've been eating there."

"Jesus, how long have you been here already?"

"A week or so, but I didn't want to bring you until I had my room set up."

She stepped away from the kitchen. "Is that it?"

"No, that's Tito's. Mine's at the other end." He led her across the floor, expecting her to resist. But she did not.

Jessica paced around, sipping her beer. She cocked her head at the mattress, which was on a sheet of plywood raised up by cinder blocks. "Pretty inventive."

As she poked around the bathroom, Johnny set his can on an end table and reclined on the bed. "Just lemme know when you're done snooping so we can fuck."

She emerged, stifling a grin. "That's a very *gangster* thing to say."

"Did it turn you on?"

She bit her bottom lip. "It kinda did." She set her beer down and went to him. They undressed and entwined. For the first time, it felt unrushed and uninhibited, and they did not stop until they were both light-headed and sore.

Jessica looked at the alarm clock on the table. "Is that the right time?"

"Yeah."

"I should probably go. If I'm late for dinner, my parents will ask questions."

Johnny rolled out of bed to dress. "Yeah. I don't think Walter needs to know about this place."

She laughed. "Oh, hell no."

"Let me find someone to get us a ride."

"Hey." Jessica took his arm before he could leave. "This was really nice. Can we do it again?"

"Baby, we can do it every day. You can spend the night if you want. Say you're sleeping over at Danni or Michelle's." He kissed her. "I'll be right back."

Johnny sprinted upstairs. Tito had returned from work and was sitting with Mario and Chico in their apartment playing cards. "Hey, you mind running me and Jessica up to her building?"

He nodded. "Jarrod has Michelle at his place. Maybe she needs a ride, too."

"Look at brother Tito," said Mario, throwing down his cards. "Chauffeur of the poontang shuttle."

Tito rolled his eyes and pushed away from the table.

By the end of the school year, many of the Dogs had relocated to the loft. There was still a lot of work to be done, but with summer coming, they would have time. There would also be more earning potential, whether from legit jobs or street performing. Or, any other opportunities that presented themselves.

Jarrod's five-piece drum set and percussion accoutrements finally had enough space after being crammed in the bedroom of his parents' apartment. Clyde no longer had to stash his guitars under his bed after every use, nor did his amplifier have to double as a laundry hamper. Patrick kept his bass with their gear, ditto Mario's sax and Johnny's Casio keyboard and electric guitar. Other brothers donated their stereo equipment, which was pieced together so the band could jam to albums or record themselves. And nobody had to worry about keeping the volume down anymore. Clyde and Jarrod's apartment was dubbed The Studio.

The crew decided to have a big loft party on the first Saturday of school break. They had spent the last week of classes inviting select students and other people they knew. Chico talked his mother into preparing some food.

When a car horn beeped, a bunch of brothers dashed downstairs. Lucinda was already pulling trays from the back of the Tempest wagon. Her flowery, thick-belted dress and beige shoes with gold buckles were more suited for church than a party. Luis emerged from the front seat, barely recognizable in a paisley shirt and black slacks.

Crew members scrambled at Lucinda's behest to carry the food up to Chico, Mario and Ramón's apartment, which they called the Mess Hall.

Luis knew better than to get in the way, so he sidled up to Johnny. "Where do you find a beer around here?" Johnny walked him to the end of the counter, where there was a trash barrel full of ice and assorted cans. They each took one and sipped. "You kids have done a lot with the place."

"We're trying. Little by little." Johnny watched Lucinda uncovering the aluminum trays on the kitchen island. One had baked ham with pineapples, another, chicken and rice, a third, macaroni and cheese. She was telling some boys where to stack paper plates and utensils. "How's she taking Chico moving out?"

Luis's lips rolled into his mouth. "You know, she loves fiercely, but she is also a realist." He faced Johnny. "She knew the day was coming."

"I should talk to her."

Johnny sidled up to Lucinda and bent to kiss her cheek. She shooed him away, saying he should make himself useful by finding her a glass of white wine. Once everything was laid out to her liking, she found a stool and sat down. Johnny set a plastic cup on the counter beside her.

"Sit," she said in Spanish. "I want to look at you."

Johnny obeyed.

"I have not seen you in a while. You are taller."

"Everyone's tall to you."

"Very funny." She sipped her wine, observing the scene. Johnny's brothers were pooling chairs from the rest of the house to split between the Mess Hall and the Studio. "You did it."

"Did you doubt me?"

"No, *muchacho*, I did not." Lucinda's eyes returned to Johnny's. "I would never bet against you. You will accomplish everything you set your mind to."

"Sounds like a lot of pressure."

"It wasn't necessarily a compliment." She brushed her lap. "So, how are you?"

"I'm fine."

"You are a good liar."

Johnny rocked his head. "There's no casual conversation with you, is there?"

"Are you still having the blackouts?"

Must she always pinpoint his weaknesses? And this last episode was clearly triggered, not just random. If that made a difference. "Did Chico say something?"

"His loyalty is with you now. He does not speak to me about you or your gang." She stuck out a finger. "But you are telling me with your eyes."

Her ability to see through him was infuriating. Still, he recognized its value. "Yes, okay? I still have them. Do you have some spell to fix it?"

"Only you can reconcile your past."

"So you keep saying."

"You are a very capable leader." Her dark eyes surveyed the room. "But these boys need your head straight. That is more important than your shame over what happened in Miami."

Guests began appearing on the third floor's landing, then drifted into the open apartment doors on either side. Some carried six-packs, others had bottles of one libation or another. Dog brothers directed them where to put stuff. Someone cranked up the stereo.

Lucinda patted Johnny's knee. "You have a party to host. We will talk another time."

"I know you want what's best for me, Lucinda. I love you for that." He got up and kissed her cheek. "And for the food."

Johnny went across the hall. The bar that had been salvaged from the street was cleaned, polished and stocked with ice and beer. On the wall behind it now hung a large neon sign that said, *McCauley's Ale House*. Found or stolen, Johnny didn't ask. A few tattered couches were positioned around a large wooden cable spool. Clyde was there, canoodling with a girl from Roosevelt, and Johnny sat across from them.

"Hi," she said, then waved at the instruments in front of a few clotheslined bedsheets, the only thing separating Clyde and Jarrod's bedrooms from the rest of the apartment. "I hear you guys are gonna play."

"Probably later."

Jarrod vaulted over the back of the couch, dropping down next to Johnny. "Hey, who the fuck invited *him*?"

"Who?" Johnny asked.

Jarrod cocked his head toward the hallway, where Hector Sarno was holding a plastic cup, talking to some classmates.

"Wasn't me," said Clyde. "Has he talked to you lately?"

"Not much," said Johnny. "He says hi and stuff, but otherwise he's backed off."

"You want me to have him leave?" asked Jarrod.

Johnny twitched a shoulder. "Nah, he's not bothering anyone." He was about to turn around when Jessica appeared with Danni and Michelle. She wore tight black jeans with a low-cut top. Her hair was extra full and her face was made up more than usual. Johnny stood to catch her eye and she came over. "Damn, you look sexy."

"It's not too much?" She grimaced. "Because it feels like too much."

"No, baby, not at all." He kissed her.

"I told my parents I was sleeping at Danni's tonight."

"You lied? I'm impressed." He took her hand. "You want a drink?"

"I should probably eat something first."

"Good strategy." On the way to the Mess Hall, they passed Hector. "Grab a plate. I'll be right in."

Jessica nodded and headed toward the buffet.

"Johnny, how's it going?" Hector stepped away from his friends. "I heard about the party at school. It was open invitation, right?"

It was a weaselly thing to say, but Johnny let it go. "It's cool, man." They shook hands.

"This is great." Hector's gaze bounced around the loft. "You live here? I always thought you were uptown."

"I am. This place is a friend of my uncle's. But he's away, so..." Johnny opened both arms.

"Really cool. And I'm sorry about being so pushy before."

"Don't sweat it." Johnny gave him a backslap. "Enjoy the party, man."

As the evening progressed, more people poured in: Tito's cousins, Jorge and Julio, some street musicians from Washington Square. Even Freddy the doorman had been invited with Jessica's okay. Many of the guests were latching onto Johnny, asking how he had found the place. Having to repeat the same lie was growing tedious, so he steered Jessica to some chairs out of the line of traffic. "Sit. I'll grab a few drinks."

"Just a beer for me."

"You got it."

Johnny went to the bar, where Mario was entertaining a crowd with his jokes and drink-mixing skills. As Johnny tried to squeeze through, someone grabbed his arm. A Roosevelt senior named Nalda. She hung around the gang sometimes, and would flirt with him if there was an opportunity. She was cute, and worth consideration for a one-night stand had he been without options, but Johnny found her abrasive.

"Hi, Johnny." She used a sing-song voice that was supposed to be alluring, but was only a tip-off to how drunk she was. "You're looking so fine tonight."

"Hey, Nalda. You having a good time?"

"It'd be better if you'd do a shot with me."

"I don't want a shot, but you go ahead. I'm just grabbing a few beers."

Her face soured. "For you and that snowflake?"

"Excuse me?"

"Nobody gets what you see in her." Nalda put her hands on his chest. "She's not your type."

"Oh yeah? What's my type, you?"

"Definitely me." She licked her lips. "I'll show you a much better time than that uppity cunt."

Johnny grabbed Nalda's shoulders and pressed her against the wall. She tipped her head to receive a kiss, then saw his eyes harden. "Don't ever talk shit about my people, you hear?"

"Let go!" She tried to push him away but he only gripped tighter.

"Now get the fuck out of this house." He released her.

Nalda looked around for a witness, but the drunken crowd was oblivious. She shot him a scowl before storming off. Once she was out the door, he got two beers and snaked back to Jessica.

She reached for the can. "Must've been a long line."

"Really long."

A while later, Clyde appeared. "People are asking when Temper's gonna play. We should round up the band."

"I'm down for that," said Johnny. "Let's find the others."

As they set off, they heard a ruckus in the stairwell. Johnny thought it might be Nalda and went to look. It was Jarrod and Michelle, having a fight on the second-floor landing.

"Fuck you," Jarrod slurred. "Just go the fuck home already."

"Make me, you prick." Michelle shoved him in the chest with both hands.

Jarrod swayed backward, then swooped to smack her face but got hair instead.

Johnny and Clyde sprinted down the steps as Joe looked out from his apartment.

Johnny pulled Jarrod away. "Enough of this shit."

Clyde put an arm around Michelle and ushered her toward the ground floor. "Why do *I* gotta leave?" She tried to duck away and almost tripped. "*He's* the asshole."

"Whatever," said Clyde. "Joey, can you get her a cab?"

He nodded.

"Bounce that bitch!" Jarrod yelled.

"C'mon, it's not worth it." Johnny guided Jarrod upstairs. "Let's play some rock and roll instead."

In the Studio, Jarrod threw up both hands. "It's all right, people. That was just the opening act. The real show's starting now." He careened toward his drums. After slapping out a few warm-up riffs, someone cut the stereo. Patrick strapped on his bass. Mario grabbed his sax. Johnny and Clyde plugged in their electric guitars and stepped up to the mics. After a brief tune-up, they launched into *School's Out* by Alice Cooper. People went wild, dancing and joining in for the chorus. They played for over an hour, slipping original songs in with the covers, all of which seemed to garner positive reactions.

By the time they called it quits, it was late and the loft had thinned out. Jessica was at the bar, yawning into her fist. Johnny brought her to his room. Their attempt at sex was impeded by alcohol, but when they woke entwined, the intimacy felt greater than ever.

After a shower, Johnny pulled on a T-shirt and gym pants. Jessica threw on some sweats from her overnight bag. When they walked into the living room, the sun beaming through the windows made them squint. "Shall we venture forth to view the carnage?" Johnny massaged his temples. "Maybe we'll get lucky and find some aspirin."

In the Mess Hall, the stench of cigarettes and stale beer met them at the door. Cans and plastic cups covered every surface, and a giant garbage barrel overflowed with food-covered paper plates. Johnny put the kettle on and rummaged through the cabinets. "You want coffee?"

"I'll have tea, if you got any."

The pair worked around the clutter to fix their drinks, which they sipped at the counter. Chico and Ramón came out of their rooms, each followed by girls Johnny didn't recognize. Clyde drifted over from across the hall, his head hanging.

"Is Jarrod alive?" Johnny asked Clyde.

"I heard him breathing. But he was pretty hammered."

Mario padded in from his sleeping area in nothing but briefs, a forearm shielding his brow as he headed for the bathroom. He emerged a few moments later clutching a bottle of Bayer aspirin, which he slapped on the counter. "Breakfast of champions."

Johnny chased a few tablets with the last of his coffee. More brothers appeared like zombies, languidly groping around the kitchen. When their heads were clear enough, everyone began cleaning up. Once the Mess Hall was done, they moved next door to the Studio until both apartments were back to normal. Danni had spent the night with Maurice and showed up midway through the process.

The mood around the loft was low key, so Johnny and Jessica went back to his room, play fighting on the way. Once inside, it turned sexual. He undressed her, kissing every section of her body as it became exposed. She did the same to him, trying to savor the moment until hormones won out and they fell into bed.

After, they kept nodding off in each other's arms. When Jessica got up to pee, Johnny rolled onto his stomach and fell deeper asleep until something jolted him awake. He felt his wrists being grabbed. Someone was straddling him from behind. Johnny's mind propelled to the cellar, where sick images of things Orlando had done flashed in his mind. He was consumed with panic and rage. In one motion he bucked the body off, leapt up and pinned it to the mattress.

Jessica shrieked. "Jesus Christ!"

He looked at her, hyperventilating. "Fuck." He reared back, palms up. "I'm sorry, baby. Shit, I—fuck."

Her expression was equal parts fear and anger. "What the hell was that?" She clawed for the sheet. "I was just playing around."

"You startled me."

"Startled?" She paddled out from under him, pressing her back against the wall to hug her knees. "That's your reaction to being *startled*?"

"I—are you okay?" He reached out to comfort her but she pulled the covers to her chin. He sat on his heels, face in hands. "Look, sometimes I get freaked out when people grab me by surprise." He forced a breath to steady his heart, grateful he hadn't lapsed into a full-on episode. "It comes from childhood shit. It fucked me up."

"You could've warned me."

"No, Jessica. I couldn't, okay? Because it's difficult and embarrassing—"

"It's better to flip me like a fucking pancake?"

"No, it's just..." His eyes locked onto hers. "Being with you makes me forget all that shit. It lets me pretend it never happened." He swiped his face. "At least I thought so."

Jessica picked at her fingernails. "Is that how you got all those scars?"

"The ones I pretend don't exist?"

She offered a weak smile. "Sometimes I imagine you had a really bad car accident."

"I might start using that."

She took his hand. Her thumb brushed the deformed skin circling his wrist. "What caused this?"

It was work not to yank his arm away. "Rope."

"And around your ankles, too?"

Johnny nodded.

"What about—" She choked on a breath and wagged a finger at his midsection.

Johnny glanced down at the lash marks across his ribs, the dozens of skinny raised scars that looked akin to having been hit with shrapnel. "Razor knife, extension cord."

She released a sound, part wretch, part wail.

The heaviness blanketing the room made Johnny want to cringe. "I think you're more disturbed by it than I am."

"Shut up." She swatted at him.

He shrunk back. "Don't do that. I might freak out again." They both smiled half-heartedly.

Johnny crawled beneath the covers and Jessica lay beside him, her head on his chest. "I get it, not wanting to think about that stuff." She caressed his shoulder. "But I'm glad you told me."

"It was either that or let you charge me with assault."

She sighed. "Again, with the deflection."

"It's cheaper than therapy."

Jessica propped on an elbow to look at him. Tears were trickling from her eyes.

"Shit. I didn't realize you were that upset." He pulled her in and rocked her. "I'm sorry, baby."

Exactly what he didn't want. Was this how it was going to be now? Him, having to apologize for shit *he* suffered? Her, viewing him forevermore as some fucking victim? It only intensified his loathing for his family. And himself.

Johnny's eyes locked on the ceiling as Jessica's wet face pressed into the nape of his neck. In her blubbering he heard something about unimaginable horror and adversity, sniffle-sniffle, perseverance and strength...

Jessica wiped her nose with the back of her hand. "It just makes me love you even more."

Johnny blinked. "Say what now?"

She sat up to look at him. "I said that I love you."

Every negative thing he was thinking and feeling blew clean out of him. How could a few piddly words do that? Instead, he felt something unfamiliar. Something exhilarating but scary, empowering yet enfeebling. It sent a buzzing sensation through his heart, brain and groin.

"Is it too soon to say it?"

Johnny snapped out of his paralysis. "No, I—no." He felt himself grin uncontrollably, which made him feel stupid. "You keep surprising me today."

Jessica bit her thumbnail. "You don't have to say it back. I know it's only been a few months."

"Look, it's just—" He finger-combed his hair with both hands. "Sometimes I feel you when you aren't here. And when we're together, it's easy, like I never want to stop learning about you." He looked into her face. "And the only time I feel really at peace, like, all of my bullshit just disappears, is when I'm inside you. Is that love?"

She smiled. "I think so."

"Then I guess I love you, too."

CHAPTER TWENTY-THREE

By late afternoon, a bunch of people around the loft made the hike to Chinatown, including Danni, who was still hanging out with Maurice. On the way, she and Jessica stopped at a payphone to call home and get permission to sleep at each other's places again.

The group chose the Hunan House on Mott Street. The dining room was compact, but it was before the dinner rush, so the staff pushed tables together to accommodate them. Lots of food was ordered and passed around for everyone to try. The ample leftovers were packed up for the brothers who had stayed behind.

On the walk home, Johnny and Jessica linked arms. They were lethargic from the food, serene from their recent declaration, and pleasantly achy from the subsequent sex. But as they got closer to the loft, Johnny's mind started to wander. He thought about how violently he had reacted to Jessica pinning him, even in play. He had barely fallen asleep, yet was so easily transported back to the nightmare of that cellar. What would happen if he had a full-blown episode? Could he seriously injure her, like that guy with the Crosses? Or worse?

"Hey, baby?"

"Yeah?"

"Are you sure you're okay to stay over again?"

"My mom sounded fine. She didn't suspect anything."

"What about your dad?"

Near the front door, Jessica released his arm and stopped walking. "What's wrong?"

"Nothing."

"I thought we were having a good time."

"We are. It's just—"

"What?"

Johnny waited for the last of his brothers to go inside. "I feel bad about before. I'm worried it'll happen again."

"Don't." Jessica laughed. "I'm never jumping on you without permission again." When he didn't share her mirth, her face dropped. "Do you not want me to sleep over?"

"No, baby, it's not that." Johnny lit a Marlboro, dragging the smoke deep into his lungs. Hadn't he confessed enough shit? Did she need to know about the blackouts also? The ones where he came to splattered with blood?

"Johnny, what happened to you was—" Her eyes drifted upward. "I don't even have words for it." She waved a hand at the building. "Do these guys know?"

Johnny nodded weakly. "Yeah."

"Okay then. You've got a support system." She stepped closer. "So, you don't need my pity."

He puffed smoke through his nostrils. "Good instincts."

"And I'm not going to tell anyone. I promise." She bit her lip. "So can I stay?"

How could he argue? "Okay. But if you ever see me acting strange, or, like, having a bad dream, you need to get the fuck away and tell one of my boys. Even if you have to wake them up. Okay?"

She sighed. "Okay."

That night, wrapped in Jessica's arms, Johnny forced himself to stay awake. What if she moved in her sleep or squeezed him too hard? Could that trigger another outburst? Was having talked about his scars enough to make him fully flip? This whole sharing a bed thing was new territory.

The more he tried to ban any Miami memories, the more they appeared. He focused on the rhythm of Jessica's breathing instead. But it was so soothing, it eventually lulled him to sleep.

Through his dreamy fog, Johnny heard an alarm. Was it time for school already? But it was summer break. And that didn't sound like his alarm clock anyway. He began to stir and so did Jessica.

"Mmm, what's that beeping?" she said into the pillow.

Were they having the same dream, and why was it still so dark? *Fuck, the pager.* Johnny slid out of bed and groped toward his bureau. He opened the top drawer, pawing through socks and underwear until he found it, then collected his pants and shirt.

"Where're you going?" Jessica mumbled.

He kissed her head. "I gotta check something. I'll be right back."

In the living room, he clicked on a light to see extra numbers on the pager's screen. Marco was out of the country. Johnny yanked on his clothes while heading to the kitchen, where he and Tito kept a jar for loose change. He stuffed a fistful of coins in one pocket, the pager in another. Before turning toward the door, he grabbed a pencil and paper plate in case there were instructions.

The crisp predawn air cleared Johnny's head as he jogged to a phone booth a few blocks north on Canal. He checked the number and dialed. The automated operator came on asking for money, and Johnny pushed coins into the slot. There was a series of clicks followed by a peculiar dial tone. After several rings, Marco's voice came through a staticky connection. "Johnny?"

"Yeah."

"How do I know it's you?"

"I don't know. It's me."

"Why aren't you asleep?"

"I *was* asleep."

"You're using a payphone, right?"

"Yes."

"Is it warm in New York?"

"It's dark." Johnny picked at an *End War!* sticker near the coin return. "Did you just call for a weather report?"

"I have a job."

Johnny's stomach flipped. "What kind of job?"

"Not the kind you're thinking of."

Thank fuck.

"Are you still there?"

"Yes."

"I need you to pick up something."

"Okay?"

"The person who was supposed to do it had an unfortunate accident." Marco let out a disturbing staccato laugh. "And I don't trust anyone else on such short notice."

"What am I picking up?"

"There's a plane landing in West Virginia. It'll have valuable cargo that you might need to hold for a while. Until I can come get it."

Johnny paced as far as the cord allowed. "How much *cargo* are we talking about?"

"A hundred."

"A hundred what?"

"Kilos."

Johnny gave the receiver an incensed face. "How the fuck am I supposed to pay for all of that?"

"You don't need money. It's my own shipment."

"Who's driving the plane?"

"Two of my people. I trust them."

"Is this, like, at an airport?"

The operator clicked on requesting more money for another three minutes, and Johnny dumped out the remaining coins. A few quarters rolled off the metal shelf. His sneaker stopped them before they made it to the curb. He hurried to feed the slot. "You still there?"

"Yeah." Marco continued. "It's not an airport. It's a landing strip. Remote. But you got friends, right? Because you can't do it alone. You'll need guns, people watching your back, making sure the delivery doesn't get ambushed."

"Jesus Christ. How dangerous *is* this?"

"You sure you got a safe place to keep shit? Not some cheap storage locker at Penn Station."

"Yeah, I got a place now."

"Look at you. Mr. Big Shot."

"Marco, you need to give me the details because I'm running out of change."

"The strip is on Patterson Creek Road. Take Route 50 to Medley, West Virginia. You'll find it on a map. The plane is a twin-engine Piper Navajo, tan and white. It's scheduled around ten o'clock tonight. I'll page you the time as it gets closer, because there could be delays on this end."

Johnny scribbled everything on the paper plate. "Should I know what I'm picking up?"

"Eighty coke and twenty dope. And Johnny? Count the bags. If it's short, kill the pilots."

"I thought you said you could trust them."

"Everyone is trustworthy until they aren't."

"Can't we just rough them up?"

"No. It sends the wrong message." Marco waited for some static to dissipate. "Guard that shipment with your life, and the lives of your boys."

Like I have a fucking choice? "Of course."

"I'll be in touch."

Johnny cradled the receiver. How far was West Virginia anyway, and how long would it take to find the place? The Brick only ever got a few kilos at a time. A dozen, tops, so how was he going to deal with a hundred? And where would they stash it? Assuming they got back without incident. Had Marco been serious about the danger, or was it one of his coked-out exaggerations?

The loft was still quiet. Even though Johnny's head was spinning, it was too early to rally the gang. He pulled off his clothes and crawled beside Jessica. He wrapped his arms around her, and she moaned before drifting off again. Her peacefulness freed his mind to do the same.

By morning, their bodies were seeking each other before their brains woke. By the end of their lovemaking, they were fully conscious.

"See?" Jessica said, getting up to use the bathroom. "Nothing bad happened last night."

Johnny sat up. "Maybe you're the antidote to my nightmares." The clock read just past eight. He needed to get busy.

Jessica cracked the door, a foamy toothbrush in her mouth. "What was that noise last night?"

"It's a pager. My uncle Casper got it for me, you know, because we don't have any phones hooked up yet."

Jessica spit in the sink and exited the bathroom. "He pages you in the middle of the night?"

"He keeps odd hours." Johnny got up to pee. "I probably didn't need to call him right back," he said through the door. "I just didn't want to miss out if he had a job."

"So, did he?"

"Yeah, and I should get ready soon." Lying through the door was easier than to her face, so he took extra time performing his ablutions. "It's out of town. Vermont." Johnny grimaced at the mirror. *Vermont*? "It's a big house, lots of furniture. Could be an overnighter."

"Where are the people moving to?"

"Westchester, I think."

"Why wouldn't they just hire a moving company out of Vermont?"

Johnny leaned against the door jamb to look at Jessica, who was sitting on the edge of the bed. "I didn't ask for details. I was half asleep."

She gave him a coquettish look. "Are you kicking me out?"

"Yeah." He winked. "After we shower."

CHAPTER TWENTY-FOUR

By mid-morning, Johnny had picked seven brothers to make the trip with him. They readied the van, packing snacks, drinks and a few blankets for concealing the goods. They also brought six guns, which was half the gang's arsenal. Tito drove the first leg, taking Interstate 78 to Harrisburg, Pennsylvania, then changed to Interstate 81. Outside the capital, Joe took over.

The scenery became lusher. There were tree-lined properties with big houses on grassy plots, and bucolic farms with silos and livestock.

JJ's face was plastered to the van's window. "Damn. This shit looks like a jigsaw puzzle I used to make with my grandma."

"The closest you've come to a cow or grass is a jigsaw puzzle?" said Clyde.

"So sad." Jarrod patted JJ's shoulder. "Your mother shoulda signed your ass up for that Fresh Air Fund."

JJ sucked his teeth. "The only green you've ever seen is the mold inside your drunk parents' refrigerator."

"You're not entirely wrong." Jarrod inhaled the fragrant air wafting through the opened windows. "Smells a lot better, too."

They pulled off the interstate to grab an early dinner before the map would have them cutting onto narrower roadways. The sun was getting low in the sky when they came upon Patterson Creek, a hilly two-lane, dotted with properties in disrepair. Many houses looked vacant. In the adjacent fields were partially collapsed corrugated outbuildings with peeling panels. Decades-old machinery sat rusting amid overgrown brush, most likely abandoned where it had stopped working. Barbed wire lay twisted between fallen fence posts.

Johnny set the atlas on the dashboard. "This looks like a country version of the South Bronx."

They came up behind a faded yellow tractor with smoke chugging from a vertical exhaust pipe. An old white guy in overalls with a hound dog on the floorboard waved them by.

"Look," said Mario. "His gang colors are denim."

Johnny smiled. "I'll bet he runs this town."

A few miles down the road was a large weather-rotted sign with faded letters reading, *Medley Air Strip*. Below, a dated advertisement for sightseeing tours and flying lessons. A cratered driveway, more weeds than gravel, disappeared into some woods. Joe pulled over. "You wanna check it out on foot?"

Johnny leaned out the window. "There's not much traffic, but these New York plates are gonna stand out like a motherfucker."

Joe inched forward as the van's shocks undulated with the swells and dips of the path. A low hanging branch slapped the windshield, lodging some leaves in the wipers. After a few shallow bends, they came to a thick chain spanning the trail. It was attached to two rotting four-by-fours. One side was padlocked to an eye hook, the other just hung from a bent nail.

Joe killed the engine and everyone got out to stretch and look around. Not far beyond the chain was a grassy opening. It was fifty feet wide and at least fifty times that long, lined with trees on all sides. In the nearest corner of the field was a rusty antique biplane on flat tires. Beside it, a pole with a tattered windsock.

"This looks promising," said Jarrod. "You wanna scope it out?"

"Yeah." Johnny pointed to JJ and Rafael. "You two stay here in case anyone comes. The rest of us will split up to check the perimeter."

The boys walked the length of the runway, inspecting the woods for anything suspicious. A few chipmunks threw up their tails and scurried under the brush. A crow cawed, breaking the silence before launching off a high branch.

Clyde shrieked from across the field.

"What is it?" Johnny looked over.

"False alarm." Joe wagged a hand from beside Clyde. "Just a snake."

"There's snakes out here?" Mario did a high knee sprint around the others. "Fuck that!"

When the canvass was complete, everyone reconvened by the gate. "I didn't see shit," said Jarrod.

"Me neither," said Johnny. "But it's still early."

"That's good. If anyone crashes the party, we'll see them coming."

The air was motionless and warm. Between patrols of the wood line, the group sat gazing at the sky, which was clear and black, the stars much brighter than they had ever seen. A rare passing car could be heard over the crickets.

Near ten o'clock, the pager beeped. The numbers 1020 were on the screen, and everyone took their positions. Tito waited by the gate. The others spread out behind trees, ready to head in whichever direction the plane came from. A faint whirring could be heard. When blinking lights appeared and rounded toward the far end of the strip, Johnny touched the gun in the back of his waistband. As it drew closer, the Piper Navajo was just as Marco had described it.

The engine shut off before the trees, and the aircraft sailed quietly onto the grass. The tires squeaked as the plane touched down and glided across the field, lurching to a halt a few dozen yards from the gate.

The crew scurried closer. Through the interior lights, two men could be seen unharnessing themselves from the cockpit. The pilot looked like a math teacher, clean-shaven, with spectacles, wearing a herringbone jacket and blue button-down shirt. The other guy, likely Marco's henchman, was scruffier, with a patchy beard. He wore jeans and a sweatshirt with a cutout collar.

Johnny approached the plane, followed by Joe, Jarrod and Rafael. The others stayed in the shadows. The pilot crouched past a few windows to open the cabin door. When the steps dropped down, light spilled onto the grass, exposing the four teens. The pilot was startled and uttered, "Adriano."

The other guy heard him and rushed to the door with an Uzi.

Johnny put up his hands. *"Tranquilo. Soy amigo de Marco."*

Adriano's grip on the gun relaxed but it remained trained.

"I'm Johnny. I was told to meet you."

"And who are these?" His chin indicated the others.

"Marco said to bring help."

"Hmm." He scanned them, looked at his partner, then set down the gun. "Okay, come get it."

Marco's men dragged five duffle bags from the rear of the plane and tossed them out one by one, until they spotted the van rolling over with the headlights cut. This time the math teacher was the faster draw, producing a handgun, but Adriano was right behind him.

"No!" said Johnny, his heart racing. "Don't shoot."

The men's mouths tightened.

"He's with us." Johnny gestured to Tito, who turned on the interior light so they could see he was alone.

"How many fucking people you got?" Adriano asked.

"Marco said to be prepared."

The pilot rolled his eyes at his partner before tucking his pistol away.

Jarrod and Rafael unzipped each bag to examine the contents before letting Joe load them into the van.

Adriano leaned a shoulder on the door frame. "You don't have to count that shit. It's all there."

Johnny shrugged. "Marco said—"

"Yes, yes, we know what Marco says." He set the Uzi back down. "Marco is like a volcano, ready to erupt at any moment." His hands simulated an explosion. "You'd be stupid to cross that guy." A scowl settled on his face as he tipped his chin at Johnny. "What I want to know is, how does a fucking kid like you get such a good grade with him?"

"Me?" Johnny shrunk back.

"Yes, you."

"I—I don't know."

"You're not related?"

"No."

"The way he talks about you, so protective, like you were his only son."

Johnny wanted to hear more, but felt a tap on his shoulder.

"It's all set," said Jarrod.

Johnny nodded, keeping his eyes on the plane. "We good here?"

"*Espera.*" The math teacher dragged a burlap sack to the door.

"Ah, yes," said Adriano. "Marco said to give you this."

"What is it?"

"Coffee."

"Coffee?" Johnny could smell the aromas of nuts and chocolate. The sack was stamped, *Product of Colombia*, with a line drawing of a sun and mountains. It felt heavy, maybe thirty-five pounds, as he passed it to Joe.

"Okey-dokey, *children.*" Adriano wiggled his fingers. "Toodeloo."

The pilot closed the hatch, and they crouched to the cockpit. The brothers got in the van, but Johnny didn't move until both men were strapped in their seats with the engine revving.

Navigating the dark back roads, everyone was guarded because Marco had made it seem like they could be ambushed at any moment. Once on the interstate, they began to relax.

"That went smoother than I imagined," said Jarrod.

"Would've went smoother without the Uzi," said Rafael.

"What'd you expect?" said Joe. "That's a lot of drugs."

"Indeed," said Mario from the back row. "And I'm so glad we risked our lives driving all the way down here for a bag of coffee." He laughed. "That's some *Jack and the Beanstalk* shit right there." He patted the sack in the cargo bed behind him. "And it ain't even ground."

Johnny wagged his head. "I'm sure we'll be compensated."

"Yeah," said Jarrod. "Your Daddy's gonna take care of you."

"Wait, what?" said Clyde.

Rafael turned to him. "You guys didn't hear?"

"Not from the woods."

"That one guy said Marco talks about Johnny like a son."

"Not *a* son," Jarrod corrected. "His *only* son."

Johnny clucked his tongue. "Shut the fuck up."

"You should be flattered," said Clyde. "Marco's kinda crazy and all, but apparently, he likes you. What's wrong with that?"

A lot was wrong with it. Maybe not the liking part, but definitely the favoritism. All that did was invoke resentment. It had happened with Dos Cruces. César telling his gang to give the Dogs of War special treatment had obviously pissed people off. Johnny turned to the back of the van. "What's wrong is I hate getting a pass from people like Marco and César because I'm covered in scars."

"Whoa, whoa." Jarrod waved a hand. "Nobody's pitying you. Do you think Marco trusted you with millions of dollars' worth of drugs because he felt sorry for you?"

Johnny's eyes dipped.

"Exactly. And the only reason César gave you a pass is because he knows you're a threat."

CHAPTER TWENTY-FIVE

Throughout the summer, the gang earned money working straight jobs and performing on the street. It was enough to get started on the loft renovations. A priority was building closets with hidden storage to stash the drugs they were holding for Marco, whose communication seemed to have lapsed. Johnny kept the pager nearby just in case.

The band hit as many open mic nights as possible. Rarely did the gigs pay anything, but it was worth it for the practice and exposure, and there were always brothers eager to schlep gear and hang out in whichever dive Temper was playing.

Tito's cousins came into possession of a neglected maroon Monte Carlo, which they said he could have if he made the repairs on his own time. They also painted over the advertising and vermin carcasses on the exterminator van. Many of the Dog brothers were heartbroken, but understood the risk of driving something so recognizable.

On July twenty-fifth, Johnny turned sixteen for real. He didn't have much enthusiasm for holidays in general, but found his birthday particularly repellent. The day he turned twelve was when he had run away—scratch that, *escaped* from his Miami home. It had taken courage, and he was proud of how far he had come, but anything connecting him to that house and those people was something better left ignored.

Jessica spent as much time at the loft as she could without raising suspicion with her parents. It helped that Danni was there almost as often, allowing them to use each other as alibis. But Michelle and Jarrod had called it quits, and he didn't want her hanging around. When Jessica did sleep over, Johnny still worried he might have an episode in front of her, but after the third or fourth time, he got over it. It was too hard to think of unpleasant things when they were together.

As the school year began, Johnny toyed with the idea of dropping out. When he was bouncing between couches and squatting at the vacant apartment, enrollment made him look less suspicious. Now that he had a legit place, his time might be better spent working. But he liked the daily routine, and the idea of finishing something he started. Roosevelt was also a good place to recruit. And there was Jessica.

Some brothers were making breakfast before school when Rafael came in and stood across the counter from Johnny. "Hey, me and Joe were watching TV last night. It was late, like close to midnight, when we heard this bass thumping from the street."

Johnny shrugged. "Yeah?"

"But there's hardly any traffic around here, so we looked out the window and saw a black car going by real slow."

Johnny put down his cereal.

"It looked like that Galaxy those Crosses were driving when they came by Roosevelt."

"You sure?" asked Jarrod.

"We weren't at first, so we turned off some lights and waited. A few minutes later, it circled by again. I swear it was the same two, the beefy bald guy and the smaller one with the mole."

"Then what?" said Clyde.

Rafael flipped his palms up. "Nothing. We kept watching, but they never came back. We even went up to the roof to get a better look, but they must've just left. I would've woken you otherwise."

"All right." Johnny swiped a hand over his face. "Tonight, we'll set up some lookouts. But all of us need to be careful at school today. No hanging around outside."

"First they're at Roosevelt," said Jarrod. "Now they're here. How the fuck are they finding us?"

"Someone from school must've said something," said Clyde. "Someone who came to the party."

"Who the fuck's friends with that gang?" asked Chico.

Johnny thought about Nalda and Michelle, both of whom had been booted rather harshly. They were still casting dirty looks at the gang when they passed in the hallway. "It could be anyone," he said. "Or it's a coincidence. But until we figure it out, we need to lay low and not have anyone over. It's too risky."

"If them motherfuckers were really out to do something shady," said Mario, "wouldn't you think they'd turn the damn radio down?" He bounced a hand off his forehead. "Like, duh."

Johnny laughed. "I don't think they're César's best and brightest." He scanned his brothers' faces. "But remember, good marksmanship does not require intelligence."

For the rest of the week, gang members took shifts watching from the roof and ground floor windows, but no one saw anything out of the ordinary.

Come Friday, Johnny and Jessica were in biology class, trying to pay attention while caressing each other's thighs under the desk. "My parents think I'm sleeping at Michelle's tomorrow night."

He pulled his hand away and straightened up. He could sense her glowering but focused on the blackboard.

When class was over, they packed up their books. "Don't you want me to stay over?" she asked.

"I can't this weekend. I got shit going on."

"If you're working, I could come afterwards."

"It's just—"

"Or I'll wait for you at the loft. Someone will be there to buzz me in, right?"

"Jessica, no." It came out harsher than intended.

She raised a brow. "Excuse me?"

"Baby, I'm sorry." Johnny raked fingers through his hair. "I want to be with you. I just can't this weekend."

"Why, are some other girls coming over?"

"What? No." She started to walk away, but Johnny took her arm. "It's not like that, okay?"

She faced him. "Then how is it?"

He should have prepared for this, thought up an excuse. A few months ago, he would have. He might have also known who was snitching. Back before he got too comfortable with his stable place to live and started playing house with his regular girlfriend. He wouldn't let that happen again.

"I need to take care of some shit, okay?" Johnny turned to walk away. "*That's* how it is."

◇◇◇

Johnny took extra shifts. He couldn't sleep anyway. He bounced between Joe and Rafael's ground floor apartment, and the one next door, where Jeff, Alex and Oscar lived, peeking through curtains in the darkened rooms. Then he would sit in the cool October air with whoever was on the roof. The whole time, his brain was spinning, looking at things from every angle. When the sun finally peeked between the buildings, he called off the watch and went to bed.

Johnny woke that afternoon with clarity and determination. There was some residual guilt over how he had treated Jessica, but this was more important.

He walked upstairs to the Mess Hall, where several brothers were hanging around. Some played cards at the table, others lounged on couches, flipping through magazines. Johnny threw together a ham and cheese sandwich, poured a glass of milk and sat at the counter. "Someone rally the others. We're having a meeting in ten minutes." By the time he finished eating, he was surrounded by the Dogs of War.

"We need a plan." Johnny pushed his empty plate aside. "We can't just hide out waiting for these assholes to make a move." He paced the length of the counter. "We know they're looking around, but they don't know we know. That gives us the upper hand."

Some brothers hummed in agreement.

"That big guy hasn't liked me from day one. And he doesn't have much respect for César's orders if he's chasing me down in the street. But, because I stabbed that guy, does that mean the truce is off? Could these guys be acting on behalf of Dos Cruces, or are they still rogue?"

157

Jarrod put up a hand. "If the whole gang was after us, wouldn't they just drive by with guns blazing? What's with all the pussyfooting?"

"There's no numbers on the buildings around here," said Rafael. "Maybe they can't find us."

"I don't think they're after *us*," said Johnny. "They're after me. That guy made it pretty clear when he drove by the school."

"But why'd they just stop?" said Clyde. "Seems like a half-assed vendetta."

"Maybe that's evidence they're acting alone," said Mario. "There might be consequences if they're caught hurting you, so they're trying to be stealthy."

"It makes sense," said Johnny. "But the only way to find out is to ask them."

"Say what?" said Chico.

"In the absence of a crystal ball, we need to fucking ask them."

"And what if we don't like the answer?" said Clyde.

"We take them out." Johnny's expression was resolute. "But I'll need to hang back because if they see me, they might try to kill me."

The rest of the afternoon was spent concocting a plan. Roles were established and rehearsed, weapons were assigned and vantage points ascertained. They parked the three vehicles strategically, with the Monte Carlo and Joe's Dart flanking the stoop. The van was one door down and across the street. When night came, everyone took their positions. But there was no sign of the black Ford Galaxy or any of the Crosses.

Another week went by. The late-night stakeouts were having an effect on the crew's mood at work and at school. For Johnny, being grumpy and overtired made it easier to avoid Jessica. She, however, didn't seem to need an excuse to steer clear of him. He would worry about that later.

Saturday night was cold and blustery with a light drizzle, further dampening the crew's enthusiasm for what was starting to feel like a futile task. Nevertheless, the brothers posted outside and shifts were rotated on schedule.

Rat Alley provided some protection from the weather, but there was no place to sit. And, of course, there were the rats. Johnny and Clyde paced back and forth to deter them from using it as an expressway, turning sideways to pass each other in the narrow space. A Winchester sniper rifle was propped by the gate, which no one had to scale anymore due to the new lock.

Johnny peeked into the street. Cigarette smoke wafted from a cracked window of the van where four brothers were stationed. He looked up to see Patrick leaning over the roof's ledge with binoculars. Rudy Grant, a tall, skinny Jamaican kid recruited from Roosevelt, was with him. Other gang members were positioned in the stairwells, ready to relay information.

Johnny had lost track of time, though it had to be near eleven. "They're not coming," he said to Clyde, who was leaning against the wall with his eyes closed. "A big gang like Dos Cruces has more important shit to do on a Saturday night."

"Absolutely. They gotta keep up their quota of assault and batteries, rapes, muggings..." Clyde yawned. "And revenge murders." He tapped his chin. "Hmm, I guess they might come after all."

"If I wasn't so tired, I'd laugh."

A whistle came from above and Johnny grabbed the rifle. He and Clyde tucked into the shadows against the wall. In the street, others were scrambling into position. A moment later, there was the faint thumping of bass, and headlights reflecting off puddles in the road.

Jarrod and Mario stepped off the stoop and exchanged the gang handshake. "We got this," said Jarrod.

Mario nodded. "You know it, brother."

Johnny positioned the rifle. It wasn't a great angle if the Crosses stayed in the car. Otherwise, he would have to trust his brothers, none of whom had as much experience as he and Joe. Everyone else had gotten a little practice in the woods of New Jersey, but they had never been to a range. Nor had they shot anything with a heartbeat.

As the Galaxy rolled through the stop sign at Vestry, Jarrod and Mario made like they were having a heated debate, each emphasizing their points in an animated manner. Johnny and Clyde tucked tighter against the wall.

The driver's window rolled down, releasing a radio station's echoing call sign: "Double-u *double-u*, Bee *bee*, Ell *ell*, Ess *ess*, Mastermix *mastermix*, *mastermix, mastermix*..." Followed by *Back Stabbers* by the O'Jays. The big bald guy stepped on the brake, cocking an elbow out the window. The passenger craned to look from his seat. It was the man with the large mole under his nose.

Jarrod eyed them intently, like he was doing long division. Then his face brightened. "I know you."

"Yeah, yeah, it's those guys from that gang." Mario shook a finger. "Dos Cruces, right?"

The big Cross turned down the radio. "Come here."

Jarrod and Mario stepped closer, but stayed behind the Monte Carlo. "You live around here?"

"Us?" Mario patted his chest. "Nah, we were tagging some shit by the river."

Baldy scrunched his nose. "Then where are your cannons?"

"Empty. We tossed them shits."

The man fiddled with the gold chains around his neck. "You sure you weren't visiting your little Dog boss?"

"Johnny?" Jarrod recoiled. "He don't live around here."

"That's not what I heard."

"Who told you that?" asked Mario.

Baldy twitched a shoulder. "I just heard it."

"You got a message for him or something?" Jarrod craned to look inside the Galaxy. He made an upside-down L behind his back, warning that the men were armed. "'Cause we could pass it along."

Mole Man leaned over his friend. "We got a message for him all right."

"That's cool." Mario shook the drizzle off his afro and pulled up his hood. "He's got César's number. I'll tell Johnny to give him a jingle."

Baldy's mouth hardened. "César ain't involved in this. It's between me and him."

Mario shrugged. "Whatever."

Jarrod swatted Mario's arm. "You know what?"

Mario feigned surprise. "What?"

"I'll bet they think Johnny lives around here because of his uncle."

"Right," Mario elongated the I. "He had that party at his place."

Baldy jutted his chin toward the stoop. "Is that it?"

"That?" Mario waved a hand. "Nah. His building's on the next block." He stepped around the Monte Carlo and into the street. "It's that one over there.

Mole Man squinted out the windshield. "Which one?"

Mario pointed. "That one further down, with the red brick. You see it?"

Now Baldy was also straining to look, and Jarrod came closer, pulling a Glock from his waistband. He stuck the gun through the window and fired into the driver's chest. The loud *pop* echoed into the night, seeming to startle Jarrod more than the recoil.

"Jesus!" Mole Man reached for his gun, but Mario's was already drawn. He pulled the trigger, hitting the man in the abdomen.

Johnny and Clyde ran out from the alley, their heads swiveling as they checked for lights flicking on anywhere in the street. Others came from their spots to surround the car. The driver was clenching the wheel, taking agonal breaths. His passenger was momentarily stunned, watching blood soak through his shirt, but then he turned to shoot his gun out the window.

Jarrod and Mario ducked as Rafael yanked open the door. He grabbed the guy's arm and they wrestled for the pistol. The driver got bumped in the struggle and slumped to the side. The Galaxy began to roll forward. JJ and Mikey were standing by the bumper and nearly got their feet run over.

"What the fuck," Rafael hollered.

"Shit, it's in drive," said Mario.

Rafael moved with the car, trying to rip the gun away, but the smaller Cross was stronger than he looked. Despite his wound, he fought back, putting a foot on the dash for leverage. The rain was coming down harder, making everything slick.

Tito dived through the driver's window. He threw the shifter into park and the car lurched to a stop mid-block. The abrupt motion allowed Rafael to rip the gun free. He handed it to Chico behind him, then punched the guy until he was unconscious.

Johnny looked at the roof, arms outstretched, but Patrick and Rudy gestured that everything was still clear. The remaining brothers poured from the loft, adding to the others who were pinging around nervously. Johnny whistled to get their attention. "Alex, Andre, grab those heavy-duty trash bags from the boiler room. Teddy, Ramón, rags and cleaning supplies."

They all nodded and jogged inside.

Johnny checked up and down the street another time. "Let's get this car out of the road."

Joe put it in neutral, working the wheel as some brothers pushed it to the curb. He shut off the engine and unfolded from the car with the keys and a blood-covered Colt .357 Magnum retrieved from Baldy's lap. "I'll take care of the guns," he said, then eyed Mario and Jarrod. "I'm gonna need yours, too."

They both complied.

After Jeff slipped a Hefty bag over the big Cross's head, Rafael and Eric helped to maneuver the guy to the trunk, where they covered him with more bags to contain the blood.

"Is the other one dead yet?" Johnny asked.

Tito put two fingers on the side of the man's neck, looked into the distance, then nodded.

He and Chico bagged up that guy and stuffed him in the back with his friend. A few brothers had to lean on the trunk to make it shut.

Johnny scanned his crew. "Anyone with blood on them needs to get cleaned up and throw their shit in the wash. If you're standing around without a job, pair up and patrol the surrounding area."

Jarrod and Mario started off with the others.

"Not you."

"Why not?" asked Jarrod.

"You've done enough. Just go relax."

"Relax?" Mario spit out a laugh.

A whistle came from above and Johnny's heart jumped. He gestured for everyone on the block to duck behind parked cars. Headlights brightened the street, but it was just an off-duty taxi. The driver barely looked awake, hypnotized by the oscillating wipers.

Once the cab passed, Johnny resumed. "Look, you both did really good tonight. Exceptional." He lay hands on their shoulders. "Have a few beers, chill out."

They nodded and went inside.

Johnny kept staring at the door even after it had closed. He knew how they must feel, part exhilaration, part shock. The need to keep busy. Even he felt like he wasn't doing enough. His brothers had everything under control. Watching each of them leap into action, playing their roles so perfectly. All to protect him? Not only were they willing, they were capable. Very capable."

"You all right?" asked Clyde.

"Yeah, but remind me to get some fucking silencers."

Joe came through the door with a dented gas can. "Those guns are wiped and stashed. I'll do a more thorough job when I get back."

Johnny nodded. "Did you decide where you're going?"

Joe watched Teddy and Ramón climb out of the Galaxy with a trash bag bulging with soiled rags and empty cleaner bottles. They stuffed it behind the front seat. "When I was younger, my uncle used to take me to this place."

Johnny shrunk back. "The Brick dragged little Joey along to dump a body?"

Joe laughed. "I wasn't *that* young, and he wasn't dumping a body. We'd go hunting in the sticks of northern Pennsylvania. It was really remote. A car could burn there a long time before anyone saw it. Especially at night." He looked at his watch. "But I better get going because it's a few hours' drive."

Tito came out with Patrick and Rudy, who had been replaced on the roof, and everyone exchanged the gang handshake. Joe climbed in the front seat of the Galaxy, with Rudy shotgun. Tito and Patrick got into the Monte

Carlo. After the two cars pulled away, Johnny checked the road for blood. It was hard to see in the dim glow of the streetlight, but if they were lucky, any evidence would wash away with the increasing rain.

CHAPTER TWENTY-SIX

Both third floor apartment doors were propped open. Several gang members had a poker game going at the Mess Hall's table. More played Risk in the Studio. Others were flopped on couches, losing the battle to stay awake. Johnny had tried to talk Mario out of a roof shift, but he said it was better than pacing back and forth.

Ultimately, that was all Johnny could do. He struggled to channel his gnarled emotions into writing lyrics. Chain-smoking while crouched over his notebook, he could only push out a few lines before the restlessness became unbearable. Then he'd pop up to resume rounds.

Jarrod, however, passed the time at his drum set. With headphones plugged into the stereo, he hammered out rhythms to song after song, using brush sticks, so he looked like Keith Moon on mute.

The sun had been up a few hours when Johnny heard the familiar chunk of the Monte Carlo's doors. "They're back!" he called out, galloping downstairs.

Joe, Tito, Patrick and Rudy filed into the foyer. They looked spent. A hint of gasoline emanated from them.

"What can we do?" Johnny asked.

Joe stripped off some layers. "We need to get these clothes washed, take showers."

"Should we clean the car?" asked Ramón.

"Can't hurt."

Oscar and JJ offered to help him.

"I'll get some more coffee going," said Chico.

Within an hour, the crew was congregated around the Mess Hall's long table, which had been lined with cereal boxes, milk, and packages of donuts and muffins. Everyone helped themselves and found places to sit. They sipped and chewed, eyeing each other as the room grew heavy with anticipation.

Joe finally set down his cereal bowl and took a swig of coffee. With the cup still at his lips, his head wobbled. "That was fucked up."

"Right?" said Patrick.

Rudy swiped a hand over his low-cut afro. "Some mad shit, man."

Tito spooned Cheerios into his mouth.

"What?" said Johnny. But did he really want to know?

Joe looked around the table. "First off, we barely got out of the Holland Tunnel before I noticed the Galaxy's gas gauge was on empty." He expelled a laugh. "Like *that's* what we need. Stuck on the side of the highway with two fucking bodies."

"But me and Tito don't know what's going on," said Patrick. "We're just following him, so when he pulls into a Shell station, we start shitting ourselves, thinking, what if blood's dripping from the trunk?"

Rudy jabbed a thumb at Joe. "My man was worried about that, too, but we didn't have much choice."

"So, Tito pulls in behind him," said Patrick. "But our car was full, so when the little zit-faced attendant asks how many gallons, Tito gives him that deadpan expression and says, 'Just clean the windshield, please.'"

Tito shrugged, slurping milk from his cereal bowl.

"Was anything leaking?" asked Jarrod.

"Not that we saw," said Patrick.

"The rest of the ride was smooth," said Joe. "North of Williamsport, it was deserted. We drove around until we found a clearing down this dirt road, poured the gasoline..." He winced, releasing a puff of air.

"Then got the fuck outta there," Rudy continued.

"But first we checked their pockets," said Patrick. "Eighty-seven dollars between them, and a packet of blow."

"IDs?" asked Johnny.

Tito pulled two driver's licenses from his shirt pocket and tossed them on the table. Johnny grabbed them. "Herbert Dawson? That asshole's name was Herbert? If I'd a known that I would've given him shit."

Clyde leaned over. "The other was Abel Torres, from University Avenue in the Bronx."

"And Herbert's at 465 East Tenth Street," said Johnny.

"Isn't that those projects on the Lower East Side?" Mario drummed fingers on the table. "My aunt lives there."

Rafael leaned back in his chair. "When César hears those guys are dead, every single one of his Crosses will be after us."

Johnny rolled the tension from his neck. "Maybe, maybe not."

"What do you mean?"

"I can't help thinking that if I'm César, and I have a few guys totally disrespecting me, disobeying my orders, I'm gonna be happy they disappeared." Johnny looked around the table. "He might even take credit for their death, you know, to send a message to the rest of his crew."

"But what if the truce got called off," said Joe, "due to that guy you stabbed?"

"That's not how it sounded," said Mario. "That Bert guy definitely said César wasn't involved."

"Johnny could be onto something," said Clyde. "As long as César is rational."

"That's just it, I think he is." Johnny rubbed his hands together. "If he finds out his own people came to kill me? Shit, that's treason." He stood to stretch. "Maybe with a few hours' sleep it'll all seem clearer."

"About that," said Joe. "I know we're all tired, but when that car gets discovered, there'll be an investigation. To be safe, we should spread out today, be seen by people."

"Joe's right," Johnny said to the others. "Visit your families, see friends, anyone who can provide an alibi."

There were some yawns and groans as the brothers pushed away from the table.

◇◇◇

When Johnny walked into Jessica's lobby, Freddy was at the desk. "What're you doing here on a Sunday?"

Freddy reached over to clasp Johnny's hand. "The weekend guy has some family shit, so that spells extra cash for me." He smiled. "What's up with you? Throwing any more wild parties?"

"I'm still recovering from the last one."

"Thanks again for inviting me." He leaned on his elbows. "You're not living uptown anymore?"

Johnny swiped his face. "No, we're out of there."

"I was talking to some of your boys that night, and I respect what you got going on."

"What do you mean?"

"You know." Freddy drummed the desk. "I've been around different crews growing up. Some even tried to recruit me. But what you got is different. It's like..." he gazed off. "Positive."

"Thanks. I didn't realize it was so obvious, meaning the gang thing."

"It's not. It's probably just my sociological perspective." He waved off the topic. "So, you looking for your girl?"

"Is she home?"

"I've been here since eight and haven't seen her leave, so go on up."

"You better buzz me. I don't want to frighten the parents."

"Right." Freddy grinned and pressed the button.

Carol's voice came over the scratchy intercom.

"Mrs. Baxter, Johnny's here for Jessica."

"Send him up."

Freddy looked at Johnny. "You're good, bro. Now they have time to hide the valuables."

Johnny laughed and slapped him five, then stepped into the elevator.

Before he could ring the bell, Jessica opened the door. Her expression was what he expected after not having spoken all week. "Baby, can we talk a minute?"

Her foot held the door. "Go ahead. Talk."

Johnny peered into the apartment to see if anyone was eavesdropping. He heard pots clanging, and Chad and Walter's voices blending with the TV. "Look, I'm sorry. I haven't been blowing you off." He stuffed hands in his pockets. "And you thinking that after all this time kinda hurts."

"What?" She stepped into the hall, leaving the door ajar. "You're putting this on *me*?"

"I'm not putting anything on you."

"It sure sounds like it."

Johnny leaned against the wall. "I didn't come here to fight. I just missed you."

Her brows raised as she waited for more of an explanation. As drained as Johnny was, he actually entertained blurting out the truth. *Sorry we couldn't hang out more, Sweetheart, but me and the boys were too busy committing a double homicide, then burning the bodies in a remote location. I'll try to be more considerate next time.* Instead, he swiped a hand over his face. "There's been some family shit going on. And you, more than anyone, know how hard that is for me. I just shut down. I can't deal."

"You could've told me."

"No, I couldn't." He tipped his head to the ceiling. "You're the remedy to that toxic bullshit. If I involve you, then you become part of it." He held her gaze. "Surely you can understand that?"

"They're not hurting you again, are they?"

"No. Not since I've been able to fight back."

"Jesus." She took a long breath. "Can we at least come up with a code word, so I'm not sitting around thinking the worst."

Her worst wouldn't come close. "Yeah, baby, whatever you want." He pulled her in for a hug and held her longer than she expected.

After, Jessica put a hand on his face. "You look like shit."

Johnny laughed. "It's been a rough week."

"I guess. You wanna come in?"

"As long as you haven't been badmouthing me to your parents. They hate me enough already."

"Shut up." She dragged him inside. "I would never."

Carol was puttering around the kitchen. Whatever she had in the oven smelled delicious, like garlic, herbs and melting fat. "Johnny. What a surprise. We haven't seen you in a while."

"Yeah, I was working a lot over the summer, and now I'm busy with school."

"That's what Jessica says."

Johnny flashed Jessica a quizzical look and she gave a tiny shrug.

Walter and Chad were at the dinner table, browsing the comics and puzzles from the Sunday Daily News. Chad offered a goofy smile with a raised palm.

"Johnny," said Walter.

"How do you do, sir," Johnny gave him a nod. "Sorry to barge in unannounced, but I was in the neighborhood."

Walter's narrowing eyes suggested he might ask what a guy like Johnny was doing in a neighborhood like theirs, but Jessica grabbed his arm. "C'mon, let's go to the living room."

They sat on the couch. The TV was playing an old Western. Jessica's loose-leaf binder was open with a textbook on the coffee table.

"A typical Sunday at the Baxter household." Johnny poked at a book. "Black and white movies and biology homework. You really are living on the edge."

Jessica jabbed him in the ribs and whispered, "We could've been fucking at your place right now, if you weren't being such a dick."

He laughed and tickled her, but they straightened up when Walter glanced over. Jessica picked up a handout and pretended to read it.

"Thanks for covering for me," Johnny said softly. "That stuff about work and school."

"You?" Her face scrunched. "If they had any idea how much I was seeing you, they'd shit themselves. Saying you weren't around let them buy all the Danni and Michelle sleepovers."

"You're more devious than I thought." He copped a feel of her breast.

She slapped his hand, giggling. "We could blow this joint, you know, say we're going for a walk and sneak over to your place."

The thought was enticing. Almost enough to make him forget all the other crap. But he didn't come here to get laid. He was here because he needed this law-abiding family to attest to his demeanor and whereabouts at a double homicide trial. And was the loft even safe? There was no telling the fallout. Not to mention the effect it was having on his crew. They certainly didn't need any outsiders hanging around while trying to process manslaughter. He had to keep her away a little longer.

"What are you kids watching?" Walter leaned in the doorway.

"Just some old movie." Jessica picked up a pencil. "Did you want to see something?"

"No dear, I was just curious."

"Walter," Carol called from the kitchen. "Why don't you ask Johnny if he'd like to stay for dinner?"

"Um, would you?" A forced smile appeared on his face. "Like to stay, that is."

Johnny nodded. "I'd love to, if it's not too much trouble."

"No trouble at all," he grumbled, "We have Sunday dinners early, so it shouldn't be much longer." He retreated to set the table.

Jessica looked disappointed.

"What?" Johnny turned up a palm. "You're always asking me to eat over."

She rolled her eyes. "In that case, you may as well help me with my homework while we wait."

Dinner was a delicious roast beef with potatoes, gravy and green beans, and everyone dug in. Jessica wasn't offering much conversation, but Chad made up for it. "I'm transferring to Roosevelt next year," he said to Johnny while forking meat into his mouth. "So, I'll probably be needing some brass knuckles or a switchblade."

Walter snorted. "Don't be so dramatic, Chad. It's a decent school."

"But there are rumors." Chad turned to his father. "And I've heard you say that the Puerto Ricans are always holding that kinda stuff."

Johnny almost spit out his green beans.

Jessica glared at Chad. "What an idiot." Then Walter. "Both of you."

"Dear, don't call your father an idiot," said Carol.

Walter put up a hand. "I never said that."

"It sure sounds like something you'd say." Jessica's lip curled in disgust.

Johnny patted her arm. "It's okay." He smiled at Chad. "First off, I'm not Puerto Rican. And second, I've never even seen a switchblade, or a pair of brass knuckles." His eyes migrated to Walter. "Not in school, or in my life."

Carol offered a strained laugh. "Don't mind them. They've been watching too many bad movies."

"Yeah," mumbled Jessica. "I'm sure that's it."

"Truth is," Johnny said, "Roosevelt *can* be difficult. Especially for freshmen. Some of the kids will try to make their presence known by exerting dominance over the younger ones." He shrugged. "But that's because deep down they're insecure, and maybe it's the only way they can feel superior."

All of the Baxters had stopped eating and were rapt with interest.

"But when that happens," Johnny speared a potato in his mouth, "your weapon of choice should be nun chucks."

Chad flopped over his plate, laughing. "That's fucking hilarious."

"Chad, language," scolded Walter.

Jessica giggled into her napkin, but Carol still looked confused.

Chad made some kung-fu moves with his knife and fork before pointing at Johnny. "This guy's great!"

Jessica walked Johnny to the elevator but they waited to push the button. They hugged and kissed until it became torturous. "I could come over for a few hours after school tomorrow," said Jessica.

"About that." Johnny repackaged the swelling in his pants. "When I said I had family shit, I meant that I had to go back home."

"What? Why?" She flung her arms in frustration. "I thought your parents were happy you moved out."

"They were." Johnny's gaze drifted down the hallway. "But everything's about control with them. Like, when I left, they were hoping I'd fall on my face. When I didn't, they got mad, and threatened to report me to social services." It sickened him to drag up his family. Even his fake family. And playing the victim felt so phony.

"Fuck." She put her arms around his neck. "I hate that this is happening to you. I want to meet these people, tell them how wonderful and brilliant you are."

Johnny brushed a lock of hair from her face. "It won't be long. They'll get tired of me again and I'll be back at the loft. I just need to wait it out."

"If I see a single new mark on you, I'll be the one calling social services."

He smiled and kissed her.

CHAPTER TWENTY-SEVEN

Things were tense. The Dogs of War did not know what to expect, but still had to keep up appearances. They stuck together as much as possible, and everyone kept one eye over their shoulder. At the loft, round-the-clock watches continued.

Jarrod, Mario and Rafael experienced waves of guilt for their roles in the killings. But if they started to withdraw, their brothers would step in with support and praise for having defended the gang, which helped convert their remorse into pride. Having made a kill also put them on par with Johnny.

By the end of the week, Johnny was in a class with Chico and Clyde. All three jumped when his pager went off. Carrying it around had become so routine, Johnny forgot it was there. The teacher and half the students turned around as he grappled to silence it. Seeing an international number, Johnny began checking his pockets for change, then caused more of a disturbance by hitting up his brothers, who also had to writhe around hunting.

At the bell, Johnny was out the door before the teacher put down the chalk. He bounded to the main floor, where there was a row of wooden phone booths. Inside one, he closed the bifold door. It felt like a mini-confessional, or so he imagined, but at least it was private. Checking the pager, he fed coins into the slot.

"What took so long?" were the first words out of Marco's mouth.

"I'm in the middle of school."

"Right. I keep forgetting you're a kid."

"What took *you* so long?"

"Me? I answered right away."

"To call," said Johnny. "It's been months."

"My men said everything went well."

"Yeah, it went fine."

"So why do I need to call?"

"I don't know." Johnny glowered at the receiver. "I just thought maybe you'd be needing your massive quantities of, um, stuff?"

"That?" Marco laughed. "It's not that much. And besides, you said you had a safe place. Should I worry?"

Johnny envisioned the NYPD ripping apart the loft looking for evidence of murder and finding a hundred kilos of drugs instead. "Nope. Nothing to worry about. Just tell me what to do next."

"How do you like the coffee?"

He cares about the fucking coffee? "We haven't tried it yet because we don't have a bean grinder."

"What? You need to get one."

"We've been a little busy."

"How many in your house drink coffee?"

A pair of teachers passed in front of the booth and Johnny shrunk deeper into the seat. "A lot."

"A lot," Marco echoed. "Look, I'm coming soon."

"When?"

"Not sure exactly, but I need the address."

Did he really want Marco knowing where he lived? "You don't need me to make a delivery or something?"

"No, I want to come."

Johnny didn't have time to think up an excuse. "It's 430 Washington Street. And I have a phone now."

"A phone? Wow. Lap of luxury."

Johnny ignored the gibe and rattled off the number.

"Good. I'll be in touch. Now go learn shit."

Johnny rubbed his temples. "Bye."

◇◇◇

Waiting was the worst part. And too reminiscent. Johnny had spent so much of his childhood waiting for bad shit to happen. In Miami, he could only tiptoe around so long before his father blew his stack over something trivial, or his brother had a psychotic outburst. Then Johnny would suffer the consequences. The anticipation became more unbearable than the punishment. But once the physical and psychological torture were over, there was this surrender. Because he knew there would be that small window, that respite. Before the waiting started all over. It was in those moments where Johnny found peace. Tranquility, even. His body would be throbbing in pain, but his brain could relax for a day. Maybe two.

Johnny was in Joe and Rafael's apartment taking out his frustrations on their gym equipment. It had been two weeks already and still nothing. He was toying with the idea of relaxing their guard when Mikey's voice came over a walkie-talkie. He was calling from the roof to say a car pulled up outside. Johnny and Rafael rushed to the window and cracked the shades. Joe stood ready to grab some guns hidden under the sink. Others heard the call and rushed downstairs.

Outside, a white Cadillac Fleetwood reflected the midday sun. A suited man in a cap walked around the car to open the rear door. He extended a hand, and Margaret emerged. She was in high heels and a black fur coat.

"False alarm," said Johnny, heading to let her in.

"It's okay," a voice hollered from the stairwell. "It's just Margaret."

"Sorry to disappoint," she said, navigating the stoop. "Were you expecting someone else?"

Johnny smiled. "You're never a disappointment."

Cradling his chin in her manicured fingers, she kissed his cheek, then turned to the chauffeur. "Will you get the boxes from the trunk, please?"

He bowed and retreated. Jarrod and Rafael followed to help.

"I apologize for my tardiness, but I've been meaning to bring you boys a little housewarming gift."

"You didn't have to do that." Johnny guided her inside and took her coat. Beneath it, she wore a red low-cut side-slit dress which accented her ample curves. Trying not to ogle, Johnny hung her fur on the end of a squat rack.

She stepped over some hand weights to sit at the table, which was littered with Joe's notepads and open college textbooks. "*Love* what you've done with the place."

"Believe it or not," said Joe, "it's the decor we were aiming for."

She eyed his chiseled physique. "It's working."

"It doesn't all look like this," said Johnny. "Would you like a tour?"

She fingered an errant black curl. "Maybe another time."

Jarrod and Rafael returned with two cases of wine and set them on the kitchen counter. Johnny and Clyde perused the assorted labels. "Can I make you a drink?" Johnny asked.

"No, sweetness, I'm on my way to a job. I just wanted to see how everything was working out."

"Great, thanks to you and Thomas. We're painting, doing some renovations, accumulating furniture..."

"I love it when hard workers catch a break." Her eyes landed on Johnny. "You deserve it."

He blushed. "So, what's on your agenda? You're looking especially dolled up today."

She laughed. "My presence has been requested in Atlantic City."

"Must be nice," Jarrod mumbled.

"Toss on a suit and some cologne, and rich horny housewives would pay a mint for a tumble with any of you young studs." She pointed at Joe. "Except you. Your uncle doesn't tolerate harlotry from family members."

"Really?" said Johnny. "The Brick's uptight about that?"

Margaret shrugged. "Some people think drug-dealing and racketeering is a fine living, but making a guy see stars is wrong."

Clyde draped over the counter. "You can make a guy see stars?"

Margaret bit her lip. "Sweetheart, I can make him see the whole solar system."

The walkie-talkie clicked on. "Cops," Mikey's voice was saying. "The fucking cops are here."

Alex and Oscar came across the hall, stating likewise.

Joe peeked out the window. "One radio car and an unmarked."

"Fuck," said Johnny, looking at his brothers. "Make sure this whole place is clean. Not even a roach in an ashtray."

"Got it." Jarrod sprinted upstairs with Oscar and Alex.

"And tell everyone to look natural," Rafael added.

"There's four," said Joe. "Two talking to Margaret's driver, the others checking out the block." He turned to Johnny. "You should get out of here."

"How?"

"Then hide," said Clyde.

Johnny exhaled toward the ceiling. "How's it gonna look when they find me crouching in a closet?" He sat next to Margaret. "Sorry about all this. You gonna be okay?"

"Me?" She slung an arm over the chair. "You're the ones who seem worried."

The doorbell rang and Johnny waved at Joe to let them in. "Everybody, just stay cool." He fingered the fake ID in his back pocket. It had his alias, with a birthdate putting him at eighteen. Clyde and Rafael grabbed seats at the table.

Joe opened the door. Two of the officers were uniformed. The other pair wore suits with guns and badges clipped to their belts.

"Good afternoon, I'm Sergeant Sullivan with the NYPD. This is Officer McCamy and detectives Grozier and Wyland. Mind if we come in and ask a few questions?"

"What's this about?" said Joe.

"Just a routine investigation. You can refuse entry, but we could come back with a warrant."

"No, please, come in." Joe stood aside, extending an arm toward the open door of his apartment.

Sullivan and McCamy scanned the rooms with a hand near their holsters. Grozier and Wyland poked around the ground floor before knocking across the hall. Jeff opened the door. Almost eighteen and burly, he could pass for older. He invited them to look around his place.

Officer McCamy cocked his head at the fur coat hanging from the gym equipment. "Who lives here?"

"I do," said Joe.

"Rental?"

"Yeah."

Sergeant Sullivan eyed the group around the table. Clyde and Rafael were perusing a Fundamentals of Macroeconomics textbook. Johnny doodled on a legal pad. "Who owns this building?"

"Not sure," said Joe. "I send checks to PDG Enterprises. Saw the apartment on the bulletin board at Medgar Evers College."

"Any tenants upstairs?"

"Probably."

The detectives were already back in the hall. Sullivan gestured with his head, and the pair started up the creaky steps.

McCamy circled the table. "You live here, too?"

"We're just friends," said Rafael.

"Yup," Clyde echoed. "Just friends."

"Got some IDs?"

Drivers' licenses and school cards were tossed on the table. Johnny braced as McCamy scrutinized them. When he felt Margaret's hand on his knee, he relaxed, then noticed that despite the notepad in the cop's back pocket, he wasn't writing anything down.

Margaret looked up at the sergeant. "Jason? Fancy meeting you here."

Sullivan froze. His pale face turned as red as Margaret's dress.

Johnny choked on a laugh. His brothers snickered into their fists.

"Margaret? What the—"

She spared him the discomfiture. "I'm just visiting these young men. They're good friends of mine." She crossed her legs, causing the slit in her dress to reveal most of her bare thigh.

He forced his focus back on Joe. "So, um, how long you been renting?"

"Not long, few months."

"Can I see the lease?"

Joe pinched his top lip. "Now, where would I have put that?" He stalled by heading for a dented file cabinet that came with the building.

Margaret half-turned in her chair. "Sweetheart, can you grab the cigarettes from my coat pocket?" Sergeant Sullivan moved toward the fur and she smirked. "I was actually talking to Joey."

"Right," said Sullivan, stepping aside.

When Joe brought her the pack, she tapped out a Virginia Slim and lit it. "So, whatcha investigating?"

McCamy tossed the IDs back on the table and muttered, "The murder of two shitbirds."

Sullivan's eyes narrowed at him. "Two men belonging to a street gang called Dos Cruces."

The officer returned a defiant look. "Who, surprise-surprise, aren't cooperating much."

"Gangs?" said Clyde. "Around here?"

Sullivan shrugged. "We got an anonymous tip, so we're looking into it."

"This neighborhood is quiet most of the time," said Joe.

McCamy's eyelids drooped. "Probably a red herring."

"A what?" said Rafael. ·

"Never mind." Sullivan pointed to the books on the table. "What are you studying?"

"Business management," said Joe. "I'm going for my bachelor's."

Margaret tapped her cigarette into an ashtray. "He's very bright." She winked at the sergeant. "I'm thinking of having him reconcile *my* books."

Footsteps could be heard descending the staircase and Sullivan turned. "Anything?" he asked the detectives appearing in the doorway, but their apathetic posture answered the question. "All right then." He offered a partial bow to the group. "Thank you for your time. If you hear anything, give me a call." Sullivan risked a tiny smile at Margaret while tossing his card on the table.

Joe saw them out the door, and the rest of the gang flooded in from above.

"That was close," Johnny said to Margaret. "You know him, huh?"

"Jason?" She grinned. "It's been a while, but I've known him many times."

"We gathered," said Clyde. "It sure was an interesting turn of events."

Margaret stubbed out her butt. "I'd love to hear him explain that to his colleagues."

"You know a lot of powerful people," said Rafael.

"When you're good at what you do, word gets around."

JJ fawned. "I'd love to find out."

"Start saving," said Jarrod.

Margaret stood. "This has been fun, boys, but I *am* on the clock." Johnny helped her into her coat and opened the door. As her high heels clicked toward the Cadillac, she turned. "It sure is exciting around here. I should swing by more often."

Johnny pressed his forehead against the closed door, his mind racing. Joe squeezed his shoulder. "Come on, brother. Let's figure this shit out."

In the apartment, crew members were milling around. Jarrod swigged from a bottle of Jack Daniels he had found.

"They didn't know shit," said Chico. "Not about our gang, nothing."

Others muttered in agreement, but Johnny shook his head. "We can't get cocky. That all could've been an act."

Chico sucked his teeth. "If they'd have known something, they'd have shown up with a SWAT team."

"Maybe the tipster didn't know this was a gang house," said Clyde.

"Possibly," said Johnny, pacing. "But those two Crosses obviously told someone they were coming here."

"But who?" said Joe.

"Not César." Jarrod took another sip and winced. "If his crew knew anything, they would've raided this place themselves."

"And they sure as shit wouldn't rat to no cops," said Chico.

Mario took the whiskey from Jarrod and raised it. "Here's to inviting law enforcement into a house with illegal guns, including two murder weapons, *and* one hundred motherfucking kilos of drugs." He took a gulp. "That's some ballsy shit right there."

Dog brothers hooted in agreement as the bottle got passed around, but Johnny stared at the floor. "I gotta get with César. Find out what the deal is."

Clyde cocked an ear over the din. "Say what?"

Johnny looked at him. "You heard right."

"Are you fucking crazy?"

Brothers hushed to hear the exchange.

Clyde exhaled. "Going to César would be a suicide mission."

"It's better to be shot in the head when I least expect it?" Johnny began to pace. "Doing nothing is a suicide mission. I need to know what the fuck is going on."

"You'd have to get him alone," said Jarrod.

Johnny nodded. "I wonder where he lives."

"Probably uptown or the Bronx," said Joe. "Since he brings his car to Tito's cousins."

"Tomorrow I can look in the records," said Tito.

"No." Johnny shook his head. "Jorge and Julio have always been good to us. I'm not putting them in the middle of our war."

"What's his last name?" Leon stood across the room, holding a phone book.

"Aguilar," said Johnny.

He squinted at the tiny print through his thick glasses. "Two in Brooklyn, one on a hundred forty-second." Leon looked up. "Where's Payson Avenue?"

"Up by Dyckman." Johnny smiled. "My old neighborhood."

Leon flicked the page. "There's a César Aguilar at fifty-five Payson."

"I should go see him in the morning."

"Who do you think he lives with?" asked Joe.

"I don't imagine it's a bunch of brothers. That neighborhood's all apartment buildings." Johnny relaxed. It felt good to have a plan. "A few of us can drive by, check it out. If it seems safe, I'll just knock on his door." He smirked. "I mean, who'd be stupid enough to shoot a rival on their own doorstep?"

CHAPTER TWENTY-EIGHT

When things came into focus, the view was upside down. Johnny tipped his head. The rope around his ankles was slung over an S-hook chained around a rafter. The hems of his pajama pants were bunched at the knees. Several streams of dried blood slalomed down his bare torso and chest. Orlando had apparently been playing with the box cutter again. Johnny's tethered hands folded into his chest to fend off the shivers. The cellar ceiling wasn't that high, but if the slipshod apparatus gave way, Johnny's neck could still break. If he was that lucky.

His brother crouched on the floor beside his bed. He was building an elaborate, multi-pronged structure with Legos. As he clicked the pieces together, he muttered to himself in mixed languages: always a good barometer of looniness. Way back, when things were still sort of normal, their mother, Aylin, used to teach them languages from foreign children's books she had amassed growing up in various countries. The lessons were fun and challenging. With a six-year age gap, it was one of few things Johnny and Orlando could bond over. They used different dialects when communicating. As they grew more fluent, they would blend them, which felt like their own secret code. Now the only time Orlando mixed languages was when he was deep in psychosis.

How long had Johnny been hanging? Hours, minutes? Used to be that his brain didn't shut down until the torture had commenced. Lately, the blackouts were starting upstairs, at the mere threat of getting tossed down here. A blessing, probably.

Johnny felt blood pooling in his head. His arms were numb.

"Orlando?"

Nothing.

"Can you let me down?"

He pushed more Lego pieces together.

"Please. My head hurts and I have to pee."

Orlando turned around, but his light brown eyes landed on everything except Johnny. "What's your problem?"

"How long have I been up here?"

"I don't know. A while."

"Can you at least let me down to pee?"

"Go fucking pee. Nobody's stopping you."

Johnny's bound hands scrubbed his mop of black curls. "C'mon, that's gross."

"Are you worried about soiling my palatial estate?" He stood to circle with outstretched arms. "Heaven forbid we make extra work for our devoted mother when she comes to clean. While our loving father protects her with a baseball bat?"

Johnny exhaled so deeply his feet slipped in the rope.

Orlando reached for a small plastic trash can under the workbench. He removed its half-full liner and slammed it on the floor under Johnny's head. "There." He put his face inches from Johnny's. "Now when you piss it won't mess up the floor."

Johnny tried to suppress tears. "What's wrong with you?"

"What's wrong with *me*?" Orlando punched Johnny in the stomach and he swung backward. "*You're* what's wrong with me."

The instinct to curl into the fetal position was thwarted by gravity and despair. Johnny let his arms dangle toward the floor and they lurched with each sob.

"Go ahead, cry." Orlando punched him again. "I'm the one locked down here, not you." He stuck out his tongue before returning to his Legos.

The gesture, coming from a seventeen-year-old, was so absurd. It made Johnny realize just how stunted Orlando was. And he'd only been

184

down here, what, a year or so? By comparison, maybe Johnny was the lucky one. But then again, he wasn't fucking insane. Unless you wanted to count the blackouts. But those would definitely stop if Johnny could just get away from this place.

Whichever body parts weren't numb throbbed. He felt faint and still had to pee. Johnny realized that his bladder was the one thing he could control. The only thing that would make hanging there a little more comfortable. He reached to hook thumbs in his elastic waistband and pushed them over his groin, then tried to relax. When warm urine raced down his torso, he turned his head to the side, but some was collected in his hair.

When Orlando heard the hollow splashing in the plastic pail, he jumped up. "HA! You really did it. I didn't think you would."

As Johnny shook pee droplets from his head, Orlando laughed, then grabbed a towel from the bathroom and pushed it into his brother's chest. "How humiliating is that?"

Johnny wiped what he could. The relief was so overwhelming it was easier to ignore whatever Orlando's intentions were, but he was surprised when his brother stretched up to unhook his feet. Was that all he had been waiting for?

Orlando set Johnny on the floor and gestured for him to hold out his hands. Johnny searched his brother's face as he untied the rope. "They don't like me, either, you know."

Orlando shot him a scowl, then started on his feet.

"Dad won't even look at me. He even makes Mom put me down here so he won't have to touch me." Johnny rubbed the abrasions around his wrists. "And she's not like she used to be. Remember how we'd read those books all the time? That never happens anymore."

Orlando's lips tightened, as if it was some small consolation. He got up and tossed the rope on the workbench, then flopped on his bed to read a book.

Johnny struggled to stand up as blood resumed circulation in his lower limbs. He tipped an ear toward the door at the top of the stairs. It was quiet. No creaking floorboards, no TV or radio. No voices, but his parents rarely spoke to each other. He remembered it was just after dinner when he got thrown down here. Aylin usually released him after Miguel fell asleep. Johnny glimpsed at the clock by the bed. Only ten after nine. It would be a while longer.

Johnny caught a whiff of urine and winced. "You care if I take a bath?"

No reply. Not that he expected one. He shut the bathroom door, undressed, and sat in the tub. As he waited for the hot water to fill, the cold porcelain made him shiver. Or was it shock? Either way, he hugged his knees, rocking back and forth to combat the chill.

◇◇◇

"And when I pulled out, there was fucking blood everywhere." Jarrod wrinkled his face from where he sat on the bathroom counter.

"She never warned you about her period?" Clyde was sitting on the toilet lid. They were both smoking. "So, what'd you do?"

"I did what any gentleman would do, I wiped my dick off with her T-shirt and I left."

"You did not."

Jarrod laughed. "I didn't really. But I thought about it."

"Did you see her again?"

"Hell no, period or no period, that girl was a skank." Jarrod took a final drag of his cigarette before extinguishing it with water from the sink. He jutted his chin toward the bathtub. "Look, I think he's coming out of it."

Clyde dropped his butt in the bowl and moved to the tub's rim. "Are you all right now?"

Johnny hugged his knees tighter, pressing his face into folded arms.

Clyde turned to Jarrod. "Get him something to drink."

Jarrod hopped off the counter and returned with a glass of orange juice. Johnny reached for it with a shaky hand and drained half of it. "How'd I get in here?" His voice was weak and raspy. He wore only pajama pants.

"Something woke me around two o'clock," said Clyde. "When I went to look, you were pacing in our living room, muttering shit in different languages."

"He got me up and we tried to snap you out of it," said Jarrod.

"But we didn't dare touch you." Clyde wagged his hands. "Never a good idea when you're in that state. We just walked beside you, trying to say that everything was okay."

"Then, like a half an hour ago, you climbed into the tub and sat down." Jarrod shrugged. "And who the fuck were we to argue?"

Johnny offered a tepid smile.

Clyde picked some crust from his eye. "Did you bring anything back from the other side this time?"

Johnny looked up at him. "The what?"

"You know, like, memories from where you go when you flip out."

Johnny pushed himself up, but felt wobbly. He sat on the edge of the tub and drained the juice. Then gestured for Jarrod to pass him the Marlboros on the counter. The first drag made him lightheaded so he rested elbows on his knees. "Yeah. I remembered something, but it's too sickening to talk about."

"You're supposed to confront this shit," said Clyde. "It'll stop the episodes."

"You don't know that." Johnny took another drag and choked on it. Didn't Lucinda tell him the same thing?

"This is better?" Clyde turned up his palms. "What have you got to lose?"

Johnny pushed out a breath, then recounted as much as he could stand.

"Damn," said Jarrod. "That's some grim shit."

"It is," said Clyde. "But I'm glad you told us. It helps to understand where you go when you..." he searched for the right word, "disappear?"

Jarrod nodded. "And if you don't want to go to César's this morning, we can always do it another time."

"No." Johnny stood and flicked his butt into the toilet. "I want to go. I just need to crash a few hours. You guys should do the same." He forced a smile. "Now get out because I gotta piss."

Alone in the bathroom, the feelings of shame and helplessness resurfaced as he urinated. Johnny tried to shove them aside. Instead, he focused on what he could control. He flushed the toilet and opened the medicine cabinet. His head was pounding so he popped two aspirins, which he washed down with cold water from his cupped hands. He also splashed some on his face.

When Johnny straightened, he caught his reflection in the mirror. He usually only glanced out of necessity, but now, the image caught his attention. He was nothing like that child from the cellar. In fact, at sixteen, there was nothing boyish about him. His dark eyes looked hard and mature beyond their years. Wispy hair budded above his top lip and jaw line. His arms were chiseled, and his once concave chest was contoured by muscles. This was no boy looking back at him, and certainly no victim.

When Johnny stepped out of the bathroom, Clyde and Jarrod had retreated to their beds. Instead of going to his own apartment, he flopped on a couch and fell asleep. A few hours later, when the house began to wake up, the sounds were comforting. Growing up, making noise was a punishable offense, so Johnny preferred the commotion. It was easier to sleep through than silence. He drifted off again.

CHAPTER TWENTY-NINE

Johnny felt a hand on his shoulder. Jarrod stood over him. "Hey, if you still want to go, we ought to get ready. Otherwise, César might go out, start his gangstering duties for the day."

Johnny swung his feet to the floor. "What time is it?"

"Eight-thirty."

"Yeah. Let's do this."

After a quick shower and a bite, Johnny strapped a .38 to his ankle: not too threatening, but would save his ass in a pinch. He chose Clyde, Jarrod, Tito, Chico and Mario to come with him. They would take the van. Now painted white, it looked like a million others. Except the windows were tinted. But who's noticing? They packed some guns under the seats just in case.

Driving uptown, Johnny was sullen. The memories of that Miami house were always difficult to deal with. The inability to predict, control, or better yet stop the blackouts made him rageful and reckless.

They circled the neighborhood. Payson Avenue was sloped, with Inwood Hill Park on one side, rows of matching five-story brick buildings on the other. Each bisected by a courtyard. It was Sunday morning, cold and blustery, so hardly anyone was out. Tito pulled into a space near the supposed address. Clyde and Chico went to poke around. They checked the park and between buildings. A few minutes later they returned.

"Aguilar is on the buzzers at fifty-five," said Chico. "3B."

"No sign of any Crosses either," said Clyde.

Jarrod turned to Johnny. "Are you ready?"

He nodded.

"If anything looks shady out here, we'll honk."

"And if you hear any shots go off, you better come with guns blazing."

"You know it, bro." Jarrod held out his hand to give Johnny the gang shake. The others did the same.

Johnny pulled up his hood and slid out of the van. He climbed the front steps to the glass-paned double doors and peeked inside. The lobby's tiled floors were scuffed and chipped. Its walls, with Romanesque crown molding, had faded to a dull grey. He was about to press the buzzer when an old couple appeared. They were heading out, bundled in coats and scarves. The man dragged a shopping cart behind them. They opened the door and Johnny rushed to hold it, offering a friendly, "Good morning." They thanked him and shuffled out as he slipped inside.

Johnny bypassed the elevator and sprinted up the stairs. In the third-floor hallway, he caught a whiff of burned toast from one apartment. Jazz was playing in another. He stopped at 3B and put an ear to the door. The goofy voices and exaggerated sound effects of cartoons competed with a crying baby. A crash made him pull away from the door. Now there were two kids crying, the yapping of dogs and a woman yelling in Spanish. Surely not the right Aguilar, but Johnny waited for things to calm down and rang the bell anyway.

The cacophony crescendoed anew, but now with feet stomping across the floor. Three locks clicked and the door opened partway. A weary-looking Latina with a wailing infant on her hip peeked through the opening while kicking away two barking dust mops. She wore sweatpants and a T-shirt. Her long dark hair was pulled into a sloppy ponytail. Still, with a nap and some eye shadow, Johnny thought she would be quite sexy. "*Buenos días, Señora. ¿César está aquí?*"

Her eyes narrowed as she looked him up and down.

He folded his hands in front of him and offered a cordial smile.

She opened the door wider, giving a side nod.

Johnny entered with his senses heightened. A male voice was negotiating with a child. Close match to César's, but were any gangmates with him? He mentally rehearsed the movements necessary to draw the gun at his ankle.

By the door was an overflowing coat closet, its top shelf stacked with diapers, formula and dog food. Below, dozens of shoes. *Could be an arsenal hidden behind all that crap.* Further cluttering the corridor was a pair of strollers and a tricycle, all of which could present a trip hazard for a hasty departure.

Two puffy cream-colored Pomeranians circled Johnny's feet, their direction being the only indicator which end was which. He stepped over them to get to the living room and halted. The décor took him aback. It was orange, gold and burgundy, and everything matched. The drapes matched the carpets matched the upholstery, down to the lace doilies on the end tables. Completely unlike the oddball, found-on-the-street stuff he lived with. Were it not for the inevitable stains and scattered toys, it looked like the tackiest furniture showroom ever.

On the paisley sofa, in gym shorts and a tank top, unshaven with tousled hair, sat César Aguilar, feared leader of the notorious street gang, Dos Cruces. He was trying to put a Band-Aid on the bloody finger of a crying toddler. A little girl was cross-legged on the floor, fixated by the TV inside a large wooden console. All three children could not have been much more than a year apart.

The woman brushed past Johnny to thrust the wailing infant into César's arms. "*Mira, tienes compañia.*" She ducked into the kitchen.

As humorless as Johnny had been feeling, it was hard not to muster some mirth. He thought of all the scenarios his brothers were imagining down in that van, worrying about the peril Johnny must be facing in the lair of an infamous gang president. Meanwhile, his greatest concern was probably hearing loss.

César repositioned the baby to look at the dogs still yipping at Johnny's feet. "*¡Cállate!*" He pointed toward the bedrooms. "Go lay down." Both fur balls slinked away, but his yelling made the baby cry louder. He stood up, patting the infant's back. Once the clamor was at a reasonable level, he could address Johnny. "What the fuck are you doing here?"

Johnny twitched a shoulder. "Did I come at a bad time?"

César jutted his chin at the toddler on the couch. "He broke a glass. We have to clean it up before someone else gets hurt."

"You need help?"

"If you could get a Band-Aid on him, I'll grab a bottle for this one."

"Can I use force?"

César stifled a grin and carried the baby to the kitchen.

Johnny looked at the little boy, whose sobs were only sporadic now. When was the last time he was around children? Probably not since he was a child. The thought caused a rush of feelings too toxic to identify. Especially after last night. He shook them off, then moved a picture book and toy train to sit on the couch. When he did, the toddler hid his face behind a cushion. Johnny did the same and the boy giggled. They played peek-a-boo until the kid cheered up enough to hold out his hand. Johnny picked the Band-Aid off the table. As he strapped it on, he wondered if being raised by gangsters instead of sociopaths would make one less mired.

"Pretty impressive." César was standing in the doorway. The baby was cradled in an arm, sucking on a bottle. "So, how'd you find me?"

"You're in the phonebook."

He rolled his eyes. "I better get unlisted." He helped the toddler off the couch to watch TV with his sister, then sat beside Johnny, his fatherly demeanor evaporating. "Why are you here, *muchacho*? You ready to come over to my side?"

At least he was consistent. "I came to check on the status of your word."

"What word?"

"Your word that your crew is supposed to lay off us."

César's brows furrowed. "That word stands, little brother. Hands off the Dogs, or face consequences."

"What kind of consequences?"

"I don't know." He twitched enough to jostle the baby. "It would depend."

Johnny locked eyes with César. "On what?"

"Jesus. What the fuck are you getting at?"

"No disrespect, but it sounds pretty vague." He raked fingers through his hair. "Like there's not much incentive for honoring the order."

"My men know what I'm capable of." It was hard for him to sound convincing, wiping a baby's cheek with a yellow duckling burp cloth.

Johnny bit his lip. "Suppose some of your men disobeyed you and found out what *I* was capable of?" He leaned forward to touch the gun beneath his pant leg while waiting for the comment to sink in.

César peered into the kitchen. His wife, or girlfriend, or whatever she was besides a baby dispensary, had the broken glass picked up, and was working on a sink full of dishes. He lowered his voice. "You better explain what the fuck you're talking about."

Johnny exhaled. "The first time was about six months ago. The big bald guy with the chains saw me in the street. He chased me down in his car. Two others got out and grabbed me. One was the guy with the, you know." He tapped above his lip and César understood. "The only way to get free was to knife one of them."

"Wait." César put up a hand. "That was *you?*"

Johnny nodded.

César's mouth hardened. "That's not the story I heard."

"How'd you hear it?"

"Burt said some random punk threw a bottle at his car. They got into it, and that's how his brother-in-law got stabbed."

"I didn't throw any fucking bottle. I was just crossing the street." Johnny straightened the book on the coffee table. "That was his brother-in-law?"

César nodded. "Burt was so angry about it he went on a big bender. Wound up in a bar fight, cops were called, but he had a warrant, so he's been locked up. Until last month."

Johnny rubbed the tension in the nape of his neck. That explained the lapse between run-ins, but not how he knew where to find Johnny. "Is he okay, the brother-in-law?"

César frowned. "He didn't make it."

"Shit. I didn't know."

"Burt had been asking me to recruit the guy." He flicked a wrist. "But I never liked him."

At least that one wasn't a Cross.

César tapped his chin. "You said the first time. There were others?"

"Two weeks ago. Burt and the guy with the mole came after me again." Johnny locked onto César's eyes. "They were gonna shoot me down in the street, but my boys were faster."

"You killed *my* men?"

Johnny watched the older gang leader's jaw tighten. "I would never start shit with your crew, but they gave me no choice." He waited for some fallout. Was the baby saving his life right now, or was it rationale? "We have an alliance."

"That explains why they've been MIA." He studied the floor, absorbing the information, then cocked his head at Johnny. "Any other shit you feel like confessing this morning?"

"That's everything."

"Is that why the cops are poking around?"

"Probably."

"What'd you do with them?"

"It's better you don't know."

César took a long, exhausted breath. "Look, *muchacho*, you know I like you. You're always straight up with me, respectful. And coming here like this? My own crew don't have the balls to say shit to my face."

Johnny's eyes swept the child-filled room. "Well, you're a little busy."

César's woman emerged from the kitchen. She took the baby from his arms and walked into a bedroom. "You wanna hear a secret?" he said to Johnny after she was gone. "We just found out she's pregnant again."

Johnny's jaw dropped. "Damn, man, you gotta slow the fuck down."

He hissed. "I can't help it."

The two gang leaders sat shaking their heads until César looked at the scars around Johnny's wrists. "When I was a boy, my father used to beat the shit out of me. A few times, bad enough to land in the emergency room." He scanned the ceiling. "I hated that fucking prick. By fourteen,

194

I started fighting back, so he turned on my baby brother instead. That's when I shot him."

"Did he die?"

César nodded. "My mother covered for me. Said the gun just went off."

"I shoulda shot my father." Johnny picked at the zipper of his jacket. "Instead, I left."

"You remind me of my little brother. He turned out to be very strong-willed, principled." César scratched his unshaven whiskers. "Never wanted anything to do with my crew either. He resisted me many times."

"What's he doing now?"

César's face pinched. "He got stabbed on the subway two years ago. For a lousy twenty-nine dollars. Bled out before the ambulance came. He was nineteen."

"I'm sorry." Johnny looked at him. "About all of it."

"I know." He brushed the fabric of a sofa cushion. "Listen, the way I see it, Burt and Abel disobeyed me and they paid the price." He raised an eyebrow. "But nobody has to know the details, do they?"

Johnny barked a laugh. "I ain't saying shit about shit."

"And if my guys mess with you again? I wanna know about it." He wagged a finger. "You're getting a big motherfucking pass, boy."

Johnny nodded. "I hear you."

César offered his hand and they shook.

At the van, Clyde slid over to let Johnny in. A barrage of questions started before Tito could drive away, but Johnny was too stunned to speak. He leaned against the backrest to collect his thoughts. "We're good," was all he could manage.

"We're good?" Jarrod mimicked. "What the fuck does that mean?"

Tito remained fixated on the road. "We're good because Johnny puts people at ease. He's confident without being arrogant. Humble without appearing weak." He shrugged. "It's an effective technique, especially in difficult situations."

"You hearing this shit?" said Mario. "We just got schooled by the great philosopher, Socra-Tito."

Chico swatted Mario. "No wonder Tito hardly ever speaks."

Jarrod leaned forward toward Johnny. "So, what? You just walked in there and said, 'Hey César, we slaughtered two of your guys, but we're still pals, right?' and he said, 'Totally. I hated those assholes anyway. Have a nice day,' and then you left."

"Yup." Johnny smiled. "Pretty much."

CHAPTER THIRTY

After the meeting with César, the gang felt they could relax. There was still some concern that cops might return with new evidence, but Joe insisted everything had been wiped clean. For the most part, the benefit of youth, and the gang's solidarity, enabled the boys to circumvent the gravity of their actions.

Johnny lifted the guest ban. He told Jessica that his parents were back to not giving a shit, so he had returned to the loft. The couple spent every day after school, and much of the weekends, rolling around in his bed until Jessica had to go home.

"So, what are your long-term goals?" She asked while draped over Johnny's chest, their legs entwined.

He laughed. "I thought those were luxury items for the well-to-do."

"I'm not well-to-do, but I still have visions for my future."

He tipped his head to look at her. "You want to be the next Picasso?"

She rested her chin on the back of her hands. "Making a living as an artist is hard. Especially for women. But I could still work in the art world, like as a curator, and do my own stuff on the side."

"Hmm."

"But I'd need college, art history and stuff. Maybe even a masters." She rubbed his foot with her foot. "Don't you see yourself doing something with music? Your band is good."

"We should rehearse more often, but we've been busy with other shit." Johnny fiddled with a lock of her hair. "Teddy likes being Temper's

197

manager. He's been trying to book us some better clubs. But do I see us playing Madison Square Garden one day?"

"You never know." Jessica smiled. "Your lyrics are intense. They obviously come from a deep place." She kissed him. "It's worth pursuing. You just have to make it happen."

"More rehearsing means less time for this." He pressed his groin firmly into her. She giggled and pushed up to straddle him, but Johnny thought he heard someone blow a warning whistle. He sat up and cocked an ear.

"Johnny!" Tito could be heard hollering. *"¡Marco está aquí!"*

"Shit." Johnny slid out from under Jessica. "Baby, I'm so sorry. I forgot I was supposed to meet someone." He threw on a pair of sweatpants. "Stay here, I'll be right back."

"How long are—"

"I don't know, but just wait *here*, okay?" He shut the door behind him.

Johnny started to rush downstairs, but Rafael and Tito were already escorting the drug lord up. Marco, despite his pale, pitted complexion, looked especially sharp. He wore a black suit with white shirt, unbuttoned to expose the top of his chest. His charcoal full-length coat matched a felt Fedora and some two-toned loafers.

Johnny saw a few brothers peeking out of the ground floor apartments. He gestured that it was all right.

"I told him you were busy," Rafael said as they approached.

"He always has time for me." Marco pressed his hat into Johnny's hands before taking a lap around the living room. "Wow. I'm impressed."

At least Marco was speaking Spanish, just in case Jessica could overhear them. Johnny did the same. "Thanks."

"Who lives in this building?"

"Just us."

"Who is *us*?" He pointed to Tito. "This one I recognize, but it's a big place. Is it safe?"

"You don't have to worry," said Johnny. "Everyone in this building is a brother."

"Right." Marco elongated the vowel. "Your *gang*." He eyed the tattoo on Johnny's shirtless arm. "Dogs of War. Interesting." He looked at Tito and Rafael. "You have that also?"

They pulled up their sleeves.

"How many are you?"

"Twenty-three, so far."

"Twenty-three?" Marco snorted. "There's more people on shift at Katz's Deli."

Had he just come here to interrupt Johnny's nooner and insult his gang?

"And why is your tattoo the same as theirs?" Marco frowned. "I'm no gangster, but shouldn't the leader have something indicating they're in charge?"

The comment was nettling. Probably because he was right. "At first, I didn't want the attention. I liked to be in the shadows, keep people guessing. But I'm getting ready to change that."

"I understand." Marco rubbed a knuckle under his chin. "It's smart, actually, because the duck with the brightest feathers gets shot first. I bet you're a good leader." He put hands on his hips. "But so far, you're a terrible host. What does a person have to do to get a drink around here?"

"Sorry. I wasn't expecting you." Johnny stole a glimpse at his bedroom door before hanging the hat from a nail in the wall. "Rafi, grab one of those cases that Margaret brought."

He nodded and sprinted downstairs.

Marco gave Tito the once-over. "What's your name?"

"Tito."

"From where?"

"El Salvador."

He turned to Johnny. "Anyone ever tell him he's got the unblinking gaze of a serial killer?"

"Everyone. All the time."

Rafael set the box of assorted wines on a folding table. Marco pulled out a few bottles to check the labels. "Where'd you get these?"

"A friend," said Johnny.

"A friend with very good taste." He thrust a cabernet at Rafael. "Open this one. You'll join me, won't you?" Marco shed his coat and draped it over a chair.

Johnny rubbed his temples. There had to be a way to move this little shindig to a different apartment, but Rafael had already uncorked the bottle and was bringing over four mismatched glasses. Marco was about to say something when he became mesmerized by a vision. Johnny looked behind him to see that Jessica had emerged from the bedroom. She was in her jeans and one of Johnny's button-down flannel shirts.

"My goodness." Marco clutched his heart and switched to English. "What do we have here?"

Jessica toggled between him and Johnny. "Um, I was just curious what was going on."

"And who might you be?"

"Jessica."

"Jessica," Marco repeated, savoring each syllable as if it were cleansing his palate. He glided across the floor to take her hand. "It is *very* nice to meet you." He kissed it. "Is that young man your boyfriend?"

She snickered. "Yes."

He nodded at Johnny. "How lucky are you to get a beauty like this?"

Johnny grunted.

"Wait. I interrupted a romantic moment, didn't I?" Marco covered his mouth. "I'm *so* sorry. I should've called first."

"Are you Johnny's Uncle Casper?" asked Jessica.

"Hmm, Uncle Casper..." Marco's eyes swept over Johnny, who twitched a shoulder.

"Yeah," she continued. "Casper Amistoso, with the moving company. Johnny's always talking about you."

Marco got the comic book reference and snorted a laugh. "Yes, my sweet, I'm Johnny's uncle Casper." He reeled her in for a hug. "You're both beautiful and perceptive." He kept an arm around her shoulder to peek down the front of her shirt.

Johnny took a protective step forward, but Marco shot him a biting look. A reminder that as charming as he was being, there was still a coked-out, gun-wielding lunatic in there somewhere.

Marco's smile returned for Jessica. "I've known this kid a long time, seen him in some hairy situations. But I've never seen him so rattled." He finally released her. "Whatever you're doing in that bedroom must be turning his brain into mush."

Rafael interrupted. "Here's your drink, *Casper*." It was a small brown water glass stolen from a diner.

Marco examined it. "I see you brought out the good crystal." He swirled the tumbler before taking a sip, then pinched one of Rafael's bulging biceps. "You like the weights, huh?"

"Mm-hmm."

"All of that lifting, up, down, over and over," he rolled his eyes. "I'd rather shoot myself in the head."

Johnny sidled up to Jessica. "Baby, I'm really sorry but I forgot we had to work today. I'll get one of the guys to hail you a cab."

"So soon?" Marco flopped onto the black leather sofa. "The party's just getting started." Rafael and Tito took the couch opposite him. The wine and glasses were set on the coffee table between them.

Jessica pouted, like she wanted to hang out, but Johnny steered her toward the bedroom. "I'll be right back."

"What's wrong with you?" she said, once the door closed.

"Nothing. I just..." he yanked on a shirt. "It's embarrassing being caught in bed."

"Your uncle didn't care. He's so funny."

"Yeah, he's funny all right." Johnny grabbed socks from a drawer while Jessica changed into her own clothes.

"And so well-dressed for a guy running a moving company. Not what I would've expected."

"We do all the heavy lifting." Johnny fished in his pocket and handed her a twenty. "Take this for the taxi."

She put her hands up. "Wow. Dismissing me like a cheap whore."

Johnny's shoulders dropped. "Look, I know the guy. He's acting all charming in front of you, but as soon as we're alone, he's gonna give me shit because I wasn't ready." He raked through his messy hair. "There's a big job out on Long Island, and I forgot all about it."

"Kinda late in the afternoon to start moving furniture."

Johnny locked onto her eyes. "I'm not involved in how he negotiates accounts. I just do what I'm told." He forced a smile. "When I remember."

She took the bill and stuffed it in her pocket.

"I'm sorry, baby. Really." He kissed her. "And if you were a whore, you'd be *the* most expensive one." He winked and she laughed.

When Johnny and Jessica came back out, Marco stood to say goodbye and get one last grope before she was ushered downstairs.

Back in his apartment, Johnny sat next to Marco. Rafael filled the other glasses and handed them out. Johnny drained half of his wine in a few gulps. Marco was watching him, grinning with a smugness that made Johnny want to punch him in the face.

"You really got the life, don't you?" Marco slung an arm over the backrest. "I should be living as well."

"I'm sure you're doing all right," said Johnny.

"I don't get women like that, so young, sweet and innocent. Most that come my way are looking for something else." Marco clutched the crotch of his pants. "But I'll be thinking about her later."

Johnny gave him an angry look.

"Stop it." Marco released his cock to pull a pack of cigarillos from an inside pocket. "I'm not interested in your fucking little girlfriend and her stupid teenaged problems." He took a long drag and reclined. "I'm trying to demonstrate something." His face turned stony. "You're usually so cool and level-headed in critical situations. But there?" He pointed to the door. "With that girl? You showed me your weakness. That shit will get you killed in this line of work. Or her."

"I get it." Johnny forced a deep breath. "Are you here to collect the stuff?"

"Christ sakes, you're all business." Marco poured more wine into Johnny's glass. "You need to lighten the fuck up." He turned to Rafael. "What's your story, Muscles?"

"Huh?"

"Where are you from?"

"Dominican."

"Born there?"

"Yeah, but we moved here when I was young."

"You got any connections down there?"

Rafael remained stern. "All my connections are right here. In this house."

"Everyone's so fucking serious," Marco mumbled into his glass, then snapped his fingers. "I almost forgot. I brought gifts. They're downstairs on the landing. Is that your kitchen?"

"Yeah, but I never cook there," said Johnny. "A third-floor apartment has the best appliances."

"You'll be able to afford new ones soon." He drained his glass and stood. "You two, Jack LaLanne, Charles Manson, go get the bags. *El Presidente* will show me to the good kitchen."

Johnny led Marco upstairs. He gave him a quick tour of the Studio, introducing whichever brothers were hanging around. At the drum kit, Marco tapped on the high-hat while looking at guitars lined up on stands. "You play?" he asked Johnny.

"Yeah, me and a few of these guys got a band."

"What are you called?"

"Temper. We play around the city, wherever we can get gigs."

"Are you any good?"

Johnny shrugged.

"Temper, huh? I used to play drums when I was a kid." He raised an eyebrow. "You gonna let me sit in one day?"

Johnny smiled genuinely for the first time, enjoying the image of him wailing like Jarrod. "Whenever you want."

In the Mess Hall, other crew members got up to greet Marco, who remained uncharacteristically stable. Johnny wondered if he was cutting back on the drugs, or had they just caught the right wave of his schizophrenia.

When Tito and Rafael brought up two Macy's bags, he flagged them over. "Where are the beans I sent?"

Chico dragged the sack from a pantry floor, while Marco unpacked boxes of appliances and set them on the counter. One was a commercial-sized coffee grinder, the other, a forty-cup urn and filters. He demonstrated how to use the equipment by making a pot. While it brewed, he drank more wine, lecturing the boys about the history and complexity of the beans. When the coffee was done, they passed around samples, commenting on its texture and different flavor notes.

Marco caught Johnny's eye to indicate it was time to round up the drugs. He tapped a few brothers, and they went to retrieve the duffel bags hidden around the loft. All five were laid out on the dining table and Marco inspected them. "Looks good." He clapped his hands. "Who's gonna bring them to the car?"

Several brothers volunteered.

Marco stopped on the second floor with Johnny. He grabbed his hat and coat, but held back a moment. "You understand what I was doing earlier, right? I was trying to teach you that emotional attachments are dangerous in this business."

"No, I get it." Johnny looked at the floor. "But if you had called first—"

"But I didn't." He put on the Fedora. "There's another box in one of those shopping bags. I think you'll find it fair."

"Okay, thanks."

"And you better put me on the guest list for that band of yours."

Johnny laughed. "You got it."

"All right, then. Until next time."

Johnny expected a handshake, but Marco reached out to pet his head instead. It was awkward, but somehow paternal.

In the Mess Hall, Johnny saw some brothers huddled around the kitchen island. "What's going on?"

"You gotta see this shit," said Clyde.

"We found another box in those bags," said Mario.

Johnny walked over. "Marco said he left something."

JJ wagged his head. "You ain't gonna believe it."

Johnny's brothers parted to let him look inside. There were two small zipper bags, each with about a half pound of powder, white and tan. Below, ten stacks of hundreds. "Fuck me."

CHAPTER THIRTY-ONE

Over the winter, the gang could afford to make more improvements to the loft. Horatio was contacted to help them put up drywall to replace the clotheslined sheets. Floors were refinished and bathrooms upgraded. Between projects, he had the boys hone their combat skills by introducing new challenges.

Separate from the renovation costs, Johnny gave each of his brothers a thousand dollars to do with as they pleased. He figured it was close enough to Christmas, so why not? He also paid Joe's tuition, since his education was ultimately helping the gang.

Combing the Village Voice classifieds, Johnny spotted a used Baldwin piano on the Upper East Side for three hundred bucks. Using the van, and several muscly volunteers, they managed to collect it and wrestle it to the third-floor apartment with the other instruments. The band dedicated a lot more time to rehearsing new songs and started creating setlists for their gigs.

By spring, five new members were inducted into the Dogs of War, all of whom moved into the loft, putting their total at twenty-eight, now maybe rivaling the staff at Katz's. Jamal Tibbets and Benji Stevens were eleventh graders from Roosevelt. Francisco Rosario, Vinnie Giordano and Gus Varga were a few years older and knew the gang from the street scene. When they went to their regular tattoo artist to get inked, other members were inspired to have more work. Johnny designed an antique dagger with an old-style handle and decorative quillons. He put it inside his right forearm so it appeared to be poking into the scar around his wrist. Across the blade was the gang's credo: *Unity*Honor*Respect*Protect*. He also had *President* scripted under the existing tattoo on his left shoulder.

Six Dog brothers were set to graduate high school and were already planning their vocations. Rafael signed up for electricians' training, and Maurice wanted to learn tile and stonework. Teddy applied for an intern position with a sound engineer at a Midtown recording studio. Even though it didn't pay, he knew whatever he learned would be valuable to the band. Jeff would be working with Tito at his cousins' garage, and Patrick and Eric were dropping applications at various bars and restaurants.

One June weekend, gang members went to Central Park to play baseball. They usurped a field by staring down a group of younger kids. The game was ruthless and penalties were nonexistent. They taunted each other with raunchy insults, used antics to distract their opposition, and sometimes "accidentally" threw a ball at the runner instead of the baseman. When people stopped to watch, it only encouraged the shenanigans.

By the end, everyone was tired, sweaty and grass-stained, but Johnny and three Temper bandmates wanted to hit the music stores on Forty-Eighth Street. They split from the others to head toward the Sixth Avenue exit via winding foot paths. When they turned a corner near the base of a rocky knoll, they saw nine guys in the distance. Some wore Dos Cruces vests, others were sporting the gang's signature green, red, and white bandanas. In the middle of the pack was Hector Sarno, a pair of superimposed crosses inked on a forearm.

"It was him," Johnny muttered. "He's the motherfucker who told those two Crosses where to look for me."

Jarrod bounced a hand off his forehead. "Shoulda fucking guessed it."

"He probably snitched to the cops, too," said Patrick.

"Come to think of it," said Clyde, "I haven't seen him around school lately."

"Me neither," said Jarrod.

When the Crosses noticed the four teens, they fanned into an offensive position.

"That doesn't look like they're honoring no fucking alliance to me," said Jarrod.

Johnny sucked his teeth. "César's too busy changing diapers."

"And no doubt Hector's stirring up animosity," said Clyde.

"There's only nine," Patrick quipped. "I think we can take them."

"We'll find out if Horatio really knows his shit," said Jarrod. "Or we could bolt."

"I'm not running." Johnny assessed the group. It looked like mostly younger recruits with a few senior members. None appeared to be armed. He turned to his brothers. "We can at least hold our own, right?"

They nodded.

As the two gangs closed in on each other, Hector's face lit up, proud to flaunt his new affiliation. "Oh look, a pack of mangy Dogs?" He halted with the others. "These mutts shouldn't be loose in the park." A few Crosses chuckled.

"You sure got a big mouth with a fucking army behind you," said Johnny. "But after years of kissing my ass, it's nice that someone finally adopted you."

"And your two faces," Jarrod added.

Hector's mouth twisted as he searched for a comeback.

One of the older men stepped forward. He had dark hair and eyes, and a thick goatee. In addition to the gang logo on his bicep, there were two small crosses tattooed above his sternum. "César said, 'hands off *los Perros*. Don't go starting shit.'" He gave the Dog brothers the once-over. "But if they start shit with *us*? That's a different story."

A skinny blond with a slick Disco Danny haircut put an arm around Hector. The word FATE was inked across the fingers of his right hand. "This boy is with us now. You better watch how you talk to him."

The Goatee stepped up to Johnny. "Especially *you*, motherfucker." He poked him in the chest.

Johnny inhaled the fresh park air and smiled. He didn't mean to look smug, but he couldn't help it. The rage that festered inside him was pervasive and historic. Rarely were there opportune moments for its release.

The senior Cross rubbed his chin. "You're about to get your ass kicked. Why're you so cheerful?" His head tilted. "Are you *slow*?"

It was all Johnny needed. He struck a blow to the man's nose, hard enough to crack the nasal bones. Goatee's head tipped back as a spray of blood cascaded down his shirt. Before he could recover, Johnny kicked him in the ribs, then took him down with a palm strike to the ear. The moves' effectiveness surprised him.

The Crosses seemed baffled too. They lurched into action, swarming the Dogs in a chaotic attack. The four made a circle to protect their backs as Crosses threw reckless punches and kicks, often missing their targets. Johnny and his boys conserved their energy, waiting for the right moments to strike. When the larger crew tired, the Dogs paired up to take out two more opponents, making it six on four.

Patrick took on a chubby teen who kept butting him like a bull. Jarrod was holding his own against a bigger guy, while Clyde sparred with Disco Danny, who landed some direct hits to the face. Johnny was working to fend off two more.

Hector circled outside the melee. "Fuck the others! Just grab Johnny!"

The battling Crosses redirected. Dog brothers tried to hold them back, but they were also fatigued. As the six piled on, Johnny's defensive blows remained forceful enough to leave a victim reeling for a few seconds, but hands and feet were coming from every direction. He dodged a lot of sloppy punches, though getting hit was inevitable.

Amid the brawl, Johnny caught the flash of a blade. Hector had elbowed his way closer and was swinging wildly. He struck Johnny across his left forearm, springing a stream of blood that dripped down his hand. The Crosses backed away as Hector lunged with the knife. Johnny ducked and got sliced across his side. He felt cool air where his T-shirt hung open before the burst of pain. Then came the blood, seeping into the hip of his blue track pants. It broke his focus, and two rivals wrenched Johnny's arms behind his back.

Even though he hadn't joined in the fight, Hector was breathing hard, and damp with sweat. His wide eyes scanned for onlookers, but any savvy New Yorker would have changed course for a group half the size.

Hector's hand trembled as he pointed the knife at Johnny's stomach. He was the only Cross posing much of a threat. The others were doubled over in various states of injury. Clyde, Patrick and Jarrod also stood catching their breath. Neither dared to rush Hector.

Johnny struggled to get free. "You outnumber us, but you gotta cut me, too, you fucking coward?"

Hector straightened his spine, feigning defiance, despite his obvious discomfort in a position of power.

"That's why I never wanted you in my gang." Johnny winced at a flash of pain in his side. "You got no balls and no honor."

"Fuck you," Hector sputtered. "And fuck your honor crap. You don't know shit about me."

The pair holding Johnny tightened their grip, making his arm wound throb.

"Just because the Dogs of War are big shots at Roosevelt doesn't mean shit."

The inability to get free was too familiar. It was stirring up flashes of the cellar, and making Johnny's brain slip, like he might mentally decamp.

"You and your tiny-ass crew think you're so fucking cool..."

Johnny closed his eyes to shut out whatever stupid shit Hector was ranting about. He focused on breathing instead, slowing his heart rate. Willing himself to stay present. They trained for this. Horatio had set up a similar scenario. Johnny recognized his impulse to lean forward against the hold. But that was exactly what these two fuckers were anticipating. Opening his eyes, he pulled harder. His captors rocked their weight back. As they did, Johnny burst backward, knocking both Crosses off balance. He ducked, twisting his shoulders, and ripped from their grip. Johnny lurched at Hector, throwing a roundhouse kick that connected with his face. Hector was knocked sideways. The knife fell from his hand before he landed on one knee.

Johnny's brothers grabbed the two who had been holding him, but like the others, the break in momentum had sapped their energy.

As Hector stumbled to his feet, Johnny could have beaten the shit out of him, but he picked up the knife instead. It was a stiletto switchblade with a decorative ivory handle, engraved with Hector's initials. "Nice," Johnny said, turning it over in his hand. "This thing must mean a lot to you."

Hector shrugged like he didn't care, but his eyes said otherwise.

Johnny held it up. "Want it back?"

"I guess."

"I'd like to be nice and return it." Johnny picked his fingernails with the blade's tip, red with his own blood. "Except I know you're the little snitch who talked to the cops."

"That—that's bullshit." Hector wiped his mouth with the back of his hand. "I don't talk to no fucking cops."

"So, you never talk to your father? Who you *live with*."

Hector's brothers leaned in to hear better.

"What's gonna happen when he finds out you dropped out of school and joined a gang?"

Jarrod cringed. "Ooh, that won't be good."

"Imagine when he sees that tattoo," said Clyde.

"Shut up," Hector sputtered.

"Oh, snap." Johnny laughed. "You didn't tell these guys what dad does for a living?"

Hector whirled to look at the Crosses. "It's bullshit. He's lying."

"You know what?" Johnny held up a hand. "Because I'm so honorable, even though I know you hate that about me, I will shut up about it, and let *you* convince these guys you're not a snitch-ass son-of-a-pig."

The Crosses were starting to rally, but their expressions suggested it was no longer against the Dogs.

"In the meantime," Johnny continued, "I'll make you a deal." He tapped the knife's blade on the palm of his hand. "If you want this back, you can have it."

Hector looked hopeful for the first time.

"But because you think it's okay to fight people with their arms behind their backs, you have to take it without using your hands."

"Huh?" Hector cocked his head.

"Take it with your mouth, like a dog." He suspended the knife horizontally, the ends pressed delicately between thumb and forefinger. "When we leave you alone with your boys, who probably have a lot of questions, you might need it."

Hector's face twitched as he weighed his options. Keeping arms by his side, he craned his neck forward. His mouth contorted into a rictus as he took the blade between his teeth, biting down to keep it balanced.

Johnny released his hold and smiled. "There. Was that so hard?"

Hector could only grunt.

Johnny looked into his face, so pathetic, so weak. He should feel sorry for the kid. Whatever Hector brought on himself was worse than anything Johnny could do. Did that not deserve some mercy?

His inner rage thought otherwise. Johnny punched Hector in the mouth, propelling the blade into both cheeks. Hector jumped back, screaming. He dropped to his knees. The knife fell from his mouth, which he covered with his hands, but blood poured through his fingers. Two younger Crosses scrambled to assist him, one pressing his bandana on the wounds.

"You want this piece of shit in your gang?" Johnny stepped back. "Take him."

Sirens could be heard in the distance and Johnny nodded to his brothers. They sprinted toward the rocks. When Johnny looked over his shoulder, he saw Dos Cruces also scattering, leaving Hector where he knelt.

CHAPTER THIRTY-TWO

"What idiot engraves a knife?" said Jarrod. "And then commits a crime with it."

The four ducked behind a tree near Columbus Circle. They were each a mess, bloodied and blotchy, with facial cuts and tattered knuckles.

"He never was the brightest kid," said Patrick, keeping an eye out for cops while the others assessed Johnny's lacerations.

"No," said Clyde, "but he will be the happiest, with that big ass smile you just gave him."

Johnny's arm was already clotting, but the slice on his back was five inches long and needed stitches. The blood stains were blending with his dark clothes, but the cut fabric exposed the gash, so he switched T-shirts with Jarrod. Clyde grabbed napkins from a hotdog vendor to slow the bleeding until they could get home. The first few taxis refused to stop, but eventually they got one.

At the loft, they trudged straight up to the Mess Hall. Mario was at the table, and lowered a magazine he had been reading. "What the fuck happened to you lot?"

"We got in a little fight," said Clyde.

"With who?" asked Ramón, coming from the living room with Chico.

"Dos Cruces," Patrick said, "fucking nine of them."

Jarrod tapped Chico. "You need to get your witchdoctor mother over here, quick."

"For that?" Chico looked at their faces. "Ice and some hydrogen peroxide will take care of it."

"No." He pulled up Johnny's shirt. "For this."

"Damn." Chico's eyes widened. "I'm calling right now."

The injured brothers were ushered to the couches. They were given cold cloths, ice packs and beer, while others rushed in to hear the story. Thirty minutes later, Luis and Lucinda appeared with two grocery bags. Lucinda took over, barking orders in Spanish and shooing away uninjured housemates. She told Luis to start boiling water, and had Chico sort the medical supplies on the coffee table. Patrick, Clyde and Jarrod were sent to wash up before being treated.

She pouted at Johnny's arm. "That's the one?"

He lifted his shirt. "This is worse."

She waved a hand. "Take it off. Lie down."

Johnny obeyed.

From a generic glass jar, she poured a brownish solution onto a stack of gauze pads. It smelled like alcohol, vanilla and espresso. She wiped around the incision, unfazed when Johnny winced. Once the area was clean, Lucinda could examine the wound more closely. "It's straight, but deep. The knife was sharp." She looked at him. "Stitches and a penicillin shot are not an option?"

"They'll ask too many questions."

"I'll do what I can, but I'll have to come every day to change the dressing."

Johnny smiled. "I believe in you."

Lucinda sucked her cheek, then smeared a thick substance on a sterile cloth with a tongue depressor. It was sweet and earthy smelling, with hints of curry. She draped it over the wound to disinfect. It stung even more than the wipe, and Johnny bit a knuckle.

"What trouble are you into?"

"We're not into anything. We just ran into some punks."

She began doctoring his forearm. "And how bad do *they* look?"

"A lot worse, believe me."

A wrinkle appeared beside her mouth. She got up to add herbs and oils to the boiling pots of water. As she set them to simmer, the other three returned. They were clean in fresh clothes. After everyone's facial wounds had been treated, Lucinda removed the cloth from Johnny's back, dried the area and applied butterfly stitches. Both lacerations were layered with pungent dried leaves before being bandaged. Lastly, she made the boys drink a mugful of warm, terrible-tasting tea before sending them to rest.

"Not you," she said to Johnny when he tried to get up. "You will stay on this couch until tomorrow morning, when I can check you again." He rolled gingerly onto his back and she passed a cushion for his head. "Then, bed rest for a few days, and no big movements for another week after that." She folded her arms. "And that means no girlfriends."

"What if I make *them* do all the work?"

Lucinda expelled an audible sigh and sat by his feet. She gave him that discerning look he both dreaded and respected. "I'm not naive, you know. Nobody has a building and supports dozens of young men by washing dishes." She handed him the mug to finish. "Whatever you're into, I don't need to know. Luis and I will be on your side." She wagged a finger. "But don't take stupid risks."

"I don't. *We* don't. Really." Johnny forced down another gulp. As putrid as it was, he could already feel the tea relaxing him. "The big stuff runs smooth. It's the little shit that bites us in the ass. Getting tripped up by people we don't even care about."

"Then walk away from them. Don't waste your time."

"It's not that easy."

"This is easier?" She waved a hand over him, then leaned closer. "It is your ego that has a hard time ignoring them, but you should listen to your instincts, your psyche."

Johnny surveyed the ceiling, as if it might make her spiritual sermon more digestible.

"You don't like to hear it, but there is something special in you. A light. Intelligent people are drawn to it, inspired by it. Ignorant people are threatened by it and want to destroy it. You can use this as a barometer to choose your path more wisely."

Johnny rocked his head.

"I know you don't see it." Lucinda's hands folded in her lap. "It's what makes your gift more alluring. One day you will understand its value."

Foggy from pain, exertion and whatever homeopathic mickey she had slipped him, Johnny wasn't about to argue. Maybe she was tapped into other dimensions.

"Don't let worthless people distract you from your goals." Her eyes narrowed. "Including those you left. The ghosts who haunt you."

Was everything tied to his shitty fucking childhood? "I'll try."

She stood and kissed his forehead. "Rest. I'll be back in the morning."

◇◇◇

Three days of convalescing was all Johnny could stand. By mid-week, against Lucinda's advice, he wrapped elastic bandages around her dressing and returned to school. When he explained his absence to Jessica, he didn't entirely lie. He told her they had been jumped, but left out that it was Dos Cruces, and Hector in particular.

Despite Johnny's resistance, Jessica insisted on pampering him after school. They would hang out in the Studio, protected from the risk of intimacy by Clyde, Jarrod and umpteen other brothers who preferred hanging out in that apartment. With Johnny reclined on the couch, she would fix them snacks and a drink before they tackled homework assignments. If he dozed off, she would pull out her sketchpad, occasionally using him or his gangmates as her subjects.

By summer break, Johnny was better, and Jessica was spending nights at the loft again. At first, she dusted off the old story about sleeping at friends' houses. But the charade grew tiresome, so she told her parents that Johnny had found a cheap rental downtown, which he paid for working with his uncle. When she said she would be spending some nights there, it caused a huge row with Walter. Jessica argued that she was seventeen and in love, and he should accept that she was sexually active.

Temper continued to rehearse and write new songs. Soon they had enough original material to fill a set, which they began to showcase in clubs. The feedback was promising, but it was undeniable that Jarrod had the most talent. His drumming was bold and creative, and always drew compliments from the more seasoned professionals.

Just as Mario had come up with the logo for the Dogs of War, he created one for Temper. It was a crazed stick figure in various rage-filled poses: pulling out his hair, jumping up and down or slamming a guitar on the ground. Mario designed posters using the character, listing upcoming club dates, which the crew would paste all over the city's lampposts and billboards. They also made Temper bumper stickers, which they handed out at clubs and affixed to street signs and subway cars. As a result of the band's growing popularity, Teddy was booking them more gigs, some into Westchester County and New Jersey.

On July twenty-fifth, Johnny woke to a thin strip of light streaming through the window. Jessica was in his arms. He pulled her closer and she stirred a moment before drifting back to sleep. As he inhaled her sweet scent, he realized it was his seventeenth birthday.

It had been five years since he left Miami. He'd been gone almost half as long as he'd lived there. In *that* house, with *those* people. Who were they again? He almost never thought of them unless the memories were foisted upon him against his will.

Johnny released Jessica's warm, naked body and got up to pee. After brushing his teeth, he caught himself in the mirror and remembered what Lucinda had said. Where the hell was this light she was talking about? Inner light was supposed to be about goodness, purity, grace. He was none of those things, and there was nothing innocent about him. Not anymore. It was obvious he had traded fear for grit long ago. He was scarred, afflicted, and haunted by abuse, but somewhere, behind all of that, there was supposed to be a light.

Johnny cracked the door and looked at Jessica. Her long auburn curls fell over the white pillow. The silky skin of her back and buttocks peeking out from the blankets. That's where the light is, he thought. Right there. He went to the bed and slid under the covers. She arched into his touch as he kissed from her lower back to her neck. She moaned and rolled onto her side to seek his lips.

"Good morning." She slithered away. "I've got to pee."

Johnny squeezed her, refusing to let go. "No."

She giggled, shoving him away. A few minutes later, she slid back under the covers, fresh-faced and minty, and they made love.

"How do you do it?" Johnny asked, as they lay entwined, catching their breath.

"Do what?"

"How are you so kind all the time?"

She propped her chin on his chest. "What do you mean?"

"You know, like, open and accepting of everyone."

"Should I think everybody's out to get me?"

"No." Johnny stroked her hair. "But do you believe all people are basically good?"

"I guess." Her fingers drew circles on his chest. "I mean, sometimes people do bad things, but that's not because they *are* bad. Maybe it's all they've been taught. Or circumstances gave them no choice. I do believe that if people are given the right opportunities, they will usually choose to do the right things. Because goodness is inherent. Evil is learned."

"Wow. That's deep." Johnny smiled. "You didn't get that philosophy from your father."

Jessica shrugged. "He does tend to be suspicious of everyone. I never understood where it came from. Maybe that's why I try to do the opposite?"

"Never judging, always trusting and forgiving. It must free up your mind."

She scrunched her face. "Are you calling me empty-headed?"

They both laughed and lay back. Johnny felt Jessica's fingers linger over the raised scars on his skin, as they tended to during intimate moments. "What about the people who did that? You think they're inherently good?"

"You haven't told me much about them."

"On purpose."

"Why?"

Johnny's arm draped over his face. Would the truth really be such a stretch? She thought he was an abused only child from Washington Heights

218

when he was an abused child with a psychotic brother from Miami. Big fucking difference. She would find out he was a runaway, but did anyone even give a shit now that he was seventeen? "It's complicated."

"I'm sure." Jessica sat up and pulled the sheet around her. "Why would your parents hurt you like that?"

Johnny propped himself up with a pillow. "Because they were miserable people who had no idea how to raise children."

Jessica tilted her head. "Whose being all kind and forgiving *now*?"

"I don't forgive them. I hate them fiercely. But if I could let it go, maybe it would free my own mind."

"What they did was criminal. They should be arrested."

"But you just said—"

"What I said was, people might have an explanation for doing bad things, but it doesn't mean they should be excused for it."

"I'm not reporting them, if that's what you're getting at." He looked at her. "Besides, how do you report people when you can't remember half the shit that happened?"

Jessica smoothed the blankets in silence. After a moment, she took his hand. "I can't forgive them for what they did to you."

He half-smiled. "Maybe you're not as kind as I thought."

"Maybe you're rubbing off on me."

CHAPTER THIRTY-THREE

Temper's reputation continued to grow amid the local music scene, and with club management, but for different reasons. They were always available on short notice, showed up on time, and were grateful to play in the diviest bars. They also came with plenty of gang brothers to act as roadies, making the place look busier than it might otherwise, thus drawing actual customers.

Teddy scored Temper a gig at a popular club in the east twenties called Rat Race. They were the first of several bands on the bill—the least-desirable time slot—but it was still a big step up. Since it was the night before Thanksgiving, there was hope it would be busier than the average Wednesday.

When the crew arrived, they unloaded gear from the van and carted it in the stage door to set up. They had time to kill so they got drinks and checked out the club. It was dimly lit, with rows of tightly packed booths on one side of an oblong bar, a stage and dance floor on the other. A smattering of people milled around.

Johnny spotted Jessica with Danni, and Michelle, all dressed to look older. He reeled her in for a kiss. "Any trouble getting in?"

"Not at all, and thanks for putting us on the guest list."

"Yeah, thanks," said Michelle, looking around.

"No problem."

Jessica leaned closer. "Jarrod won't mind that we brought her, will he?"

"Nah," said Johnny. "He's moved on, as long as she has." He ushered them to the bar. "You want drinks?"

As Johnny paid the bartender for four Rolling Rocks, Teddy appeared. He took his role as band manager seriously, dressing the part in a pressed shirt and slacks. At eighteen, he already had a respectable beard and passed for much older. "Get this." He tapped Johnny. "The act that was supposed to go on at eleven-thirty bailed. The manager said we could take their spot if we wanted to stick around."

"Hell yeah," said Johnny. "This place will be packed by then. You tell the others?"

He nodded. "Everyone's down with it."

"I won't be able to stay," said Jessica. "I gotta be home by ten."

Johnny swigged his beer. "Is Walter trying to exercise some authority?"

She shook her head. "We're going to my grandmother's in Katonah for Thanksgiving, and catching an early train upstate, so I gotta be home at a reasonable hour."

He squeezed her bum. "If you decide to stage a revolt, you can always do it from my bed."

By the time Temper took the stage, the bar was a bit more crowded and tables were filling. They performed some original up-tempo songs to try to entice the sober crowd. Jarrod's explosive percussion played off Patrick's bass. Clyde's lead guitar and harmonies wailed between Johnny's rhythm guitar and vocals, punctuated by Mario's sax. The boys had a cocky, animated stage presence, honed from years of playing on the street, and before long, a dozen patrons had migrated to the stage to bop up and down.

When the set was done, Johnny found Jessica near a wall by the dance floor. He corralled her with his arms and kissed her, despite being winded and damp with sweat. "How was it?"

"So good. Best I've seen so far."

"C'mon, I need a drink."

Jessica held him back. "Sherry's here."

"Huh?"

"That girl Sherry. She's here with Betsy, from Roosevelt."

Johnny saw them at the far end of the bar, flirting with two men in their forties. "Christ, I haven't seen her in ages."

"That's what she said. Since Betsy graduated, she doesn't hang out at the school anymore."

"You talked to her?"

"A little, but then they wanted drinks."

"Whatever. Come on." They went to where some of his brothers were standing.

Once Sherry spotted Johnny, she beelined over. She wore a low-cut top, short skirt and go-go boots. "Hey stranger." She leaned in for a hug and kiss, but he turned sideways to minimize contact. Were it not for her high heels, they would have been the same height for the first time. "Since when are you in a band?"

"Since quite a while, actually." He took hold of Jessica's hand. "What brings you here?"

"Betsy's friend's brother is the barback or some shit." She flicked her wrist. "He got us on the guest list."

"Must be a long list."

"Huh?"

"Nothing." At a loss for anything to say, Johnny began introducing his crew members. Before he could finish, Sherry leaned into his ear. "You got any blow?"

He pulled away. "No." A lie.

"Pity." She pouted.

"If I hear something, I'll let you know."

"Cool." She flashed a fake smile at Jessica. "Guess I'll leave you two alone." She traipsed back to Betsy.

Jessica let go of Johnny's hand to sip her beer. "Will she stay for the late set?"

"I don't know."

"She has a thing for you, you know."

"She has a thing for a lot of guys."

"When I leave, she'll probably be all over you."

Johnny connected with Jessica's eyes to assuage her fears. "She'll be all over whoever has the most coke."

Jessica looked down at her bottle. "Don't suppose you want to come for Thanksgiving."

"Right." Johnny laughed out loud. "Your dad likes me so much, your grandmother ought to *love* me."

Jessica couldn't help but grin. "Anything happening at the loft?"

"Chico's mother is cooking for everyone who doesn't have someplace else to go."

"That sounds nice." She wrapped her arms around Johnny's waist. "I should go. If I'm late, I'll have to hear about it all day tomorrow."

"I'll walk you out."

Jessica scooped up Danni and Michelle along the way. Near the door, Tito and Rafael stood rigid, eyeing Johnny with intent. Tito held a Manila envelope.

Johnny turned up his palms. "What?"

"Nothing." Rafael cast a glance over the mixed company.

Johnny nodded. "I'll be right back. I'm just gonna see that they get a cab." Minutes later, he returned alone. "Okay, spill it. And what the fuck's that?" He jutted his chin at the package.

Tito raised his eyebrows. "You have a job."

"Another gig?"

Rafael shook his head.

"Then what?"

Tito flicked the envelope. "You got an assignment from Marco."

"Shit." Johnny raked his scalp. "He was here?"

"Yeah," said Rafael. "But you were on stage and he couldn't wait."

"Why didn't he just page me?"

Tito shrugged.

"How'd he know I'd be here?"

"The Temper posters," said Rafael. "They're all over the city."

Johnny was about to ask more questions when a couple interrupted to compliment him on the set. They spoke with a German accent, so Johnny made the mistake of thanking them in German. That prompted a longer conversation, which Johnny regretted. Still, he was intrigued by how fluidly the foreign words tumbled out of his mouth.

Rafael caught his eye and mouthed, "Later." Then disappeared into the crowd with Tito.

When the couple finally left, Johnny went to find his bandmates. On the way, he flagged Francisco. He was nineteen, tough-looking, with a diamond stud earring. Johnny palmed him an eight-ball. "You see that blonde?"

Sherry was easy to spot in a crowd. Not just for her height, but for the swarm of men that materialized the second she stood still.

"Go turn her and her friend on."

"Are you shitting me?" Francisco took a step back. "I heard that's one of *your* girls."

Johnny wagged his head. "I like her, but not like that."

"Why don't you just give her the packet?"

"Because I don't want her hanging on me."

"Whatever you say, boss." Cisco twitched a shoulder. "Need me to check it for quality control?"

"You like that shit?"

"I've done it a few times."

"Whatever, bro, just don't go crazy because it's pure."

By Temper's second set, the club was packed and the energy infectious. They threw in a few cover songs to mix things up, including a rocked-out version of *The Night Chicago Died*, by Paper Lace. Folks in the crowd were pumping their fists and cheering, while others pinballed off each other dancing. When the set was over, people yelled for an encore, which the band obliged. Afterward, they received accolades from the club's manager, and gratitude for filling in.

The last act of the night was a punk rock group called Catacoma. The crew had crossed paths with them at other gigs. They knew some of the guys and liked their sound so they stuck around to watch.

Cisco found Johnny in the crowd. "Damn man, that girl is *crazy*."

"What happened?"

"We did a line in the bathroom, and she was all over me."

Johnny laughed. "I'm not surprised."

"I was trying to be respectful, but she's all grabbing down my pants and shit."

"You should go for it."

"Nah, man, that's your territory."

"It's not. Really."

As they stood together watching the band, Sherry popped up from behind, draping her arms around both of them. "Where's the afterparty?"

The brothers eyed each other.

"Come on." She shook them. "Surely one of you guys knows someplace we can hang out."

The high of performing for such an electrified crowd, mixed with the half dozen beers he had drank, made Johnny want to keep the party going, too. "Yeah. I know a place."

CHAPTER THIRTY-FOUR

At the loft, the group headed to the Studio, but a few brothers were tired and broke off for their apartments. Jarrod put on some music while Mario went behind the bar to make drinks. Johnny grabbed a beer and sat on a couch with Clyde and Eric. Patrick and Betsy had started drinking together at the club. They were both tipsy and collapsed on another couch to canoodle. Cisco scooted over to make room.

"This place is great," said Sherry, her syllables slipping into each other. She kicked off her boots to wander around the big open apartment. "Where'd you get the funky furniture?"

"Most of it came from the street," said Mario. He handed her a vodka and tonic, then squeezed beside Cisco. "The rest we improvised."

"Wait." A revelation stopped Sherry mid-stride. "All of you guys found apartments in the *same building*?" She flipped some hair from her face. "How does that even happen?"

"Just lucky, I guess," said Johnny.

She circled the table made of plywood and sawhorses; its primitiveness contrasted by a knightly red tablecloth. The centerpiece was the vintage brass candelabra plucked from someone's trash, now polished, with white taper candles in all but the missing cup. "Whose apartment is this one?"

Jarrod raised his hand from an overstuffed chair. "Me and Clyde's."

Sherry batted her lashes at Johnny. "Which one's yours?"

Johnny reached for a pack of Marlboros on the spool coffee table. "That's anyone's guess."

"How long have you been here?" Betsy asked Patrick.

"About a year and a half," he said.

Sherry came closer. "Apparently I've missed a lot."

"Why, where've *you* been?" said Johnny.

She gazed at the reflections in the industrial windows. "Last year my tight-ass, bible-thumping parents sent me to my grandparents' farm in North Carolina." She groaned. "Apparently, they were concerned about my partying."

Johnny cocked his head. "But aren't you, like, not a minor anymore?"

Cisco laughed. "I would've hightailed it the fuck outta there."

Her steel-blue eyes swept the ceiling. "At first, I sorta liked it, getting away from the vultures who run the modeling agencies and the crazy hours. Instead, I'm in the middle of nowhere, surrounded by nothing but animals, green fields, trees. And it was summer, so there were lots of babies. Cute little cows and lambs, chicks and ducklings. It was kinda cool, getting up early, feeding them, caring for them…" Her expression turned uncharacteristically melancholy. She shooed it away. "But I'm back now, so fuck it." She downed her drink and went to refill it.

Johnny looked at Betsy. "How long was she there?"

"Over a year." Betsy sipped her wine. "She just got back a few months ago."

Sherry bounced on the balls of her feet to stand behind Cisco. She set her glass on the floor and rubbed his shoulders. Her hands drifted down the front of his shirt and she nibbled his ear. He cringed because it tickled and she looked at Johnny. "Does this bother you?"

What?" Johnny blew a stream of cigarette smoke toward the ceiling. "That?"

"Yeah." Her tongue swiped Cisco's neck.

Johnny shrugged. "Guess I'm not the jealous type."

She pulled away to grab her drink. "How about laying out some lines then?"

Still buzzing from the band's performance and several beers, Johnny was feeling reckless. He had never been tempted by anything harder than weed. Nor had his brothers. But there were no pending threats or commitments, and they were safe inside the loft. He stubbed out his butt and nodded to Cisco. "Why not?"

Jarrod passed over a record album and Cisco emptied out the remains of the eight-ball. As he chopped it into lines with a matchbook, Sherry leaned over his shoulder with a rolled-up twenty. Annoyed by her impatience, he plucked the bill from her fingers and handed it to Johnny with the album.

Johnny snorted a line. A warm tingling sensation washed over him. As he gave Clyde the drugs, colors seemed brighter, sounds were crisper, and everything was interesting and important.

"How do you guys always find the best blow?" Sherry asked after everyone had a hit.

Johnny felt an impulse to blurt out the truth. A side effect of getting fucked up, and a reminder why he preferred keeping his wits intact.

"Maybe it's you." She walked around the couch, put her drink on the coffee table, and sat on Cisco's lap. "Are you the connection for this good blow?" She leaned back, swaying to the music. Her spine arched as she grinded into Cisco's groin. Sherry was oblivious that she kept bumping into Mario, who took advantage of his proximity by brushing his fingers against her breasts.

The scene was as provocative as it was uncomfortable. No one could look away, except Betsy, who seemed bored by her friend's antics and slurped her wine instead.

"That girl ain't too bright," said Clyde, breaking the silence.

Jarrod nodded. "You think?"

"You come into a gang house, dressed like that, acting like that?" Clyde shook his head. "It's just stupid, that's all."

Ignoring the comments, or not hearing them, Sherry met Johnny's gaze and bit her index finger. It was supposed to be sexy, but her faded lipstick was smudged, and her mascara had deposited black clumps around her bloodshot eyes. When she massaged her breasts with her free hand, Cisco scooted out from underneath her.

"Bitch, I don't know what kinda game you're playing, but I'm done."

She tumbled into his place on the couch.

"You told me I could get with her," he said to Johnny. "But I ain't gonna find out you changed your mind, and next thing I got a bullet in my head." He stormed out of the apartment and down the stairs.

"Party pooper," Sherry huffed. She stood to straighten her clothes. "Who wants another drink?" She swayed over to the bar. The others also got up to shake off the tension.

◇◇◇

Both girls were so drunk, the cocaine could no longer sober them. Sherry dragged out a chair to sit at the dining table. It took three tries to light her cigarette. "Who said something about a gang house?" she slurred. "What even is that?"

Mario, Eric, and Clyde ignored her, continuing their conversation around the bar. Patrick was piloting Betsy out of the apartment. He had to make several hitches to get her through the door. Their laughter echoed in the stairwell.

Jarrod had kicked back on the couch next to Johnny. He was going on about John Bonham, and how he was hands-down the best drummer of all time. He talked about his early beginnings, influences and kick-ass technique. "If I die playing half as good as that guy, I'd be happy. You know what I mean?"

Johnny didn't answer.

"Hellooooo. Earth to Johnny." Jarrod leaned forward to look at his face. Johnny's vacant eyes were fixed across the room. "No fucking way." He scooted to the edge of the couch. "Clyde. Help."

"Huh?" Clyde turned around.

"Get over here. I think our boy's flipped."

Clyde rushed over to kneel in front of Johnny. He bobbed around a bit, waved a hand, but got no reaction. "Shit. I'm way too fucked up to deal with this right now."

"What do we do?" Eric asked, coming over with Mario.

"For one, we don't touch him," said Jarrod. "He can get violent when he's in this state."

"Maybe he's just high," said Mario.

Clyde rubbed his forehead. "No. It's like the other times."

The rocking back and forth started small, then the bizarre foreign word stew. Both increased in intensity as the others gathered closer. Suddenly, Johnny sprang from the couch, making Clyde almost fall over. He began pacing the length of the loft, becoming more agitated with each lap.

Sherry jutted out a thumb as he passed. "What's wrong with him?"

"Mind your damn business," said Mario. "And keep your flat ass in that chair." But when Johnny made his next pass, she stood up to grab him. It was meant to be playful, though she was so unsteady she fell into his chest. The brothers gasped.

Johnny flung her off, and she banged into the table. Annoyed, she regained her balance, then made a half-assed attempt to slap his face. He grabbed her wrist mid-swing. The other hand clutched her throat.

"What do we do?" asked Eric.

"Nothing yet," said Clyde. "He's fucking manic. And now he's coked up too."

Sherry weakened in his grip and croaked, "You're so sexy when you're mad."

The crew watched Johnny's hollow eyes sweep across her reddening face.

"Hey, Johnny," Clyde said. "She didn't mean it."

"Yeah, she's no threat," Jarrod added. "She's nothing. Fuck her."

Whether Johnny could hear them or not, he released his hold.

Sherry groped for a chair to keep from falling, and Clyde breathed a sigh of relief. But then Johnny bolted out of the apartment and up the stairs. "Motherfucker!"

The brothers scrambled after him. The commotion woke some gang members, who burst from their apartments to follow the pack. Jarrod and Mario were one flight behind Johnny as he ran out to the roof. When they opened the door, he was on the ledge with arms spread wide. They both halted. Clyde and Eric barged out seconds later, almost bowling them over.

"Fuck," Jarrod whispered to Clyde. "You gotta talk him off there."

"Me?" Clyde tried to swallow but had no spit. "Why always me?"

"Because he listens to you when he's batshit. Like, your voice reaches him wherever it is he goes."

Before anyone could act, Johnny began walking around the perimeter, talking in mixed languages. Clyde kept pace from a distance. He spoke calmly, trying to locate Johnny, wherever he might be, and convince him to return.

Chico, Ramón and Maurice appeared. They were given the run-down by Jarrod as they stood shivering in their pajamas and bare feet.

"Johnny, please." Clyde struggled to mask the panic in his voice. "I don't know what's going on in your brain right now, but over here? On *this* side? Shit's pretty good. As long as I don't have to scrape your ass off the sidewalk." He choked on an unexpected sob. "Do not make me have to do that."

The others remained fixed on Johnny afraid to make a sound.

The door burst open. Sherry clung to the knob, swaying. "What're you people doing up here?"

"Jesus," said Mario. "Get that cunt outta here!"

Chico and Maurice tried to grab her, but she was slippery for someone so fucked up.

She headed toward Johnny. "Hey, why're you ignoring me?"

Jarrod and Mario got hands on her and held her back.

Johnny stopped. He looked over the city skyline, then down toward the street.

Clyde doubled over, covering his face.

"You guys throw *the worst* afterparties." Sherry blew a raspberry that was mostly spit. Mario dug his fingers into the flesh of her upper arm and she grimaced.

Johnny spun and jumped onto the roof. He blew past everyone, ripping open the door to sprint downstairs. The herd of brothers galloped after him.

"I hope someone locked the door behind that bitch," said Mario, skimming steps a handful at a time.

On the ground floor, Johnny took off down the street. Jarrod and Mario had him in sight, with Clyde and Eric not far behind. Chico, Ramón and Maurice stayed back to dress and rally more gang members.

Johnny cut over to Greenwich Street and ran south. The drugs mixed with his psychosis gave him the ability to outpace the others. It was twenty-five degrees at three-thirty on Thanksgiving morning, so the area was even more desolate than usual. A lucky break, as they sprinted in nothing but house clothes, which might have otherwise drawn attention.

By the time they passed the World Trade Center, the gaps between them had grown. At Battery Park, they lost sight of Johnny entirely. The four stood around a bench, catching their breath.

"What the fuck?" said Eric. "Is this normal?"

"Ain't nothing normal about him when he's like that," said Mario.

Jarrod ruffled his hair, where the sweat was crystalizing in the cold. "In the good old days, we'd just find him rocking in a corner. Now he's out running marathons, stabbing guys..." He turned to Clyde. "So much for your theory. You said if he confronted everything in Miami, these episodes would stop. But he's remembered a bunch of shit already." Jarrod opened his arms. "Yet here we are."

"I'm not a fucking doctor, okay?" Clyde punted an empty Sprite can onto the path. Its tinny sound echoed in the silence. "I looked up some shit in the library, that's all. But I don't even know the diagnosis." Holding the bench's backrest, he grabbed a foot to stretch his quads. "What have *you* done?" He eyed the others. "Any of you."

Johnny appeared from between some trees. He was walking uptown at a brisk clip. His brothers exchanged looks of bewilderment before falling in behind him.

"Hey, I didn't mean to lay it all on you," Jarrod said to Clyde.

Clyde shrugged. "Whatever. Let's just deal with this."

"Is he still even flipped?" asked Eric.

Clyde quickened his pace to get closer. "Hey, Johnny? Are you there?"

Jarrod got on the other side. "Yeah, man. Say something."

Johnny marched ahead, unreactive. Clyde jumped in his path, walking backward. "C'mon, Johnny, I know you see me. You'd be running into shit otherwise." He wiped his nose with his sleeve. "Aren't you tired yet? I know I am. It's fucking cold and we all want to go to bed."

"Yeah, Johnny," said Jarrod. "Snap out of it already."

Clyde skipped in reverse, waving his hands. "Don't you remember us? Me and Jarrod have been with you from the beginning. Since you first came to New York. We were twelve for Christ sakes." Clyde's jaw clenched. "How do you not know who the fuck I am?"

"Clyde."

The four boys gaped at each other.

Clyde dropped back beside Johnny. "What'd you say?"

"Clyde."

"Yeah." He laughed a little. "But why didn't you answer me earlier?"

"You weren't talking to me."

Clyde huffed out a misty cloud of breath. "I said your name like a hundred times."

Johnny's pace remained consistent, his eyes inanimate. "Not my name."

"What do you mean it's not your name?" said Jarrod. "Who the fuck are you then?"

"Javier."

CHAPTER THIRTY-FIVE

"So, um, Javier, do you know where you're going?" asked Clyde.

"Home."

"Where's home?"

"The loft."

"He knows that much," said Mario.

The five walked abreast. "You know that you're safe with us, right?" said Jarrod. "That we have your back no matter what."

Johnny nodded.

"Then why were you running?" asked Clyde.

"Sometimes I feel trapped."

"By us?"

"No."

"Then trapped by what?"

Johnny didn't answer.

Clyde looked at the others. "Let's just get home then."

As they neared the loft, brothers who had been looking out from the roof gave a thumbs-up. Tito, Alex and Chico were on the stoop. They stood aside to let the others file in.

"What's the deal?" Chico asked after Johnny disappeared into his bedroom.

Jarrod slapped him on the back. "He's all yours."

"Yeah," said Clyde. "I think the worst is over, but you'll still need to watch him."

"Us?" said Alex. "You know how to deal with this shit better than us."

Clyde spun toward him. "Listen, I just played two sets, watched someone I love almost jump off a goddamn roof, then sprinted halfway around Manhattan. All while fucking wasted." He swiped a hand over his mouth. "We got his ass home, now it's someone else's turn."

Jarrod folded his arms. "I second that." Mario and Eric nodded in agreement.

"It's okay," said Tito, stepping between Chico and Alex. "Of course we will watch him. You guys go get some rest."

The four brothers dragged themselves upstairs. Others were coming down, asking what happened, and were ignored.

Jarrod's voice boomed from above, "Get this drunk bitch the fuck outta *my bed*!"

◇◇◇

Water was running in the bathtub. A striped Terrycloth mat lay scrunched in the corner. From his vantage point, Johnny could see that his father had done a shoddy job installing the peel-and-stick vinyl flooring. There were sizable gaps between the tiles and the base of the toilet. And the cuts were crooked. Miguel must have been in a hurry to get Orlando locked up.

Again, Johnny tried to wiggle out of the rope tying his hands behind his back. He could hear Orlando rustling around, ranting in mixed languages. Every second he stayed out there was a blessing because Johnny knew what was coming would be bad. He had been down here enough to recognize the patterns. When Orlando hung him from the rafter to slice him with the box cutter, it was playful by his standards. A fun little game to watch blood droplets trickle this way and that. Sadistic, yes, but Johnny knew the goal was not to kill him. Other times, Orlando was so thoroughly unhinged he wasn't sure.

This was one of those times. Orlando's erratic movements, along with his unfocused eyes, warned of something grimmer than usual. And he sounded like six foreigners arguing at once. Johnny's terror was peaking so acutely he could not even produce tears. So, he lay there, willing himself to be anywhere else.

Orlando burst through the door. "Why didn't you tell me it was full?" He stepped over Johnny to shut off the tap. A menacing grin appeared. "Are you ready?"

Johnny's body trembled against the floor as Orlando pulled off his shirt. There wasn't much room for him to maneuver; still he knelt between the toilet and sink. He lifted Johnny from behind to swivel him toward the tub. His closeness was repellent. The stale musky scent, the flaccidity of his body, his sour breath. But Johnny had no fight. It had been scared out of him.

Orlando grabbed a clump of Johnny's hair with one hand. The other pressed between his shoulder blades to fold him over the rim. Johnny looked into the clear flat water. Some chips in the porcelain were starting to rust, and two of the no-slip butterfly stickers were missing wings.

Without warning, Orlando shoved his head into the tub. Johnny sealed his mouth shut. He held his breath as long as he could until panic set in. He began to struggle and Orlando pulled him up. Johnny gasped and spit, his eyes blinking. Water had gotten in one ear, which muffled sound, but not enough to keep from hearing his brother's demented laugh.

"That was just a test run." Orlando wiped his nose on his forearm before taking hold again.

This time, Johnny took a preparatory breath, but Orlando held him deeper, shoving his face to the bottom. Johnny tried to stay calm as the weight of Orlando's body draped over his back, jamming his ribcage into the tub's rim. He resisted the instinct to breathe, hoping his brother would tire before he did. Eventually his involuntary reflexes won out and he gasped. Despite the coldness of the water, Johnny felt a scorching heat in his lungs. The pain coursed through his body before everything went limp.

◇◇◇

"New shift," Joe said, walking into Johnny's room with Leon. "Any change?"

"He stopped pacing." Tito jutted his chin toward the corner. "But now he's sitting on the floor."

"It's after ten already," said Leon. "How much longer can he stay like that?"

"Shit, it's that late?" Chico stood to stretch. "My parents are gonna be here soon to start cooking. What's the status upstairs?"

Joe leaned on Johnny's dresser. "Jarrod's asleep on the couch, because that crazy bitch is still passed out in his bed, but Rafi's on his way to bounce her now. Jeff is getting Patrick and Betsy up so we can boot her, too. Other than that, most everyone else is awake."

"Cool," said Chico.

Tito's eyes lingered on Johnny before he turned for the door. "It's hard seeing him like that. But keep talking. It lets him know somebody's here."

Joe smiled. "We will, brother."

◇◇◇

Johnny thought he should be floating. His skin and bones felt weightless, but his organs were leaden, anchoring him to the ground. He wondered how it was possible to be light and heavy at the same time. Something shone from above. It pierced his closed lids, but he was unable to open his eyes. Sounds were faint, distant, but there was a presence. It was close.

A fist crashed onto Johnny's chest, jolting his whole body. It happened again, and he coughed, but it felt like he was expelling razors. The third time sent him into a fit of spasms so bad he was going to vomit. Johnny rolled onto his side, gasping for air between convulsions. He wanted to sit up, but his hands were still tied. He curled his knees into his chest instead, until the fits subsided.

When Johnny opened his eyes, Orlando was on all fours, his face inches from his own. He was sporting a goofy grin. "That was fucking amazing!" He tipped his head back to laugh. "Did you see that?" He got back down to Johnny's level. "Did you?"

Johnny tried to swallow but it hurt.

"You drowned. I drowned you. But then I brought you back." He cackled. "That was really cool, right?"

Johnny closed his eyes and prayed for oblivion.

CHAPTER THIRTY-SIX

As the curtain of consciousness lifted, everything hurt. The muscles in his legs ached, his back was stiff, and his head throbbed so badly there was a heartbeat in his ears. Johnny's face had become one with the pillow, its feathery softness the only comfort. He inhaled cautiously, expecting searing pain. Instead, he was hit with delicious aromas. Herbs and spices, the succulent smell of roasting meat. Was that pie? His stomach growled, piling onto the misery, and he realized he was famished.

Johnny rolled onto his back, throwing an arm over his face to shield it from the daylight. There was another smell. This one was floral, like perfume. It was nearby. He sensed that someone was close to him, and flashes of the cellar sprung into Johnny's head. The bathtub. His face under water. The panic, choking. Orlando cackling. He lurched up, gasping for air.

Lucinda leaned back, palms up. *"Tranquilo, hijo mío, todo estará bien."*

Johnny looked at her. His bed. The room. His brain rationalized that he was safe, but his autonomic nerve system was slow to catch up. Heart racing, he could not stop hyperventilating. Then came the tears.

Lucinda flicked a hand at Maurice and Diego, telling them to wait outside. Once alone, she pulled Johnny close, rocking him and stroking his head.

In her hold, he wept convulsively. With his face pressed against her bosom, Johnny experienced a wave of unfamiliar feelings. A kind of release. Like mourning something he never had—if that were even possible. He wondered if his mother had shown him comfort like this, or offered the

238

slightest acknowledgement of what went on in that house, would the atrocities have been more bearable? If she had, would he ever have left?

When his breath regulated, Lucinda lay him back, but kept hold of his hand. "I've been checking on you since I arrived," she said in Spanish.

"What time is it?" he muttered.

"Near five. Dinner is almost ready, but we have time. Tell me what happened."

"Last night?"

"No. Just then, when you woke."

Johnny looked at the ceiling. Could he even describe such horror? When Lucinda rested her palm over his heart, he tried. Single words stretched into sentences. Fortunately, it did not require much elaboration.

She cast up her eyes and crossed herself. "That boy was very sick. It's no surprise you blocked it out." She brushed a curl from his face. "You get angry for not remembering. You feel defective, but how could a child confront that? Any of it?" Her head tilted to the side. "Your brain did what it had to under the circumstances. And the second you were able? You had the courage and strength to get away." She smiled. "Every day you should rejoice that you are alive. That you are not him."

Johnny rubbed his temples. "But how do I know that?"

"What do you mean?"

"What if I am like him? What if we suffer from the same illness?"

Lucinda waved the suggestion away. "He was born like that. What happens to you, with these episodes, is circumstantial. Had you been raised different, you would be fine."

She sounded so confident he wanted to believe her. Despite her exceptional intuition, she didn't have all the facts. She didn't know about the people he had killed. How easy it had been.

Lucinda caught the doubt in his eyes and patted his cheek. "You will feel better with a shower and some food."

He nodded. "Thank you."

"You know, I love you like my own son. And I would never repeat a word of what you have told me."

"I do know that. I trust you with all of my heart." Johnny swung his feet to the floor and caught a whiff of himself. "Jesus, I do need a shower."

In the Mess Hall, food was being brought to the table and people were taking their places. Only half the residents were eating at the loft, but a few had invited guests, including Chico's two older sisters who had come with his parents. Johnny felt self-conscious as he crept in, but brothers greeted him with the usual nod or handshake. He took a seat next to Jarrod, who gave him the once over. "You look like shit."

Johnny plucked his fresh T-shirt. "I look better than I feel."

"How about a few beers?"

He grimaced. "No thanks." Johnny glanced around. Luis was carving the turkey while Lucinda and her daughters carried over the final trimmings. "Where's Clyde?"

"He went to have dinner with his family."

"I thought he was gonna eat here."

"He needed to get away for a while."

Johnny sighed. "That bad, huh?"

"Look, we can get into it later." Jarrod handed him a bowl of mashed potatoes. "For now, let's just eat."

Johnny piled food onto his plate. As he forked portions into his mouth, he struggled to erase the heinous images in his head, tuning into different conversations. He was grateful no one was trying to reel him into their stories, nor were they making him feel awkward for not participating. Whatever happened last night must have been bad, judging by how sore he was and how long he had been...away. Yet his Dog brothers were still here. Where would he be without this family? The thought was almost as disturbing as the memory.

After dinner, gang members cleared the table and packed away leftovers. Rudy brewed an urn of coffee while plates were set out for pumpkin and apple pies. Chatter slowed as everyone grew too lethargic to do much more than loll in their chairs. Lucinda sipped the remains of her wine, deflecting compliments on the food.

Johnny got up and went to her. Laying hands on her shoulders, he bent to kiss her cheek. "My brothers need to know what I remembered," he whispered in her ear. "But I can't repeat it. Will you pull some aside and tell them?"

She tipped her head to face him. "Are you sure?"

"Yes. They should know."

"If you say so."

"Thank you. For everything." He kissed her again.

Johnny went across the hall to the Studio and flopped on a couch. Stuffing a throw pillow under his head, he surveyed the room. He recalled Sherry's performance with Cisco. And doing the coke. But after Patrick staggered out with Betsy, everything was blank. He tried to force his brain to give him something, anything, but it only caused anxiety. He looked at the water stains on the ceiling instead, shaping them into different animals.

Jarrod, Chico and Mario came in and sat on the couch opposite. Johnny adjusted the pillow to view them better. Their expressions were funereal. "She told you."

Jarrod wagged his head. "Jesus fuck, Johnny."

"That's the most messed-up shit I ever heard," said Mario.

"Oh yeah?" Johnny rolled his eyes. "Maybe it's just the beginning."

"You can't think like that," said Chico.

They were quiet for a moment. Jarrod lit a cigarette. "So? Do you want to hear what went down last night?"

"May as well," said Johnny. "I can't feel much worse."

Jarrod ran down the basics until the part on the roof. "We're buzzed off our asses and you're trying to do a fucking swan dive." Jarrod folded forward, cradling his head. "I've never been so scared in my whole life."

"You were walking back and forth on the ledge." Mario expelled an audible breath. "We were frozen. Helpless."

"Wait." Johnny sat up. "But I wouldn't actually jump, right?"

"Do *you* know that?" Chico turned up his palms. "Because I don't fucking know that."

"And now?" Jarrod looked at Johnny. "Knowing what was in your mind while that shit was going down?"

"Yeah," said Mario. "I could see why you'd wanna get away from it all."

Johnny rubbed his face, trying to marry what he couldn't remember with what he only just remembered. It made his brain feel squeezed, distressed. He leaned back on the couch. "Then why am I still here?"

"Clyde," all three said in unison. They took turns adding the rest of the story. The chase, the walk home, the fact that he had actually spoken to them. The aftereffects in his room, pacing and rocking, and how, like a toy with a dying battery, he finally crawled into bed and passed out.

"You were flipped almost twelve hours," said Jarrod. "That's the longest I know about, but I'm blaming the coke."

Johnny flashed a palm. "I'm all done with that shit."

"No doubt."

"What ever happened to Sherry?"

"That skanky ho better never set foot in this house again." Mario sliced the air with his hands. "Her bullshit could've turned a bad situation into a disaster."

"And the bitch passed out in *my bed*," said Jarrod. "So now I gotta burn them damn sheets."

Johnny laughed. It chipped away a small bit of tension. The others laughed with him.

Clyde returned and tossed his coat on a bench by the apartment door.

"Look who's back," said Chico. "How was dinner?"

"All right." He sat on the same couch as Johnny, but at the far end.

"Just all right?" asked Mario.

Clyde shrugged.

"Your mother musta been happy to see you," said Chico.

"She was."

The five of them stared at the spool coffee table until Johnny cocked a knee toward Clyde. "Thank you."

He scrunched his face. "For what?"

"For not pushing me off the roof."

Clyde tapped out a Marlboro. "I fucking should have."

"You'd have been within your rights."

"Would've been too messy." He blew a stream of smoke toward the ceiling. "I'm gonna wait till you're asleep. Put a pillow over your face."

Johnny chuckled into his chest. "Look, man, I don't know what to tell you, except I'm sorry."

Clyde's eyelids drooped. "It's not like you can control it."

"True. But it always seems to fall on you to fix it."

"Then maybe next time take some fucking Quaaludes so we can catch your ass." Clyde flicked the ash off his cigarette.

"No doubt." Mario laughed.

"Or go see someone," Clyde continued. "Like a doctor or something. You're seventeen now. No one's gonna question you." He looked at Johnny. "My sisters were telling me about this place on Twelfth Street, a free clinic. Confidential services, no parents required. You could at least talk to someone, try to find out what the fuck is going on."

Johny pulled his knees to his chest, pressing into the corner of the couch. "And when I tell them Orlando drowned me in the bathtub, then performed some spastic version of CPR, so I didn't *actually fucking die*, you don't think they'll report that shit?"

Clyde tipped an ear. "Say what?"

Jarrod waved at him. "I'll tell you later."

They labored to digest the conversation along with the food. Their breath, mixed with an occasional sigh or grunt, was the only sound as they melted into the furniture. Eventually, Chico leaned forward. "Since we're having this fireside chat..." He looked at Johnny. "I got a confession. But it might be helpful."

The others sat up, curious.

"Last night, after they got you back in your room, me and Tito were watching you while you were talking all that gibberish."

Mario shrunk back. "What Puerto Rican uses the word *gibberish*?"

"Shut the fuck up." Chico backhanded him in the chest. "I'm an eloquent motherfucker."

"Hey!" Clyde glared at them. "Can we get to the point?"

Chico regrouped. "We were trying to analyze it, like, understand the patterns, but neither of us speak six languages."

Johnny raised his eyebrows. "And?"

"But *you* do."

"Yeah. So what?"

"So, I got my boombox, a blank cassette, and we taped it."

Jarrod expelled a laugh. "That's brilliant." He slapped Chico's shoulder. "We shoulda thought of that before."

Chico grinned. "Exactly. Now Johnny can translate his own gibberish."

"Maybe he shouldn't hear it," said Clyde. "What if it triggers something?"

"No," said Johnny. "I want to hear it. Anything that might help us understand these episodes is worth it." He turned to Clyde. "Because I can't keep putting you guys through this."

Clyde circled the tension from his neck. "Do we have permission to restrain the shit out of you if you start to flip?"

Despite Clyde's sarcastic tone, Johnny knew he wasn't joking. "Yes. But be careful because I don't know what I'm capable of in that state, and I don't want to hurt you."

Clyde smiled through tight lips. "I'll take a black eye over scraping your body parts off the sidewalk."

"Do whatever you need to because I don't want to die." Johnny locked eyes with each of his brothers. "I really don't."

"Okay, hermano." Chico stood. "I'll be right back."

He returned from across the hall and set the boombox on the table. He handed a pen and paper to Johnny before sitting. "Ready?" Chico put a finger on the *play* button.

Everyone nodded.

The voice on the tape seemed so distant, alien. Sometimes fading to a whisper. Johnny gestured for Chico to turn it up, but that made the sound quality scratchier. He leaned closer. It was hard to decipher which word was what language because they were alternating at an impossible pace, but any time Johnny identified one, he would scribble it down. He had to replay the tape several times.

Finally, he hit *stop*. "You're right," he said to Chico. "It's a pattern. With every single word I switch languages, cycling through all six, then start over again." He swiped his face. "But I'm not just repeating the same sentence. Do you know how much concentration that requires? It would be hard to do with *two* languages. Also, I thought I forgot most of that stuff."

"So, what are you saying on the tape?" asked Jarrod.

Johnny smiled. "Remember that rhyme, the one about the old lady who swallowed a fly? 'I don't know why she swallowed a fly. Perhaps she'll die.'"

"Yeah," Mario snapped his fingers. "Then she swallowed a spider that wriggled and jiggled and tickled inside her."

"It doesn't make sense," said Clyde. "You're having these fucked-up flashbacks about all the shit that happened to you as a kid, but meanwhile, you're reciting some nonsensical nursery rhyme?"

Johnny nodded. "I told you how my mother tutored me and Orlando with all those foreign kids' books."

"Why would you be spewing that shit while you're reliving being tortured?"

"I don't know." Johnny stared at the paper peppered with words. "Maybe I'm doing it to distract myself from the memories."

His brothers nodded like it was plausible.

"Or mimicking something I did back then, when I was locked up with Orlando." It felt like he was getting closer. "What if I started alternating languages on purpose? Like, to force my brain to check out when shit got bad." The hypothesis seemed to fit. And if he taught himself to mentally detach from reality, that meant he also had the power to stop it.

Johnny tossed the pen and paper on the table. "Thank you. This was huge. Really." He smiled. "But I'm tapped. I gotta go crash."

"Of course," said Jarrod. "But we're still gonna be checking on you, so keep your door open."

He stood up. "You know I can't stand being locked in anywhere."

CHAPTER THIRTY-SEVEN

Despite his recent resolution and general exhaustion, Johnny didn't sleep well. Every time he started to drift off, Orlando or his parents would jolt him awake. They weren't doing anything in particular. Just benign figures passing through the background of a shallow dream. Regardless, it was unnerving, and by morning his sheets were damp and knotted.

With all the doors open, it was easier to hear the loft come alive. The creaky staircase as gang members traveled to the Mess Hall or off to work, their conversations fading in and out as they passed. Johnny found the noise more comforting than silence and finally fell into a deep slumber. He was enjoying a generic dream when a buzzer woke him. It was disorienting at first because hardly anyone rang the front door. He heard Rafael calling from below. "Hey, Johnny. It's Jessica. You want me to let her in?"

Johnny shuffled to the landing to tell him it was okay. When the door opened, a frigid gust of wind whipped up the stairwell. It halted his breath as he stood in nothing but pajama pants.

Jessica greeted Rafael with some small talk, loosening her scarf and coat before climbing the steps. As she got closer to Johnny she hesitated. "Wow. You look terrible."

"So I've been told."

"Are you okay?"

"Yeah. Come in." He ushered her inside.

"I probably should've called first."

"It's okay. But I'm not gonna be good company."

"Do you want me to go?"

"No." He took her coat and hung it from a nail in the wall. Inside his room, he made a halfhearted effort to straighten out the sheets before flopping onto the bed.

"Rough night?" She kicked off her shoes.

He grunted while scooting over to make room for her. Jessica stripped down to her shirt and panties. She crawled beside him and he pulled her close. "Mm, yeah. This is exactly what I needed." He kissed her head. "Tell me all about your Thanksgiving."

"Right." Jessica cocked an elbow. "Because nothing's more exciting than a Baxter family dinner."

Johnny smiled. "I don't care. I want to hear it."

"Fine."

She stroked the stubble budding on his face and began to recount the day. How Walter insisted they get to Penn Station early, only to have the train be forty minutes late. Then, it was so overcrowded they couldn't even sit together. But her face softened as she described Katonah, where her grandmother lived, with its quaint streets and pretty houses, and reminisced how the family used to visit more often, back when she and Chad were younger.

Johnny closed his eyes. He was soothed by her voice as she listed all the delicious dishes Grandma Baxter had cooked, some of them especially for her, since she was the firstborn grandchild. He found the banality refreshing. The normalness of her family was loosening some of the contaminated feelings still clinging to him.

When she finished, he tipped his head to look at her. "Why are you *really* here so early?"

"Huh?"

"You never show up unannounced."

"I missed you and wanted to—"

"You thought you were gonna catch me with Sherry, didn't you?"

She bit her lip. "It crossed my mind."

He pressed the back of his head deeper into the pillow. "Well, she *was* here."

Jessica's face withered. "In this bedroom?"

"No." Johnny propped up to look at her. "At Clyde and Jarrod's. She was trying to get with Cisco."

"Which one is he?"

"Tough-looking, diamond earring."

"He was at the club, right?"

"Yeah."

She plucked a piece of lint from the sheet. "I can't keep up with all the new guys."

"A bunch of us came here after the show and went upstairs. I had a drink, then left. When I woke up, she was gone." It wasn't untrue.

"Does that mean she'll be hanging around now?"

"No, baby." Johnny stroked her arm. "Cisco wasn't even into her."

"But now she knows where you live."

"I think we got enough manpower to keep her out." Johnny put his arm around Jessica and scooched down. "But if she breaches the line of defense, we'll shoot at her from the window."

She chuckled, snuggling closer. "So, how come you're feeling rough?"

"I haven't been sleeping."

"Any reason?"

Johnny closed his eyes. "Fucked-up memories."

"Do you want to talk about it?"

"Not really."

"You sure?" She kissed his neck, then chest.

"Yeah."

She scooted lower to kiss his belly. "Is there anything I can do to help?" Then lower still.

Johnny moaned. "You're doing it."

After the sex, Johnny fell deeply asleep. Jessica napped with him for a while, but when she got up, he stirred. "Mm, where are you going?"

"I can't sleep anymore. I'm gonna go putz around, maybe look for something to eat."

"Gimme a minute, I'll get up."

"Don't." She kissed the top of his head. "Sleep. I'll be fine."

Johnny rolled tighter into the blankets. He was out before she even got dressed.

When he next cracked an eye, his clock said one-fifty. He threw an arm out, but the bed was empty. Had he only dreamed that Jessica was there? But his pajama pants were off, and her strawberry shampoo lingered on the pillows. He put on some sweats and jogged up to the Mess Hall. Jessica was at the table, playing poker for sunflower seeds with Jarrod, Mario and JJ. The pile of seeds in front of her was respectable.

"There's nothing good that can come from this," Johnny said, walking up behind her. She tipped back her head for a kiss.

"Thanks a lot," said Mario. "Sending her up here to kick our asses."

JJ clucked his tongue. "This bitch is cheating."

Jarrod looked at Johnny over his hand of cards. "Feel better now?"

"Yeah, but I'm starving."

"We figured, bro. We left the food out for you."

Johnny stroked Jessica's hair. "Did you eat?"

"I did. Your boys are taking very good care of me."

"And letting your ass win," Mario mumbled.

Gus and Vinnie came in and grabbed sodas from the fridge, then flopped on the couch to watch TV. Jessica whispered to Johnny. "More new guys?"

Johnny opened his arms. "Who can resist being part of all this?"

At the island counter, Johnny was carving turkey for a sandwich when Tito and Rafael appeared. He barely looked up. "You having lunch?"

Neither one answered. They just eyed him with arms folded.

"Shit." Johnny set down the knife. "I totally forgot."

"You've been kind of busy," said Rafael.

"Do you need me right now?" Johnny peered between them to see Jessica shuffling cards.

"No." Tito's brow furrowed. "But don't take all day."

"I hear you." Johnny piled turkey onto his bread. "I won't."

He brought his sandwich to the table with some chips and a glass of milk. After eating, he sat in on a few hands of poker before complaining that the food wasn't agreeing with him. He apologized to Jessica, saying he needed to go back to bed, and that he would call her tomorrow. After walking her out, Johnny found Tito and Rafael in the Studio drinking beer with Clyde. The Manila envelope sat in the middle of the coffee table. Johnny picked it up. "This is what Marco gave you?"

"Yup." Rafael slurped from his can.

"D'you look in it?"

"Mm-hmm."

Johnny undid the fasteners and pulled out two stacks of hundreds. "Twenty grand? What for?"

Tito jutted his chin. "Look."

Johnny turned the envelope upside down. A business card fell out along with a grainy Polaroid. "What the fuck's this?" He examined the photo. It was unposed. A sixtyish-year-old man at some type of corporate function. Johnny picked up the business card.

Vanguard Securities

Gregory H. Chandler, Vice President

A phone number and Times Square address were inscribed below.

"And I care about this guy why?"

Rafael leaned forward. "Because you're supposed to kill him."

"Ah-ha," Jarrod said, walking in. "The unveiling of the mystery envelope." He went to the fridge to grab a beer. "What'd I miss?"

"You better bring me one of those too." Johnny sat.

Jarrod set down the cans of Coors and looked at the items on the table. He picked up a stack of bills. "Nice. But what's it for?"

Johnny stayed focused on Tito and Rafael. "Did he say anything else?"

Tito shrugged. "Just to have it done as soon as possible."

"And that he was sorry he couldn't stay to watch the set," Rafael added.

"Fuck me." Johnny swigged the beer.

Jarrod looked at Johnny. "He wants you to kill a guy?" Then Clyde. "He wants him to kill a guy?" When nobody answered, he tossed the money back.

"He paid up front," said Clyde. "That means he assumes you're gonna do it."

"Seriously," said Jarrod. "He could have asked first."

Clyde pinched the corners of his mouth. "I don't like Marco expecting you to be at his beck and call. Especially for this type of shit. The guy might be loaded, but he's also nuts."

"I got to agree," said Jarrod. "And this time he's not holding a gun to your head."

Johnny glanced again at the Polaroid. Gregory Chandler had a drink in one hand, a cigar in the other. The tie of his expensive suit was loosened, his top shirt button undone. Behind him, some fancy-looking banquet hall, with a bunch of other suits yukking it up. "Marco's pretty powerful." He took another pull of his beer. "He's got connections. Might even know people in the music business."

"Are you shitting me?" Clyde threw up his hands, standing. "You think Aerosmith got signed because they killed a guy?"

Johnny clawed his scalp. "That's not what I meant."

"The more you do for him, the more he's gonna expect." Clyde stuffed his fists into his hips. "Do we really want to be tied up in all of his shit?"

"No, but with the Brick out of commission, we don't have a steady income."

"So *this* is our thing now? Killing people?" He ripped the Polaroid from Johnny. "Do we even know why this Chandler person deserves to die?"

"Obviously he crossed Marco."

"And that concerns us how?"

"Look, I get it. I don't want to be tied to him either." Johnny leaned back. "I mean, maybe for the drug running, because that went pretty smooth." Johnny eyed the stacks of bills on the table. Who was he trying to convince? "It won't hurt to do some research, check out the guy's routine. And if I'm not feeling it—"

"You think it's that easy?" said Jarrod. "How do you know he won't have *you* bumped off?"

"We have a connection."

"Yeah," Clyde muttered. "You're both mental."

Johnny narrowed his eyes at Clyde. "Last time I checked, *President* was inked on my arm, not yours."

Rafael put up both hands. "C'mon, guys, don't do this. If Johnny wants to look into it, we'll look into it."

"Rafi's right," said Tito. "It's his call, and we will stand with him."

CHAPTER THIRTY-EIGHT

By the second week of December, the Dogs of War had compiled all the information they could on Gregory Chandler. Johnny held a meeting in his apartment to go over the details.

"He's most predictable on weekdays," said Chico.

Mario checked his notes. "He lives alone in Astoria, on Twenty-Eighth Street, by Twenty-First Avenue. A small house, wedged between a bunch of lookalikes. Leaves for work seven thirty, seven forty-five, walks to the Ditmars Boulevard train station and takes the N to Forty-Ninth Street in Manhattan."

"Most mornings, he stops at a diner," said Maurice, "grabs coffee and a bagel before heading to the eighth floor of a building on Forty-Seventh and Sixth."

"Vanguard Securities does investment banking," said Chico. "Whatever the fuck that is."

"But you'll never get him near work," added Eric. "Way too crowded. His neighborhood is your better bet."

"What time does he get home?" Johnny asked.

"Between five-thirty and six," said Rafael. "If he goes straight there, but half the time he has drinks with colleagues near work, and that can turn into dinner. A few times he met up with some blonde and spent the night at her place on the Upper East Side."

"What's his street like?"

"Residential," said Joe. "Busy in the morning. By dark, it's quieter, but rarely deserted, unless it's very late."

"A car would be pretty visible," said Jarrod. "If you're planning a drive-by."

"Either way," said Chico. "I don't think you can pop him with no witnesses."

Johnny looked around at his crew, alert and excited to have a common task. They worked well together. That was proven with Dos Cruces. And despite Jarrod's initial hesitation, he had also jumped on board. It was only Clyde who sat slumped in the corner of the couch.

Johnny told himself they were just looking into things. Tracking the guy merely as an exercise. Nobody was getting smoked, bumped off, taken out. Or any other term that diluted the gravity of *murdered*. At this rate, it seemed undoable anyway. Surely, he could convey that to Marco, explain how he had tried everything but just couldn't pull it off. If he survived Orlando, he ought to be able to get out of this.

JJ's voice broke Johnny's thought. "There's an abandoned house a block from his."

"Say what?"

"It's across the street from where Chandler walks to the train. You could get a decent shot from the window."

Johnny scratched his chin. "Isn't it sealed up? I'd have to break in."

"Already done." JJ grinned. "Tito drove me and Benji there last night with a prybar. The back door popped like a cherry."

Mario coughed out a laugh. "Like *you'd* know."

"I got *charisma*."

"Your tiny ass can't spell charisma."

"Hey!" Johnny snapped his fingers to shut them up. "Did anyone see you?"

"Nope," said Benji. "Not that we could tell."

"How is it inside?"

"Empty, cold. Everything's shut off."

"You could slip in late at night, like we did," said JJ, "hang out till he leaves for work."

Johnny bit his lip. "But if I can't get a clean shot, I'd be stuck there all day waiting for him to come home, or risk blowing the only cover."

"That's a lot of waiting," said Jarrod. "Sitting there alone..."

Johnny looked at him, then Clyde. "I won't be alone. You two will be with me."

Clyde sat up. "Huh?"

Fuck." Jarrod punched the air. "Me and my big mouth."

◇◇◇

At two a.m. the following Monday, Johnny packed sandwiches, snacks and drinks into a duffel bag along with a sniper rifle, silencer, and a couple of .38s. Just in case. Clyde and Jarrod, who looked dressed for the Arctic, met him outside where Joe was idling in his Dodge Dart. Rarely did they have the luxury of such light traffic and zipped across town in silence.

"Listen," Clyde said, once they hit the FDR. "I wanna be clear about something."

Johnny turned from his position up front.

"I'm in this, Johnny. I stand behind you and the Dogs of War one hundred percent. So don't think my concern for your mental health, and general safety for that matter, are a sign of disrespect. Or weakness." He puffed out a breath. "You're the president, but I *am* third in command, so you could make more room for me at the table when it comes to the big shit." Clyde paused to allow a reply but changed his mind. "And don't tell me we're doing this for money, because getting that loft was more than we could've dreamed of. If we never commit another crime, it'll be enough." His head tipped toward his lap. "At least for me, anyway."

Johnny set his chin on the backrest. "I get it. And you're right." He watched Clyde pick at the zipper of his parka. "About all of it. You're the voice of reason, and I want your perspective. I'd never compromise that. But I'm backed against a wall here with Marco. I have to at least give the appearance that I made every effort to do this. Because who knows how far his reach is."

"If he's that powerful, I'm sure he's got access to a more qualified assassin."

"I'm questioning the same thing." The sound of the tires hollowed out as Joe drove onto the Queensboro Bridge, and Johnny gazed out the window. "Is he a legit kingpin who saw something in me and wants to give me a leg up, or just some has-been who's so coked-up no one will work with him anymore?"

"According to my uncle," said Joe, "it's the latter."

Johnny turned to face front. "Either way, his instability is the only thing I'm clear about."

"Yeah," said Clyde. "Exactly why you need to get his hooks out of you."

"Wait," said Jarrod. "So you're not gonna actually kill this guy?"

"I don't know." Johnny bit his lip. "But if not, at least I'll be able to honestly say that I tried. Maybe then he'll stop throwing this kinda shit at me."

Once in Astoria, Joe circled around so Johnny could get a feel for the neighborhood. It was charming. Low-rise apartment buildings compressed against single family homes, some with garages or walled-in yards. And there were more trees, giving it a suburban slant.

Joe pointed out Chandler's house and the vacant one, showed which streets led to the train station, in addition to alleys and cut throughs. A few interior lights were on but no one was stirring. He pulled up to a curb on Ditmars Boulevard, which still had some through traffic. "You should get out here and walk in. Less conspicuous."

"No doubt." Johnny picked up the bag between his feet. Cold air rushed in the opened door. "And don't drive around all night either. That'll also be too obvious."

"You want to put a few shifts on foot, so we'll know what's what?"

"No. If anything is going down today, I don't want our boys involved."

"Great." Jarrod looked at Clyde. "That means we get to go home."

"Nice try." Johnny slid out of the car, then ducked to look at Joe. "Post someone near his office. If he shows up, you'll know I didn't get the shot, and that we'll be waiting for him to come home."

"You got it." Joe stuck out a hand for the gang shake all around. "Good luck."

The Dog brothers skulked down side streets to the vacant house. It was a small brick two-story, partially illuminated by a distant streetlight. They could see a few broken steps below a weathered front door. They ducked behind a row of hedges clinging to life by the sidewalk and listened for activity. All that could be heard was the distant hum of traffic. New York's unimaginative soundtrack.

Crouching down, they scurried single file over cracked, uneven squares of cement leading to the right side of the house. Johnny flattened against the wall. He pulled open a screen door, not much more than a twisted aluminum frame. It creaked louder than expected, and they all froze. When nothing happened, Clyde reached out to steady it. Johnny saw where the lock of the wooden door had been jimmied. He grabbed the knob and turned. It stuck but came open with a shoulder bump. They all slinked inside, gently pulling both doors closed behind them.

The house smelled of mold and pet urine. Gusts of wind rattled its emptiness. Johnny groped his way to the kitchen, where light from the street illuminated a counter under a row of windows. Blinds hung askew, only half their slats intact. He unlocked a window and opened it partway. He took out the rifle and tried lining up the sights from different positions.

Clyde and Jarrod each grabbed a handgun before checking upstairs. The house creaked with every footstep. "Nothing but a whole bunch of nothing," Jarrod reported upon returning. He searched his pockets for a Bic lighter to guide them down the rickety basement steps. They returned brushing cobwebs off their hoods.

"Tiny down there," said Clyde. "Just a boiler, but the floors are dirt. Good pee spot." He walked over to Johnny. "Did you figure it out?"

"He's gonna pass from left to right, but on the opposite sidewalk. I should be able to get a clear shot between those parked cars. But if I miss, the bullet could go through someone's house."

"I guess you better not shoot then."

Johnny shut the window and pushed off the counter.

"What do we do now?" asked Jarrod.

"We wait." Johnny leaned the rifle against the cabinets and sat on the bare kitchen floor. Jarrod and Clyde huddled beside him. "You know not to touch anything, right?"

Jarrod rubbed his gloved hands together. "You couldn't pay me to take these off."

The three brothers leaned against each other for warmth, drifting in and out of a semi-sleep. When the neighborhood began to come alive at dawn, they stretched and spread out to peek from various windows. House lights were popping on. Cars could be heard starting, along with the occasional clopping of heels on the sidewalk.

"What time is it?" Johnny cracked open the window.

"Seven-twenty," said Clyde.

He stuck the rifle's muzzle through the opening. Jarrod and Clyde picked vantage points from the living room which provided a broader view.

A woman walking a Weimaraner stopped in front of the yard. The dog lifted its leg on a bush. It must have caught a scent because it began barking at the vacant house, lunging from the end of the leash. The three boys tensed up but didn't dare move. The woman surveyed the building for a moment, then tightened her coat and yanked the dog back. It refocused on a new spot to mark.

"Seven-forty-one," said Clyde after several minutes. "Just FYI."

Johnny circled his neck muscles and took a breath, then repositioned.

"There," said Jarrod. "Tan coat, briefcase."

Johnny slid his sights to the far end of the block. Gregory Chandler appeared in the crosshairs. He was at the corner, looking both ways, bracing against the wind. A black scarf was wrapped around his neck and tucked into his three-quarter length wool coat. Chandler stepped from the curb and took off at a good clip, but Johnny held steady, tracing his path.

"Hold up," said Clyde. "A truck's coming."

Johnny used the opportunity to blink. After a mid-sized freightliner rattled by, Chandler returned to view. A woman was several paces behind him, a man a quarter block ahead. Johnny realigned his target.

"It's clear here," said Clyde.

"Here, too," said Jarrod.

Johnny's index finger rested on the trigger. A pair of grade-schoolers exited the house in front of Chandler. They were too bundled up to see him, and he had to stop short to avoid tripping over the smaller one. At the same moment, three teens with backpacks bounded out of the house abutting the vacant one. They were yelling and play-fighting as they cut through the yard right in front of Johnny's sights before merging with the pedestrians.

Johnny tipped up the gun. "Fuck."

"It was a good call," said Clyde. "You can try again on the way home."

Jarrod sighed. "We gotta sit in this shithole another ten hours?"

Johnny resumed his position on the floor. "Just think of all this quality time we're getting."

"Quality time freezing our balls off." He hunkered beside Johnny and Clyde. "What do you think we're missing in school today?"

"Shit. Jessica." Johnny tipped his head against the cabinet. "I better make an excuse for why I'm not there."

"The old ball and chain." Jarrod chuckled. "At least I don't have to worry about that shit anymore."

"Right," said Clyde. "Mr. Bachelor over here. How many girls have you fucked in that janitor's closet since breaking up with Michelle?"

Jarrod eyed the ceiling. "Eight, nine?"

"Liar."

"Am not."

"I hope you're dousing your dick in the bleach afterwards."

"You know how many girls will spread for the ink on our arms?" Jarrod leaned forward to better address Clyde and Johnny. "Just wait until Temper takes off. Then we'll be in a rock band *and* a gang. There'll be so much pussy, we'll be knee-deep in it."

"But Johnny won't want any," said Clyde, "because he's *in love*." He sang the last two words.

"Loving and fucking are different," said Johnny. "You can do both."

"Isn't anybody faithful anymore?" Clyde shook his head. "Look at all the married men Margaret fucks. Hell, it's probably why my father split."

"Aw." Johnny nudged him. "You're such a romantic."

Clyde brushed his hand away. "It's got nothing to do with romance. It's about honor." He smirked. "But I bet you don't know how many times *I've* gotten a piece in that closet, do ya? Four, motherfuckers. Four."

Johnny laughed. "You both got me beat."

Jarrod flicked his wrist. "That's because you don't have to get your dick sucked next to a mop bucket. You can do it in Sherry's fancy Upper West Side apartment, or a penthouse overlooking the park."

"Penthouse?" Johnny scrunched his face. "You mean Margaret's?"

Jarrod shrugged. "Yeah."

"I never fooled around with Margaret."

He snorted. "Please."

"A little kiss here and there, but it's just affectionate."

"Would you?" asked Clyde. "If you could?"

"In a heartbeat."

Jarrod shrunk back. "Really?"

"Of course."

"Even knowing all the guys she's been with?"

"Who am I to judge? Besides, she's smart, sexy, classy. And she can probably do stuff you've never imagined."

Jarrod grimaced. "Don't you think her snatch is all stretched out from taking so much dick?"

Johnny laughed. "You take a shit every day and your asshole doesn't get stretched out. I'm no fucking specialist, but why would a vagina be any different?"

"I'm pretty sure it is."

"How?"

"I don't know."

"Okay, genius." Johnny crossed his arms. "Since we've got all day, let's talk it out. What stretches a pussy, size or frequency?"

Jarrod contemplated. "Probably size."

"You think all of Margaret's clients are huge?"

He stuck out his bottom lip. "I guess not."

"Are you suggesting that if a woman fucks a guy with a big dick, even once, her pussy is stretched out forever?"

Clyde backhanded Jarrod in the arm. "You definitely don't know the answer to that question."

Jarrod shot him a look. He rethought his answer. "Maybe it is frequency."

"Okay," said Johnny. "But sometimes Jess and I have sex a few times a day, and I'm never bouncing off the walls in there. How do you explain that?"

Clyde turned to Jarrod. "I think Johnny just fucked a big giant hole in your dumbass theory."

CHAPTER THIRTY-NINE

After eating sandwiches, the brothers were able to catch some sleep in an upstairs bedroom. The wall-to-wall carpet was thin and blotchy, but a passing sunspot warmed it enough for them to shed a layer to use as a pillow.

Aside from small spurts of activity, the neighborhood was quiet in the middle of the day. It picked up again as people returned from work and school. By four-thirty, it was already getting dark. To ease the boredom, the boys took turns smoking in the pitch-black basement, where no one would spot the glow from the cigarette. By five-thirty, Jarrod and Clyde were growing more restless. They kept trading places between the kitchen and living room, spying out each of the windows. Johnny, however, was calm. This time he knelt on the counter, his back against the cabinets. The top half of the window was cracked, with the rifle's silencer resting on its rail.

"What if we missed him?" said Jarrod.

"We didn't miss him," said Clyde.

"He could've come home at lunch, when we weren't looking."

"We know sometimes he goes out after work. And that's a good thing because there'll be less traffic."

"If he takes a cab, we'll never see him."

Clyde peered through the slats of a living room window. "Are you just trying to be annoying?"

"Let's say we do miss him tonight." Jarrod folded over the kitchen sink. "Then that's it, right? We're not gonna sit here another day, are we?" He turned to Johnny. "Are we?"

Johnny didn't answer.

"Fuck."

Clyde walked over. "Fuck what?"

Jarrod nodded his head toward Johnny. In the darkness it was hard to see for sure, but his face had a familiar blank stare.

"Shit," said Clyde. "I was wondering why he was so quiet."

"He's got a gun," Jarrod mouthed. "Should we just..." He gestured toward the back door.

Clyde shook his head small and fast, then stepped closer to Johnny. "Hey man, are you, um, okay?"

No reply.

"I know you're concentrating really hard, but can you say something? One word maybe, so I know that you're all right?"

Still nothing.

Clyde checked the street. There was a lull, so he inched in front of the window to get a better view of Johnny's face. His detached expression was unmistakable. The only difference from the other times was that he seemed eerily calm. Clyde crept back out of view.

"What do we do?" Jarrod asked.

"How the fuck should I know?"

"Aren't you gonna talk to him?"

"What? Right now?" They stood paralyzed as minutes ticked by.

"He's coming." Johnny's voice sliced the silence.

Clyde and Jarrod craned out the window. Gregory Chandler was walking up the block, just like before only less hurried. Unlike the morning, there were only a few other people out.

"I thought we weren't actually doing this," said Jarrod.

"As long as it looks like we tried." Clyde glanced up at Johnny. "You said that'd be enough, right?"

Johnny was so still he had become one of the shadows. His breathing was barely perceptible. Clyde and Jarrod toggled between him and Chandler, who was passing straight across from them now. Clyde clung to Jarrod's arm as Johnny drew back his index finger, one millimeter at a time. A muffled *pop* cut through the empty house. The rifle's recoil forced Johnny's back into the cabinet.

Clyde and Jarrod gasped. They inched toward the window, leaning forward in time to see a camel-colored coat crumble to the sidewalk.

"Fuck," Jarrod whispered. "We gotta get outta here." He spun for the back door.

"No." Johnny retracted the rifle and slid off the counter. "Not yet."

Clyde flattened himself against a wall. "What do you mean not yet?"

Dogs barked from different locations. A couple rushed to Chandler. They stood over him. The woman screamed. Outside lights turned on. Neighbors swung open their doors or windows to find out what happened.

"Calm down." Johnny knelt to pack the gun into the duffel bag. He was unalarmed, methodical. "Just wait."

"He's been shot," yelled the man. "Get the fuck outta here!" He and the woman bolted around the corner. The onlookers pulled themselves back inside, slamming their doors. A passing car slowed to view the scene, then peeled off with tires screeching.

Johnny gripped the bag's handles and stood. He walked to the back door, Clyde and Jarrod close behind. Stopping short, he held up a hand. A guy emerged from the abutting house, pulling on a coat. The three teens they'd seen earlier were watching through the curtains. At the end of the walkway, he turned around, waving his arms at the kids. "Get away from the windows! Call 9-1-1!" The drapes pulled closed as he scrambled inside. Sirens blared in the distance.

Johnny lowered his hand. "Now." He yanked open the door. Crouching below hedges that divided the properties, he led his brothers out back. They stepped over a collapsed wood fence, around a cluster of garbage cans, into the yard of the house behind them. One block over, panic had yet to spread. When they hit the sidewalk, Jarrod and Clyde started to take off, but Johnny grabbed their coats. "Walk normal."

As the three teens turned onto Ditmars, a police car was barreling toward them with lights flashing, but Johnny's pace never faltered. Clyde and Jarrod struggled to do likewise. When the cruiser turned right, they crossed the boulevard and zigzagged to the train station. The last of the day's commuters were slogging down the stairs from the elevated platform. The brothers jogged up, weaving around them, then flashed their bus passes to the semi-comatose man in the booth. From the platform, more cruisers and an ambulance could be seen passing below.

The N train was already at the station preparing for the turnaround with doors open. Johnny walked in and sat at the end of a bench seat. He dropped the bag between his feet. Clyde sat next to him, then Jarrod. The car was unheated but still felt like a sauna due to the surging adrenaline. Johnny remained unaffected, perusing the graffiti with eyelids at half-mast, while Clyde and Jarrod evaluated passengers' demeanors, searching for any hint of a threat. When the doors finally shut and the train lurched into motion, they both exchanged a sigh of relief and unzipped their coats.

At each stop, more passengers trickled in. Clyde kept stealing glances at Johnny, worried that his claustrophobia would be triggered, causing him to bolt. But he didn't seem the least bit agitated. If anything, he was calmer now than he had been at the house. Jarrod, however, was bouncing his knee up and down. Clyde put a hand on it to make him stop.

At the Lexington Avenue/Fifty-Ninth Street station, the majority of passengers exited. Clyde craned over his shoulder to look out the window but nothing seemed abnormal. He took the opportunity to search Johnny's face once again.

"Stop already." Johnny said once the train was moving.

"Stop what?"

"Why do you keep staring at me?"

"I don't know." Clyde shrugged. "Your hair looks particularly nice today?"

Jarrod mouthed, *What the fuck?*

Clyde cleared his throat. "So, um, Javier, you remember us then?"

"Clyde, Jarrod." Johnny's eyes never strayed from the wall. "We covered this the last time."

Clyde cocked his head. "The last time?"

"The last time you both…" he opened his hands to the air, "… appeared."

Jarrod barked a spontaneous laugh. "What are we, *illusions*?"

Clyde shushed him. "At least he knows who we are."

A tiny crease appeared near Johnny's mouth. "It was wild, right?"

"What was wild?"

"Back there. Getting that guy."

Clyde and Jarrod checked the people half a car away. No one was paying attention, and the hollow clacking was most likely drowning out their conversation. "Are you okay with it?" Clyde asked.

"Shooting a guy?" Johnny faced them for the first time. "Yeah. I'm good with it."

Jarrod leaned forward. "It was a great shot."

Johnny grinned. "Right between the eyes."

Clyde shifted in his seat. "So, um, Javier, how did you know he was the one?"

"I just knew."

"Then you remember seeing the photograph from Marco?"

Johnny's smile faded.

"I mean, if you recognized him, you gotta remember that part, right? Do you remember his name?"

Johnny turned forward again.

Jarrod nudged Clyde. "Don't push him."

Clyde's eyes locked with Jarrod's. "If we can just get him to connect this one dot, maybe it'll carve a path back to…" he dropped to a whisper. "Lucidity."

Jarrod bit his cheek. "Be careful, man."

Clyde resumed. "So, Javier, you know where you've seen that guy before?"

Now Johnny's knees were bouncing.

"At the loft. Remember the envelope? The polaroid, the business card? I know you know his name. It starts with a G." He clutched Johnny's arm. "C'mon, think."

Johnny spun, grabbing both of Clyde's wrists. He squeezed them tight, looking at him with cold, blank eyes.

"I-I'm sorry, Javier. I didn't mean to touch you."

"He really didn't," Jarrod said, leaning over. "It won't happen again."

Johnny released his grip and Clyde and Jarrod exhaled. But then the rocking and muttering of languages began.

"Don't ask anything else," said Jarrod. "Let's just get him the fuck home."

◇◇◇

At the loft, Joe burst from his ground floor apartment. "What happened? How'd it go?"

"It's done," said Clyde. "But he's flipped."

Johnny brushed by, climbing the stairs to his apartment.

"I'll keep an eye on him," Jarrod said to Clyde. "Go tell the others, then grab a hot shower and some food."

"I'm coming with you," Joe said to Jarrod as they started upstairs. "In case he tries to make another run for it."

In the apartment, Johnny dropped the duffel bag and shook off his coat. The muttering continued as he paced the length of the loft. From the back wall of his bedroom, through the long open living room, into the alcove kitchen and back again. Occasionally a layer of clothing would get peeled off mid-lap and dropped to the floor.

Joe centered a chair over the apartment's threshold and sat down. Now almost twenty, he'd maxed out at 6'3". His chiseled frame filled the space between the moldings.

Jarrod stripped down to his jeans and T-shirt, then grabbed a beer from the refrigerator. He kicked back on the couch to light a cigarette. "Hey Javier, I'm gonna tell Joey about our day, okay?" He stuffed a throw pillow behind his head as Johnny walked past. "Feel free to jump in any time."

Johnny offered no reaction.

"He was pretty chatty on the way home." Jarrod took a long pull off his beer. "Even more than the last time." Johnny emerged from the bedroom. "Hey Javier, is that one of those nursery rhymes you're reciting?"

"From my mother's books."

Jarrod shrugged at Joe, then continued. "Right. Your mother. What was her name again?"

At the kitchen, Johnny turned around. "Aylin."

"Yeah. That's it." Jarrod dragged from his Marlboro. "So, can I ask why you're walking back and forth like that?"

"It takes the edge off."

"No edges around here, my man. Just smooth surfaces." Jarrod jutted his chin toward the door. "You see Joey over there? No one's getting by him, so you can relax."

"That's right, brother," said Joe. "Me and everyone in this house will protect you."

Johnny stopped walking. "You can't protect me."

"Sure, we can." Joe stood up. "Whoever you imagine is coming for you will get the living shit kicked out of them."

Johnny turned, his inanimate eyes looking more through Joe than at him. "But *you're* the ones I'm imagining." He resumed pacing.

Jarrod's jaw clamped tight as he stuffed his butt into the ashtray. "Joey, I'm gonna smack this motherfucker so hard he'll *know* I'm real."

Rafael and Patrick appeared. Patrick carried a plate with pot roast, potatoes and carrots. The succulent smell filled the apartment. Joe scooted over to let them in.

"We're here to take over so you can get dinner," Patrick said to Jarrod. "Chico reheated everything for you guys."

"Great, I'm starving." Jarrod began collecting his things.

Patrick set the plate on the kitchen counter. As Johnny walked by, he pinched a potato and popped it in his mouth.

Jarrod waited to let Johnny pass by. "Bet that food doesn't taste so fucking *imaginary*, does it?"

Rafael scrunched his nose at Joe. "Huh?"

Joe wagged his head. "I'll explain later."

CHAPTER FORTY

Johnny unburied his face from the pillow and rolled onto his back. The light streaming through the open blinds suggested it was late morning. His pounding head suggested a batshit crazy hangover. He was hot and peeled back the blanket. His jeans were still on, one cuff bunched around his calf, a wool sock half off. His fingers brushed the waffle knit of his thermal Henley. No wonder he was warm. But why was he so overdressed?

"Fuck."

The image hit him. Kneeling on the counter of that cold, vacant house, the rifle in hand. The frustration, the waiting. His muscles sore from holding one position. Eyes twitching from staring into the sights for so long. Then nothing.

"Double fuck." He scrambled to the living room.

"Whoa, easy," Joe looked up. "You all right?" He was on the couch, his textbooks spread over the coffee table.

"No." Johnny put a hand on the wall to steady himself. "Where is everybody?"

"The usual. School, work."

"Even Clyde and Jarrod?"

"They thought it best to keep up appearances."

"What the fuck happened?"

Joe put down his pencil and leaned back.

"That bad, huh?" Johnny sat on the sofa across from him. "Did I pull a bunch of crazy shit again?"

"The opposite. Clyde and Jarrod said you were calm and collected, took charge of the whole situation."

"So, I never shot him?"

"Oh no," Joe's head bobbled. "You shot him."

"Jesus." Johnny clawed at his hair. "Is he dead?"

"Mm-hmm."

"What are they saying on the news?"

"Witnesses saw a car speed off. Otherwise, not much else has been reported." Joe twitched a shoulder. "It wasn't even the top story last night. Some chick getting shoved in front of the A train was. Chandler was like fifth. Today's papers didn't say much more, but I'm sure they're investigating."

"Did they name him?"

"Yeah."

"Then at least Marco will know." Johnny massaged his neck. "Has he called?"

"No, but Jessica has. Twice. I told her you pulled a back muscle moving shit for your uncle, and that you were sleeping."

"Thanks. I can't deal with her right now." Johnny exhaled. "What happened after?"

Joe repeated what Jarrod had told him. "It was actually a pretty mild episode. And you were sociable."

"Great." Johnny rolled his eyes. "What was I saying?"

"Stuff about your mom and those nursery rhymes," Joe stifled a smirk, "and how you think we're your imaginary friends."

"Are you fucking kidding me?" Johnny stood and stormed toward his bedroom. "I'm taking a shower."

"Hey," Joe called behind him. "When you're done, come with me to the Bronx. Tito's gonna do an oil change on the Monte Carlo, check that squeaky fan belt. It'll take your mind off this shit."

The long hot shower helped a little, but the anger burning in Johnny's stomach wouldn't surrender quite so easily. The hunger pangs weren't helping. He threw on fresh clothes and left his room. Joe had returned to his own apartment, so he climbed a flight to the Mess Hall. It was usually a common hangout spot, but at this hour it was empty. Johnny peeled back the tin foil covering a platter in the fridge. It was a hunk of leftover pot roast surrounded by cut potatoes and carrots. He set it on the counter. Stuffing a potato in his mouth, he reached for a knife. A strong wave of déjà vu passed through him and he paused. He shook off the thought and hacked off some meat for a sandwich.

Johnny sat on a stool at the island to eat. Fuck these episodes. After the last one, and the revelation that he might actually have been their architect, he thought they would stop. Now, instead of coming to with some deranged memory, he was holding chat sessions with his crew of imaginary friends. *Really?*

As he chewed, his eyes swept the spacious loft. The handmade furniture mixed with stuff from the street. Bedrooms Chico, Mario and Ramón had framed and sheet rocked for themselves with Horatio's help. The industrial grade appliances that now furnished the kitchen to accommodate house meals. Maybe Clyde was right. Maybe it was enough. They could afford the building's upkeep with straight jobs, so why this need to bank cash through illegal means? For what? And how was getting tangled up with lunatic criminals helping?

Fucking Marco. Whatever this draw, this urge to impress a man so unpredictable, so lethal, it had to stop. Johnny would just tell him he was done. But when? It wasn't like he had Marco's number. The guy only called from payphones. Would he have to sit around and wait until the next time he was summoned in order to end this? It made him feel trapped.

There it was again. That old familiar pattern. Johnny had already acknowledged that Marco tripped these emotional wires, so why was he still drawn to him? Even after everything that just happened, this fierce attraction remained. Like walking away would mean leaving part of himself behind.

"Fuck this." He dumped the remains of his sandwich in the trash and jogged downstairs to meet Joe.

◇◇◇

Joe parked the Monte Carlo, and he and Johnny walked into the garage. Jorge was in the office on the phone but gave them a nod.

Julio set down a parts catalogue. "Cousin Tito said someone was coming by, but I wasn't expecting the big boss." He offered a hand to Johnny, then Joe. "How've you been, man?"

"Great." Johnny forced his face to match the lie.

"Your boy's just finishing something, but you know your way around."

"Thanks." Johnny and Joe walked into the bay.

Tito was beneath a battered Mercury Cyclone. Its front tire had been removed and he was pounding out a dent in the fender. Johnny put a hand on the hood. "What happened to this poor thing?"

"The owner needs driving lessons." Tito rolled out on the creeper and stood. "You okay?"

Johnny's jaw clenched. "As okay as I can be."

Tito stuck out his bottom lip. "Don't be so hard on yourself. There are positive signs, like how you're talking to us now. It means you're not drifting as far as you used to."

"*Drifting*." Johnny expelled a disgruntled laugh. "It's still bullshit."

"And you remembered the task. Don't you think that's good?"

"But I didn't want to do it. I shouldn't have." Johnny pushed off the Mercury. "Look, I came here to forget about this shit."

Joe gave Tito a nod. "Want me to pull the car in?"

"Sure." He pushed a button to raise the overhead door, then guided Joe inside.

Johnny saw that Jorge and Julio were in the street now, standing in front of a GTO with its hood up. Johnny didn't pay them much mind until the bay door started to close and the car's owner ducked under it. "We have to stop meeting like this."

Johnny's pulse throbbed behind his eyes and ears. It was César Aguilar. The last motherfucker he needed to deal with right now. He swallowed hard and extended a hand. "You must own stock in this place. You're here enough."

"Tell me about it." César clasped Johnny's hand. "Damn car is more trouble than it's worth, but I can't bring myself to part with her." He tipped his head at Tito and Joe, who did likewise before stepping away to give the

two gang leaders some space. They popped the Chevy's hood and began poking around the fan belt.

César's eyes slanted. "So, little dog, I heard about some shit that went down in the park with one of my new recruits."

"Hector Sarno."

"Yeah."

"I didn't start that."

"That's what I figured." César rolled his eyes. "Because I got nine different versions of what happened."

"And our shit with him goes back," said Johnny. "Before he was with you."

"I get it." César turned up his palms. "But you're putting me in a tight position. I'm *trying* to keep the peace here, but if you keep punking my boys, whether they deserve it or not, there isn't a lot I can do."

"They disrespected our truce."

César chuckled into his chest. "It's funny. You don't want to join Dos Cruces, but here you are, doing my bidding by weeding out all the bad seeds."

Even though Johnny hadn't had much choice in any of those incidents, hearing it from that perspective annoyed him more than he already was. He punted an errant lug nut across the floor.

"You ought to just make it official," César continued. "With skills like yours, I'll promote you quick."

This guy was like a broken fucking record. "So, what'd you do to him?"

"Hector?" César sucked his cheek. "I gave him the boot."

"The *boot*?" Johnny felt his face ignite.

"His pops is five-O. I don't need that kind of heat." César shrugged. "Besides, he's gotta go through life with that scar you put on him. It tells the world he's a snitch and a liar who crossed the wrong people."

"But he's wearing *your* ink."

"Nah, we covered that shit up."

"And the other guys?"

"Your boys smacked them around pretty good. I thought it was enough."

273

"Wow." Johnny tipped his head to the ceiling. "I guess that's the difference between you and me. And why your crew doesn't listen."

César stepped up to Johnny. "You gonna tell *me* how to run shit? I got hundreds in my army, and they're managing a fucking enterprise. Dos Cruces distributes product throughout the Tri-State area, while you got what?" His head swiveled around the garage. "One guy wrenching on cars? Another competing for Mr. Atlas?"

Joe and Tito stepped out to wait for a cue.

"You got no goddam idea what I do." Johnny hissed. *I'm killing motherfuckers when I'm not even conscious.* "Besides, what good are the numbers if they don't respect you. Maybe you should spend more time on the street and less time fucking that wife of yours." The last sentence slipped out before he could stop it. Even Joe and Tito winced.

"Mm-hmm." César took a step back. "I see how it is."

"Look, I shouldn't have said—"

"Too late, *muchacho*." César's lips tightened. "You got balls, that's for sure. But lemme give you some advice, and *only* because you remind me of my little brother." He closed the gap between them. "When you're looking at the big picture, it's best not to waste time on the small stuff." He emphasized the last two words by poking Johnny's chest, and Johnny let him because he knew he had crossed a line. "One day, when you're running a *real* gang, you'll understand."

Jorge returned to the garage and waved César into the office to make an appointment.

"You *do* remember what happened to my little brother, right?" César said before leaving.

Johnny nodded. "He got killed."

"Over nothing." His eyes locked on Johnny's. "Over small stuff."

Johnny held his gaze, struggling to think of a way to apologize that didn't sound insincere. "I hope they can fix your car," was all he came up with.

"Yeah." César laughed, turning away. "Me, too."

CHAPTER FORTY-ONE

Johnny and his crew watched the TV news and combed through local papers, but only one article surfaced about Gregory Chandler. It painted him as quite the swindler. He and a few others at the firm had been skimming money off clients for years. There was no shortage of suspects, all of whom would have been happy to see him dead. He also had an affinity for cocaine. Between his home and office, cops recovered more than an ounce of the stuff.

Given that the other guy Marco had whacked was also in banking, some brothers joked that it would be safer for everyone if he just kept his money in a mattress.

Johnny remained buried in a cavalcade of emotions. The pulled back muscle story Joe had fed Jessica seemed to be working, so he milked it another day. He needed more time to process shit. To concoct a strategy for living with himself. Johnny spent much of the day in bed, staring at the ceiling, taking breaks to lift weights, eat, or just wander around the loft, tackling each issue as it swirled by.

It was hard to know where he stood with César. Had his big mouth just blown their truce? Surely César wouldn't let one snide comment offend him bad enough for that. He did, after all, seem to espouse the don't-sweat-the-small-stuff motto.

Still, it was a stupid gaff, and one that never would have happened had it not been for those fucking episodes. And Gregory Chandler would still be alive. That Johnny was capable of murder while flipped was jarring.

But was it? Really? Apparently, he had no problem stabbing a guy during a blackout or almost throwing himself off a roof. And, for all he knew, he might have killed Orlando. The very last time Johnny had come to in that cellar, his brother was face down, blood pooling on the floor under his head, a piece of chain nearby. He had been too scared to check if Orlando was breathing, so he waited at the top of the stairs until his mother released him. Then, in the middle of the night, he left that house for good, never finding out what happened. Of all the lost memories, smacking Orlando across the head was the one he would love to recover the most.

The only upside to his abominable childhood was that it taught him discipline. It took discipline to endure brutality, to keep the family secrets, to get out of bed and face that insanity, day after day, just waiting for an opportunity to escape. It was a practice Johnny carried to this day. Discipline served him, in work and school, and helped him to acquire everything surrounding him.

And he would implement it now. To live with what he had done.

◇◇◇

Though Johnny had no sentimentality for holidays, Christmas offered a pleasant distraction. Some Dog brothers were more enthusiastic than others about decorating their spaces. They put up trees or hung wreaths and lights. There was also an unofficial Christmas cookie bake-off, where each day one resident would try to top the others with their recipe. Half the time it ended with a sheet pan full of hockey pucks, but the sugary aroma from the oven, mixed with evergreen, wafted throughout the building, lifting one's mood whether they liked it or not.

After spending Christmas morning with her family, Jessica came by so she and Johnny could exchange gifts in the privacy of his room. They sat cross-legged on the bed.

Johnny peeled the festive paper off a box. "What's this?"

Jessica beamed. "It's a Wah pedal. For your guitar."

"I can see that, but how did you know to get one?"

"I asked Clyde and Jarrod. Don't you like it?"

He examined the packaging. "I love it, but you shouldn't have spent so much money."

"Please. I was happy to get something you really wanted."

"Well, you did." He leaned over for a kiss. Then he handed her his present. She unwrapped it carefully to savor the moment. Inside was a black jewelry box, adorned with birds and flowers, made from Mother of Pearl. When she lifted the lid, it played the theme to *Love Story.* A pair of earrings matching her necklace lay atop the red velvet liner.

"Oh my god. These are so beautiful." She held them up. "Are they from the same store?"

Johnny nodded.

"I love it." She checked the box for more surprises, pulling out each drawer while the rotating metal comb plinked out its melody. In the bottom compartment she saw a tiny piece of paper that looked like a manufacturing label. Then she noticed the handwriting. It was so small she had to squint.

Jessica, you've opened my heart in ways I never thought possible. For that I will always love you. — Johnny.

Her eyes welled up. "This is—I don't even know what to say." She set the gifts aside and pushed him down onto the bed.

◇◇◇

Piles of filthy snow flanked the sidewalks. In heavily trafficked parts, it had compressed into the concrete. The only thing making it less slippery was the ground-in dirt. Johnny leaned on a car in front of Roosevelt, puffing on a Marlboro. A handful of Dog brothers stood around him. Some bobbed up and down to keep warm. As Jessica approached, he flicked his butt into the gutter. "It's cold, baby. Gimme some heat." He wrapped his arms around her.

She pressed into him. "I didn't think you'd still be here."

"Believe me, if the others don't show soon, we're leaving without them." He slid his hands in her coat pockets. "You wanna come over?"

"I got a shitload of homework."

He bit his lip. "Just for a little while?"

"You know how that plays out." She pulled his collar closed. "I'll stay too long and never get anything done."

"Hey Johnny, how's it going?" Jessica's brother was standing beside them. He wore an electric blue down jacket, with a striped woolen beanie, complete with pom-pom, pulled to his eyebrows. He held out his mittened hand stiffly, like he was begging for spare change.

Johnny glanced down at him, then realized he was waiting to be slapped five. Johnny gave him a nod instead. Chad retracted his arm to wave at the Dog brothers by the curb. None of them noticed.

"What do you want?" Jessica hissed.

"We catching the bus together?"

"No." She pulled away from Johnny to cross her arms. "Never. And don't speak to me again, you little shit."

Johnny winced into his chest.

"You and your big mouth can just leave me the fuck alone."

"Jeez." Chad rolled his eyes at Johnny. "She must be on the rag."

"Come here you dorky asshole!" Jessica lunged at him, but Johnny held her back. Chad turned to march away, an untied shoelace flitting in the slush.

"Wow." Johnny stood slack-jawed. "What was that about?"

Jessica's fists clenched. "I didn't want to say anything to you, but I'm so fucking mad at him."

"Apparently." Johnny lay hands on her shoulders. "What happened?"

She took a deep breath. "You know he thinks you're the coolest, right?"

Johnny shrugged.

"Ever since he transferred, he sees you hanging with your boys. He hears the rumors, and knows no one will fuck with you. The only reason he isn't getting his ass kicked like all the other freshmen is because he keeps bragging about how his sister is your girlfriend."

"Can you blame him?"

"Yes, I can." Her eyes narrowed. "Last night he told my parents that you're in a gang."

Johnny's head tipped back. "Fuck."

"Yes. Fuck." Jessica fought back tears. "My father went ballistic. He's insisting we end our relationship. He threatened to get the cops involved if I don't."

"Of course he did."

"I'm hoping if we just chill out for a few weeks, things will blow over. And I'll talk to my mom. Maybe she can get him to relax."

"And if not?"

"I'm seventeen for Christ's sake. What can they really do?"

Johnny looked at the ground. They could make her nice, normal life miserable. Disown her, possibly. And then what? No way he could let her move into the loft. He had enough money to rent her an apartment. But realistically, how much time would he stay there with her because he wasn't leaving his gang.

Everything in Johnny's life had been ramping up so fast lately, and growing more dangerous. Including him. It was selfish to keep putting Jessica at risk.

Johnny put his arms around her. "You're right, baby." He swallowed the lump in his throat. "Just give Walter a little time. He'll realize that Chad is full of shit."

CHAPTER FORTY-TWO

Johnny was struggling to concentrate on his homework when the front door buzzed. Thinking it might be Marco, he bounded downstairs. Through the peephole, he saw Freddy's face haloed by the fuzzy hood of a parka. Johnny opened the door. "Sup, man, what brings you here?"

"Sorry for coming by like this, but I didn't have your number." His eyes bounced on everything except Johnny. "I wasn't even sure I'd find you."

"You all right?"

Freddy rubbed his forehead. "Yeah—I mean, I'm not sure."

Johnny opened the door wider. "Come in."

Freddy entered the foyer and pushed back his hood. "Look, I don't know if I'm doing the right thing by coming here, but Jessica talks to me."

Johnny's stomach dropped. "What is it?"

"Have you spoken to her?"

"I saw her at school a few hours ago. Said she was going home."

"She was later than usual." He pulled off his gloves. "And she didn't look good."

"Didn't look good how?"

"She was crying. Like someone hurt her."

"Hurt her how?" Johnny struggled to measure the surge of emotions. "Like, beat her up?"

"No. I mean, I don't know. And when I asked if she was okay, she ran into the elevator."

"Then what?"

"It was shift-change, but I stuck around because I was concerned."

"And?"

"A while later, an ambulance came." He lowered his head. "They took her."

"A fucking ambulance?" Johnny smacked the wall with his palm before he could stop it. Some ground floor residents appeared from their units.

"I know I'm taking a liberty," Freddy continued. "But you and I have hit it off from the get-go." His eyes passed over Johnny's brothers standing in their doorways. "And I respect what you got going on here."

"Where would they take her?"

"The closest hospital is on First Avenue."

"Were her parents there?"

"Yeah. They rode with her."

Johnny folded forward to take some deep breaths. Why hadn't he walked her to the bus stop? Or better yet, to her building. He could've at least given her cab fare.

"What do you want to do?" asked Rafael.

Johnny straightened. "I need to see her."

"If she was mugged, you can't just rush in," said Joe. "The cops will be there."

"Mugged?" Johnny stepped within inches of Freddy's face. "You're not implying she got *mugged* are you. You think it was something worse."

Freddy put up his hands and took a step back. "Johnny, man, I don't know shit. I'm just telling you what—"

"But you were there. You caught a vibe."

"Yeah." Freddy blinked back tears. "And it wasn't good."

Jarrod was coming down the stairwell with more brothers. "Whatever happened, Joe's right. There'll be cops."

"And you're already on her parents' shit list," said Mario. "Thanks to her turd of a brother."

Johnny's teeth gritted. "Whoever hurt her, I'll fucking kill them."

"Don't think the worst," said Clyde. "All we know is that she went to the hospital. Let's just stick with that before we jump to conclusions."

"Good advice," said Joe. "And if you want to see her, we'll need a plan."

Freddy nodded. "What can I do to help?"

"Let's swap numbers, keep each other posted." Johnny lay a hand on Freddy's shoulder. "You did the right thing bringing me this. I won't forget it."

◇◇◇

The van double-parked a block from the hospital's entrance. Johnny leaned forward to address Joe and Mario up front. "I don't know how long we'll be."

"Don't sweat it," said Mario.

"Yeah," said Joe. "We'll be circling around here somewhere."

Johnny slipped out with Clyde and Jarrod. Leon and JJ fell in behind them. When they entered the lobby, it was too bright. The benches in the waiting area were nearly full, and the semicircular front desk was bustling. Johnny kept his eyes peeled for the Baxters as they drifted down a hall to a gift shop, where it was quieter.

"See what you can find out," Jarrod said to JJ and Leon, who were chosen for their demure, boyish looks. "We'll stay here." He steered Johnny and Clyde into the shop.

Johnny read the entire greeting card selection twice before Leon returned alone. They rushed to meet him in the hallway. "Anything?"

"Based on your descriptions— Mom: strawberry hair, pale as a sheet. Dad: a constipated Clark Kent—they were arguing in front of a room on the third floor, but the door was closed."

"What were they saying?"

"They were too quiet, and I was trying to be discreet. But JJ?" A twinkle appeared in Leon's eye. "He marched straight into the room next door."

Jarrod smiled. "'Atta boy."

"After the Baxters went back inside, he came out. Said there's some old geezer in there. JJ claimed to be his grandson and he didn't know the difference. Apparently, he's so out of it that JJ can listen through the wall without him noticing."

"How'd you get by the front desk?" asked Clyde.

"We blew right by. But if we get stopped, the old guy is Conrad Fishbourne in 321."

"Were there any cops?" asked Johnny.

"No." Leon gestured for them to follow him. "But that doesn't mean they're not coming."

They weaved around gurneys, visitors, and medical staff, until they came to a stairwell. On the third-floor landing, Leon put up a hand. "Hang here. When it's clear, I'll come get you."

Johnny sat on a step and folded forward. He was filled with rage, but it was paralyzed by fear. It felt more familiar than he cared to acknowledge. He pressed his eyes closed, swaying back and forth to alleviate tension.

Jarrod put a hand on Johnny's shoulder. "Don't do that. It scares me."

"It might not be as bad as you think," said Clyde.

Johnny looked up. "Then why is my gut saying it's exactly that bad."

The three waited in silence. When the stairwell door finally opened, they lurched.

It was JJ. "C'mon, it's clear."

"How long for?" asked Clyde.

"Not sure. A nurse said it'd be at least an hour before they can do an exam, so Mom ran home to check on the brother, and Pops is going to some restaurant."

Jarrod's head cocked. "You heard all that?"

JJ laughed. "You know that shit about putting a glass to the wall, like you see on The Three Stooges? It really works."

Clyde ruffled JJ's hair. "Only you, man."

JJ led them down the hall and around a corner. "This is it." He stopped. "Leon's watching the elevators, but I'll stay here and whistle if anyone's coming."

Clyde and Jarrod gave a tight-lipped smile to Johnny before he cracked the door. The room was small, bisected by a half-drawn curtain, a bed by the far wall. Jessica's auburn hair was unmistakable, splayed over a blanket pulled up to her neck. Her body was curled in a ball with her back turned, but he could hear her quiet sniffles. Johnny tried to vacate any preconceived notions as he crept closer.

"Baby? You all right?"

"Johnny?" She turned and sat up. Her face was puffy and pale. "What are you doing here?"

"If you'd rather be alone, I'll go."

"No." Her arms opened. "Don't leave me."

As Johnny sat beside Jessica, she began sobbing convulsively. He cradled her, rocking and kissing her head until she calmed. "How'd you know I was here?" she asked, pulling back.

"Freddy." His thumb brushed some tears from her cheek. "I've been waiting for your parents to leave."

"They're driving me nuts." She rolled her bloodshot eyes. "They won't stop hovering, and they keep berating the nurses. I insisted they give me a break."

"How'd you pull that off?"

"I told them I needed fresh clothes, and that I was craving a cheeseburger. But it had to be from my favorite diner, like five blocks from here." She offered a weak smile. "They couldn't argue. But they're freaking out. My father even made me come in an ambulance." Her head dipped. "I just feel so...numb."

Johnny scooped up Jessica's hands. "What happened, baby?"

Her tears returned and he wrapped his arms around her. She burrowed her face in his coat. "They raped me."

Her muffled words were barely comprehensible, but it didn't matter. He couldn't deny what he had heard. *They?* His heart pulsed with an urgency that dispersed the dread.

Jessica sat back to blow her nose with the stiff hospital tissues on the tray table. Johnny went to get a damp cloth and a cup of water from the bathroom. He dabbed her eyes. After taking a drink, she patted the bed for him to lie with her. He shed his coat to the floor and scooted in.

"I have to tell you what happened."

"Baby, if you don't want to—"

"Are you not *able* to hear it?"

"No. It's not that."

"Will it change the way you feel about me?"

He looked her in the eyes. "No, it won't."

"Okay, because I need to tell you."

They scooched down so she could rest her head on his chest, like they always did in Johnny's bed.

"This car pulled up to the bus stop."

"By the school?"

She nodded. "It might've followed me because it appeared just after I got there. A brown four-door, with three men inside. They made like they knew me. Said they were with the Dogs."

"What?" Johnny started to sit up.

"They weren't." She pulled him down. "I know that now." She puffed air through her cheeks. "The guy in the back seat said you'd been in an accident. That you told them to find me."

"They knew my name?"

"Yeah."

"What'd they look like?"

"The guy that spoke was older, thirty maybe, dark hair, goatee. I didn't see the driver because he had a hat and sunglasses. And he never touched me. The one next to him was early twenties, pale and thin with slicked-back hair." Her lip curled in revulsion. "He was staring at me the whole time the guy in the back was...you know." Jessica reached for more tissues. "Before they traded places and he did the same."

It took all the self-control Johnny could muster to remain reclined. He stroked her hair.

"The car drove around the whole time. When it was over, they stopped to let me out. It was on East Fifty-something, so I just walked home." She wiped her nose. "My father asked why I didn't get the license number or call for help."

She shivered and he tightened his arms around her. "But you were in shock."

"I just—I needed to go home."

"I get it." He kissed her head.

"I did see that the skinny guy had the word FATE tattooed across his knuckles. The other one had two crosses."

Johnny's insides ignited. "Where?"

"On his neck." She sat up and pointed to her sternum. "Here."

Johnny knew exactly who it was. Those motherfuckers from Central Park, in that group with Hector. Their tattoos were unforgettable. His thought got sideswiped. "Where's your necklace?"

More tears trickled from her eyes. "He yanked it off."

"Which guy?"

"The one with the crosses. He said he wanted something to remember me by."

Johnny fought to keep his tone gentle. "Don't worry, baby, I'll buy you another one."

"He said something else, too. Something I'm supposed to tell you."

"What's that?"

Jessica looked at the ceiling to make sure she repeated it exactly. "'César said to keep our hands off the Dogs, but he didn't say anything about their bitches.'"

Until that moment, Johnny didn't think it was possible to feel any worse.

"Who's César?"

Johnny peeled his tongue from the roof of his mouth. "He runs a gang called *Dos Cruces*, the Two Crosses. I don't know him well, but we've bumped up against his men a few times."

"I never should have gone with them. But when he said you were in trouble—"

Johnny lifted her chin. "Don't *ever* blame yourself. This is not your fault."

She looked down to pick at the blanket. "I didn't mention that part."

"Huh?"

"To the police. That those guys said they knew you. In case you'd get in trouble."

"You talked to the cops already?"

"When I got admitted. They took a statement, said a detective would come by to get more details after the exam. But they need a special doctor for that." She attempted a smile. "And apparently the city is having a busy rape day."

Johnny put a hand on Jessica's shoulder. "You don't have to protect me. You tell them the truth. Whatever you need to do." A tear escaped and dripped down his face. So what if they came after him? None of it mattered anymore. Let them uncover his identity, tie him to every crime he had ever committed. He deserved it.

"My father's convinced you're responsible somehow."

For once he and Walter agreed. "Don't mind him. I just want you to be okay."

They sat in silence, staring at their entwined fingers. "You're sure you didn't see the driver?" Johnny asked eventually.

"Yeah. He never turned around." She cocked her head. "Are you going after those guys?"

He didn't answer.

"No, Johnny. Let the cops handle it." She released his hands. "Please. I just want this over with."

Johnny nodded.

"Promise?"

"I promise." He kissed her.

"Will you stay until the exam?"

"Are you nuts?" He shrunk back. "Your parents won't permit that."

"But I don't want to be alone, and they're not helping."

"Jessica, I would but—" Three staccato whistles came from the hall and Johnny turned. "They're coming."

"You've got people out there?"

"Yeah."

"Please don't leave." She clutched his forearm. "This is the most normal I've felt since it happened."

Another whistle sounded, but Johnny stayed put.

"I'm back," Walter said with fabricated enthusiasm. He held up a paper bag. "Extra pickles, just like you—" He halted, glaring at Johnny. "What the hell are you doing here?"

Jessica clung tighter to Johnny. "I want him here."

Walter jabbed out a finger. "*He* is responsible for this! Him and his *gang.*"

"It wasn't his gang," Jessica snapped.

"So, he *does* have a gang."

"It's not what you think."

"If he had nothing to do with it, how did he know you were here?"

"Freddy told him."

Walter dropped the to-go bag on the tray table. "Freddy?" He planted his fists on his narrow hips. "The Puerto Rican doorman?"

"He's Dominican," Johnny muttered. He swung his feet to the floor, but kept hold of Jessica's hand.

"Freddy's part of those thugs, too?"

Jessica threw back the covers. "No. He was just concerned."

"Wait till I talk to building management." Walter grabbed Johnny around the bicep and pulled. "And you! Get the hell away from my daughter."

It was a bold move, since Johnny could have flattened Walter with a single punch. But he offered no resistance.

"Dad, no!" Jessica lunged for Johnny's hand.

Walter stepped between them. "Look what you've done. You've ruined her life. Isn't that enough for you?"

Johnny had no argument.

"I want him here."

"And will he stay when the cops come back, too?" Walter turned to Johnny. "Will you?"

Johnny fought to remain calm. "Walter, I'm not doing this with you. Not in front of your daughter." He locked eyes with Jessica. "Baby, you don't need this right now, so I'm gonna go."

Walter overdramatized a laugh. "What'd I tell you? One mention of the police and he's running away."

Johnny ignored him. "Sweetheart, if you need anything, just call. I'll be there in an instant."

Jessica scrambled around her father to embrace Johnny. "I love you."

Her tears were streaming again and Johnny cried with her. "I love you, too. That's why I'm leaving." He kissed her one last time, before grabbing his coat from the floor.

CHAPTER FORTY-THREE

In the van, Johnny only managed to run down the basics before folding forward with his head between his knees. Of all the feelings plaguing him—rage, misery, worry—the most unbearable was the helplessness. How many times had he emerged from his parents' cellar beaten, carved with a razor and whipped—drowned even. It was still easier than seeing someone he loved get hurt. For once he beckoned those memories. He deserved them. Even the darkest one. The one he refused to acknowledge in his most private moments. One that might have even given Jessica a shred of comfort and hope. That he had endured a similar assault as a child. By his own brother.

Was putting his shame above her pain selfish, or business as usual? Just another fucking lie to pile on all the others. If he had bothered pulling his head from her tits for one goddamn minute, he would have seen this coming. There had already been narrow misses, when the corrupt parts of his life oozed closer to hers. But he was too fucking arrogant, or horny, to heed the warning.

Johnny didn't need a dissociative episode to want to throw himself off a roof. The urge was as present as he was lucid. He looked out the window to interrupt the thought. They were approaching the West Side Highway. "Where are we going?"

"Home."

Johnny raked his scalp. "We should go look for those motherfuckers."

His brothers exchanged looks before Clyde wagged his head. "No. Not like this."

"Yeah," said Jarrod. "You're too emotional. We don't have the numbers and we're not armed."

"It'd be crazy," said Mario. "We don't even know where they hole up."

"And besides," Clyde continued, "your strategy has always been to be patient. To be smart and plan ahead."

Johnny rubbed his temples. "But if I don't do something I might flip."

Joe pulled over by the river and turned to the back. "We definitely don't want that to happen."

"Maybe if you tell us what's going through your head it'll help," said Clyde.

Johnny searched the van's roof. "It's like everything is pulling me in different directions. I feel manic but paralyzed. Full of rage...yet totally drained." He blew out a breath. "It feels like I'm shackled to something rotting and rancid, but that thing is me." Johnny's eyes swept over each of his brothers. "Like maybe being tied up and tortured is all I deserve."

The others waited in case there was more.

JJ broke the silence. "I hope somebody's writing this shit down. These lyrics could put Temper on the map."

Even Johnny smiled. Leon picked an old band flyer off the floor. Mario handed him a pen from the glovebox.

Clyde squeezed Johnny's shoulder. "What do you need to keep your head straight?"

Johnny shook off his coat. "I need to run."

Jarrod groaned. "Why do you always gotta run when it's twenty fucking degrees?"

"You better not try to ditch us again," said Mario.

Johnny shrugged. "If you're worried, you'll have to keep up."

"Fuck this shit." Jarrod peeled off his jacket.

"I guess I'm in, too," said Mario.

The wind off the Hudson made the air even more punishing, and they bounced in place to warm up.

"You ready?" asked Johnny.

Jarrod put up a hand. "On your marks—"

"Mark *this*." Mario grabbed his crotch before sprinting off.

Johnny and Jarrod bolted after him. The van followed, with Clyde, Leon and JJ hanging out the window razzing them. Cars came from behind, honking before driving around. After several blocks the pace regulated, with the three runners remaining evenly matched. Johnny felt the frigid air numbing his face and burning his lungs but he welcomed it, urging his legs to keep up with the thoughts spinning in his head.

After about a mile, Jarrod began dropping back, then Mario. When it looked like Johnny had no intention of stopping, they both got in the van to follow him home.

At the loft, Johnny broke off to shower and throw on pajamas. When he opened the bathroom door, Jarrod was sitting on his bed. "This is how it's gonna be."

"How what's gonna be?" Johnny grabbed socks from his dresser.

"You're coming upstairs to eat something, then you're staying with me and Clyde." He grabbed one of Johnny's pillows. "You're not just gonna hole up in this room making yourself nuts."

"Fine."

Jarrod's face pinched. "Really?"

Johnny sat beside him to pull on the socks. "I don't want to be in this bed anyway. It'll hurt too much."

"Okay then." Jarrod stood. "But can you make it *seem* like you put up a fight? As Vice President, I got to appear to have *some* value around here."

"Believe me, you're valuable." Johnny offered a weak smile. "I don't know what the fuck I'd do without you."

The next morning, Johnny debated whether or not to attend school, but figured he could hate himself there as much as anywhere. The day dragged. When it ended, he didn't want to be home either, but his brothers were unrelenting in their campaign to keep him busy. Several of them pushed him to go for a run around the neighborhood. When they returned, his bandmates were setting up for a jam session. Johnny offered little resistance because he didn't know what else to do.

After dinner, he went to his apartment. He sat on the couch and dialed Jessica's number. After a few rings, Walter's voice said, "Hello."

"Can I please talk—"

Click.

When he redialed, the line was busy. Johnny set the phone beside him. He muddled through some homework before trying again. Still busy.

Johnny lay back with his head on the armrest. Closing his eyes, he envisioned the Baxter's apartment. The parquet floors, worn in the high traffic spots. Their aging furniture passed down from previous generations, its oaky scent saturated by decades of lemon polish. Carol's all-American cooking lingering in the walls. Johnny wondered where Jessica would be, in this place she had lived all her life. Her bed, surrounded by stuffed animals? The oversized chair by the hall? Where was she finding the most comfort? He hoped she had been able to sleep a little, had eaten something.

Exhaustion took hold and Johnny drifted off. When a ring jolted him awake, he fumbled for the receiver. "Jessica?"

"Pathetic."

Marco. His fucking timing was always so perfectly flawed. Johnny sat up. "I was expecting—"

"You're a lost cause for that girl, and it's gonna get you killed." He tsked a few times. "I tried to warn you."

"It's not what—"

"I, for one, will miss you."

Johnny latched onto the phone's base, tempted to hurl it at the wall.

"Speaking of which, I should've called sooner to commend you on your work, but I got tied up with other projects."

The line was staticky with little pops and clicks. Was he calling from Antarctica? Prison, maybe? "About that—"

"For obvious reasons, we can't go into details, but I found a spare minute and wanted to reach out…"

Was this coked-up motherfucker gonna let him get a word in or what? "Hey!"

Marco's words yielded to the static.

"I'm not working for you anymore."

"Excuse me?"

"Not like that last thing." Johnny leaned back. "The other shit, like we did with the plane? I'll do that, but only that."

"Wow. That girl really has your balls in a vice."

"Will you shut the fuck up about her already?"

"Jesus. Why so sensitive?"

"I'm not fucking sensi—" Johnny grimaced at the wall. "You know something? Forget all of it. Don't call me anymore." He slammed down the receiver and slumped into the couch. Seconds later the phone rang. Johnny let out a sigh and picked it up. "What."

"I would advise not hanging up on me."

"Why? What are you gonna do?"

"I can't say on an unsecured line."

"You think I give a shit?" Johnny stood up to pace the length of the phone cord. "You wanna come at me? I'll pull the fucking trigger myself. I'm about to do it right now."

"Whoa, whoa. Calm down." There was a long pause while Marco... what? Did some more coke? Maybe a snort of dope to take the edge off? "Look, I shouldn't have teased you. I'm sorry."

Johnny sat on the armrest.

"Tell me. What's going on with you?"

"I just can't anymore."

"Can't what?"

Johnny picked at the upholstery. "Anything."

"I get it. It's a lot." More popping and clicking. "Believe it or not, I've been there, too. But you're still young..."

Drained and deflated, Johnny lowered the receiver to his lap. So many things had been wrested from his control lately. But not this one. He had told himself he was done with Marco, and that could still happen. He just had to resist the man's demented vortex. The crazy but familiar patterns that tugged at Johnny's core. He should just pinch him off, like an umbilical cord. Johnny looked down at the tinny, distant voice coming from the earpiece. He raised it to his face.

"...because, after all, you're probably one of the most reliable people I know."

Finally, a pause. "Are you finished?"

"Excuse me?"

"Because I'm gonna talk now." Johnny stood to sound more decisive. "First off, don't pretend to know what I'm feeling, or what the fuck's going on with me."

"I'm not pretend—"

"And second, I was pretty clear about what I said before. I'm grateful for your confidence in me, and your generosity, but I'm done."

"*Muchacho*, I'll be in the city next month. Let me take you to dinner. A nice place, fancy, like you've never been. We'll talk."

"I'm sorry, Marco. I can't."

His tone turned grave. "Don't do something stupid."

"You don't have to worry about me blabbing to—"

"That's not what I meant."

"Oh. You mean blowing my brains out?"

"Yeah."

Johnny tipped his head back. "I gotta go."

"Yeah, yeah, okay. Take some time, think about things. We'll talk later."

"Whatever." Johnny hung up the phone. He walked to the kitchen, opened a beer from the fridge and drained it in a few gulps. He grabbed another and returned to the couch as Tito came through the door.

"You talk to her?"

"The phone's off the hook."

Tito pouted. "You sleeping at Clyde and Jarrod's again?"

"Nah. I'll probably crash here on the couch."

"Okay. I'm going to bed, but I'll keep my door cracked in case you need anything."

"You mean in case I flip?"

Tito smiled. "That, too."

Johnny thumbed through some car magazines, smoking cigarettes and sipping beer until he finally fell asleep. He had been out a few hours when the phone rang again. He grabbed it mid-ring. "Hello?"

"It's me." Jessica's voice was hushed. "Sorry it's so late."

"It's fine, baby. I've been trying to call you."

"I figured. I had to wait till my parents fell asleep. They won't let me talk to you. Or anyone. Not even Danni and Michelle." She sniffled and blew her nose. "My mom won't stop asking how I'm doing, and my father is losing his shit. You'd think it was him who got attacked.

"They're just worried about you, that's all."

Jessica paused. "Did I dial the wrong number?"

Johnny smiled. "I know, right? I'm sorry."

"I thought I could count on you, of all people, not to give me a line of bullshit."

"I guess none of us knows how to be anymore."

Jessica's voice faltered. "I never should have said anything. I should've just pretended it didn't happen. Then I wouldn't have to babysit everyone else's emotions."

Johnny wiped a tear with the back of his hand. "That's a big secret to walk around with. It would change you."

"I'm already changed."

They listened to each other breathe a moment. "Are you ever coming back to school?"

"My mom's gonna talk to the principal, see if I can finish out the semester at home."

"Is that what you want?"

"I'm scared, Johnny." She muffled some sobs. "I can't imagine ever having to wait at that bus stop."

The comment pierced Johnny's heart.

"How will I ever feel safe again? Or, how will I ever be safe with you?"

And there it was. The million-dollar question, finally said out loud.

"I haven't been able to stop thinking about everything. My mind keeps flashing on all these little details. Things I didn't see before, but now seem so clear. Times when I caught a vibe, but because I was so in love with you, I let it go." She set the phone down to blow her nose. "I don't think you've lied to me about who you are. I believe your feelings for me are sincere. But you've been lying about other things."

"You're right." Johnny squeezed back tears.

"I'm gonna need some time. If you keep calling, it'll only make things harder."

"I understand."

"I love you, Johnny."

"I love you, too, Jessica." They sat in silence. "And I'm sorry."

CHAPTER FORTY-FOUR

For the next few weeks, Johnny plodded through his daily routine. His only reprieve from the clamoring emptiness was in the seconds between sleep and consciousness. The dreamy moment of bliss before reality smacked him awake.

Never before had he experienced such sorrow. Such inertia. The two fed off each other, creating a spiral of depression neither he nor his brothers could pry him from. To everyone's astonishment, he was remaining lucid.

After school, Johnny was looking in his bedroom closet when his foot tapped the hollow floor. He'd forgotten about the hidden storage. Kneeling down, he removed the cover. There sat the two baggies. Marco's bonus for the drug run at the airstrip. Johnny picked up one of them and examined it. The crystally whiteness of the cocaine induced a wave of nausea. He wasn't doing that shit again.

But the other bag.

He had snorted heroin once before, at fourteen. It was during his first meeting with Marco, when Johnny was picking up drugs for the Brick. Marco had insisted he do it, maybe to prove Johnny wasn't a narc, or to try and hook a new customer. Either way, he recalled how all of his negative feelings just melted away. The euphoria.

He dabbed his pinky on his tongue, then into the bag, tasting the bitter granules. Johnny saw junkies nodding out almost every day, on the streets and subways. The risks were evident. But what if he did a little? Just enough to break the cycle of depression. And how nice would it be to have control over a dissociative episode?

Johnny dropped the baggie and sat back on his heels. What the fuck was he thinking? He smacked one cheek. Then the other. Was he really that stupid? The thought made him mad. It flushed his face even more than the slap. His heart, which had been so lethargic, began to knock in his chest. His spine straightened. Emerging from beneath all the despair was Johnny's old familiar steady: Anger.

Why not embrace that? It was better than being despondent. Anger was exhilarating. It was a motivator. Fuck all this sadness shit, it was time to reconnect with his inner rage.

Johnny sealed the drugs back in storage. He jogged to the Mess Hall, where several brothers were congregating before dinner. Gus and Eric were cooking pots of spaghetti and meatballs. Bread slices and a big bowl of salad were on the island counter beside stacks of plates and silverware.

Jarrod came from behind. "Are you gracing us with your presence tonight?"

"Yeah." Johnny faced him. "And we're having a meeting."

"Great. I'll make sure everyone knows."

When all twenty-eight gang members were seated and eating, Johnny put up a hand. "I want to discuss how to deal with Dos Cruces."

The room hushed.

"These motherfuckers need to pay for what they did."

Brothers exchanged looks. "How?" asked Chico. "The Crosses have hundreds of members, and we don't know where they live."

"They gotta hang out somewhere," said Johnny.

"Okay," said Mario. "But even if we find them, you think we can outshoot them?"

"It's nice you came out of your funk," Jarrod said through a mouthful of bread. "But thinking we can mow them all down is nuts. And trying to weed out the ones who grabbed Jessica could be complicated."

"And she told the cops," said JJ. "So those guys will probably get arrested anyway."

Johnny threw down his fork. "What the fuck should we do then, just let it go?" He surveyed his brothers' faces.

Clyde picked at his food to avoid eye contact. "Jessica's not one of us," he muttered.

Johnny folded his arms, head cocked.

"Is it worth blowing up everything we've built?" Clyde looked up. "Or getting killed? Over someone who's not even in the gang?"

"We all care about Jessica," said Jarrod. "But Clyde's right. Ever since leaving Miami you've been careful, staying under the radar. Now you wanna go out guns blazing, risking everything?"

Johnny stood up. "Is that what everyone thinks? Just let it go?" He circled the table. "And then what happens? The Crosses see that we're weak, so maybe they decide to rape Chico's sisters," he put a hand on Clyde's shoulder, "or mow down your mother with a car." He looked at Tito. "Maybe they throw a Molotov cocktail into your cousins' garage." Johnny returned to his chair. "I get it. Jessica's just collateral damage, right? But so are all those people."

"You could take out César's wife," said Rafael. "A civilian for a civilian."

"I'm not killing someone's wife."

Rafael shrugged. "But you killed people for Marco."

The whole room got quiet.

"Rafi didn't mean it like that," said Jarrod.

"It's okay." Johnny pinched the corners of his mouth. "Everyone here gets to speak their mind." He leaned back. "And maybe he's right. Maybe it *is* all the fucking same."

"Why not pop César then?" asked Teddy.

"Killing César won't stop his crew," said Mario. "Those motherfuckers don't listen to him alive."

"It's true," said Patrick. "Also, how many Crosses did Hector talk to about this loft before getting booted? Was it just those two goons in the Galaxy, or were there others? If we retaliate, there could be a full-on war right outside our door."

"Johnny, you know we'll stand behind you," said Joe. "Whatever you decide. But part of our job is to keep you grounded, to make sure you think this shit through."

Johnny mopped his face with both hands. "The Dogs of War come first. I haven't forgotten that. But it wouldn't hurt to do some investigating and see what comes up." He speared a meatball. "Whether or not we act on what we find will be another decision."

For the next few weeks, the Dogs of War set out on reconnaissance missions. They took turns circling the city in search of Dos Cruces, but it proved to be a waste of gas. Occasionally, they would watch César's building, in hope of tailing any crew members who came calling, but no one did. And César hardly left the house anymore, which they guessed was due to the birth of his fourth child. Whenever someone slipped into the building to listen by his door, at least one kid was wailing, the adults were arguing and the little mutts were yapping. JJ joked that if an ambush did go down, César would probably throw himself in front of a bullet.

Despite the lack of results, having a common task resurrected the gang's camaraderie and lifted the general mood. As Johnny drove around the city, however, he kept digging up old wounds to toss into his anger well. It wasn't hard. His Miami family alone would have been enough, but he didn't stop there. He remembered all the people who had underestimated him. Kids who fucked with him when he was new to the city, adults who tried to rip him off, snitches, like Hector. And, of course, Dos Cruces.

Johnny conjured up images of every member he had encountered. One by one, he picked apart their features and mannerisms, imagining what he would do to them. Especially Mr. Goatee. How nice would it be to plunge a dagger through his heart? And Disco Danny? Johnny would chop off his arm and flog him to death with his stupid fucking FATE tattoo.

Johnny made an occasional pass down Jessica's block. He wasn't sure why, because he didn't expect to see her. Maybe it was out of nostalgia. But doing so only evoked a bitter brew of longing, regret and self-loathing. Absent from the lobby desk, Johnny noticed, was Freddy.

The last Sunday in March was sunny and warm. Dirt-covered mounds of snow remained solely in the darkest corners of the city. Citizens trickled from hibernation to get their first reprieve from the long, bitter winter.

Johnny and some Dog brothers were in the street washing the vehicles. Tito left to gas up the Monte Carlo, with Mario and Patrick. Thirty minutes later they returned, honking the horn.

"We saw Dos Cruces," Mario said, crawling from the car. "They're shooting hoops on Houston Street."

"How many?" asked Johnny

"Ten or so."

"One of the guys from Central Park was there," said Patrick. "The goatee with the neck tattoo."

Johnny's jaw tightened. "Are you sure?"

"Pretty sure." Patrick shrugged. "We drove around the block twice."

"Let's have a meeting at Joe and Rafi's."

They filed into the ground-floor apartment while the remaining residents were summoned. It was the most alive Johnny had felt in weeks. "This could be our best shot," he told the gang. "They won't be packing if they're playing ball."

"There could be weapons somewhere," said Patrick.

"But we can get every one of them before they know what's going on." Johnny looked at the blank faces staring back at him. "It'll happen so fast. We'll be gone before the cops roll up."

"What do you mean by *get*?" asked Clyde. "Because when they see us coming, they're going for their guns."

Johnny stood with arms akimbo. "If it comes to that, we'll be ready to shoot first."

"If you want Jessica's rapist, wouldn't it be less drastic to take him out with the sniper rifle?"

That felt too unsatisfying. Too...humane. Johnny expelled a breath. "This isn't about Jessica. When those guys grabbed her, that's not who they wanted. They made it very clear. They wanted us. Me in particular." He rubbed the scarring around his wrists. It felt tight, like it was cutting off circulation to his hands. "If you think this is over, just because they won a round, you're wrong." Johnny walked among his gang. "What if that was us playing ball? You think they'd just smile and wave?"

Some brothers shook their heads.

"Of course not. They would—" Johnny corrected himself. "They *will* come at us. Are we supposed to live like that? Never knowing when we're gonna bump into them next?"

Murmurs rose amid the crowd.

"The truce is bullshit. These motherfuckers don't care. But right now, we have the advantage." Johnny held up his fists at Clyde. "You wanna go in there, put up our dukes and see if they'll fight fair?" He expelled a wry laugh. "Good luck with that." He lay a palm on his chest. "Look, if anyone wants to sit out, that's fine. But I can't."

Energy was ramping up as Jarrod moved to the front of the room. "Johnny's right. It's never gonna be over with these guys. We didn't start this war, but we're in it. Whether we like it or not." He looked at Clyde. "You get that, right?"

Clyde gave a pained smile. "Yeah. I get that."

"You could be a driver," Johnny said to him. "We're gonna need all three cars to get us there."

"No." Clyde rubbed his forehead. "Why don't we grab all the weapons, see what we got."

Johnny gave a nod and several crew members scattered. Minutes later, the dining table was covered with guns.

"Everybody knows that park," Johnny continued. "It's surrounded by a chain-link fence, with gates on Houston, MacDougal and Sixth Avenue. The hoops are by the north wall." His hand brushed one of the Glocks. "If we split up and rush them from three sides, they'll be trapped." Johnny fingered Joe, Teddy and Gus to operate vehicles. Others chose weapons. "The goal is to take down as many of these motherfuckers as we can. Hit and run. It's the middle of the day, so we need to be quick. Drivers, if it's not safe to wait, leave. We'll run our asses off and meet back here."

Jarrod looked at Johnny. "You want us to save the rapist for you?"

He bit his lip. "No. Anyone with an opportunity needs to take it. No hesitation."

"Even if it's César?" asked Chico.

Johnny searched the ceiling. "Yeah. Even César."

As the crew was grabbing coats, Tito relinquished a gun to Mikey.

"What's up with that?" said Johnny. "You're a decent shot."

Tito shrugged. "I'm more comfortable with a knife."

Mario laughed. "How the fuck would you know?"

Tito's deadpan turned into a smirk as he lifted his shirt. An eight-inch Bowie knife was holstered to his belt. "You joke about me being a serial killer, but maybe I did leave a few bodies in El Salvador."

"You crazy motherfucker." Mario threw his arms around Tito. "I fall more in love with you every day."

Johnny laughed for the first time in a long time.

Gus drove the van up Sixth Avenue. As it approached Houston, Johnny peeked out the window. The Crosses were still playing ball, but there were eighteen of them now. Some were hanging around benches on the sidelines, razzing their gangmates. They smoked butts and drank from bottles in brown paper bags. A boombox surrounded by coats cranked *Feels Like the First Time* by Foreigner. Across the park, people tried to ignore them. Adults tipped their faces to the sun, read newspapers or played with their dogs. A handful of kids traded tricks on skateboards.

Gus double-parked by the entrance. Jarrod leaned over to Johnny. "They multiplied."

"But we still have the numbers." Johnny jutted his chin toward the hoops. "And look. They're both here now."

Spinning for a jump shot was Disco Danny, his helmet hair barely moving. Goatee tried to bat the ball away.

"Bonus," said Jarrod.

Johnny broke his gaze to see the Monte Carlo idling on MacDougal Street, the Dodge Dart on Houston. He and Jarrod shared a tight-lipped smile before securing the guns in their waistbands. Johnny turned to the others. "Ready?"

There were nods all around.

He swung open the side door and gang members poured from the van. As they raced through the gate, Mario, Jeff and Cisco jumped on two Crosses near the entrance. They began pummeling them with fists, but the Crosses had good reflexes, blocking and hitting back. One was slippery, twisting to grab the .38 in Cisco's belt. Jeff shot him in the stomach. Mario got the other guy in the shoulder.

The gunfire created havoc throughout the park. Skateboarders ducked behind their boards and bolted toward MacDougal Street, brushing past the crew members charging in. Other civilians also fled, dragging their dogs and children behind them.

Johnny was rushing toward the hoops with more brothers, but the ballplayers were alert to the ambush now and charged at the younger gang. A big guy grabbed Mikey. He picked him up and threw him on the ground. Tito came from behind and sliced his throat. Mikey had to roll sideways to avoid him as he dropped. Tito offered Mikey a hand and they moved together into the fray.

JJ never even saw the Cross that bowled him over. "My gun!" he yelled as it skidded across the asphalt.

"Thanks, asshole." The Cross picked it up and aimed at him.

Chico saw them. "No you don't, motherfucker." He shot the guy in the back.

JJ scrambled to retrieve his gun, then shot the man again for good measure.

The Crosses on the sidelines dove for their belongings, hunting for weapons. Rafael and Eric fired at them. Some bullets hit the boombox, knocking it backward, silencing the tape deck.

The men shot back, causing both crews to scatter. Andre was hit in the calf. He let out a yell and rolled to the ground, clutching his leg.

"I got you, man." Rudy scooped him up and dragged him out of the crossfire toward the van.

Some Crosses had produced knives. They were whirling around the court, slicing at Dogs as they rushed by. Maurice got cut in the hip, Oscar on the hand. Jamal was stabbed in the side. As he folded over, a rival tried to rip the 9 mm from his grip. "Get the fuck off me!" his deep voice boomed.

Johnny spun in the chaos trying to find a clean shot. There were clusters of skirmishes everywhere, and he couldn't risk hitting his own brothers. He ducked as a bullet whizzed over his head. When he straightened, Johnny saw him. The rapist with the goatee was rifling through a coat on the ground. As Johnny ran closer, his shirt was grabbed by another Cross, who punched him in the head. Johnny winced from the pain, but managed to kick the guy in the stomach. The attacker stumbled backward and Johnny shot him in the chest. When he looked again, Goatee was waving a gun, heading toward two Crosses who were kicking Alex where he lay on the ground.

"Move!" Goatee yelled at them. "I'll finish him off."

Johnny fired at Goatee's chest. The bullet missed, but made him turn. His eyes locked on Johnny and he sneered. Was that Jessica's pendant around his neck? A wave of rage obliterated every distraction. Goatee raised his barrel. Johnny centered himself and fired first. The bullet hit the two crosses tattooed on the man's throat. Blood streamed over the diamond-encrusted heart before he crumbled to the ground.

Johnny stood waiting to feel some vengeance. Some satisfaction. But when the two guys kicking Alex dove for Goatee's gun, he refocused. He shot one in the side while the other swept up the weapon, firing haphazardly until the clip was empty.

Dos Cruces were carrying their wounded brothers out of the park. The Dogs of War were doing the same. Johnny scanned the area a final time and saw Jarrod. He was under a basketball hoop with Disco Danny, who was crouching with hands over his head. Jarrod shot him through his tattooed fingers.

Sirens echoed in the distance. Johnny blew a warning whistle. "We gotta go! Now!"

Some Dogs piled into waiting vehicles, which sped off. Others scattered.

Two shots rang out in succession. Through the dissipating crowd, Johnny saw Clyde. He was frozen, his gun still clenched in his shaking hands. It was trained on a rival across the park. Clyde had hit him from behind. The Cross was on his knees, groping for his dropped gun. Patrick, sprinting out of the park, shot the guy twice more as he ran by.

Johnny looked to see what Clyde's target had fired at and saw Jarrod on the ground. He ran over to kneel beside him. Clyde followed. Jarrod was bleeding from the abdomen but he was conscious. "Did you see it? I got Disco Danny."

"I saw it, man. Don't talk." Johnny ripped off his sweatshirt. He pressed it into the most blood-soaked part of Jarrod's stomach.

Clyde looked at Johnny. "We gotta get him out of here."

Jarrod's eyes widened. "You can't move me."

"Don't worry," said Johnny. "We're not moving you."

Sirens grew louder.

"Johnny, you can't stay here." Tears were trickling down Clyde's face. "The cops are coming."

"I don't care."

"I'll stay with him, but you should go."

"You should both go." Jarrod's voice was weak.

"I'm not leaving you." Johnny turned to Clyde. "But there's no need for us both to get caught."

Jarrod squeezed Johnny's hand. "You stubborn fuck. If you're not leaving, at least get rid of the guns."

Johnny couldn't help but smile. "You're right." He grabbed the discarded weapons and looked at Clyde. "Ditch these or we're all fucked."

Clyde didn't move. "I should've pulled the trigger faster."

"There's no time for that."

"I-I wasn't fast enough." He was fixated on the blood pooling underneath Jarrod.

"Clyde!" Johnny shoved the guns at him. "Take these and run."

Clyde fumbled for the weapons, slipping them in his coat pockets. He stood up, mopping his wet face with a sleeve before racing toward MacDougal Street. At the same time, four police officers appeared from Sixth Avenue. They were about to chase him until they caught sight of the carnage. They halted, furiously radioing for more back up.

Johnny kept pressure on Jarrod's wound. "You gotta stay with me."

"Where am I gonna go?" Jarrod whispered.

"I can't believe you're being a smartass right now."

"Don't say anything."

"You want me to shut up?"

"No." Jarrod met Johnny's gaze. "Don't say anything to the cops. Not a fucking word." He gasped and began to tremble.

Johnny knew the police were surrounding them with guns drawn, but he couldn't look away. "Come on, my brother, don't do this. You can make it."

Jarrod's breath slowed. Then it stopped.

"Jarrod."

Nothing.

"Come on man, don't leave me." Tears streamed down Johnny's face as he pulled Jarrod into his arms.

"Hands behind your head," said one cop. More came through the gates.

"Jarrod, please." He cradled Jarrod's lifeless body.

"Move away from that kid and put your hands in the air!"

Johnny looked up. All four officers had their guns aimed at him. Behind was a line of others. Johnny took one last glance at his brother of choice, his second in command, as cold steel pressed into his forehead. Johnny's vision narrowed as he released Jarrod's body. His fingers inched up to link behind his neck.

He was tackled face down on the ground. Knees pressed on his back and legs. Fire trucks and ambulances drowned out the yelling and scratchy radios. The sounds muffled together as Johnny's hands were yanked behind him. Handcuffs tightened around his wrists. On the ground in front of him were some faded chalk drawings. Childlike sketches of trees and animals. Was that a sun? Or maybe a spider. *That wriggled and jiggled and tickled inside her.* He adjusted his head to look closer. *She swallowed the spider to catch the fly.* He zeroed in on the image. *I don't know why she swallowed a fly.* It drew all of his attention. *Perhaps she'll die.*

Acknowledgements

I owe much gratitude to Cindy Caughey, Harris Thompson, Daphne Vlachojannis, Nathalie Erika Langner, Jim Childers, Stephanie Page, Meredith Lobur, and my posse of oldest and dearest—you know who you are!—all of whom helped corroborate the details of our youth. Mark, as always, thanks for your continued love and support.

About the Author

A.D. Metcalfe is the author of the award-winning novel *Street*, the first in a series. She has had several short pieces featured in various publications, and her children's book, *Mousebound*, was published under the pen name, Leslie Ann George. She is a member a Grub Street and Vice President of the Cape Cod Writers Center.

To read more by A. D. Metcalfe, and to sign up for her newsletter, Fearless Ink, go to www.admetcalfe.com

Connect on social media:

FACEBOOK facebook.com/admetcalfeauthor
INSTAGRAM instagram.com/admetcalfeauthor
TWITTER x.com/admetcalfe

What risks would you take if you had nothing left to lose?

STREET

A.D. METCALFE

BOOK 1

amazon.com/dp/1962834034

1970s New York City is borderline bankrupt. Police departments, public schools and other municipalities are struggling under massive layoffs, buildings are abandoned, and the streets are rife with crime and drugs. For Johnny Alvarez, a precocious young runaway, the decay and lawlessness offer camouflage and opportunity. He squats in an empty apartment in a derelict Washington Heights tenement and gathers a gang of streetwise kids, most of whom struggle with their own issues. Johnny is haunted by the abuse he suffered at the hands of his sadistic older brother. The crew tries to keep his head straight with belonging and levity, but the turbulent nature of the street triggers unwanted memories, which spin Johnny into recklessness amid the city's seedy underbelly.